Linnet by Grant Allen

A ROMANCE

Charles Grant Blairfindie Allen was born on February 24th, 1848 at Alwington, near Kingston, Canada West (now part of Ontario).

Home schooled until 13 when his family moved to England, Grant was to become a highly regarded science writer who branched out to a fiction career and became enormously popular.

His work helped propel several genres of fiction and whilst his career was short it was enormously productive.

Grant's scientific background enabled him to root much of his work in a plausibility that was denied to others. He had little fear in challenging a society that treated women as second class citizens and creating best sellers from such works.

On October 25th 1899 Grant Allen died at his home in Hindhead, Haslemere, Surrey, England. He died just before finishing Hilda Wade. The novel's final episode, which he dictated to his friend, doctor and neighbour Sir Arthur Conan Doyle from his bed appeared under the appropriate title, The Episode of the Dead Man Who Spoke in 1900.

Index of Contents

CHAPTER I

"TO INTRODUCE MR FLORIAN WOOD"

'Twas at Zell in the Zillerthal.

Now, whoever knows the Alps, knows the Zillerthal well as the centre of all that is most Tyrolese in the Tyrol. From that beautiful green valley, softly smiling below, majestically grand and ice-clad in its upper forks and branches, issue forth from time to time all the itinerant zither-players and picturesquely-clad singers who pervade every capital and every spa in Europe. Born and bred among the rich lawns of their upland villages, they come down in due time, with a feather in their hats and a jodel in their throats, true modern troubadours, setting out on the untried ocean of the outer world, their voice for their fortune, in search of wealth and adventures. Guitar on back and green braces on shoulders, they start blithely from home with a few copper kreuzers in their leather belts, and return again after a year or two, changed men to behold, their pockets full to bursting with dollars or louis or good English sovereigns.

Not that you must expect to see the Tyrolese peasant of sober reality masquerading about in that extremely operatic and brigand-like costume in the upper Zillerthal. The Alpine minstrel in the sugar-loaf hat, much-gartered as to the legs, and clad in a Joseph's coat of many colours, with whom we are all so familiar in cosmopolitan concert-halls, has donned his romantic polychromatic costume as an integral part of the business, and would be regarded with surprise, not unmixed with contempt, were he to appear in it among the pastures of his native valley. The ladies in corset-bodices and loose white lawn sleeves, who trill out startling notes from the back attics of their larynx, or elicit sweet harmonies from mediæval-looking mandolines in Kursaals and Alcazars, have purchased their Tyrolese dress direct from some Parisian costumier. The real cowherds and milkmaids of the actual Zillerthal are much more prosaic, not to say commonplace, creatures. A green string for a hat-band, with a blackcock's plume stuck jauntily or saucily at the back of the hat, and a dirty red lappel to the threadbare coat, is all that distinguishes the Tyrolese mountaineer of solid fact from the universal peasant of European Christendom. Indeed, is it not true, after all, that the stage has led us to expect far too much, in costume and otherwise, from the tillers of the soil everywhere? Is it not true that the agricultural and pastoral classes all the world over, in spite of Theocritus and Thomas Hardy, are apt, when one observes them impartially in the flesh, to be earthy, grimy, dull-eyed, and unintelligent?

Florian Wood didn't think so, however, or affected not to think so, which in his case was probably very much the same thing; for what he really thought about anything on earth, affectation aside, it would have puzzled even himself not a little to determine. He was a tiny man of elegant proportions: so tiny, so elegant, that one felt inclined to put him under a glass case and stick him on a mantelpiece. He leant his small arms upon the parapet of a wall as they were approaching Zell, shifted the knapsack on his back with sylph-like grace, and murmured ecstatically, with a side glance at the stalwart peasant-women carrying basketfuls of fodder in huge creels on their backs in the field close by, "How delicious! How charming! How essentially picturesque! How characteristically Tyrolean!"

His companion scanned him up and down with an air of some passing amusement. "Why, I didn't know you'd ever been in the Tyrol before," he objected, bluntly. And, in point of fact, when they started together from Munich that morning on their autumn tour, Florian Wood had never yet crossed the Austrian frontier. But what of that? He had got out of the train some five hours back at Jenbach station, and walked the sixteen miles from there to Zell; and in the course of the tramp he had matured his views on the characteristics of the Tyrol.

But he waved one lily-white hand over the earth none the less with airy dismissal of his friend's implied criticism. "How often shall I have to tell you, my dear Deverill," he said blandly, in his lofty didactic tone, the tone which, as often happens with very small men, came most familiarly of all to him—"that you unduly subordinate the ideal to the real, where you ought rather to subordinate the real to the ideal. This, you say, is the Tyrol—the solid, uncompromising, geographically definite Tyrol of the tax-gatherer, the post-master, and the commercial traveller—bounded on the north by Bavaria, on the south by Italy, on the east by the rude Carinthian boor, and on the west by the collection of hotels and pensions marked down on the map as the Swiss Republic. Very well then; let me see if there's anything Tyrolese at all to be found in it. I have instinctive within me a picture of the true, the ideal Tyrol. I know well its green pastures, its upland slopes, its innocent peasantry, its fearless chamois-hunters, its beautiful, guileless, fair-haired maidens. Arriving by rail to-day in this its prosaic prototype, cast up, as it were, from the train on the sea-coast of this Bohemia, I turn my eyes with interest upon the imitation Tyrol of real life, and strive earnestly to discover some faint points of resemblance, if such there be, with the genuine article as immediately revealed to me."

"And you find none?" Deverill put in, smiling.

Florian waved that dainty Dresden china hand expansively once more over the landscape before him, as if it belonged to him. "Pardon me," he said, sententiously; "in many things, I admit, the reality might be improved upon. The mountains, for example, should be higher, their forms more varied, their peaks more jagged, their sides more precipitous; the snow should drape them with more uniform white, regardless of the petty restrictions of gravity; the river should tear down far rockier ravines, in more visible cataracts. But Nature has sometimes her happy moments, too. And I call this one of them! Those women, now, so Millet-like in their patient toil, how sympathetic! how charming! A less primitive society, a less idyllic folk, would have imposed such burdens upon a horse or a donkey. The Tyrol knows better. It is more naïve, more picturesque, in one word, more original. It imposes them on the willing neck of beautiful woman!"

"It's terribly hard work for them," Deverill answered, observing them with half a sigh.

"For them? Ah, yes, I admit it, of course, poor souls!—but for me, my dear fellow—for me, just consider! It gives me a thrill of the intensest sensibility. In the first place, the picture is a beautiful one in itself—the figures, the baskets, the frame, the setting. In the second place, it suggests to the observant mind an Arcadian life, a true Dorian simplicity. In the third place, which is perhaps the most important of all, it affords me an opportunity for the luxury of sympathy. What is the trifling inconvenience of a heavy load on their backs to these poor ignorant creatures, compared with the refined and artistic pleasure, of an altruistic kind, which I derive from pitying them?"

"Florian!" his friend said, surveying him comically from head to foot, "you really are impayable. It's no use arguing with you; it only flatters you. You know very well in your heart you never mean a word of anything you say; so stop your nonsense and put yourself in marching order again. Let's get on to Zell, and see what sort of quarters we can find in the village."

Florian Wood came down at once from his epicurean clouds, and strode out with his little legs in the direction of their resting-place. In spite of his tininess, he was a capital walker. If Nature, as he averred, has sometimes her happy moments, she certainly had one when she created her critic. Florian Wood was a young man of a delicate habit of mind and body, a just and pleasing compromise between a philosopher and a butterfly. His figure was small but extremely graceful; his limbs were dainty but well-knit and gazelle-like; his face, though small-featured, was very intelligent, and distinctly good-humoured; his voice was melodious and exquisitely modulated. And what Nature had left undone, his godfathers and godmothers did for him at his baptism when they christened him Florian. As plain John Wood, to be sure, he would have been nobody at all; as William or Thomas or Henry or George, he would have been lost in the multitudinous deep sea of London. But his parents had the glorious inspiration of dubbing him Florian, and it acted like a charm: all went well in life with him. A baronetcy would have been a far less valuable social passport, for there are many baronets, but only one Florian. Before the romantic rarity of that unique Christian name, the need for a surname paled and faded away into utter nothingness. Nobody ever dreamt of calling him "Wood": they spoke of Florian as they once spoke of "Randolph." On this somewhat illogical but very natural ground, he became from his schooldays upward the spoiled child of society. He was a toy, a plaything. Clubs hung on his clear voice; women petted and made much of him. When you talk of a man always by his Christian name alone, depend upon it, he becomes in the end as one of the family: mere association of ideas begets in you at last a friendly, nay, almost a fraternal feeling towards him.

They walked along briskly in the direction of Zell, Florian humming as he went a few stray snatches of Tyrolese songs (or what pass in the world for such), by way of putting himself in emotional harmony with the environment. For Florian was modern, intensely modern. He played with science as he played with everything else; and he could talk of the environment by the hour with the best of them, in his airy style, as if environments and he had been lifelong companions. But Zell itself, when they got to it, failed somehow to come up to either of their expectations. Florian would have made the valley narrower, or transplanted the village three hundred feet higher up the slope of the hill. As for Will Deverill, less critical of Nature's handicraft, he found the inns over-civilised; the Post and the Bräu were too fine for his taste: they had come thus far in search of solitude and Alpine wilds, and they lighted instead on a sort of miniature Grindelwald, with half-a-dozen inns, a respectable café, experienced (or in other words extortionate) guides, and a regular tourist-trap for the sale of chamois-horns and carved models of châlets. "This will never do!" Will Deverill exclaimed, gazing round him in disgust at the Greiderer Hotel and the comfortable Welschwirth. "This is pure civilisation!"

And Florian, looking down instinctively at his dust-encumbered boots, murmured with a faint sigh, "A perfect Bond Street!" For Florian loved to do everything "consummately,"—'twas his own pet adverb; he aimed at universality, but he aimed quite as much at perfection in detail of the most Pharisaical description. In Piccadilly, he went clad in a faultless miniature frock-coat, surmounted by the silken sheen of Lincoln and Bennet's glossiest; but if he made up his mind to Alps and snow-fields, then Alps he would have, pure, simple, and unadulterated. No half-way houses for him! He would commune at first hand with the eternal hills; he would behold the free life of the mountain folk in all its unsophisticated and primitive simplicity.

So he gazed at his Tom Thumb boots with a regretful eye, and murmured pensively once more, "A perfect Bond Street!"

"What shall we do now?" Will Deverill asked, stopping short and glancing ahead towards the glaciers that close the valley.

"See that village on the left there," Florian answered, in a rapt tone of sudden inspiration, seizing his arm theatrically; "—no, not the lower one on the edge of the level, but that high-perched group of little wooden houses with the green steeple by the edge of the ravine: what a magnificent view of the snow-fields to the south! From there, one must look at a single glance over all the spreading fingers and ramifications of the valley."

"Perhaps there's no inn there," Will responded, dubiously.

"No inn! You prate to me of inns?" Florian exclaimed, striking an attitude. "In full view of these virgin peaks, you venture to raise a question of mere earthly bedrooms—landlord, waiter, chambermaid! Who cares where he sleeps, or whether he sleeps at all, in such a village as that?" He struck his stick on the ground hard to enforce and emphasise the absoluteness of his determination. "The die is cast," he cried, with the Caesaric firmness of five-feet-nothing. "We cross the stream at once, and we make for the village!"

"Well, there's probably somewhere we can put up for the night and reconnoitre the neighbourhood," Will Deverill answered, as he followed his friend's lead. "If the worst comes to the worst, we can fall back upon Zell; but the priest will most likely find us a lodging."

No sooner said than done. They mounted the steep slope, and rose by gentle zig-zags towards the upland hamlet. At each step they took, the view over the glacier-bound peaks that close the glen to southward, opened wider and wider. Near an Alpine farmhouse they paused for breath. It was built of brown wood, toned and darkened by age, with projecting eaves and basking southern front, where endless cobs of Indian corn in treble tiers and rows hung out drying in the sunshine. Florian drank in the pretty picture with the intense enjoyment of youth and health and a rich sensuous nature. There was a human element, too, giving life to the foreground. Three Tyrolese children, a boy and two girls, in costumes more obtrusively national than they had yet observed, stood playing with one another on the platform in front of the farmhouse. Florian beamed on them, enchanted. "What innocence!" he cried, ecstatically. "What untrammelled forms! What freedom of limb! What Hellenic suppleness! How different from the cramped motions of our London-bred children! You can see in a moment those vigorous young muscles have strengthened themselves from the cradle in the bracing air of the mountains, so fresh they are, so lithe, so gracious, so lissom! I recognise there at once the true note of the Tyrol."

As he spoke, the younger girl, playing roughly with the boy, gave him a violent push which nearly sent him over into a neighbouring puddle. At that, the elder sister clutched her hard by the wrist and gave her a good shaking, observing at the same time in very familiar accents:

"Naow then, Mariar-Ann, if you do like that to 'Arry agin, I'll tike you stright in, an' tell your mother."

It was the genuine unmistakable Cockney dialect!

In an agony of injured nerves, Florian seized the elder girl by the collar of her dress, and, holding her at arm's-length, as one might do some venomous reptile, demanded of her, sternly, in his severest tone: "Now, where on earth did you ever learn English?"

The little Tyrolese, trembling violently in his grasp, stammered out in deadly fear: "Wy, o' course, in London."

"Pa was a waiter at the Criterion," the younger sister volunteered in a shrill little voice from a safe distance; "and ma's an Englishwoman. We've come 'ere to retire. Pa's tiken the farm. But we can't none of us speak any German."

Florian relaxed his grasp, a dejected, dispirited, disappointed mannikin. "Go, wretched little mudlark!" he exclaimed, with a frank gesture of discomfiture, flinging her from him as he spoke. "There isn't, there never was, any objective Tyrol!"

The child retreated prudently to the safe shelter of the doorway, before venturing on a repartee. Then she put out her tongue and took up a stone in her hand. "Who are you a-callin' a mudlark?" she answered, with the just indignation of injured innocence. "If my pa was 'ere 'e'd punch yer bloomin' 'ead for yer."

It ill became Florian Wood, that man of taste, to bandy words before the eternal hills with social waifs from the slums of Drury Lane. He strode on up the path in moody silence. It was some minutes, indeed, before he had sufficiently recovered from this crushing blow to murmur in a subdued voice: "What an incongruous circumstance!"

"Not so unusual as you'd suppose, though," his companion answered with a smile; for he knew the Tyrol. "There are no people on earth so vagrant in their ways as the Tyrolese. They go away as pedlars, musicians, or waiters; but when they've made their pile, almost without exception, they come back in the end to their native valleys. I've more than once met hunters or farmers in these upland glens who spoke to me in English, not always without a tinge of American accent. Perhaps it's not so much that these people emigrate as that they always come back again. They think other countries good enough to make money in, but the Zillerthal's the one place where they'd care to spend it."

Florian answered nothing. He strode on, sore distressed. The only Tyrol worth tuppence, he now knew to his cost, was the one he had erected, anterior to experience, in his own imagination.

CHAPTER II

A FRESH ACQUAINTANCE

It was a steep pull up to the little village on the hill, which Florian had selected by pure intuition for their immediate headquarters. But once they had arrived there the glorious panorama which disclosed itself in one burst to their enchanted eyes made them forget the fatigues of their long tramp to reach it. The village was a tiny one, but comely and prosperous; composed of great farm-houses with big boulders piled high on their shingled roofs to keep them in place, and a quaint old church, whose tall and tapering spire was prettily tiled with bright green slates, after the country fashion. Moreover, what was more important just then to the footsore travellers, a hospitable wirthshaus or village inn occupied a place of honour on the small green in the centre. It was cheerful though homely, and clean in a certain rough countrified way; and it faced due south, toward the sun and the snow-fields. Florian saw at a glance there would be a ravishing outlook from the bedroom windows; and Will Deverill, more practical, and better accustomed to these out-of-the-way nooks, felt inclined to believe they might count at least on decent beds, plain wholesome fare, fresh trout from the stream, and sweet venison from the mountains.

The name over the door was Andreas Hausberger. Will entered the inn with a polite inclination of the head, and inquired in his very best German of the first man he saw if he could speak with the landlord.

"I am he," the stranger said, drawing himself up with much dignity. "This inn is my Schloss. My name is Hausberger."

Will Deverill surveyed him with a critical air. He had seen such men before; they are not uncommon in the rural Tyrol. Tall, powerful, big-built, with a resolute face and a determined mien, he looked like a man well able to keep order among the noisy frequenters of his rustic tavern. For the wirth or innkeeper of these remote villages is often, after the priest, the most important personage of the little community: he represents the temporal as the pfarrer represents the spiritual authority. The owner of four or five horses, the entertainer of strange guests, the dispenser of liquor to the countryside, the organiser of festivals, marriage-feasts, and dances, the proprietor of the one club and assembly-room of the village, the wirth is necessarily a man of mark and of local position, beyond anything that is usual with his kind elsewhere. In the communal council his voice is supreme; the parlour is his court-house: he settles all quarrels, attests all deeds, arranges all assemblies, and assists, as a matter of course, at all rural ceremonies.

"Can we have rooms here for a week?" Will inquired, still in German.

The landlord led them upstairs and showed them two bedrooms on the first floor, roughly furnished, but neat, and, as Florian had foreseen, with a glorious outlook. Will proceeded to inquire, as interpreter for the party, about various details of price, possibilities as to meals, excursions in the neighbourhood, and other practical matters. The landlord answered all in the same self-respecting and almost haughty tone as before, assuring him in few words as to the excellence of the bread and the meat, the cleanliness of the beds, the soundness of the beer, and the advantages and respectability of his establishment in general. "You will be as well here," he said, summing up, "as in New York or London, a little less luxury, perhaps, but quite as much real and solid comfort."

"What does he say?" Florian asked, languidly, as the landlord finished. For, though in his capacity as man of culture, the philosopher of taste was prepared to give a critical opinion offhand at any moment, on Goethe or Heine, the Minnesänger, or the Nibelungenlied, he was innocent of even the faintest acquaintance with the German language. Two words in it amply served his turn: with wieviel and ja wohl, he made the tour of the Fatherland.

Will explained to him in brief, and in the vulgar tongue, the nature of the landlord's somewhat high-flown commendations.

By way of answer Florian unslung his knapsack, which he flung on the bed with as much iron determination as his height permitted. "This'll do," he said, decisively, this time in his character as the man of impulse. "I like the house; I like the place; I like the view; I like the landlord. He's a dignified looking old boy in his way, the landlord, with that independence of mien and that manly chivalry which forms an integral part of my mental conception of the Tyrolese character. No bowing and scraping there; no civilised flunkeydom. And that scar on his face, you observe; what a history it conceals: some free fight on the hills, no doubt, or some tussle with a wounded bear in his native forest!"

"Wal, no; not pre-cisely that," the landlord answered, in very Teutonic English, strangely tinged with an under-current of a most Western flavour. "I got that mark in a scrimmage one day on a Mississippi steamer. It was a pretty hard fight, with a pretty hard lot, too, he was a real rough customer, one of these professional monte-sharpers that go up and down on the boats on the lookout for flats; but I settled him, anyway. He didn't want another when we'd squared accounts over that gash on my face. He retired into private life at the St Louis hospital for the next few voyages."

Poor Florian collapsed. This was too, too much! He sank on the sofa with a dejected face, drew a very long breath from the innermost depths of his manly bosom, and at last gasped out with a violent effort: "Are there no Tyrolese in the Tyrol at all, then?"

The landlord smiled, a restrained and cautious smile. He was a self-contained sort of man, very large and roomy. "Why, I'm a Tyroler, myself," he said, opening the second window, and bustling about the room a little—"as Tyrolese as they make 'em; but I've been around the world a bit, for all that, both in Europe and America."

"You play the zither?" Will inquired, guessing at once what quest was most likely to have taken him there.

The landlord shook his head. "No; I sing," he answered. "It was in charge of a troupe that I went over the water. You know Ludwig Rainer?"

"Who has an hotel on the Achensee?" Will replied. "The well-known jodel singer? Yes; I've stayed there and heard him."

"Wal, he set the thing going," Herr Andreas Hausberger continued, still bustling about the room; "he took over a troupe to New York and Chicawgo. The first time, he fell in with a pack of scoundrels who cheated him of everything he made by the trip. The second time, he came back with a few hundred dollars. The third time, he got into a very good thing, and made money enough out of his tour to start the Seehof. So I followed suit, but I only saved enough on my first venture to set me up here in this house in the village. It's a one-horse affair for a man like me. Next time, I hope I shall make a little capital to start a big hotel for foreign tourists and kur-guests at Meran or Innsbruck."

"Then you mean to go again?" Will Deverill asked, sitting down.

"Why, certainly," the landlord answered, retreating to the door, "as soon as ever I can get another good troupe together again." And with a ceremonious bow, like a courtly gentleman that he was, he retired downstairs to superintend the preparation of those fresh mountain trout he had promised them for dinner.

As soon as he was gone, Florian raised himself on one elbow like a startled butterfly, with an air of studious vacancy, and stared hard at Will Deverill. "What an extraordinary country," he murmured, with a pensive sigh. "It's Babel reversed. Everybody seems to speak and understand every European language. The very babes and sucklings call one names as one passes, in vile gutter English. It's really quite uncanny. Who'd have thought, now, of meeting in an out-of-the-way lost corner of earth like this, a village innkeeper who's a man of the world, a distinguished traveller, an accomplished linguist, and an intelligent impresario? The ways of Providence are truly mysterious! What a place to bury such a shining light! Why dump him down so, in this untrodden valley?"

"Oh, it's not by any means such a singular case as you suppose," Will answered, looking up from the knapsack he was engaged in unpacking—"above all, in the Zillerthal. I've never been here before myself, but I've always been told in other parts of the Tyrol that the Zillerthalers, men and girls, are every one of them born musicians. And as for our landlord here, the Tyrolese wirth is always a man of light and leading in his own society. He opposes the priest, and heads the liberal party. All the popular leaders in the war of independence in the Tyrol were monks or innkeepers. Andreas Hofer, himself, you know, had an inn of his own in the Passer valley."

"Ah, to be sure," Florian ejaculated, in an acquiescent tone of a peculiar calibre, which showed his friend at once he hadn't the remotest idea who Andreas Hofer was, or why one should be expected to know anything about him. Now, want of knowledge on such a point is, of course, most natural and pardonable in a stranger; but there was no sufficient reason, Will Deverill thought, for Florian's pretence at its possession where he really knew nothing. That, however, was poor Florian's foible. He couldn't bear to have it thought he was ignorant of anything, from mathematics or music to esoteric Buddhism. If a native of Siberia had addressed him casually in the Ostiak dialect of the Tungusian language, Florian would have nodded and smiled a non-committing assent, as though Ostiak had always been his mother-tongue, and he had drunk in Tungusian at his nurse's bosom.

"You know who Andreas Hofer was, of course?" Deverill went on, persistently. He was a devil of a fellow for not letting you off when he caught you out in an innocent little piece of social pretension, was Deverill.

Florian, thus hard pressed, found himself compelled to do what he hated most in the world—confess his ignorance. "I remember the gentleman's respected name, of course!" he said, dubiously, with a sickly smile and a little forced pleasantry; "but his precise claims to distinction, as Men of the Time puts it in its cheerful circular, entirely escape my memory for the moment."

"He was the leader of the spontaneous Tyrolese peasant movement, you know, for the expulsion of the French and their Bavarian allies in 1808 or thereabouts," Will went on, still unpacking. "Napoleon caught him at last, and had him shot at Mantua. You'll see his tomb when you go to Innsbruck, and lots of other mementos of him all over the country everywhere. He pervades the place. He's the national hero, in fact, the martyr of independence, a sort of later and more historical William Wallace."

"Dear me, yes; how stupid of me!" Florian cried, clapping his hand to his head in a sudden burst of pretended recollection. "It comes back to me now, of course. Good old Andreas Hofer! How could I ever forget him? The Tyrolese William Tell! The Hampden of the Alps! The undaunted Caractacus of these snow-clad mountains!"

Deverill pulled off his coat. "If I were you," he said, drily, "instead of rhapsodising here, I'd go into my own room, have a jolly good wash, and get ready for dinner. We must have walked about twenty-two miles since we got out at Jenbach, and this bracing air gives one a positively Gargantuan appetite."

Florian roused himself with a yawn, for though vigorous enough for his size, he was a lazy creature, and when once he sat down it was with difficulty he could be prevailed upon to put himself in motion again. Ten minutes later they were seated at the white-covered table in the tidy little salon, doing the fullest justice to the delicious broiled trout, the foaming amber ale, the fresh laid eggs, and the excellent home-made bread, provided, according to promise, by Herr Andreas Hausberger.

CHAPTER III

WITHIN SIGHT OF A HEROINE

Next morning early, aroused by the cloister bell, Will Deverill rose, and looked out of his window. Oh, such an exquisite day! In that clear, crisp air the summits of the Floitenspitze, the Löffler, and the Turnerkamp glistened like diamonds in the full morning sunlight. 'Twas a sight to rejoice his poetic soul. For Will Deverill, though too modest to give himself airs, like Florian, was a poet by birth, and a journalist by trade. Nature had designed him for an immortal bard; circumstances had turned him into an occasional leader-writer. He stood there entranced for many minutes together. He had pushed the leaded window open wide when he first rose, and the keen mountain air blew in at it most refreshingly. All, all was beautiful. He looked out on the fresh green pastures, the deep glen below, the white stream in its midst, the still whiter tops of the virgin mountains beyond it. A stanza for his new poem rose spontaneous in his mind as he leaned his arms on the low sill and gazed out upon the great glaciers:

"I found it not where solemn Alps and grey
Draw crimson glories from the new-born day,
Nor where huge sombre pines loom overhanging
Niagara's rainbow spray."

He was just feeling in his pocket for a pencil to jot down the rough draft of these few lines, when of a sudden, at the window in the next room at the side, what should he see but Florian's pale face peeping forth most piteously.

"What's the matter? Haven't you slept?" Will inquired of his disconsolate friend with a sympathetic nod.

The epicurean philosopher shook a sad, slow head with a painfully cheerful air of stoical resignation. "Not a wink since three o'clock," he answered, gloomily. "Those dreadful creatures have bothered me without ceasing."

"Surely," Will began, somewhat surprised, "not—"

Florian shook his head wearily. "No, no; not them," he murmured with melancholy emphasis. "I don't mind about them. They, at least, are silent, and, besides, if you like, you can get up and catch them. Bells, bells! my dear fellow; bells, bells, all the morning. They've been tinkling in my ear every blessed minute since the clock struck three. It's unendurable, horrible."

"Oh, the cow-bells!" Will answered, laughing. "Why, for my part, I like them. They're a feature of the place; they sound so countrified. I hardly hear them at all, or if I hear them, they come to me drowsily through the haze of my dreams like the murmur of water or a nurse's lullaby. I find them, to tell you the truth, positively soothing. Besides," he added, mischievously, with a malicious little smile, "in such a village as this, who cares where he sleeps, or whether he sleeps at all? He should be able to subsist here on scenery and the affections."

At the words, Florian's head disappeared incontinently. That, surely, was the unkindest cut of all. Thus convicted out of his own mouth, by his familiar friend, he could but retire abashed to complete his toilet. That Deverill should have slept all night long, while he lay awake, and tossed, and turned, and wished ill to the whole ill-omened race of cows, was bad enough in all conscience; but that he should pretend he liked those disgusting bells was nothing short of atrocious.

He descended a little later to the homely parlour. Will was down there before him, and had succeeded in ferreting out an old violin from a corner cupboard. He was musical, was Will—not, to be sure, in the grand perceptive and critical way, like Florian himself, who played no instrument and understood all perfectly, but, after the inferior fashion of the mere dexterous executant, who possesses a certain physical suppleness and deftness of fingers to elicit from dumb strings the most delicate fancies of a Mendelssohn or a Chopin. In pursuance of this lesser gift of his—"the common faculty of the fiddler," as Florian called it—Will was just then engaged by the open window in playing over to himself a pretty little song by some unknown composer. He played it very well, too, Florian admitted, condescendingly; Will had a capital ear, indeed, and was not without feeling of a sort, for the finer touches in musical composition—up to a certain point, you know; not quite, of course, to the high and delicate level of Florian's own cultivated and refined perceptions. It was a charming piece, however, a very charming piece, and, after a while, Will began singing the words to it. Florian listened with pleasure and a forgiving smile to the clever twists and turns of that well-arranged melody.

As he stood there, listening, a little behind, one impressive forefinger held up in an attitude of discriminative attention, he was aware of two voices in the street outside catching up the tune naturally, and fitting it as if in sport to shapeless syllables of their own invention. They were women's voices, too, young and rich and powerful; and what was odder still, to Florian's immense surprise, they took up their proper parts as second and third in a concerted piece, like trained musicians. Strange to find such finished vocalists in a mere peasant hamlet!, but, there, no doubt they were some of Herr Hausberger's Transatlantic performers. Florian moved closer to the window to observe the unknown but silvery-tongued strangers. As he did so, two plump and rosy-cheeked mountain lasses, in homespun kirtles, fled, blushing and giggling, with their hands to their mouths, away from the close scrutiny of the foreign Herrschaft. Accustomed as he was by this time to marvellous incongruities in this land of surprises, Florian could hardly believe his own eyes when he further observed that the two girls with the divine voices were driving cows home from the pasture to the milking shed. Great heavens, yes! there was no gainsaying it. Shade of Wagner, incredible! The accomplished vocalists whose fine sense of melody so delighted his acute and critical ear were nothing but a pair of common country milkmaids!

Will Deverill, too, had risen, and, with a friendly nod, was gazing out appreciation at his unknown accompanists. Florian turned to him, all amazement. "They must have practised it before," he cried. "They must know it all of old. It must certainly be one of their own national pieces."

"Oh, no," the poet replied in a very confident voice. "They can't possibly have heard it. It's quite, quite new. I'm sure about that. It's never yet been published."

"But, my dear fellow," Florian exclaimed, with much argumentative heat, "I assure you, none but the most instructed musicians could possibly take up the right chords like that, and sing them second and third, without having practised them beforehand. Allow me to know something of the musical art. Even Patti herself—"

"Why, the song's my own," Will broke in, much amused, and unable to restrain himself. "I ought to know; it was I who wrote it."

"The words! ah, yes, to be sure; the words are nothing. They didn't sing them, of course; 'twas the melody they caught at. And the melody, I venture to assert, without fear of contradiction, the melody, from the peculiar way it modulates into the sub-dominant, must certainly be one of their own love songs."

"But I composed the tune too," Will made answer with a quiet smile. "It's never been played before. It came up into my head in the railway carriage yesterday, and seeing this old fiddle in the cupboard this morning, I thought I'd try it over before scoring it down, just to hear how it sounded."

"You wrote it!" Florian repeated, dazzled and stunned at the news. "You compose as well as rhyme! You set your own songs to music, do you? Well, upon my soul, Deverill, I hadn't till this moment the slightest idea you had such an accomplishment."

"Oh, I'm only a beginner," Will answered, with a faint blush, laying down the violin, "or rather an amateur, for I've always dabbled in it. But I've only published one song. I just strum to amuse myself. Good morning, Herr Hausberger; what an exquisite day! We'd better take advantage of it for a climb up the Rauhenkopf."

The landlord, dish in hand, bowed his courteous and courtly bow. There was deference in it, without a tinge of servility. Florian noted with approbation that mixture of independence and a just self-respect which formed a component part of his preconceived idea of the Tyrolese character. Andreas Hausberger was "right," because he was very much as Florian would have pictured him. "Yes; a very good day for the ascent," the landlord said, quietly. "We will put up some lunch, cold meat and Pilsener. You'll get a fine view, if you start in good time, over the Zementhal glaciers."

Florian sat down to the table, a trifle crestfallen; but the poached eggs were excellent, and the coffee fragrant; and he consoled himself for the cow-bells and the mishap about the song by the reflection that, after all, these idyllic milkmaids, with the voice of a prima donna and the manners of Arcadia, were in exact accordance with the operatic ideal of his own imagined Tyrol. They sang like the Chorus of Happy Peasants; they behaved as the mountain lass of poetry ought always to behave, and as the mountain lass of reality often utterly fails to do.

That morning on the Rauhenkopf was to Florian a day of unmixed delights. He was At Home with Nature. In a vague sort of way, without troubling himself much to know anything about them, the town-bred philosopher loved the fragrant fields, the beautiful flowers, the mossy rocks, the bright birds, the chirping insects. And Will Deverill knew them all, their names, and where to find them. The ragged, sweet-scented pinks still loitered late in deep clefts of the glacier-worn rock; a few stray sky-blue gentians still starred the rich patches of Alpine pasture; emperors and orange-tips still flaunted their gaudy wings in full autumn sunshine. Florian drank in all these things with pure sensuous delight; the sweet sounds of the fields, the smell of tedded kine filled his æsthetic soul, not so much with direct pleasure, as with some faint afterglow of literary reminiscence.

At one of the little alp-huts among the higher pastures, Will Deverill murmured a cheerful "Guten Morgen," as he passed, to a buxom peasant lass in a woollen kirtle, who stood busy at her churn by the door of her châlet. The girl curtseyed, and looked back at them with such a good-humoured smile that Florian, as an admirer of female beauty, couldn't resist the temptation of standing still for a moment to take a good long gaze at her. "What's she doing up here alone?" he asked at last, turning curiously to Will, as the girl still smiled at him. "Does she come up here every day? It's a fearful long pull for her. But then—this charming air! such strength! such agility!"

"Why, she lives here," Will answered, surprised that anyone shouldn't know what to him was such an obvious and familiar fact. "She doesn't come up at all, except once in the spring; and in autumn she goes down again. It must be nearly time for her to go down now, I should say. There's not much fodder left in these upper alps here."

"Lives here!" Florian exclaimed, taken aback. "What?—and sleeps here as well? You don't mean to say she sleeps in that little wooden box there?"

"Certainly. She's a sennerin, you know; it's her business to do it. All the alp girls live like that; they've been born and brought up to it."

In his innermost soul, Florian was dying to know what manner of wild beast a sennerin might be—being undecided in his own mind as to whether it was most probably the name of a race, a religion, a caste, or a profession. But it would have been treason to his principles to confess this fact, so he compromised with his curiosity by murmuring blandly in reply, "Oh, ay, to be sure, a sennerin! I might have guessed it! Do you think now, Deverill, if we asked her very nicely, she'd let us go in and inspect her châlet?"

"I'm sure she would," Will answered, half repressing a smile. "They see so little of any outsiders while they're up here on their alps that they're only too glad, as a rule, when a stranger visits them. We'll give her a couple of kreuzers for a glass of milk; that'll serve as an introduction."

He raised his hat jauntily, and approached the hut with a few words of apology. The sennerin smiled in return, bobbed, curtseying low, and welcomed them affably to her hospitable shelter. After a minute's parley with Will, the good-humoured young woman brought out a jug of fresh milk, still frothy from the cow, and poured it out for them liberally in a blue stoneware mug. Will drank his off at a draught; Florian hated milk, but as admirer of female beauty, she was a good-looking wench, he gulped it down to the dregs without even a grimace, and handed the mug back again. Then Deverill talked for a while with their sunburnt entertainer in that unknown tongue which Florian didn't understand; though he could see from their laughing faces and their quick tones of repartee that she was a merry brown lass, shy and bashful indeed before the foreign gentlefolk, but frank and fearless for all that as his soul could wish, and absolutely free from the absurd conventionalities and mauvaise honte of the women who dwell in our too civilised cities. She was no more afraid of men than of oxen. Florian liked that well. Here, at least, was true freedom; here, at least, was ancestral simplicity of life; here the woman held her own on equal terms with the man; here love was unfettered by law or by gold, untrammelled by those hampering inconvenient restraints of parental supervision, society, or priestcraft, which impede its true course in our too complex communities. Florian's lungs breathed freer in this rarified air: he had risen above the zone of Mrs Grundy.

At the end of their brisk colloquy, which he followed but in part, the sennerin, with a gesture of countrified courtesy, turned to the door with a pretty smile and waved Florian into her châlet. "She says you may look over it and welcome," Will Deverill explained, interrupting. Florian, nothing daunted, entered and gazed around. It was a rough log hut, divided into two rooms by a wooden partition, a big one, with a door behind, for the cows and calves; and a little one, with a door in front, for the sennerin's own bedchamber, kitchen, and parlour. The chief article of furniture seemed to him to consist of a great black cauldron, suspended from a crane over the open fireplace, and used, so Will assured him, as the principal utensil in the manufacture of cheese. The fire itself blazed in a hole, dug roughly in the floor of native turf; the edge of this hole, cut out into a rude seat, did duty as sofa, couch, chair, and chimney-corner. Florian sniffed somewhat dubiously. "And she sleeps here all alone?" he said, with a suppressed shudder. This was Arcadian simplicity, he felt, with quite too much of the bloom off.

"Yes; she sleeps here all alone," Will answered, undisturbed. "Comes up in May, when the snow first melts, and goes down in October, when it begins to lie thick again."

The sennerin, laughing aloud, confirmed his report with many nods and shrugs, and much good-humoured merriment. It amused her to see the stranger's half-incredulous astonishment.

"And aren't you frightened?" Florian asked, Will interpreting the question for him.

The sennerin laughed the bare idea to scorn. "Why should I be?" she exclaimed, brimming over with smiles of naïve surprise at such a grotesque notion. "There are plenty more girls in all the other huts on the alps round about. This hut's Andreas Hausberger's, and so are that and that. He owns all these pastures; we come up and herd cows for him."

"Isn't it terribly lonely, though?" Florian inquired with open eyes, reflecting silently to himself that after all there were advantages, of a sort, in Bond Street.

"Lonely!" the sennerin cried, in her own country dialect. "We've no time to be lonely. We have to mind the cows, don't you see, worthy well-born Herr, and give milk to the calves, and make cheese and butter, and clean our pots and pans, and do everything ourselves for our food and washing. I can tell you we're tired enough when the day's well over, and we can creep into our loft, and fall asleep on the straw there."

"And she has no Society?" Florian exclaimed, all aghast at the thought. For to him the companionship of his brother man, and perhaps even more of his sister woman, was a necessary of existence.

The girl's eye brightened with an unwonted fire as Will explained the remark to her. "Ah, yes," she said half-saucily, with a very coquettish toss of her pretty black head; "when Saturday night comes round then sure enough our mountain lads climb up from the valley below to visit us. We have Sunday to ourselves, and them, till Monday morning; for you know the song says—" and she trilled it out archly in clear, quick notes—

"With my pouch unhung,
And my rifle slung,
And away to my black-eyed alp-girl!"

She sang it expressively, in a rich full voice, far sweeter than could have been expected from so stalwart a maiden. Florian saw an opportunity for bringing out one stray phrase from his slender stock of German. "Das ist schön," he cried, clapping his hands; "sehr schön! So schön!" Then he relapsed into his mother-tongue. "And you sing it admirably!"

Their evident appreciation touched the alp-girl's vanity. Like most of her class she had no false modesty. She broke out at once spontaneously into another native song, with a wild free lilt, which exactly suited both her voice and character. It was excellently rendered; even Florian, that stern critic, admitted as much; and as soon as she ended both men clapped their hands in sincere applause of her unpremeditated performance. The sennerin looked down modestly when Will praised her singing. "Ah, you should just hear Linnet!" she cried, in unaffected self-depreciation.

"And who's Linnet?" Will asked, smiling at the girl's perfect frankness.

"Oh, she's one of Herr Hausberger's cow-girls," the sennerin answered, with a little shake of her saucy head. "But you needn't ask her; she's a great deal too shy; she won't give you a chance; she never sings before strangers."

"That's a pity," Will replied, lightly, not much thinking what he said; "for if she sings better than you, worthy friend, she must be well worth hearing."

The sennerin looked down again. Her ruddy cheek glowed ruddier. Such praise from such lips discomposed her serenity. Will glanced at his watch. "We must be going, Florian," he said. "Half-past twelve already! I've no coppers in my pocket. Have you anything you can offer this lady gay for her agreeable entertainment?"

Florian pulled out his purse, and took from it gingerly a well-worn twenty-kreuzer piece—one of those flimsy silvered shams which the Austrian Government in its paternal stinginess imposes as money upon its faithful lieges. The sennerin accepted it with a profusion of thanks, and smothered the generous donor's hand with unstinted kisses. So much happiness may a man diffuse in this world of woe with a fourpenny bit, bestowed in due season! But Florian mistook that customary symbol of thanks on the alp-girl's part for an expression of her most heart-felt personal consideration; and not to be outdone when it came to idyllic courtship, he lifted her hand in return to his own gracious lips and kissed it gallantly. Will raised his hat and smiled, without commenting on this misconception, and with a cheery "Auf wiedersehen!" they went on their way rejoicing once more up the slopes of the mountain.

CHAPTER IV

ENTER LINNET

Lunch on the summit was delicious that day, and the view was glorious. But when they returned in the evening to the inn at St Valentin, that was the name of their village, and described to Andreas Hausberger how an alp-girl had sung for them in a mountain hut, the wirth listened to the description with a deprecatory smile, and then said with a little shrug: "Ah, that was Philippina; she can't do very much. Her high notes are too shrill. You should just hear Linnet!"

"Is Linnet such a songstress then?" Florian cried, with that dubious smile of his.

The wirth looked grave. "She can sing," he said, pointedly. His dignity was hurt by the young man's half-sceptical, half-bantering tone. And your Tyroler is above all things conservative of his dignity.

These repeated commendations of this unknown Linnet, however, with her quaintly pretty un-German-sounding name, piqued the two Englishmen's curiosity in no small degree as to her personality and powers, so that when the wirth next morning announced after breakfast, with a self-satisfied smile, "Linnet's coming down to-day," Florian and Will looked across at each other with one accord, and exclaimed in unison, "Ah, now then, we shall see her!"

And, sure enough, about five o'clock that afternoon, as the strangers were returning from a long stroll on the wooded heights that overhang the village, they came unexpectedly, at a turn of the mountain footpath, where two roads ran together, upon a quaint and picturesque Arcadian procession. A long string of patient cows, in the cream-coloured coats of all Tyrolese cattle, wound their way with cautious steps down the cobble-paved zig-zags. A tinkling bell hung by a leather belt from the neck of each; garlands of wild flowers festooned their horns; a group of peasant children assisted at the rude pageant. In front walked a boy, with a wreath slung across his right shoulder like a sash, leading the foremost cow most unceremoniously by the horns; the rear was brought up by a pretty sunburnt girl, with a bunch of soft pasque-flowers stuck daintily in her brown hair, and a nosegay of bluebells peeping coquettishly out of her full round bosom. Though vigorous-looking in figure, and bronzed in face by the sun and the open air, she was of finer mould and more delicate fibre, Will saw at a glance, than most of the common peasant women in that workaday valley. Her features were full but regular; her mouth, though large and very rich in the lips (as is often the case with singers), was yet rosy and attractive; her eyes were full of fire, after the true Tyrolese fashion; her rounded throat, just then trembling with song, had a waxy softness of outline in its curves and quivers that betrayed in a moment a deep musical nature. For she was singing as she went, to the jingling accompaniment of some thirty cow-bells; and not even the sweet distraction of that rustic discord could hide from Will Deverill's quick, appreciative ear the fact that he stood here face to face with a vocalist of rare natural gifts, and some homespun training.

He paused, behind the wall, as the procession wound round a long double bend, and listened, all ears, to a verse or two of her simple but exquisite music.

"This must be Linnet!" he cried at last, turning abruptly to Florian.

And the boy at the head of the procession, now opposite him by the bend, catching at the general drift of the words with real Tyrolese quickness, called out with a loud laugh to the singer just above: "Sagt er, das musz ja Linnet seyn!" and then exploded with merriment at the bare idea that the Herrschaft should have heard the name and fame of his companion.

As for the girl herself, surprised and taken aback at this sudden interruption, she stood still and hesitated. For a moment she paused, leaning hard on the long stick with which she guided and admonished her vagrant cows; then she looked up and drew a long breath, looked down and blushed, looked up once more and smiled, looked down and blushed again. They had overtaken her unawares where the paths ran together; but as each was enclosed with a high wall of granite boulders, overgrown with brambles, she had no chance of perceiving them till they were close upon her. She broke off her song at once, and stood crimson-faced beside them.

"Ah, sing again!" Florian cried, folding two dainty palms in a rapture on his breast, and putting his delicate head on one side in a transport of enchantment "Why, Deverill, how she sings! what a linnet, indeed! and how pretty she is, too! For the first time in my life, I really regret I can't speak German!"

The singer, looking up, all tremulous to have overheard this unfeigned homage, made answer, to Florian's equal delight and surprise, "I can speak a little English."

It would be more correct, perhaps, to put it that what she actually said, was: "Ei kann schpiek a liddle Ennglisch"; but Florian, in his joy that any means of inter-communication existed between them at all, paid small heed at the time to these slight Teutonic defects in her delivery of our language.

"You can speak English!" he exclaimed, overjoyed, for it would have been a real calamity to him to find a pretty girl in the place, with a beautiful voice, and he unable to converse in any known tongue with her. "How delightful! How charming! How quite too unexpected! I'm so glad to know that! For had it been otherwise, I should really have had to learn German to talk with you!"

This overstrained compliment, though it rose quite naturally to Florian's practised lips, and was far more genuine than a great deal of his talk, made the girl blush and stammer with extreme embarrassment. She was unaccustomed, indeed, to such lavish praise, above all from the gentlefolk. Was the gnädige Herr making fun of her, she wondered? She grew hot and uncomfortable. Fortunately for her self-possession, however, Will Deverill intervened with a more practical remark. "You speak English, do you?" he repeated. "That's odd, in these parts. One would hardly have thought that! How did you come to learn it?"

"My father was a guide," the girl answered, slowly, making a pause at each word, and picking her way with difficulty through the insidious pit-falls of British pronunciation. (She called it fahder.) "He taked plenty Ennglish gentlemen up the mountains before time. I learn so well from him, as also from many of the Ennglish gentlemen. Then, too, I take lesson from Herr Hausberger in winters, and from Ennglish young lady at the farm by Martinsbrunn."

Florian gazed at his companion with an agonised look of mingled alarm and horror. "Do you know who she means?" he cried, seizing Will's arm. "This is too, too terrible! The girl on the hillside who sticks out her tongue! that horrible little Cockney! She'll teach this innocent child to say 'naow,' and 'lidy'! At last I feel I have a mission in life. We must save her from this fate! We must instruct her ourselves in pure educated English!"

"And how do you come to be called Linnet?" Will inquired with some interest, a new light breaking in upon him. "That's surely an English name. Who was it first called you so?"

"An Ennglish gentleman when I was all quite small," the girl replied, with much difficulty, searching her phrases with studious care. "He stop at my father's hut on our alp many nights, I know not how man says it, so must he go up the mountains. I sing to him often when he come down at evening. My right name is called in German, Lina; but the gentleman, says he, that I sing like a bird. A linnet, that is in Ennglish a singing-bird. Therefore, Linnet he call me. The name please my father much, who make a great deal of me; so from that time in forwards, all folk in the village call me also Linnet."

Will broke out into German. "They're quite right," he said, politely, though with less ecstasy than Florian; "for you do indeed sing like a real song-bird. I'm so sorry we interrupted you; pray go on with your song again."

But Linnet hung her head. "No, no," she answered, hastily, in her own native tongue, glad to find he spoke German. "I didn't know I was overheard. If I'd been singing for such as you, I'd not have chosen a little country song like that. And besides"—she broke off suddenly, with a coy wave of her brown hand, "I can't sing before strangers the same as I can before my own people." And she tapped the hindmost heifer with her rod as she spoke, to set the line in motion; for the cows, after their kind, had taken advantage of the pause to put down their heads to the ground, and browse placidly at the green weeds that bordered the wayside.

At one touch of her wand the bells tinkled once more; the long string got under way; the children by the side recommenced their loud shouts of rustic merry-making. For the return of the cows from the alp is a little festival in the villages; it ends the long summer's work on the mountain side, and brings back the unmarried girls from their upland exile to their homes in the valley. Linnet drove her herd now, however, more soberly and staidly. The free merriment of Arcadia had faded out of the ceremony. One touch of civilisation had dispelled the dream. She knew she was observed; she knew the two strangers were waiting to hear if she would trill forth her wild song again, for they followed close at her heels, talking rapidly among themselves in their own language, so rapidly, indeed, that Linnet could hardly snatch here and there by the way a single word of their earnest conversation. Once or twice she looked back at them, half-timidly, half-provokingly.

"Sing again!" Florian cried, clasping his hands in entreaty.

But the wayward alp-girl only laughed her coy refusal.

"No, no," she said in her patois, with a little shake of her beautiful head; "that must not be so. I sing no more now. I must drive home my cows. They are tired from the mountains."

"But, I say," Florian cried at last, bursting in upon his mountain nymph with this very colloquial and unpoetic adjuration; "look here, you know, Fräulein Linnet, you say you learn English from our landlord, Herr Hausberger. Now, what does he want to teach you for?"

Linnet turned round to him with a naïve air of unaffected surprise. "Why, when he teach me Ennglish songs," she said, "I will know what mean the words. Also, I have remembered a little, a very little, since the Ennglish gentleman teach me at my father's. Besides, too, shall I not need it when I go to Enngland?"

"Go to England!" Florian repeated, all amazed at the frank remark. She seemed to take it for granted they must know all her plans. "When you go to England! Oh, he means to take you there, then! You're one of his troupe, I suppose; or you're going to be one."

"I am not gone away yet," Linnet answered, not a little abashed to find herself the centre of so much unwonted interest; "but I go next time; I will sing with his band. All summers, I stop on the mountain and milk; with the winter, come I down to the house to practise."

"But you don't mean to say," Will put in, in German (it was easier so for Linnet to answer him), "he lets a singer like you live out by herself in a châlet on the hills with the cows all summer?"

Linnet held up her hands, palm outward, with a pretty little gesture of polite deprecation. Her movements were always naturally graceful. "Why not?" she said, brightly, in German, with no little suppressed merriment at his astonished face. "That's Andreas Hausberger's plan; he believes in that way; he calls it his system. He says we Zillerthalers owe our beautiful voices, for they tell us we can sing a great deal better than the people in any other valley about, to our open-air life on the very high mountains. The air there is thin, and it suits our throats, he says." She clasped her hand to her own as she spoke, that beautiful, well-developed, clear-toned organ, with a natural gesture of unconscious reverence. "It develops them, that's his word; he believes there's nothing like it. Entwickelung; entwickelung! I get more good, he thinks, for my voice in the summer on the alp than I get from all my lessons in the winter in the valley. For the throat itself comes first, that's what Andreas holds, and afterwards the teaching. Not for worlds would he let me miss my summer life on the mountains."

"And how long has he been training you?" Will inquired with real interest. This was so strange a page of life thus laid open before him.

"Oh, for years and years, gnädige Herr," Linnet answered, shyly, for so much open attention on the young man's part made her awkwardly self-conscious. "Ever since my father died, he has always been teaching me."

"Has your father been dead long?" Will inquired.

Linnet crossed herself devoutly. "He was killed eight years ago on the 20th of August last," she said, looking up as she spoke towards the forest-clad mountains. "May Our Dear Lady and all holy saints deliver his honoured soul from the fires of purgatory!"

"But your mother's alive still, I suppose, Fräulein," Florian put in with a killing smile; he had been straining his ears, and was delighted to have caught the general drift of the conversation.

"Yes; thanks to the Blessed Virgin, my mother live still," Linnet answered in English. "And I keep her comfortable, as for a widow woman, from that which Andreas Hausberger pay me for the summer, as also for the singing. But for what, mein Herr, do you make to call me Fräulein? Do you wish to mock at me? I am only an alp-girl, and I am call just Linnet."

She flushed as she spoke, and turned hastily to Will. "Tell him," she said in German, with an impatient little toss of one hand towards Florian, "that it isn't pretty of him to make fun of poor peasant girls like that. Why does he call me such names? He knows very well I am no real Fräulein."

Florian raised his hat at once in his dimpled small hand, with that courtly bow and smile so much admired in Bond Street. "Pardon me," he said, with more truth and feeling than was usual with him; "you have a superb voice; with a gift like that, you are a Fräulein indeed. It extorts our homage. Heaven only knows to what height it may some day lead you."

CHAPTER V

THE WIRTH'S THEORY

In the evening, while they dined, the landlord came in to see how they fared, and wish them good appetite: 'tis the custom with distinguished guests in the Tyrol. The moment he entered, Florian, all agog, attacked him at once on the subject of their wonderful find that afternoon on the hillside. "Well, Herr Hausberger," he cried in his high-flown way, "we've seen and heard your Linnet, heard her warbling her native wood-notes wild, to the tune of her own cow-bells on her lonely mountains. Now, what do you mean, sir, by turning out a divine singer like that, I'm a musical critic myself, and I know what I'm talking about, what do you mean by turning her out to make butter and cheese in a solitary hut on an Alpine pasture? It's sheer desecration, I tell you, sheer wicked desecration; there's nothing, almost, that girl couldn't do with her voice. She's a genius, a prodigy; she ought to be clothed in purple and fine linen, and fare sumptuously every day on champagne and turtle. And you, sir, you send her up to herd cows all alone, in an inclement clime, on a barren hill-top!"

Andreas Hausberger gazed at him with a self-contained smile that was extremely characteristic. He bowed a sarcastic bow which Florian misinterpreted for polite subservience. "Are you running this show or am I?" he asked, after a fresh pause, with a quaint reminiscence of his Western experience.

"You are, undoubtedly," Florian answered, taken aback at this unexpected assault. "But you ought to run it, all the same, on rational and humane and intelligent principles. You owe this girl's voice, as a delight and a treasure, to US, the enlightened and critical connoisseurs of two eager continents. Nature produced it that we might enjoy it. It was intended to give us some of those exquisite moments of artistic pleasure which are the sole excuse creative caprice can plead for the manifold defects of the Universe."

Andreas Hausberger looked down at him with a half-pitying curl on those stern thin lips of his. Florian had attacked him lightly where his position was strongest. "That's all right," he said, slowly, with a chilly drawl—'twas his favourite expression. "And do you think then," he went on, bursting forth almost scornfully, in spite of his outward deference, "we Zillerthalers get our fine singing voices and our musical ears by pure chance and accident? Not so, you may be sure of it. It's no mere coincidence that our men and women can almost without exception sing like birds from their childhood upwards by the light of Nature. What gives them this power? Why, they live their lives long, in summer especially, in the thin clear atmosphere of our higher mountains. There isn't much sour-stuff in it—what do you call it in English?—oh, oxygen, don't you? Wal, there isn't much oxygen in that thin upper air, rarefied, I think you say, and therefore they're obliged to fill their lungs well and expand their chests"—he swelled himself out as he spoke, and showed off his own splendid girth to the fullest advantage—"and that gives them large reservoirs and rich, pure-toned voices."

"I never thought of that before," Will Deverill interposed, much struck by the landlord's plausible reasoning. "I suppose that's why mountain races, like the Welsh and the Tyrolese, are so often musical. The rarefied air must tend to strengthen and develop the larynx."

"No; you never thought of that before," Andreas Hausberger echoed. "You haven't had to think of it. And you haven't had to select and train a choir of our Tyrolese peasants. But I have thought of it for years, and satisfied myself it's true. Is it for nothing, do you suppose, that on our cold mountain tops the vocal chords, as they say, are braced up and tightened? Is it for nothing that in that clear, pure, limpid air the very nerves of the ear, strained hard to catch quickly at distant sounds, are exercised and educated? Do you think, if I wanted to pick out voices for a musical troupe, I would go for them to Holland, or to Lombardy, or to Hamburg? No, no; I would go right away to the gründe there, the upper forks of the Zillerthal, in the crystal air just below the glaciers, and pick out my best singers from the cow-boys and the alp-girls."

He spoke of what he knew and had long reflected upon. Acquaintance with his subject supplied in part the unimportant deficiencies of his English vocabulary; and, besides, he had said the same things before a dozen times over, to other English travellers.

"Perhaps you may be right," Florian responded, blandly, as the wirth paused for breath in his eager harangue. It was a way of Florian's to be bland when he saw he was getting the worst of an argument.

"Right!" Andreas Hausberger repeated. "Never mind about that! You'd know I was right if only you'd seen as much of these people as I have. Look here, Mr Wood, you say it's desecration to send a girl like Linnet after butter and cheese in a sennerin's hut on the lonely mountains. You say I owe her voice as a treasure to humanity. Wal, I acknowledge the debt, and I try to discharge it to the best of my ability. I send her to the hills, the free open hills, where she will breathe fresh air, develop her throat and lungs, eat wholesome food, grow strong and brown and hearty. If I clothed her in purple and fine linen, as you wish, and fed her every day on champagne and turtle, do you really imagine I'd be doing her a good turn? I'd be ruining her voice for her. In the summer, she gains breath and good health on the grassy mountains; in the winter, she gets training and advice and assistance from Lindner and myself, and whatever other teachers we can find in the Zillerthal."

"I surrender at discretion," Florian answered, with a yawn, rising up and flinging his small person lazily on the home-made sofa. "I admit your contention. You interest me strangely. Your peasants and your country girls have finely developed ears and capital voices. No doubt you're correct in attributing these splendid gifts to the clearness of the atmosphere and the wild life of the mountains. I'm a musical critic in London myself, and I know what a voice is the moment I hear it. Indeed, after all, what does it matter in the end if these divine creatures spend a joyless life for years in sordid and squalid surroundings, provided only, when they burst forth at last in the full effulgence of their musical prime, they afford us, who can appreciate them, and for whose sake they exist, one vivid thrill of pure artistic enjoyment?" And he stroked his own smooth and girlish cheek with one plump hand, lovingly.

"You're a musical critic, are you?" Andreas Hausberger repeated, with marked interest, disregarding the last few words of Florian's flowing rhapsody. "Then you shall hear Linnet sing. You can say after that whether I'm right in my system or not." He opened the door hastily. "Linnet, Linnet," he called out in the Tyrolese dialect, "come in here at once. I want the Herrschaft to hear you singing."

For a minute after he spoke, there was a flutter and a rustling at the door outside; somebody seemed to be pushing some unwilling person bit by bit along the passage. A murmur of whispered voices in the local dialect floated faintly to Will's ears. "You must!" "But I can't." "You shall!" "I won't." "He says you are to." "Ah, no; I'm ashamed! Not before those gentlemen!"

In the end, as it seemed, the first voice had its way. The door opened brusquely, and Linnet, all trembling, her face in her hands, and crimson with shame, was pushed bodily forward by unseen arms into the strangers' presence. For a moment she stood there like a frightened child. Will's cheek burned hot with sympathetic tingling. Florian leaned back philosophically as he lay, and regarded this pretty picture of beauty in distress with observant complacency. She was charming, so, to be sure! That red flush became her.

"Sing to the gentlemen," Andreas Hausberger said, calmly, in a tone of command. "Take your hands from your face at once; don't behave like a baby."

He spoke in German, but Florian followed him all the same. 'Twas delicious to watch this pretty little comedy of rustic ingenuousness.

"Oh, I can't!" Linnet cried, all abashed, removing her hands for a second from her burning cheeks, and clasping them hard on her throbbing breast for one fiery moment before she clapped them up hastily again. "To bid one like this! It's so hard! It's so dreadful!"

"Don't ask her just now," Will Deverill put in pleadingly. "One can see she has such a natural shrinking and disinclination at first. Some other night, perhaps. When we've been here a little longer, she may be less afraid of us."

Linnet let her hand drop once more, and gave him a grateful glance, sidling away towards the door like a timid child in her misery. But Andreas Hausberger, for his part, was not so to be put off. "No, no," he said, sternly, fixing his eye with a determined gaze on the poor shrinking girl; "she must sing if I tell her to. That's all right. This shyness is absurd. How can she ever appear on a platform, I should like to know, before a couple of hundred people, if she won't sing here when she's told before just you two Englishmen? Do as I bid you, Linnet! No nonsense, my girl! Stand here by the table, and give us 'The Bride of Hinter-Dux.'"

Thus authoritatively commanded, poor Linnet took her stand where Andreas Hausberger motioned her, steadied herself with one trembling little fist on the edge of the table, raised her eyes to the ceiling away from the two young men, and, drawing a deep breath, with her throat held out and her mouth opened tremulously, began to trill forth, in her rich, silvery voice, a deep bell-like song of her own native mountain. For the first minute or two she was nervous, and quivered and paused unduly; after awhile, however, inborn artistic instinct overcame her nervousness: she let her eyes drop and rest in a flash once or twice on Will Deverill's. They were kindly eyes, Will's; they reassured and encouraged her. "Bravo!" they seemed to say; "you're rendering it admirably." Emboldened by his friendly glance, she took heart and went through with it. Towards the end, her courage and self-possession returned, for, like all Tyrolese, she was brave and self-reliant in her inmost soul, though shy at first sight, and bashful on the surface. The two last stanzas she sang to perfection. As she finished, Will looked up and said simply, "Thank you; that was beautiful, beautiful." But Florian clapped his hands in obtrusive applause. "Well done!" he cried; "well done! you have given us such a treat. We can forgive Herr Hausberger now for insisting on a performance."

"And you must accustom yourself to an audience," the wirth said in German, with that same quiet air of iron resolution Will had already marked in him. "If ever you're to face a whole roomful of people, you must be able first to come in upon the platform without all this silly fuss and hang-back nonsense."

Linnet's nostrils quivered. She steadied herself with her hand on the table once more, and made answer boldly, "I think I could more easily face a roomful of people I'd never seen than sing before two in the parlour of the inn here; that seems less personal. But," she added shyly, with half an appealing glance towards Will, "I'm not so nervous now. If this gentleman wishes, I—I would sing another song to him?"

And so she did—a second and a third. As she went on, she grew braver, and sang each time more naturally. At last the wirth dismissed her. Linnet curtsied, and disappeared. "Well, what do you say to her now?" the landlord asked in a tone of triumph, turning round to the young men as the door closed behind her.

Florian assumed his most studiously judicial air. The perfect critic should, above all things, be critical. Before Linnet's face, indeed, he had been enthusiastic enough, as politeness and due respect for her sex demanded; but behind her back, and in her teacher's presence, regard for his reputation compelled him to adopt the severest tone of incorruptible impartiality. "I think," he said slowly, fingering his chin in one hand, and speaking with great deliberation, like a recognised authority, "with time and training she ought to serve your purpose well for popular entertainments. Her organ, though undeveloped, is not wholly without some natural power and compass."

"And I think," Will Deverill added, with a glow of generous enthusiasm, "you've lighted on one of the very finest voices in all Europe."

CHAPTER VI

THE ROBBLER

A day or two passed, and the young men from time to time saw, by glimpses and snatches, a good deal of Linnet. For now the summer season on the hills was over, and the cows had come back to their stall-fed existence, the musical alp-girl had leisure on her hands for household duties. In the morning she helped in the general work of the inn; in the afternoon she practised much in the parlour upstairs with Andreas Hausberger and his little company. But in the evenings, ah, then, the landlord brought her in more than once, by special request, to sing her native songs to Will Deverill's accompaniment on the lame old fiddle from the corner cupboard. Those were pleasant meetings enough. Gradually the mountain lass grew less afraid of the strangers; she talked German more freely with Will Deverill now, and considerably enlarged her English vocabulary by listening to Florian's richly-worded harangues on men, women, and things, and the musical glasses. It surprised Florian not a little, however, to see that this child of Nature, unlike the ladies of culture in London drawing-rooms, positively preferred Will's society to his own, if such a fact seems credible; though he explained away in part this unaccountable defect of taste and instinct in one female heart by the reflection that, after all, Will was able to converse with her in her own language. His own finer points she could hardly understand; his words were too deep, his thoughts were too high for her. Still, it annoyed him that even an unsophisticated alp-girl should display so singular and so marked a predilection for any other man when he was present. Indeed, he half made up his mind, irksome as he felt sure the task would prove, to learn German at once, as a safeguard against so humiliating a contretemps in future.

In the early part of the next week, Will proposed one day they should mount the hills behind St Valentin, in search of a rare fern he was anxious to secure before the snows of winter. Andreas Hausberger, nodding his head, had heard of it before. It was a well-known rarity; all botanists who came to the Zillerthal, he said, were sure to go in search of it. "But I'm not a botanist," Will burst out deprecatingly, for to admit that fell impeachment is to number yourself outright in the dismal roll of scientific Dryasdusts; "I only want the plants because I love them."

"That's all right," Andreas answered, in his accustomed phrase. "You want the plant, anyway. That's the chief thing, ain't it? Wal, there's only one place anywhere about St Valentin that it ever grows, and that's the Tuxerloch; without somebody to guide you there you'd never find it."

"Oh, I won't have a guide," Will responded, hastily. "I hate to be guided. It's too ignominious. If I can't find my own way about low mountains like these, in the forest region, I'd prefer to lose it; and I certainly won't pay a man to show me where the fern is."

"Certainly not," the wirth answered, with true Tyrolese thrift. "I didn't mean that. Why waste your money on one of the regular guides, who charge you five florins for eating half your lunch for you? But Linnet knows the way as well as any trained guide of them. It's not a hard road; she'll go along with you and show you it."

"Oh, dear no," Will replied, with a little hurried embarrassment, for he felt it would be awkward to be thrown all day into the society of a young girl in so equivocal a position. "I'm sure we can find the way all right ourselves. There are woodcutters on the hills we can ask about the path; and if it comes to that, I really don't mind whether I find it or not—it's only by way of goal for a day's expedition."

Andreas Hausberger, however, was an imperious soul. "Linnet shall go," he said, shortly, without making more words about it. "She has nothing else to do. It's bad for her to be cooped up in the house too much. A long walk on the hills will be no end of good for her. That's what I always say; when young women come down from the mountains in winter, they do themselves harm by changing their mode of life all at once too suddenly, and living in close rooms without half the exercise they used to take on the alp with their milking and churning."

So, whether they would or not, the two young men were compelled in the end to put up as best they might with Linnet's guidance and company. No great hardship either, Will thought to himself, as Linnet, bare-headed, but in her Sunday best, led the way up the green slopes behind the village inn, with the bounding gait of a holiday alp-girl. As to Florian, his soul was in the seventh heavens. To see that Oread's light foot trip gracefully over the lawns was to him pure joy—a stray breath of Hellas. What Hellas was like, to be sure, the arid Hellas of reality, with its dusty dry hills and its basking rocks, Florian had not in his own soul the very faintest conception. But still, the Hellenic ideal was none the less near and dear to him. From stray scraps of Theocritus and his inner consciousness he had constructed for himself an Arcadia of quite Alpine greenness, and had peopled it with lithe maidens of uncircumscribed affections. So, whenever he wanted to give anything in heaven or earth the highest praise in his power, he observed with an innocent smile that it was utterly Hellenic.

Linnet led them on, talking unaffectedly as she went, by long ridge-like spurs, up vague trails through the woods, and over spongy pastures. As elsewhere on their walks, Florian noted here and there little whitewashed shrines at every turn of the road, and endless rude crucifixes where ghastly white limbs seemed to writhe and struggle in realistic torture. Of a sudden, by one of these, Linnet dropped on her knees, all at once without a word of warning; she dropped as if mechanically, her lips moving meanwhile in muttered prayer. Florian gazed at her curiously; Will stood by expectant, in a reverent and mutely sympathetic attitude. For some minutes the girl knelt there, murmuring low to herself. As she rose from her knees, she turned gravely to Will. "Here my father has died," she said, with solemn slowness in her broken English. "He has slipped from that rock. The fall has killed him. Will you say, for his soul's repose, before you go, a Vaterunser?"

She looked up at him pleadingly, as if she thought the prayers of so great a gentleman must carry weight of their own in Our Lady's councils. With infinite gentleness, Will bowed his head in acquiescence, and, after a moment's hesitation, not to hurt her feelings, dropped on his knees himself and bent his neck in silent prayer before the tawdry little oratory. It was one of those rough shrines, painted by unskilled fingers, where naked souls in rude flames of purgatory plead for aid with clasped hands and outstretched arms to placidly unheeding blue-robed Madonnas. Underneath, an inscription, with N's turned the wrong way, and capitals mixed with smaller letters, informed the passer-by that, "Here, on the 20th of August 188-, the virtuous guide and experienced woodcutter, Josef Telser of St Valentin, perished by a fall from a slippery rock during a dangerous thunderstorm. The pious wanderer is hereby implored to say three Paternosters, of his charitable good-will, to redeem a tortured soul from the fires of purgatory."

Will knelt there for a minute or two, muttering the Paternosters out of pure consideration for Linnet's sensitive feelings. When he rose from his knees again, he saw the girl herself had moved off a little way to pick a few bright ragworts and Michaelmas daisies that still lingered on these bare heights, for a bouquet to lay before the shrine of Our Lady. Like all her countrywomen, she was profoundly religious, or, if you choose to put it so, profoundly superstitious. ('Tis the point of view alone that makes all the difference.) Florian, a little apart, with his hand on his cheek and his head on one side, eyed the oratory sentimentally. "How sweet it is," he said, after a pause, with an expansive smile, "to see this poor child, with her childlike faith, thus throwing herself on her knees in filial submission before her father's cenotaph! How delightful is the sentiment that prompts such respect for the memory of the dead! How eloquent must be the words of her simple colophon!" Florian was fond of colophons; he didn't know what they were, but he always thought them so very Hellenic!

Will's face was graver. With one finger he pointed to the uncompromising flames of that most material purgatory. "I'm afraid," he said, seriously, "to her, poor child, this act of worship envisages itself in a very different fashion. She prays to hasten the escape of her father's soul from what she takes to be a place of very genuine torture."

Florian looked closer. As yet, he had never observed the subsidiary episode of the spirits in their throes of fiery torment, which forms a component part of all these wayside oratories. He inspected the rude design with distant philosophical interest. "This is quaint," he said, "most quaint. I admire its art immensely. The point about it all that particularly appeals to me is the charming superiority of Our Lady's calm soul to the essentially modern vice of pity. There she sits on her throne, unswerved and unswerving, not even deigning to contemplate with that marked squint in her eye the extremely unpleasant and uncomfortable position of her petitioners beneath her. I admire it very much. I find it quite Etruscan."

"To you and me, yes, quaint, nothing more than that," Will responded, soberly; "but to Linnet, it's all real—fire, flames, and torments; she believes what she sees there."

As he spoke, the girl came back, with her nosegay in her hand, and, tying it round with a thread from a little roll in her pocket, laid it reverently on the shrine with a very low obeisance. "You see," she said to Will, speaking in English once more, for Andreas Hausberger wished her to take advantage of this unusual opportunity for acquiring the language, "my poor father is killed in the middle of his sins; he falls from the rock and is taken up dead; there is no priest close by; he has not confessed; he has not had absolution; he has no viaticum; no oil to anoint him. That makes it that he must go straight down to purgatory." And she clasped her hands as she spoke in very genuine sympathy.

"Then all these shrines," Florian said, looking up a little surprised, "are they all of them where somebody has been killed by accident?"

"The most of them," Linnet answered, as who should say of course; "so many of our people are that way killed, you see; it is thunderstorms, or snow-slides, or trees that fall, or floods on rivers, things that I cannot say, for I know not the names how to speak them in English. And, as no priest is by, so shall they go to purgatory. For that, we make shrines to release them from their torments."

They had gone on their way by this time, and reached a corner of the path where it turned abruptly in zig-zags round a great rocky precipice. Just as they drew abreast of it, and were passing the corner, a young man came suddenly on them from the opposite direction. He was a fiery young man, dressed in the native Tyrolese costume of real life; his hand held a rifle; his conical hat was gaily decked behind, like most of his countrymen's, with a blackcock's feather. The stranger's mien was bold—nay, saucy and defiant. He looked every inch a typical Alpine jäger. As he confronted them he paused, and glared for a moment at Linnet. Next instant he raised his hat with half-sarcastic politeness; then, in a very rapid voice, he said something to their companion in a patois so pronounced that Will Deverill himself, familiar as he was with land and people, could make nothing out of it. But Linnet, unabashed, answered him back once or twice in the same uncouth dialect. Their colloquy grew warm. The stranger seemed angry; he waved his hand toward the Englishmen, and appeared, as Will judged, to be asking their pretty guide what she did in such company. As for

Linnet, her answers were evidently of the sort which turneth away wrath, though on this hot-headed young man they were ineffectually bestowed. He stamped his foot once or twice; then he turned to Will Deverill.

"Who sent you out with the sennerin?" he asked, haughtily, in good German.

Will answered him back with calm but cold politeness. "Herr Hausberger, our wirth," he said, "asked the Fräulein to accompany us, as she knew the place where a certain fern I wished to find on the hills was growing."

"I know where it grows myself," the jäger replied, with a defiant air. "Let her go back to the inn; it is far for her to walk. I can show you the way to it."

"Certainly not," Will retorted, in most decided tones. "The Fräulein has been good enough to accompany us thus far; I can't allow her now to go back alone to the village."

"She's used to it," the man said, gruffly, with half a sneer, his fingers twitching.

"That may be," Will retorted, with quiet self-possession; "but I'm not used to allowing her to do so."

For a minute the stranger put one sturdy foot forward, held his head haughtily, with his hat on one side, and half lifted his fist, as if inclined to rush forthwith upon the offending Englishman, and settle the question between them then and there by open violence. But Linnet, biting her lip and knitting her brow in suspense, rushed in to separate them. "Take care what you do," she cried hurriedly in English to Will. "Don't let him strike. Stand away of him. He's a Robbler!"

"A what?" Will replied, half smiling at her eagerness, for he was not at all alarmed himself by her truculent fellow-countryman.

"A Robbler," Linnet repeated, looking up at him pleadingly. "You know not what that is? Then will I tell you quickly. The feather in his hat, it is turned the wrong way. When a Tyrolese does so, he wills thereby to say he will make himself a Robbler. Therefore, if any one speaks angry to him, it is known he will strike back. It is—I cannot say what it means in English, but it invites to fight; it is the sign of a challenge."

"Well, Robbler or no Robbler, I'm not afraid of him," Will answered, with quiet determination; "and if he will fight, why, of course, he must take what he gets for it."

"Perhaps," Linnet said, simply, gazing back at him, much surprised, "in your own country you are also a Robbler."

The naïveté of her remark made Will laugh in spite of himself. That laugh saved bloodshed. The Tyrolese, on his part, seeing the absurdity of the situation all at once, broke into a smile himself; and, with that unlucky smile, his sole claim to Robblerhood vanished incontinently. Linnet saw her advantage. In a moment, she had poured into the young man's ear a perfect flood of explanatory eloquence in their native dialect. Gradually the Robbler's defiant attitude relaxed; his face grew calmer; he accepted her account. Then he turned to Will with a more mollified manner: "You may go on," he said, graciously, with a regal nod of his head; "I allow the sennerin to continue her way with you."

As for Will, he felt half inclined, at first, to resent the lordly air of the Robbler's concession. On second thoughts, however, for Linnet's sake, in his ignorance of who the young man might be, and the nature of his claim upon her, he judged it better to avoid any quarrel of any sort with a native of the valley. So he raised his hat courteously, and let the stranger depart, with a very bad grace, along the road to the village.

"What did you tell him?" he asked of Linnet, as the Robbler went his way, singing defiantly to himself, down the grassy zig-zag.

"Oh, I told him," Linnet answered, with a little flush of excitement, "Andreas Hausberger had sent me that you might teach me English."

"Is he your brother?" Will asked, not that he thought that likely, but because it was less pointed than if he had asked her outright, "Is this young man your lover?"

Linnet shook her head. "Ah, no," she answered, with a very decided air; "he's nothing at all to me— not even my friend. I do not so much as care for him. He's only Franz Lindner. But then, he was jealous because he see that I walk with you. He has no right of that; I am not anything to him; yet still he must be jealous if somebody speak to me. It is because he is a Robbler, and must do like that. A Robbler shall always fight if any man shall walk or talk with his maiden. Though I am not his maiden, but he would have me to be it. So will he fight with anyone who shall walk or talk with me. But when I tell him Andreas Hausberger send me that I may learn English, then he go away quietly. For Franz Lindner, or any other Robbler, will not fight with a stranger so well as with a Tyroler."

CHAPTER VII

WAGER OF BATTLE

That evening at the Wirthshaus, as things turned out, Will and Florian had an excellent opportunity afforded them of observing for themselves the manners and customs of the Tyrolese Robbler. There was a dance at the inn—a prodigious dance, of truly national severity. It was the eve of a wedding, and, as is usual on such occasions, the peasants of the neighbourhood had assembled in full force to drink good luck to the forthcoming union. The Gaststube or bar-room was crowded with a gay throng of bright and merry faces. The young men were there, jaunty, bold, and defiant; the old men, austere and stern of feature from the hardships of long life among the grim-faced mountains. Groups of black-eyed lasses stood about the room and bandied repartee with their gaily-dressed admirers; matrons, unspoilt by conventional restraint, instead of checking their mirth, looked on smiling and abetting them. Through the midst, the Herr Vicar strolled, stout and complaisant, an easy-going man; not his to stem the tide of their innocent merriment; so long as they confessed twelve times a year, and subscribed to release their parents' souls from purgatory, he sanctified by his presence the beer and the dances. Andreas Hausberger, too, flitted here and there through the crowd with an anxious eye; 'twas his task to provide for and protect the bodies of his guests, as 'twas the Herr Vicar's to save their priceless souls from undue temptation.

At one end of the room, on a little raised platform, the music sat installed;—a trombone, a zither, and a wooden hackbrettle made up the whole orchestra. Scarcely had the performers struck up an enlivening tune when the men, selecting as partners the girls of their choice, began to dance round the hall in the very peculiar and (to say the whole truth) extremely ungraceful Tyrolean fashion. Will and Florian had heard from the landlord beforehand of the expected feast, to which they were not invited; but, "at the sound of the harp, sackbut, psaltery, and all kinds of music," as Florian phrased it, their curiosity was so deeply aroused that they crept from their sitting-room and peeped cautiously in at the door of the Tanzboden. The sight that met their eyes in that close-packed hall was sufficiently striking. Even Florian allowed this was utterly Arcadian. For a minute or two, just at first, the young men and maidens, grasping each other wildly round the neck and waist with both their arms, in a sort of bear-like death-hug, whirled and eddied in a maze round and round the room, stamping their heavy boots, till Will almost trembled for the stability of the rafters. For some time that was all: they twisted and twirled in closely-coupled pairs, clasped breast to breast, like so many dancing dervishes. But, of a sudden, at a change of the music, as if by magic, with one accord, the whole figure altered. Each man, letting his partner go, began suddenly to perform a series of strange antics and evolutions around her, the relics of some pre-historic dance, of which the snapping of fingers and uttering of heuchs in a Highland fling are but a faint and colourless reminiscence. As the reel went on, the music grew gradually faster and faster, and the motions of the men still more savage and fantastic. The two Englishmen looked on in astonishment and admiration. Such agility and such verve they had never before seen or even dreamt of. Could these rustic cavaliers be really made of india-rubber? They twisted and turned and contorted themselves all the time with such obliviousness of their bones, and such extraordinary energy! They smacked their lips and tongues as they went; they jumped high into the air; they bent back till their heads touched the ground behind; they bounded upright once more to regain their position like elastic puppets, and, in between whiles, they slapped their resounding thighs with their horny hands; they crowed like cocks; they whistled like capercailzie; they stamped on the ground with their hob-nailed shoes; they shouted and sang, and clicked their tongues in their cheeks, and made unearthly noises deep down in their throats for which language has as yet no articulate equivalent. Florian gazed and glowered. And well he might; 'twas an orgie of strange sound, a phantasmagoria of whirling and eddying motion.

While all this was going on, the two young Englishmen stood undecided and observant by the lintel of the door, even Florian half-abashed at so much unwonted merriment. But after a while, the Herr Vicar, whose acquaintance they had already made among the stones of the churchyard, spied them out by the entrance, and, with one hospitable fat forefinger extended and crooked, beckoned them into the Tanzboden. "Come on," he cried, "come on; there's room enough for all; our people are still glad to entertain the Herr strangers: for some, unawares, have thus entertained angels."

So encouraged by the authorised mouthpiece of the parish, Will and Florian stepped boldly into the crowded room, and watched the little groups of stalwart young men and nut-brown lasses with all the interest of unexpected novelty. The scene was indeed a picturesque and curious one. Every Tyrolese is, or has been, or wishes to be thought, a mountain hunter. So each man wore his hat, adorned with the trophies of his prowess in the chase; with some, 'twas a gamsbart, or so-called chamois' beard—the tuft of coarse hair that grows high like a crest along the creature's back in the pairing season; with others, 'twas the tail-feathers of the glossy blackcock, stuck saucily on one side, with that perky air of self-satisfied assurance so characteristic of hot youth in the true-born Tyroler. Glancing around the room, however, Will saw at a single look that two young men alone among that eager crowd wore their feathers with a difference—the "hook" being turned round in the opposite direction from all their neighbours'. One of these two was a tall and big-built young man of very florid complexion, with a scar on his forehead; the other was their fiery friend of that morning on the hills, Franz Lindner. From what Linnet had said, Will guessed at once by the turn of the feather that both young men went in for being considered Robblers.

As he turned to impart his conjecture to Florian, Linnet caught his eye mutely from a corner by the mantelpiece. She wasn't taking part in the reel herself, so, undaunted by his experience of Franz Lindner that day, Will strolled over to her side, followed close at heel by Florian. "You don't dance?"

he said, bending over her with as marked politeness as he would have shown to a lady in a London drawing-room.

"No; I may not," Linnet answered, in her pretty broken English, with a smile of not unnatural womanly pleasure that the strangers should thus single her out before all her folk for so much personal attention. "I have refuse Franz Lindner, so may I not dance this time with any one. It is our custom so. When a girl shall refuse to dance with a man first, she may not that turn accept any other. Nor may he, in turn, ask her again that evening."

"How delightful!" Florian cried, effusively. "Franz Lindner's loss is our gain, Fräulein Linnet. No; don't frown at me like that; it must be Fräulein; I've too much respect for you to call you otherwise. But, anyhow, we'll sit out this dance and talk with you."

"And I," Will put in with a quiet smile, "I'll call you Linnet, because you prefer it."

"Thank you," Linnet said, shyly, with a grateful flash of her eyes, and a side glance towards Franz Lindner; "it seems less as if you mock at me."

As they spoke, the figure changed of a sudden once more to a still stranger movement. The women, falling apart, massed themselves together in a central group, in attitudes expressive of studied indifference and inattention to the men; their partners, on the contrary, placing themselves full in front of them, began a series of most extraordinary twists and twirls, accompanied by loud cries or snapping of fingers, and endeavoured by every means in the power, both of lungs and limbs, to compel their disdainful coquettes to take notice of their antics. While they stood there and watched, Linnet with eyes askance on Franz Lindner's face, Andreas Hausberger strolled up, and took his place beside them.

"Why, that's the blackcock's call!" Will exclaimed, with a start of recognition, as the dancers, with one accord, uttered all in a chorus a shrill and piercing note of challenge and defiance. "I've heard it on the mountains."

"Yes," the wirth assented; "that's the blackcock's call, and this, that they're doing, is the blackcock's love-dance. In the springtime, on the mountains, you know, the blackcocks and the grey hens assemble in their dancing place, their Tanzboden we call it, just the same as we call this one. There, the hens stand aside, and pretend to be coy, and take no notice of their mates, like the girls in this dance here; while the blackcock caper in front of them, and flap their wings, and fluff their necks, and do all they know to display their strength and beauty. Whoever dances the most and best, gets most of the hens to join his harem. So our young men have got up this love-dance to imitate them; they flap their arms the same way, and give the blackcock's challenge. Nature's pretty much the same above and below, I guess—especially here in the Tyrol, where we haven't yet learned to hide our feelings under smooth silk hats as you do in England. But it's all good for trade, and that's the great thing. It makes them thirsty. You'll see, after this bout, the beer will flow like water."

And, sure enough, the wirth was right. As soon as the dance was ended, young men and maidens, with equal zest, betook themselves, all alike, to the consolations of the beer-jug. Their thirst was mighty. And no wonder, indeed, for this Tyrolese dancing is no drawing-room game, but hard muscular exercise. Andreas Hausberger looked on with a cynical smile on those thin, cold lips of his. "It's good for trade," he murmured again, half to himself, once or twice, as the girls at the bar filled the beer-mugs merrily; "very good for trade. So are all amusements. That's the way the foolish get rid of their money—and the wise get hold of it."

After the beer came a pause, a long, deep-drawn pause; and then two young men, standing out from the throng, began to sing alternately at one another in short Tyrolese stanzas. One of them was Franz Lindner; the other was the young man with the scar on his forehead, whom Linnet described as her cousin Fridolin. What they sang, neither Florian nor Will could make out, for the words of the song were in the roughest form of the mountain dialect; but it was clear from their manner, and the way they flung out their words point blank at one another's heads, that they improvised as they went, like Virgilian shepherds, and that their remarks were by no means either polite or complimentary in substance or character. The rest stood round in a circle and listened, laughing heartily at times as each in turn scored a point now and then off his angry rival; while Linnet and the other girls blushed again and again at some audacious retort, though the bolder among the women only tittered to themselves or looked up with arch glances at each risky allusion. Andreas Hausberger too, stood by, all alert to keep the peace; it was plain from the quick light in his resolute eye, and the rapid upward movement of his twitching hand, he was ready at a moment's notice to intervene between the combatants, and put a stop in the nick of time to the scoffing contest of defiance and derision.

The song, however, passed off without serious breach of the peace. Then more dances followed, more beer, and more bucolic contests. As the evening wore on, the fun grew fast and furious. On the stroke of twelve, the Herr Vicar withdrew—not one hour too early; his flock were fast getting beyond control of his counsels. Linnet and a few others of the more modest-looking girls now sat out from the dance; the rest continued to whirl round and round the room in still wilder and more fantastic movements than ever. Andreas Hausberger was now yet more clearly on the alert. A stray spark would raise a flame in that magazine of gunpowder. Suddenly, at the end of the first dance after the priest's departure, the young man with the scar on his forehead, called Cousin Fridolin, came forward unexpectedly to where Linnet sat aside between Will Deverill and Florian. He had danced with her once before in the course of the evening, and Will observed that through that dance Franz Lindner's eyes had never been taken off his rival and Linnet. But now the tall young man came forward with a dash, and without one word of warning, placed his conical hat, blackcock's feather and all, with a jodel of challenge, on Linnet's forehead. They had seen the same thing done before more than once that evening, and Linnet had explained to them that the custom was equivalent to a declaration of love for the lady so honoured—'twas as much as to say, "This girl is mine; who disputes it?" But as the tall young man stood back with a smile of triumph on his handsome lips, one hand on his hip, staring fixedly at Linnet, Franz Lindner sprang forth with a face as black as night, and a brow like thunder. Trembling with rage, he seized the hat from her head, and tore hastily from its band the offending plume. "Was kost die Feder?" he cried, in a tone of angry contempt, holding it up in his hand before the eyes of its owner; "Was kost die Feder?" which is, being interpreted, "How much for your feather?"

Quick as lightning, the answer rang out, "Fünf Finger und ein Griff"—"Five fingers and a grip." It is the customary challenge of the Tyrolese Robbler, and the customary acceptance.

Before Will had time to understand what was happening next, in the crack of a finger, in the twinkle of an eye, the two young men had closed, with hands and arms and bodies, and were grappling with each other in a deadly struggle. All night long they had been watching and provoking one another; all night long they had vied in their attentions to Linnet, and their studious interchange of mutual insults. Sooner or later a fight seemed inevitable. Now, flown with insolence and beer, and heated from the dance, they flung themselves together, with one accord, like two tigers in their fury. Linnet clapped her hands to her ears, and shut her eyes in horror. For a minute or two, it seemed to every looker-on as though there would be bloodshed in the inn that evening. Florian observed this little episode with philosophic interest; 'twas pleasant to watch these simple dramas of the primary emotions, love, jealousy, passion, still working themselves out as on the stage of Hellas. He had never before seen them so untrammelled in their play; he stood here face to face with Homeric simplicity.

In five minutes, however, to his keen disappointment, the whole scene was finished. Andreas Hausberger, that cool, calm man of the world, perceiving at a glance that such contests in his inn were very bad for trade, and that 'twould be a pity for him to lose by a violent death so good a singer, or so constant a customer, interposed his heavy hand between the angry combatants. Your half-tipsy man, be he even a Tyrolese, though often quarrelsome, is usually placable. A short explanation soon set everything right again. Constrained by Herr Andreas, with his imperious will, the two Robblers consented, after terms interchanged, to drown their differences in more mugs of beer, and then retire for the evening. The young man with the scar, whom they called Cousin Fridolin, regretted that he had interfered with Franz Lindner's maiden, but excused his act as a mere hasty excess of cousinly feeling. Franz Lindner in return, not to be outdone in magnanimity, though still with flashing eyes, and keen side-glance at Linnet, regretted that he had offered such indignity in his haste to the dishonoured symbol of his comrade's championship. Hands were shaken all round; cuts and bruises were tended; and, almost as soon as said, to Florian's infinite disgust, the whole party had settled down by the tables once more, on an amicable basis, to beer and conversation.

But before they retired from that evening's revel, Linnet murmured to Will in a tone of remonstrance very real and aggrieved, "Franz Lindner had no right to call me his Mädchen."

CHAPTER VIII

THE HUMAN HEART

Next morning Will woke of himself very early. He jumped out of bed at once, and crossed, as he stood, to the open window. The sun had just risen. Light wisps of white cloud crawled slowly up the mountains; the dewdrops on the grass-blades sparkled in the silent rays like innumerable opals. 'Twas the very time for an early stroll! But the air, though keen, had the rawness and chill of an autumn morning. Will sniffed at it dubiously. He had half a mind to turn in again and take an hour's more sleep. Should he dress and go out, or let the world have time to get warmed and aired before venturing abroad in it?

As he debated and shivered, however, a sight met his eye which determined him at once on the more heroic course of action. It was Linnet, in her simple little peasant dress, turning up the hill-path that led behind the wirthshaus. Now, a chance of seeing Linnet alone without Florian was not to be despised; she interested him so much, and, besides, he wanted to ask her the whole truth about the Robblers. Without more ado, therefore, he dressed himself hastily, and strolled out of the inn. She hadn't gone far, he felt sure; he would find her close by, sitting by herself on the open grass-slope beyond the belt of pinewood.

And so, sure enough, he did. He came upon her unseen. She was seated with her back to him on a round boulder of grey stone, pouring her full throat in spontaneous music. For a minute or two, Will stood still, and listened and looked at her. He could see from his point of vantage, a little on one side behind the boulder, the rise and fall of her swelling bosom, the delicate trills under her rich brown chin. And then, oh, what melody! Will drank it in greedily. He was loth to disturb her, so delicious was this outpouring of her soul in song. For, like her namesake of the woods, Linnet sang best when she sang of her own accord, delivering her full heart of pure internal impulse.

At last she ceased, and turned. Her eye fell upon Will She started and blushed; she had expected no such audience. The young man raised his hat. "You're alone," he said, "Linnet?"

The girl looked up all crimson. "Yes; I came out that I should be alone," she answered, shyly, "I did not wish to see anyone. I wished for time to think many things over."

"Then you don't want me to stop?" Will broke in, somewhat crestfallen, yet drawing a step nearer.

"Oh, no; I do not mean that," Linnet answered in haste, laying her hand on her bosom. Then she burst into German, which came so much easier to her. "I wanted to get away from all the others," she said, looking up at him pleadingly, and, as she looked, Will saw for the first time that big tears stood brimming in her lustrous eyes; "I knew they would tease me about, about what happened last evening, and I didn't wish to hear it till I had thought over with myself what way I should answer them."

"Then you're not afraid of me?" Will asked, with a little thrill. She was only an alp-girl, but she sang like a goddess; and it's always pleasant, you know, to find a woman trusts one.

"I want you to stop," Linnet answered, simply.

She motioned him with one hand to a seat on a little heap of dry stones hard by. Will threw himself down on the heap in instant obedience to her mute command, and leaned eagerly forward. "Well, so this Robbler man wants to have you, Linnet," he said, with some earnestness; "and you don't want to have him. And he would have fought for you last night, against the man with the scar; and the girls in the inn will tease you about it this morning."

"Yes; the girls will tease me," Linnet answered, "and will say cruel things, for some of them are not fond of me, because, you see, Franz Lindner and the other man, my cousin Fridolin, are both of them Robblers, and would both of them fight for me. Now, a village that has a Robbler is always very proud of him; he's its champion and head; and if a Robbler pays attention to a girl, it's a very great honour. So some of the other girls don't like it at all, that the Robblers of two villages should quarrel about me. Though Gott in Himmel knows I've not encouraged either of them."

"And would you marry Franz Lindner?" Will asked, with genuine interest. It seemed to him a pity, nay, almost a desecration, that this beautiful girl, with her splendid voice, and all the possibilities it might enclose for the future, should throw herself away upon a Tyrolese hunter, whom the self-confidence engendered by mere muscular strength had turned for local eyes into a petty hero.

"No; I don't think I would marry him," Linnet answered, after a short pause, with a deliberative air, as though weighing well in her own mind all the pros and cons of it. "He'd take me if I chose, no doubt, and so also would Fridolin. Franz says he has left three other girls for me. But I don't like him, of course, any better for that. He ought to have kept to them."

"And you like him?" Will went on, drawing circles with his stick on the grass as he spoke, and glancing timidly askance at her.

"Yes; I like him, well enough," Linnet responded, doubtfully. "I liked him better once, perhaps. But of late, I care less for him. I never cared for him much indeed; I was never his Mädchen. He had no right to say that, no right at all, at all—for with us, you know, in Tyrol, that means a great deal. How much, I couldn't tell you. But I never gave him any cause at all to say so."

"And of late you like him less?" Will inquired, pressing her hard with this awkward question. Yet he spoke sympathetically. He had no reason for what he said, to be sure, no reason on earth. He spoke at random, out of that pure instinctive impulse which leads every man in a pretty girl's presence, mean he little or much, to make at least the best of every passing advantage. 'Tis pure virility that: the natural Adam within us. I wouldn't give ten cents for the too virtuous man who by "ethical culture" has educated it out of him.

Linnet looked down at her shoes, for she possessed those luxuries. "Yes; of late I like him less," she answered, somewhat tremulously.

"Why so?" Will insisted. His lips, too, quivered.

Linnet raised her dark eyes and met his for one instant. "I've seen other people since; perhaps I like other people better," she answered, candidly.

"What other people?" Will asked, all on fire.

"Oh, that would be telling," Linnet answered, with an arch look. "Perhaps my cousin Fridolin, or perhaps the young man with the yellow beard, or perhaps the gnädige Herr's honoured friend, Herr Florian."

Will drew figures with his stick on the grass for a minute or two. Then he looked up and spoke again. "But, in any case," he said, "you don't mean, whatever comes, to marry Franz Lindner?" It grieved him to think she should so throw herself away upon a village bully.

Linnet plucked a yellow ragwort and pulled out the ray-florets one by one as she answered, "I shan't have the chance. For, to tell you the truth, I think Andreas Hausberger means himself to marry me."

At the words, simply spoken, Will drew back, all aghast. The very notion revolted him. As yet, he was not the least little bit in his own soul aware he was in love with Linnet. He only knew he admired her voice very much; for the rest, she was but a simple, beautiful, unlettered peasant girl. It doesn't occur, of course, to an English gentleman in Will Deverill's position, to fall in love at first sight with a Tyrolese milkmaid. But Andreas Hausberger! the bare idea distressed him. The man was so cold, so cynical, so austere, so unlovable! and Will more than half-suspected him of avaricious money-grubbing. The girl was so beautiful, so simple-hearted, so young, and Heaven only knew to what point of success that voice might lead her. "Oh no," he burst out, impetuously; "you can't really mean that?—you never could dream, don't tell me you could, of accepting that man Andreas Hausberger as a husband!"

"Why not?" the girl said, calmly. "He's rich and well to do. I could keep my mother in such comfort then, and pay for such masses for my father's soul, far more than if I took Franz Lindner or my cousin Fridolin, who are only jägers. Andreas Hausberger's a wirth, the richest man in St Valentin; he has horses and cows and lands and pastures. And if he says I must, how can I well refuse him?"

She looked up at him with a look of childlike appeal. In a moment, though with an effort, Will realised to himself how the question looked to her. Andreas Hausberger was her master, and had always been her master. She must do as he bid, for he was very masterful. He was her teacher, too, and would help her to make her fortune as a singer in the world, if ever she made it. He was rich, as the folk of the village counted riches, and could manage that things should be pleasant or unpleasant for her, as it suited his fancy. In a community where men still fought with bodily arms for their brides, Andreas Hausberger's will might well seem law to his sennerin in any such matter.

"Besides," Linnet went on, plucking another ragwort, and similarly demolishing it, "if I didn't want to take him, the Herr Vicar would make me. For the Herr Vicar would do, of course, as Andreas Hausberger wished him. And how could I dare disobey the Herr Vicar's orders?"

To this subtle question of religion and morals Will Deverill, for his part, had no ready-made answer. Church and State, it was clear, were arrayed against him. So, after casting about for a while in his own mind in vain for a reply, he contented himself at last with going off obliquely on a collateral issue. "And you think," he said, "Andreas Hausberger really wants to marry you?"

"Well, he never quite told me so," Linnet replied, half-deprecatingly, as who fears to arrogate to herself too great an honour, "and perhaps I'm wrong; but still I think he means it. And I think it'll perhaps depend in part upon how he finds the foreign Herrschaft like my singing. For that, he says little to me about it at present. But if he sees I do well, and am worth making his wife, for he's the best husband a girl could get in St Valentin, in that case, ja wohl, I believe he'll ask me."

She said it all naturally, as so much matter of course. But Will's poetic soul rebelled against the sacrifice. "Surely," he cried, "you must love someone else; and why not, then, take the man you love, whoever he may be, and leave Andreas Hausberger's money to perish with him?"

"So!" Linnet said quickly, the pretty German "so!" Her fingers trembled as she twitched at the rays of the ragwort. She plucked the florets in haste, and flung them away one by one. First love's conversation deals largely in pauses. "The man one might love," she murmured at last with a petulant air, "doesn't always love one. How should he, indeed? It is not in nature. For, doesn't the song say, 'Who loves me, love I not; whom I love, loves me not?' But what would the Herr Vicar say if he heard me talking like this with the foreign gentlefolk? He'd tell me it was sin. A girl should not speak of her heart to strangers. I have spoken too much. But I couldn't help it, somehow. The gnädige Herr is always so kind to me. You lead me on to confess. You can understand these things, I think, so much better than the others."

She rose, half-hesitating. Will Deverill, for his part, rose in turn and faced her. For a second each paused; they looked shyly at one another. Will thought her a charming girl, for a common milkmaid. Linnet thought him a kind, good friend, for one of the great unapproachable foreign Herrschaft. Will held out one frank hand. Linnet gave him the tips of her brown fingers timidly. He clasped them in his own while a man might count ten. "Shall you be here . . . to-morrow . . . about the same time?" he inquired, before he let them drop, half hesitating.

"Perhaps," Linnet answered, looking down demurely. Then blushing, she nodded at him, half curtsied, and sprang away. She gave a rapid glance to right and left, to see if she was perceived, darted lightly down the hill, and hurried back to the wirthshaus.

But all that day long, Will was moody and silent. He thought much to himself of this strange idea that Andreas Hausberger, that saturnine man, was to marry this beautiful musical alp-girl.

CHAPTER IX

THE MAN OF THE WORLD

For some four or five mornings after this hillside interview, Florian noticed every day a most unaccountable fancy on Will Deverill's part for solitary walks at early dawn before breakfast. Neither dew nor hoar-frost seemed to damp his ardour. Florian rose betimes himself, to be sure, but Will had always already distanced him. And on every one of those five mornings, when Will said farewell to Linnet by the big grey boulder, he used the same familiar formula of leave-taking, "You'll be here again to-morrow?" And every time, Linnet, thrilling and trembling inwardly, answered back the same one conscience-salving word, "Perhaps," which oracular and highly hypothetical promise she nevertheless most amply fulfilled with great regularity on the following morning. For, when Will arrived at the trysting-place, he always found Linnet was there before him; and she rose from her rocky seat with a blush of downcast welcome, which a less modest man than he might easily have attributed to its true motive. To Will, however, most unassuming of men and poets, she was only an interesting alp-girl, who liked to meet him on the hillside for a lesson in English. Though, to be sure, why it was necessary to give the lesson alone in the open air at six o'clock in the morning, and, still more, why the professor should have thought it needful to hold the pupil's hand in his own for many minutes together, to enforce his points, Will himself would no doubt have been hard put to explain on philological principles. Moreover, strange to say, for Linnet's sake, the conversation was conducted mostly in German.

Lookers-on, however, see most of the game. On the sixth such morning, it occurred casually to Florian as he lay abed and reflected, to get up early himself and go out on the hillside. Not that the airy epicurean philosopher was by any means afflicted with the essentially vulgar vice of curiosity. He was far too deeply occupied with Mr Florian Wood to think of expending much valuable attention on the habits and manners of less-interesting personalities. But in this particular case he felt he had a positive Duty to perform. Now, a Duty had for Florian all the luxury of novelty. He was troubled with few such, and whenever he found one, he made the most of it. Just at present, he was persuaded Will Deverill was on the eve of "getting himself into an entanglement" with the beautiful milkmaid who so paradoxically preferred his society to Florian's. Plain Duty, therefore, to Will himself, to Mrs Deverill mère, to the just expectations of the ladies of England (who had clearly a prior claim on Will's fortune and affection), compelled Florian to interfere before things went too far, so as to save his friend from the consequences of his own possible folly. Animated by these noble impulses, Florian did not even shrink from leaving a very snug bed at five o'clock that cold morning, and waiting at the window, like a private detective, till Will took his way up the path to the hillside.

About six, Will emerged from the door of the inn. Florian gave him law, five minutes law, just rope enough to hang himself. Then, marking from the back window which way Will had gone, he followed the trail up hill with all the novel zest of an amateur policeman. Skulking along the pinewood, he came upon them from behind, by the same path which Will himself had taken on the morning when he followed Linnet first to the boulder in the pasture. Then, treading softly over the green turf with muffled footfall, he was close upon the unconscious pair before they knew or suspected it. The ill-advised young people were seated side by side on a little ledge of rock that protruded from the green-sward. Will leant eagerly forward, holding Linnet's hand, and looking hard into her eyes; the girl herself drew back, and cast down her glance, as if half fearing the ardour of his evident advances. Respect for the conventions made Florian cough lightly before disturbing their interview. At the sound, both looked up. Some five feet nothing of airy observant humanity beamed blandly down upon them. Linnet gave a little cry, started up in surprise, hid her crimson face hurriedly between two soft brown hands, and then, yielding to the first impulse of her shy rustic nature, fled away without one word, leaving Will face to face with that accusing moralist.

The epicurean philosopher seated himself, like stern justice in miniature, beside his erring friend. His face was grave: when Florian did gravity, he did it, as life did everything else, "consummately." For a minute or two he only stared hard at Will, slowly nodding his head like an earthenware mandarin, and stroking his smooth chin in profound meditation. At the end of that time, he delivered his bolt, point blank. "Tomorrow," he said, calmly, "we go on to Innsbruck."

"Why so?" Will asked, with a dogged air of dissent.

"Because," Florian answered, with crushing dialectic, "we never intended to spend our whole time on the upper Zillerthal, did we?"

This sudden flank movement took Will fairly by surprise. For Florian was quite right. Their plan of campaign on leaving London included the South Tyrol, Verona, and Milan. "But a day or two longer," he put in, half-imploringly, thus caught off his guard. "Just a day or two longer to . . . to settle things up a bit."

Stern justice was inexorable. "Not one other night," Florian answered, severely. "The lotus has by this time been sufficiently eaten. I see what this means. I know now why you've kept me here so long at St Valentin. With Innsbruck and Cortina and the untrodden Dolomites beckoning me on to come, you've planted me plump in this hole, and kept me here at your side, all for the sake of one Tyrolese cow-girl. In the name of common morality," and Florian frowned like a very puisne judge, "I protest against these most irregular and improper proceedings."

"I never meant the girl any harm," Will answered, with a faint flush.

"That's just it, my dear fellow. I know very well you didn't. That's the head and front of your offending. If you had meant her harm, of course I could much more readily have forgiven you."

"Florian," Will said, looking up, "let's be serious, please, for once. This is a serious matter."

Florian pursed his thin lips, and knitted his white brow judicially. "H'm, h'm," he said, with slow deliberateness. "It's as bad as that, is it? Why, Deverill, I assure you, I've rarely, if ever, been as serious as this in all my life before. Don't look at me like that. I mean just what I say. I'm not thinking about the girl, but about you, my dear fellow. The morals of these parts, as you very well know, are primitive—primitive. It won't do her much harm, even if it gets noised about, to have been seen on the hills, alone in the grey dawn, hand in hand with an Englishman. This is no place for Oriental seclusion of women. Indeed, from what I hear, the Arcadian relations of these unchaperoned alp-girls with their lovers from the plains must be something truly sweet in their unaffected simplicity. Herr Hausberger was telling me last night that when an alp-girl marries, all the hunters and peasants, her discarded lovers, whom she has admitted to the intimacy of her châlet on the mountains, leave a cradle at the door of her chosen husband on the night of the wedding. The good man wakes up the morning after his marriage to find staring him in the face, on his own threshold, these tangible proofs of his wife's little slips in her spinster existence. . . . It's a charming custom. I find it quite economical. He knows the worst at once. It saves him the trouble, so common among ourselves, of finding them out for himself piecemeal in the course of his later relations."

"You are wandering from the question," Will interrupted, testily. He didn't quite relish these generalised innuendoes against poor Linnet's character.

"Not at all, not at all," Florian went on very gravely. "The point of these remarks lies in the application thereof, as Captain Cuttle puts it. . . . When Linnet marries, you mean, I suppose, to increase the number of the delicate little offerings presented at her door by—"

Will started up and glared at him. "You shall not speak like that," he cried in a very angry voice, "of such a girl as Linnet."

The little man waved one dainty white hand with a deprecating gesture towards his excited friend. "This is too bad," he said, sighing, "very bad indeed, far worse than I imagined. I said it on purpose, just to see what you were driving at. And I find out the worst. If you mean the girl no harm, and take a slighting little jest on her to heart like that, why your case is desperate—an aggravated attack, complicated by incipient matrimonial symptoms. You need change of air, change of scene, change of company. Law of Medes and Persians, it's Innsbruck to-morrow! You go with me as I bid, or I go without you. Demur, and I leave you at once to your fate. You may stop with your cow-girl."

"Don't speak of her by that name!" Will broke in, half-angrily.

But Florian, for his part, was provokingly cool. "All A is A," he said, calmly, with irresistible logic—"and every cow-girl's a cow-girl. I'll call her a boutrophista, or a neat-herding Phyllis, if it gives you any pleasure. That's neither here nor there. The point's just this—You mean the girl no harm: then what the deuce do you mean? Are you going to marry her?"

"No; certainly not," Will answered. She was a very nice girl, and he loved to talk with her—there was something so sweetly unsophisticated in her ways that she charmed and attracted him. But marry her? No; the very word surprised him; he had never even dreamt of it. In the first place (though as yet he hadn't as much as thought about that), he had nothing to marry upon. And in the second place, if he had, could he take a Tyrolese milkmaid fresh from the cowsheds in his tow to London, and present her to his friends as Mrs Will Deverill?

"Then what the deuce do you mean?" Florian repeated, persistently. His sound common-sense, when he chose to let it loose from his veneer of affectation, was no mean commodity.

Thus driven to bay, Will was forced to reply with a somewhat sheepish air, "I don't know that I mean anything. I've never tried to formulate my state of mind to myself. She's a very nice girl . . . for her class and sort . . . and I like to talk to her."

"And when you talk to her, you like to hold her hand and lean forward like this, and stare with all your eyes, and look for all the world as if you wanted to devour her! Oh yes; I've seen you. No, no, Will, it won't do; I've been there myself, and I know all about it. Looking at the matter impartially, as a man of the world"—and Florian, drawing himself up, assumed automatically, as those words rolled out, his most magisterial attitude—"what I'm really afraid of is that you'll get gradually dragged into this rustic syren's vortex, and be swallowed up before you know it in the treacherous sea of matrimony. However, you don't believe that, and I know enough of the world to know very well it's no use, therefore, arguing out that aspect of the case with you. No fellow will ever believe he can be such a fool—till he catches himself in church face to face at last with the awful reality. I prefer, accordingly, to go on the other tack with you. If you don't mean to marry the girl, then, whether you know it or not, you mean no good to her. I dare say you've got all sorts of conventional notions in your head, which, thank heaven, I don't share, about honour and so forth . . . how a cow-girl's virtue, I beg your pardon, a boutrophista's, or a neat-herding Phyllis's, is as sacred at your hands as the eldest daughter's of a hundred marquises. But that's neither here nor there. If you don't marry the girl, and you don't ruin the girl, there's only one thing left possible—you must break the girl's heart for her. Between ourselves, being, I flatter myself, a tolerable psychologist, I don't for a moment suppose that's what would actually happen; you'd get yourself entangled, and you'd go on and on, and you'd flounder and struggle, and you'd marry her in the end, just to save the girl misery. But we'll do poojah to your intellect at the expense of your heart, and we'll put it the other way, as you seem to prefer it. Very well, then; sooner or later you'll have to leave this place. No doubt, after what I've seen this morning, it'll cost the girl a wrench—her vanity must be flattered by receiving so much undisguised attention from a real live gentleman. But, sooner or later, as I say, come it must, of course; and sooner, on the whole, will be better for her than later. The longer you stop, the more she'll fall in love with you; the quicker you get away from her the less it'll hurt her."

He spoke the words of wisdom—according to his kind. Will rose again with an effort, and started homeward. As they walked down the pasture, and through the belt of pinewood, he said never a word. But he thought all the more on Florian's counsel. Till that morning, he had never tried to face the question himself: he liked the girl—that was all; she sang like a linnet; and he loved to be near her. But the longer he stopped, the harder for her would be the inevitable breaking off. Just beyond the pinewood Florian halted and fronted him. "See here, Will," he said, kindly, but with the world's common sense, "it isn't that I care twopence myself what becomes of the girl—girls like that are just made for you and me to play skittles with; if you meant her any harm I wouldn't for the world interfere with any other man's little fancies. All I want is to get you away from the place before you've time to commit yourself. I use the other argument as an argumentum ad hominem only. But as that it has its weight. The longer you stop, the harder it'll be in the end for her."

Will drew a deep breath. His mind was made up now. "Very well, then," he said, slowly, though with an evident struggle; "if I must go, I must go. I won't haggle over a day. Let us make it to-morrow."

CHAPTER X

HAIL, COLUMBIA!

And next morning, indeed, saw them safe at Innsbruck.

'Twas a pull to get away; Will frankly admitted to his own soul he felt it so. But he saw it was right, and he went accordingly. Linnet, he knew, had grown fond of him in those few days; when he asked her once how it was she liked Franz Lindner less now than formerly, she looked up at him with an arch smile, and, after a second's pause, made the frank avowal: "Perhaps it's because now . . . I think Englishmen nicer." At the moment his heart had come up in his mouth with pleasure, as will happen with all of us when a pretty woman lets us see for ourselves she really likes us. But he must go all the same: for Linnet's sake—he must go: if illusion there were, he must at once disillusion her.

As for Linnet herself, she accepted the separation much more readily, to say the truth, than Will ever imagined she could. It half-piqued him, indeed, to find how easily she seemed to acquiesce in the inevitable. She trembled when he told her, to be sure, and tears started to her eyes; but she answered, none the less, in a fairly firm voice, that she always knew the gnädige Herr must go away in the end; that she hoped he would remember her wherever he went; and she, with a deep sigh, she could never forget his kindness. That, however, was all. Just a pressure of her fingers, just a kiss on his hand, just a tear that dropped wet on his outstretched palm as she bent her head over it in customary obeisance, and Linnet was gone, and he saw no more of her that evening. In the morning when he stood at the door to bid farewell to the household, he fancied her eyes looked red with crying. But she grasped his hand hard, for all that, and said goodbye without flinching. He gave a florin or two as Trinkgeld to each of the servants at the inn; but to Linnet he felt he couldn't give anything. She was of different mould. Linnet noticed the omission herself, with a glistening eye, and took it, as it was meant, for a social distinction.

The plain truth was, she had always expected Will must soon go away from her. Nor was she indeed as yet what one might fairly call quite in love with him. The very distance between them seemed to forbid the feeling. He was kind, he was sympathetic, he was musical, he was a gentleman, he divined her better qualities, her deeper feelings; he spoke to her more deferentially and with truer respect than any of her own equals had ever yet spoken to her; she couldn't help feeling flattered that he should like to come out upon the hillside to talk with her; but, as yet, she hardly said to herself she loved him. If she had, what good? Was it likely such a great gentleman from over the seas would care to marry a mere Tyrolese milkmaid? Was it likely, if he did, the wirth and the priest would allow her to marry a Protestant Englishman?

So, from the very outset, save as a passing affection, Will Deverill stood wholly outside poor Linnet's horizon. She regarded him as a pleasant but short-lived episode. Besides, light loves are the rule with the alp-girl. It was quite in the nature of things for Linnet that a man should take a liking to her, should pay her brief court, should expect from her far greater favours than ever Will Deverill expected, and should give her up in the end for a mere freak of fancy. That was the way of the Zillerthal! So, though the thorn had gone deep, she accepted her fate as just what one might have anticipated, and hardly cried for an hour in her own bed at night, to think those sweet mornings on the pasture by the pinewood were to be over for ever. For of course, in the end, if the wirth so willed, she must marry herself contentedly to Andreas Hausberger.

Acting on Florian's advice, Will did not even tell his tremulous little friend he was going to Innsbruck. "Better break it off at once," Florian said, with practical common-sense, "once for all and absolutely. No chance of letters or any nonsense of that sort, if the dulcinea can write, which of course is doubtful." And Will, having made up his mind to the wrench, acquiesced in this sage council. So for Linnet, the two strangers who had loomed so large, and played so leading a part on the stage of her little life for one rapturous fortnight, vanished utterly, as it were, at a single breath, like a dissolving cloud, into the infinite and the unknowable.

By seven that night, the young Englishmen found themselves once more in the full flood of civilisation. The electric light shed its beams on their hotel; a Parisian chef de cuisine turned out sweetbreads and ices of elaborate art to pamper their palates. Once more, Florian donned with joy the black coat of Bond Street. They had penetrated the Zillerthal with their knapsacks on their backs; but two leather portmanteaus, enclosing the fuller garb of civilised life, awaited their advent at Innsbruck. Thus restored to society, with a rosebud in his buttonhole, the dainty little man descended radiant to the salle-à-manger. He welcomed the change; after three whole weeks of unadulterated Nature, he had tired of Arcadia. And he loved tables-d'hôte: 'twas a field for the prosecution of social conquests. "A man goes there on his merits," he said briskly to Will, as they dressed for dinner, "neither handicapped nor yet unduly weighted. Nobody knows who he is, and he knows nobody. So he starts there on the flat, without fear or favour; and if at the end of ten minutes he hasn't managed to make himself the centre of a conversational circle, he may retire into private life as a social failure."

On this particular evening, however, in spite of several brilliant and manful efforts, Florian didn't somehow succeed in attracting an audience quite so readily as usual. The environment was against him. On his right sat a lady whom he discovered by a side glance at the name written legibly on the napkin ring by her plate, to be the Honourable Mrs Medway, and who was so profoundly filled with a sense of the importance of her own Honourableness that she feared to contaminate herself or her daughter by conversation with her neighbours till she had satisfied her mind by sure and certain warranty that they too belonged to the Right Set in England. Pending proof to that effect, her answers to his questions were both curt and monosyllabic. This nettled Florian, who prided himself with truth on his extensive knowledge of all the "smart people." To his left, beyond Will, on the other hand, sat a stolid-looking gentleman of nonconformist exterior and provincial garb, whose conversation, though ample, betrayed at times the inelegant idiom and accent of the Humber. Him Florian the silver-tongued carefully avoided. Opposite, was a vacant place, on either side of which sat two young girls of seventeen or thereabouts in the acutest stage of giggling inarticulateness. Florian listened, and despaired. Here was a coterie, indeed, for a brilliant talker and a man of culture!

But just as they finished the soup, to his intense relief, a ray of light seemed to pierce of a sudden the gathering gloom of the dinner table. The drawing-room door opened, and through its portal a Vision of Beauty in an evening dress floated, Hellenic goddess-wise, into the salle-à-manger. It made its way straight to the vacant chair, nodded and smiled recognition to the bread-and-butter gigglers and the Honourable Mrs Medway, bowed demurely, continental-way, to the newly come strangers, and glided off at once, without a pause or break, into a general flow all round of graceful, easy conversation. Florian gazed, and succumbed. This was a real live woman! Ripe, but not too ripe, soft and rounded of outline, with a bewitching mouth, a row of pearly teeth, and a cheek that wore only its own natural roses, she might have impressed at first sight a less susceptible heart by far than the epicurean sage's. As she seated herself, she drew from her pocket a little cardboard box, which she handed with a charming smile to one of the giggling inarticulates. "Those are the set you admired, I think," she said, with unconscious grace. "I hope I've got the right ones. I was passing the shop on my way back from my drive, and I thought I'd just drop in and bring them back as you liked them so."

The giggling inarticulate gave a jerky little scream of unmixed delight as she opened the box and took out from it with tremulous hands a pretty set of coral necklet, brooch, and earrings. "Not for me!" she cried, gasping; "not for me—for a present! You don't really mean to give them to me! They're too lovely, too delicious!"

"Yes, I do," the Vision of Beauty responded, beaming. "I wanted to give you some little souvenir some time before you went, and I didn't know what you'd like; so, as you said you admired these, I thought I'd best go in at once as I passed and buy them. They're pretty, aren't they?"

Florian eyed them with the lenient glance of a man of taste who appraises and appreciates a beautiful woman's selection. When the bread-and-butter gigglers had exhausted upon them their slender stock of laudatory adjectives—their oh's and just look's, and dear me, aren't they beautiful's—he broke in with his bland smile, and, laying the necklet in a curve on the white tablecloth before him, began to discourse with much unction in the Florianic tongue, on the æsthetic points of this pretty trifle. For it was a pretty necklet, there was no denying that; its lance-like pendants were delicately shaped and most gracefully arranged; it was one of those simple half-barbaric designs which retain to our day all the naïve beauty of primitive unsophisticated human workmanship. Florian found in it reminiscences of Eve in Eden. And he said so in that luxuriantly florid style of which he was so great and so practical a master. He called attention with suave tones to the distinctly precious suggestions of archaic influence in the shaping of the pendants; to the exquisite nature of coral as a decorative object, cast up blushing on our shores by the ungarnered sea—a material whose use we inherit from our innocent ancestors, when wild in woods the noble savage ran, his limbs untrammelled by clinging draperies—when beauty unadorned was adorned the most in the subtle and sinuous curves of its own lissome figure. Necklets and armlets, he observed, with one demonstrative white forefinger held poised above the salmon, are the string-courses, so to speak, of this our natural human architecture; they serve to emphasise and throw out into stronger relief the structural points of the grand design, to call attention to the exquisite native fulness of a faultless torso.

The giggling inarticulates dropped their chins and stared. They were not quite sure whether such talk was proper. But the Vision of Beauty, more at home in the world, was not in the least alarmed at Florian's torrent of eloquence. On the contrary, she answered him back, as he himself remarked a little later to Will, like the lords of the council, with grace, wisdom, and understanding. Florian brightened, and flowed on. He loved a listener who could toss the ball back to him as fast as he tossed it. And the Vision of Beauty answered him back with lightning speed, and bore her share with credit in the conversation. It was evident as she went on that she knew her Europe. Was it Munich Florian touched upon with the light hand of his craft?—she discoursed of the Van der Weydens and Crivellis in the Pinakothek, like one to the manner born, and had views of her own which were bold, if not prudent, about the meaning and arrangement of the Aeginetan marbles. Was it Florence he attacked?—she was at home at San Marco, and knew her way like a Baedeker round the rooms at the Pitti. Will listened and marvelled, talking little himself, but giving Florian and the Vision of Beauty their heads. It surprised him much to find one female brain could store in its teeming cells so much miscellaneous knowledge.

At last, at a brief break in Florian's flood of speech, Will found space to inquire, for a purpose of his own, "Would you mind my asking where you got that necklet?"

The Vision of Beauty handed the lid of the box to him. It bore, on a label, the name and address of the jeweller at whose shop she had bought it. "It's on the way up," she said, carelessly, "to this hotel from the city."

That one Shibboleth betrayed her. Florian started in surprise. "Why," he cried with open eyes, "then you must be an American."

The beautiful stranger smiled and nodded. "Yes, sir," she said with marked emphasis, as if to clinch the assertion of her western nationality. "I am an American, and I don't want to hide it. But you pay what you consider a compliment to the purity of my English all the same, if you mean that till now you haven't even suspected it."

Florian made some politely condescending remark, of the sort so obnoxious to the late Mr Lowell, as to the correctness and delicacy of her English accent, and then, in order to show himself quite abreast of the times, inquired expansively if she knew the Van Rensselaers.

"No; I haven't had that pleasure," the Vision of Beauty answered, curtly.

"The Livingstones, perhaps?" Florian adventured, in tentative tones.

The Vision shook her head.

"My friends the Vanderbilts?" Florian essayed once more, eager to find a connecting link. "I stayed with them at Newport."

"No; nor yet the Vanderbilts," the Vision answered, smiling.

Florian paused and reflected. "Ah, then, you're from Boston, no doubt," he suggested, with charitable promptitude. The fine friends he had mentioned, at whose houses he had stopped, were all New Yorkers.

"No; not from Boston," the Vision answered with prompt negation.

"Washington, I suppose?" Florian adventured again. They were the only three places a self-respecting American could admit she came from without shipwreck of her dignity. He would not pay so much grace and eloquence the very bad compliment, as it seemed to him, of supposing it could "register" from St Louis or New Orleans.

The pretty woman smiled once more, a self-restrained smile. "I come from New York," she said, simply. "I've lived there long. It's my native place. But there are a good many of us there who don't aspire to know the Roosevelts or the Livingstones."

Florian withdrew, with quiet tact, from this false departure. He led aside the conversation, by graceful degrees, to the old Dutch families, the New England stock—Emerson, Longfellow, Channing, the Concord set: Howells, James, and Stedman, the later American poets. On these last he waxed warm. But the Vision of Beauty, herself cosmopolitan to the core, was all for our newest school of English bards. She doted on Lang and Austin Dobson.

"And have you seen the last Illustrated?" she asked, after awhile, with a burst of enthusiasm. "It's on the table in the salon there. And there are three, oh, such lovely, lovely stanzas in it, 'Among Alps,' by Will Deverill."

Her words sent a thrill of pleasure through Will's modest soul. He had published but little, and 'twas seldom he heard his own name thus familiarly unhandled. Still, a harassing doubt possessed his soul. Could the Vision of Beauty have seen his name in the visitors' book of the hotel, noticed the coincidence with the lines in the Illustrated, which he had sent from the Zillerthal, and managed this little coup with feminine adroitness, on purpose to deceive him? Yet she didn't look guileful. With poetic trustfulness, he cast the evil suggestion at once behind him. "I'm so glad you liked them," he said, timidly, looking down at his plate, and playing in nervous jerks with his fork in the chicken. "I wrote them in the Tyrol here. They're fresh-fed from the glaciers."

The Vision laid down her knife and fork and stared at him, speechless. "You're not Will Deverill," she exclaimed, in some excitement, after a moment's pause.

"That's my name," Will answered, somewhat abashed, still perusing his plate. "But I'm very little used to—to—to meeting people who have heard of it."

The pretty American clasped her hands with delight "Well, I am glad to meet you," she said, "though I'd have given you the benefit of the Mr, of course, if I'd known it was you. I just love your verses. I have 'Voices from the Hills' in my box upstairs, bound in calf, this minute."

"No; not really?" Will cried, with a young author's delight at unexpected recognition.

"I'll go upstairs after dinner and fetch it down to show you," his pretty admirer answered, with some pride. "And your friend, too, is he a poet?"

"In soul; in soul only!" Florian interposed, airily, dashing in at a tangent; for it irked him thus to play second fiddle to Will's first hand, and he longed to assert his "proper position." "I string no sonnets; I play no harmonies; I take the higher place. I sit on a critical throne, weighing and appraising all arts impartially. Deverill rhymes; another man paints; a third man strums; a fourth acts, or carves stone—and all for me. I exercise none of these base handicrafts myself; but I live supreme in the Palace of Art they build, subordinating each in due place to my soul's delight, like a subtle architect."

"Just the same as all the rest of us," the pretty American put in, interrupting his period. "We all do that. We sit still and listen. The difficulty is—to produce, like Mr Deverill."

Florian stood aghast. To think a mere woman should thus slight his pretensions! But the pretty American, disregarding him, turned to Will once more. "And your friend's name?" she said, interrogatively.

"My friend's name," Will answered, "is Florian Wood. You must know it."

"Ah, Mr Florian Wood," the pretty stranger echoed; "I've heard of him, of course. I'm glad to meet him. It's so nice to see people in the flesh at last one has often heard talked about."

"But you've heard about everybody, Mrs Palmer," the first giggling inarticulate interposed, with a gurgle of admiration.

Florian clapped his hand to his head in theatrical disappointment. "Mrs Palmer!" he cried, markedly. "Did I hear aright, Mrs Palmer? This is indeed a blow! Then, I take it, you're married!"

From anyone else on earth, the remark would have been rude; from Florian, it was only exaggerated compliment. The Vision of Beauty accepted it as such with American frankness.

"Well, you needn't go and take a draught of cold poison offhand," she retorted, a little saucily, "for there's still a chance for you. Remember, a woman may be maid, wife, . . . or widow."

"Dear me," Florian ejaculated, half-choking himself in his haste, "I never thought of that. You don't mean to say—"

"Yes, I do," Mrs Palmer responded, cutting him short with a merry nod. "Any time these last five years. Now, you're sorry you spoke. Mr Deverill, may I trouble you to pass the mustard?"

CHAPTER XI

PRIVATE INQUIRY

During the rest of the young men's stay at Innsbruck the pretty American was, as Florian remarked, "a distinct feature." Such is the fickleness of man, indeed, that she almost superseded poor Linnet in their minds as an object of interest. She was attractive beyond a doubt; she was clever; she was lively; and she was so delighted to make a real live poet's acquaintance, that Will hardly knew how to receive her almost obtrusive attentions. She brought him butter in a lordly dish, as Florian phrased it. That same evening, in the salon, according to promise, she came down with "Voices from the Hills," Will's thin little volume of fugitive verse, which she had had gorgeously bound in red calf in Paris, and made that sensitive young bard blush up to his eyes with modesty, by insisting on pointing out which pieces she liked best, in a voice that was audible to half the guests in the establishment. Ossian's Tomb was her favourite—she knew that one by heart; but Khosru Khan was sweet too; and Sister Clare made her cry; and then Gwyn!—ah, that dear Gwyn was just too lovely for anything!

And yet, Will liked her. In spite of her open praise, and his blushes, he liked her. The surest way to a poet's heart is to speak well of his poetry. And besides, he said to himself, Mrs Palmer had discrimination. She noted in his verse the metrical variety, the pictorial skill, the strong sense of colour—just the qualities of his poor muse on which he himself most prided himself. No artist cares for praise except for those characteristics of his art which he feels to be his strong ones. Mrs Palmer gave Will that, and he liked the incense.

Florian had said at St Valentin that Will needed change of air, change of scene, change of company. And at Innsbruck he got them. The pretty American, having found her poet, didn't mean to let him slip again too soon from her clutches. With the pertinacity of her compatriots, she fastened herself at once upon the two young Englishmen. Not obtrusively, to be sure, not ungracefully, not awkwardly, not as a European woman might have done the same thing, but with that occidental frankness and oblivion of sex which makes up half the charm of the charming American. The very next morning, at the early breakfast, she happened to occupy a small table close by them. They chatted together through the meal; at the end of it Will mentioned, in a casual sort of way that he was going down the street to the shop where Mrs Palmer had bought the coral necklet. The dainty young widow seized her cue. "I am going down that way myself," she said. "Let me come and show you. I won't take a minute to run up for my hat. I'm not one of those women who can never go out for a morning stroll without spending half-an-hour before their mirrors, tittivating." And, in spite of Will's assurance that he could find the shop very well by himself, she was as good as her word, and insisted on accompanying them.

She had been charming in evening dress; she was more charming still in her girlish straw hat and neat tailor-made costume, as she tripped lightly downstairs to them. Florian, by her side, while they walked through the streets, cast sheep's eyes askance up at her. Even Will, more mindful of poor Linnet's desertion, was not wholly insensible to that taking smile, those pearly white teeth, that dainty small nose, those rounded contours. They turned down the road in the direction of the Maria-Theresien Strasse. Will knew of old that quaintest and most picturesque of European High Streets, with its queer gabled roofs, its rococo façades, its mediæval towers, its arcades and pillars. But to Florian, it all came with the added charm of novelty. Twice or thrice on their way, the spirit moved him to stop and perorate. Each time, the pretty widow cut him short at once with some quick retort of truly American practicality. At the shop, Will selected a second necklet, exactly like the one Mrs Palmer had chosen. "I gave her nothing before I came away," he said, turning to Florian, and only indicating by that very indefinite pronoun, the intended recipient of his beautiful gift. "One couldn't give her money. 'Twould have been a positive insult. But this ought to look well on that smooth brown neck of hers."

"For your sister, of course," Mrs Palmer said, pointedly.

"No; not for my sister," Will admitted, with a quiet smile. "For a girl at the inn we've just left at St Valentin."

Mrs Palmer said "Oh!" 'Twas an American oh. It deprecated the fact—and closed the episode. Cosmopolitan though she was, it surprised her not a little that Will should allude to such persons in a lady's company. But there! these poets, you know—so many things must be condoned to them. Because they have loved much, much must be forgiven them. They have licence to break hearts and the most brittle of the commandments, with far less chance of blame than their even Christians.

Will's transaction completed, Mrs Palmer proceeded to buy a second similar set on her own account, for presentation to the second of the giggling inarticulates. "Poor girl!" she said, good-humouredly, "she looked so envious last night when I gave the other to Eva Powell, I couldn't bear to think I'd left her out in the cold. Thirty florins, I think you said? Ah, yes; that's twelve dollars. Not much to make a poor little girl so happy!"

From this, and various other circumstances which occurred in the course of their first few days at Innsbruck, it began to dawn dimly upon Florian's open mind that their American friend, though she knew not the Van Rensselaers, the Vanderbilts, and the Livingstones, must have been "comfortably left" by the late Mr Palmer. It was clear she had money for every whim and fancy. She took frequent drives, up the Brenner or down the Innthal, in a roomy two-horse carriage specially ordered from the livery stables; and she always gave a seat to one at least of the giggling inarticulates; and then, "on the girl's account, you know," with good-natured zeal, asked Will and Florian to take part in the expedition. "It's so good for them, of course," she said, "to see a little, when they can, of young men's society. They're each of them here with an invalid mamma, throat and lungs, poor things, you know the kind of person; and before I came, they had nobody to talk to, not even one another, for they were far too much afraid of a mutual snub ever to utter a syllable. I've tried to bring them out a bit, and make life worth living for them. But without a young man, at that age, no amusement's worth anything. Do come, Mr Deverill, there's a good soul, just to humour them."

And Will and Florian, it must be candidly allowed, fell in with a good grace with her philanthropic projects. Though, to be sure, when once the carriage got under way, they seemed much more desirous of amusing the pretty American herself, than of seconding her schemes for drawing out the latent conversational powers of the giggling inarticulates, who contented themselves chiefly with leaning back in their seats, and listening open-mouthed to Florian's flamboyant disquisitions. That, however, is a detail. Will attempted at first to pay his share of the carriage; but such interference with her plans Mrs Palmer most manfully and successfully resisted. She wanted to give the girls a little outing, she said; Will might come or he might stop; but she wasn't going to let any other person pay for her well-meant attention to her poor little protégées. To that point she stuck hard, through thick and thin. They must come as her guests if they came as anything.

From this, and sundry other events that came under his knowledge by occulter channels, Florian grew strengthened in his idea that the late Mr Palmer, whoever he might have been, had at least "cut up well," and, what was more to the point, had cut up entirely in his widow's favour. Now this was business; for Florian, incurious as he was by nature where mere gossip was concerned, liked to know what was what in the matrimonial market. As he was wont to put it sweetly to his friends at the Savile, he wasn't going to throw himself away on a woman for nothing. He had an income of his own, just sufficient to supply him with the bare necessaries of life, such as stalls at the opera and hansoms ad libitum; and, this being so, he had no intention of giving up that singular franchise which young men call "their liberty," except in return for valuable consideration. But if good things were going, he liked at least to know of them; some day, perhaps, if some lady bribed him high enough, he might possibly consent to retire by her side into the Philistine gloom of wedded respectability.

So he pushed his inquiries hard into the Vision's antecedents, wholly without effect, during the first few days of their stay at Innsbruck.

A few nights later, however, as they sat in the salon after a long day's tramp to the summit of the Patscher Kopf, Florian found himself cast casually into conversation with an American old maid, belonging to the most virulent type and class of old maidhood—"of the cat-kind, catty," he said afterwards to Will Deverill; one of those remarkable persons who have pervaded cosmopolitan hotels for years together, and are on intimate terms with the domestic skeletons in every cupboard. Miss Beard, as she was called, favoured Florian at full length with the histories and antecedents of the giggling inarticulates, their papas and mammas, and all their forebears; informing him with much gusto how one of them had paid ninepence in the pound to his creditors, and another had been cashiered from the navy for embezzlement. Then she proceeded in the same strain to demolish the unprepossessing gentleman of nonconformist exterior, who had been guilty, it seemed, of the social crime of retail business. Miss Beard was inclined, indeed, to believe he was nothing more than a retired chemist; but she wasn't even sure, with hushed and bated breath, that it mightn't be as bad as grocery and provisions. All these, and many other unimportant details, Florian's soul endured, possessing itself in patience for many minutes together, in the fervent hope that at last this living encyclopædia of genealogical knowledge would come round to the character of the Vision of Beauty.

"And Mrs Palmer, who sits opposite me," he adventured gently after awhile, when Miss Beard reached a pause in her caustic comments; "she seems a nice little thing in her way, though, of course, a mere butterfly. She comes from New York. I suppose you know her?"

Miss Beard drew herself up with that offended dignity which only an American woman of the "very best class" can exhibit in perfection when you suspect her of an acquaintance with a person moving in a social grade less exalted than the sphere she herself revolves in. "I don't know her," she said, markedly, "but I know, of course, who she is. She's the widow of Palmer, the well-known Palmer, the notorious Palmer, who—but there!—you've been in the States; you must know all about him."

"Not Palmer the murderer!" Florian exclaimed in surprise. "She's too young for that, surely."

"No; not Palmer the murderer," Miss Beard responded in a very shrill voice with considerable acerbity. "He was at least a gentleman. I can't say as much for this lady's husband. She's the widow of Palmer, the dry-goodsman in Broadway."

"Oh, indeed," Florian cried, deeply interested in this discovery, for it meant much money. "I remember the place well, a palatial building in the Renaissance style at the corner of a street near the junction with Fifth Avenue. These princes of commerce in your Western world represent in our midst to-day the great signiors of the Adriatic who held the gorgeous East in fee, and whose Gothic façades, rich in arch and tracery, still line the long curve of the Grand Canal for us. They are the satraps of finance. The world in our times is ruled once more, as in Venice of old, in the heyday of its splendour, by the signet-ring of the merchant. Palmer was one of these, a paladin of silken bales, a Doge Dandolo of Manhattan, a potentate in the crowded marts of the Samarcand of the Occident."

"I don't know what you mean," Miss Beard retorted in an acrid tone, eyeing him sternly through her pince-nez, "but I say he was a dry-goodsman."

Florian descended at a bound from the open empyrean to the solid earth of commonplace. "Well, at any rate, he was rich," he said, letting the paladins slide. "He must have died worth millions."

"His estate was proved," Miss Beard said, curtly, "at a sum in dollars which totals out, let me see, fives into 35, ah, yes, to exactly seven hundred and eighty-four thousand pounds sterling."

Florian gave a little gasp. "That'll do," he said, with slow emphasis. "And he left it?" he suggested, after a second's pause, with an interrogative raising of his broad white forehead.

"And he left it, every cent," Miss Beard responded, "without deduction of any sort, to that fly-away little inanity."

Florian drew a deep breath. "Then she's rich," he said, musing; "rich beyond the utmost dreams of avarice."

"Well, of course she is," Miss Beard answered, with a sharp little snap, as though every one knew that. "If she wasn't, could she go tearing about Europe as she does, herself and her maid, buying everything she sees, and making presents right and left—to everyone she comes across. She'd give her own soul away if anybody asked her for it. Little empty-headed fool! She's not fit to be trusted with the use of money. But, of course, one can't know her, however rich she may be. We draw the line in the States at keeping shop. And, besides, she was never brought up among cultivated people."

As she spoke, Florian noted several things silently to himself. He noted, first, that Mrs Palmer spoke the English tongue many degrees more correctly, and more pleasantly as well, than her would-be critic. He noted, second, that her very generosity was counted for blame to her by this narrower nature. He noted, third, that in republican America, even more than in monarchical and aristocratic England, Mrs Palmer's cleverness, her information, her reading, her culture, were as dust in the balance in Society's eyes, compared with the damning and indelible fact that her late lamented husband had owned a dry-goods store. But, being a worldly-wise man, Florian noted these things in his own heart alone. Externally, he took no overt notice of them. On the contrary, he continued his talk in the same bland and honey-sweet tone as ever. "Still, she'd be a catch in her way," he said, with a condescending smile, "for any man who didn't object to swallow her antecedents."

"She would," Miss Beard replied, with austere self-respect, "if people care to mix in that sort of society. For myself, I've been used to a different kind of life. I couldn't put up with it."

Florian was audacious. He posed the one last question he still wished to ask, boldly. "And there's no awkward clause, I suppose," he said, without even the apology of a blush, "in her husband's will, of that nasty so-long-as-my-said-wife-remains-unmarried character?"

Miss Beard took up her Galignani with crushing coldness. She didn't care to discuss such people's prospects from such a standpoint. Their matrimonial affairs were beneath her notice. For fine old crusted prejudice of a social sort, commend me, so far as my poor knowledge goes, to the members of good New Yorker families. "To the best of my knowledge and belief," she murmured, acridly, without raising her eyes, "the property's left for her own sole use and benefit, without any restriction. But I'm sure I don't know. If you want to find out you'd better ask her. I don't burden my mind with these people's business."

Then Florian knew the Vision of Beauty was a catch not to be despised by a man of culture. Such wealth as that, no gentleman could decline, in justice to himself, if she gave him the refusal of it.

CHAPTER XII

THE MADDING CROWD

Andreas Hausberger was a dictator. He kept his own counsel till the moment of action grew ripe for birth in the womb of time; then, heeding no man, he gave his orders. Three days after Will Deverill's departure from St Valentin, he called up Linnet to his office suddenly. "The dressmaker has brought home your new costume," he said in his curt way. "Go upstairs and put it on. Then come down and let me see you."

Linnet, much wondering what this mood might portend, went up to her own room and tried on her new gew-gaws. Puffed white sleeves, laced corset, crimson kirtle, high shoes, flowered kerchief at her bosom, silver dirk in her hair; Linnet wasn't over-vain, as girls go in this world, but tricked out in such finery, she gazed in her glass, and, to tell the whole truth, admired herself consumedly. If only her Englishman could have seen her in that dress! But she stifled her sigh, and tripped lightly downstairs again, with the buoyancy of youth, when conscious of a perfectly becoming costume, for Andreas Hausberger's scrutiny.

The wirth scanned her, well satisfied. "On Monday," he said, briefly, in that iron voice, "we set out on our tour, and go first to Innsbruck."

It was earlier by a week than he at first intended; but he saw it would be hard, if he stopped at St Valentin, to keep Fridolin's hands from Franz's throat much longer. So, by way of minimising the adverse chances, he made up his mind to start as soon as possible for his winter season. He meant to begin modestly with entertainments at hotels among the Tyrolese winter resorts, and the towns of the Riviera; and then, when his troupe had got over its first access of stage fright, and grown used to an audience, to go across for the summer to England or America.

So, for the next few days Linnet was busy as a bee with preparations for her first journey into the great wide world outside the Zillerthal. As yet, her native valley had bounded her view—she had never gone even as far as Jenbach. Expectation and preparation kept her mind well employed during that busy week, and prevented it from dwelling too much or too long on the kindly Engländer, who had vanished from her ken across the sea to England. For, that he had gone straight home, Linnet never even doubted. On the afternoon of Andreas Hausberger's exciting announcement, indeed, a little registered parcel came by post for her to St Valentin. It bore the postmark of Wilten, where Will had intentionally dropped it into the letter-box, on purpose to conceal from her his exact whereabouts. Linnet scanned it close, and read the name correctly, but was too innocent of the topography of her native country to know that Wilten is the name of a village on the outskirts of Innsbruck. When she asked Andreas Hausberger where Wilten was, a little later in the day, without showing him the postmark, he confirmed her belief by answering at once that 'twas a town in England, not far from Salisbury. So he had thought of her over sea, then, and sent her this beautiful costly present from his own country. She tried it on that night before her tiny square mirror. As Will had rightly judged, it set off the rich tints of her creamy brown neck to the best advantage.

A beautiful gift! A real lady might have worn it! Later on, when Linnet had diamonds and rubies at command, there was no trinket she prized among all her jewels like Will Deverill's coral.

At last the eventful morning itself arrived. The little troupe set out on foot down the mountain to Mairhofen. There, their boxes, sent on over-night, awaited them. They drove in a large open brake to Jenbach—Andreas Hausberger, Franz Lindner, Linnet herself, Philippina, and the two other singers who composed the party. At Jenbach, they descended at the door of the railway station. For the first time in her life, Linnet saw, half-alarmed, a puffing and snorting machine, a sort of iron devil, breathing flames like purgatory, burst with smoke and stench upon the crowd by the waiting-room. Though she had heard all about it often enough before, and could see for herself that this great scurrying creature, for all its noise and bustle, kept rigidly to the rails as it approached the platform, she yet drew back in pure physical terror and surprise at the swiftness and irresistibility of the fire-fiend's motion.

She had scant time to think, however, for scarce had it come to rest when Andreas Hausberger, little heeding, bundled them all unceremoniously into a third-class compartment; and before Linnet had leisure to recover her self-possession, the engine had uttered one wild discordant shriek, and with ringing of bells and rattlings of wheels in her ears, she found herself, willy-nilly, beyond hope of release, whirled along at the break-neck pace of what you and I know as an Austrian slow train, over the jolting rails, up the broad Inn valley.

In spite of her terror—for she knew the railway as yet chiefly by hearing reports of collisions and accidents—Linnet enjoyed to the full that first steam-borne journey. She whirled past turreted towers like Hall and Volders, which to you and me commend themselves as the absolute quintessence of old-world quaintness, but which, to Linnet's young eyes, accustomed only to St Valentin and the grassy Alps, envisaged themselves rather in glowing hues as the kingdoms of the world and all their glory. They had been late to start, and their drive from Mairhofen had been tolerably leisurely, so dusk was closing in when they arrived at Innsbruck. Oh, the bustle, the din, the whirling awe of that arrival! Electric lamps lighted up the broad Platz in front of the station; on either side rose great hotels, grander and more palatial than any buildings on earth Linnet's poor little fancy had ever yet dreamed of. Not to one of these, however, of course, did Andreas Hausberger take his little troupe of minstrels. But even the humbler inn on the south side of the Theresien Strasse, to which they repaired on foot, bearing their boxes between them, seemed to Linnet's inexperienced and impressionable eye a most princely caravanserai. After the noise and bustle in that busy railway junction, which made her brain whirl with the unaccustomed dizziness of a great city, the comparative rest and quiet of the Golden Eagle seemed a positive relief both of mind and body. That night she slept little. Her head swam with excitement; for this was the first step on her journey through the world, which might lead her perhaps at last to England. And in England, she thought to herself once or twice with a little thrill, who could tell but peradventure she might meet . . . Will Deverill?

For she knew little as yet of how big the world is, and how long you may live in it, going to and fro, without necessarily knocking up against this one or that of its component units.

Next morning they rose betimes, and went out into the street to view the city. For to Linnet, as to Mrs Palmer, a city it was—and a very great one. Such streets and streets seemed to frighten and appal her. Florian had admired in that picturesque old capital of a mountain land, the antiquated tone, the eighteenth-century flavour, the mediæval survivals, the air as of a world elsewhere gone from us utterly. But to Linnet, though it was beautiful and impressive too, it was above all things magnificent, grandiose, stately, imposing. She gazed with open eyes at the Golden Roof, admired the bronze statues at the base of the Anna Column, looked up with silent awe at the front of the Landhaus, and thought the Rudolfsbrunnen, with its attendant griffins and dragons, a wonderful work of art for the world's delectation.

Philippina went with her, her companion on the alp. Linnet noticed with much surprise—for she knew not as yet the difference in fibre between them—that Philippina, though as interested as herself in the shops and their contents, seemed wholly unimpressed by these other and vastly more attractive features of a civilised city. For Linnet had been gifted by nature, to the fullest degree, with the profound Tyrolese artistic susceptibility. Though her mind came to art as a blank page, it responded to the stimulus, once presented to its ken, as the sensitive plate of a photographic camera responds in every line to the inspiring picture.

As they strolled through the town, by Andreas Hausberger's express desire—for the wise impresario had arranged their first appearance for that very evening, and wished the girls to come to it fresh, after a morning's exercise, they paid comparatively little heed to what most of us regard as by far the most striking characteristic of Innsbruck, the great limestone crags that seem on every side to tower and overhang the very roofs of the city. They were accustomed, indeed, to crags, and made very small case of them. It was the houses, the shops, the noise, the crowd, the gaiety, that chiefly struck them. Innsbruck to Linnet was as a little Paris. But as they went on their way through the bustling streets, they came at last to a church door, which Linnet's profound religious nature could hardly pass by without one minute's prayer for Our Lady's aid at this critical turning-point of her artistic history.

Philippina, nothing loth, for her part, opined it could do them no harm to make favour above with the blessed saints for this evening's work by a little Pater Noster. The blessed saints dearly love attentions: much may be done with them by a small wax candle! So they opened the door, and stepped into the Hofkirche.

Even those of us who know well the world and its art, can remember vividly the strange start of surprise with which we gazed round for the first time on that oddest and most bizarre of Christian temples. It isn't so much beautiful, indeed, as unexpected and startling. To push open the church door and find oneself at once ringed round and guarded close, as it were, by that great circle of mailed knights and bronze-wimpled ladies, who watch the long sleep of the kneeling Maximilian on his cenotaph in the centre, gives one a thrill of a novel sort from which some tinge of dim awe can hardly ever be wholly absent. There they stand, on their low pedestals, a congregation of bronze ancestors round their descendant's tomb—Theodoric the Ostrogoth and King Arthur the Briton, Mary of Burgundy and Eleonora of Portugal—strange efforts of struggling art in its first faint steps towards the attainment of the beautiful—naïf, ungainly, crude, rising only once or twice within measurable distance of the ideal in the few figures cast in metal by Peter Vischer of Nuremberg. But to Linnet, a woman grown, instinct with the innate artistic taste of her countrymen, yet innocent till then of all forms of art save the saints and purgatories of her mountain chapels, the Hofkirche was a glimpse of some new and unseen world of infinite possibilities. She went through it all piecemeal with open-mouthed interest. Philippina could only laugh at the quaint vizors of the knights, the quainter dresses of the ladies. But Linnet was almost shocked Philippina should laugh at them. She herself half forgot her intended prayer to Our Lady in her delight and surprise at those wonderful figures and those beautiful bas-reliefs. She read all the names on the bases conscientiously; they didn't mean much to her, to be sure—her historical ideas didn't get as far as "Clovis, King of the Franks," or even as "Count Frederick of Tyrol with the Empty Pockets"; but in a vague sort of way she gathered for herself that these were statues of archdukes and mighty heroes, keeping watch and ward silently round the great dead emperor who knelt in the centre on his marble sarcophagus. Good luck, too, attended them. The little hump-backed sacristan, seeing two pretty girls looking through the grating at the reliefs on its sides, relaxed his stony heart without the customary kreuzers, and admitted them within the railing to inspect at their leisure those exquisite pictures in marble which Thorwaldsen declared the most perfect work of their kind in the whole of Christendom. Philippina found the dresses quite grotesquely old-fashioned; but Linnet, hardly knowing why she lingered so long, gazed at each scene in detail with the profoundest interest.

While down in the town Linnet was thus engaged, high up in the hills Will Deverill sat alone by Mrs Palmer's side on an outcrop of rock near the summit of the Lanser Kopf. Florian had gone off for a minute or two round the corner by the mountain indicator, with the giggling inarticulates. Mrs Palmer, pointing her moral with the ferrule of her parasol on the grass in front of her, was discoursing to Will earnestly of his work and his prospects. "I want to see you do something really great, Mr Deverill," she said, with genuine fervour, looking deep into his eyes; "something larger in scale and more worthy of your genius—something that gives full scope to your dramatic element. I don't like to see you frittering away your talents on these exquisite little lyrics—beautiful gems in their way, to be sure, but that way not the highest. I want to see you settled down for a long spell of hard work at some big undertaking—an epic, a play, a grand opera, a masterpiece. I know you could do it if only you took the time. You should go to some quiet place where there's nothing to distract you, and make your mind up to work, to write something more lasting than even that lovely Gwyn, or that exquisite Ossian!"

Will looked down and sighed. 'Tis pleasant to be appreciated by a beautiful woman. And every man thinks, if he had but the chance, he could show the world yet the sort of stuff that's in him. "I only wish I could," he answered, regretfully. "But I've my living to earn. That ties me down still to the treadmill of journalism. When my holiday's over, the first for two years, I must get back once more, well content, to Fleet Street and drudgery."

Mrs Palmer sighed too. She felt his difficulty. Her parasol played more nervously on the grass than before. She answered nothing, but she thought a great deal. How small a matter for her to secure this young poet whom she admired so much, six months of leisure for an immortal work, and yet, how impossible! There was only one way, she knew that very well; and the first step towards that way must come, not from her, but from this modest Will Deverill.

'Twas a passing thought, half formed, or scarce half formed, in the pretty widow's mind. But nothing came of it. As she paused, and sighed, and played trembling with her parasol, and doubted what to answer him, Florian came up once more with the giggling inarticulates, "Well, Mr Wood?" she said, looking up, just by way of saying something, for the pause was an awkward one.

"Pardon me," the mannikin of culture answered in his impressive way; "my name is Florian."

"But I can't call you so," Mrs Palmer answered, recovering herself, with a merry little laugh.

"It's usual in Society," Florian responded with truth. "Just ask Will Deverill."

Will nodded assent. "Quite true," he admitted. "Men and women alike in London know him only as Florian. It's a sort of privilege he has, an attribute of his own. He's arrogated it to himself, and the world at large acquiesces in his whim, and grants it."

"It makes things seem so much more real and agreeable, you see, as Dick Swiveller said to the marchioness," Florian continued blandly. "Now suppose we five form an elective family, a little brotherhood of our own, a freemasonry of culture, and call one another, like brothers and sisters, by our Christian names only! Wouldn't that be delightful! I've just been explaining to Ethel and Eva that I mean henceforth to Ethel and Eva them. Soul gets nearer to soul without these flimsy barriers. I'm Florian; this is Will; and you, Mrs Palmer, your Christian name is—?"

The pretty widow drew back with a little look of alarm. "Oh no," she said, shortly; "I never could tell you my given name for anything. It's much too dreadful." She pulled out a pencil from the pocket at her side. "See here," she said to Will, writing down one word for him on the silver-cased tablets that hung pendant from her delicate Oriental chatelaine, "there's a name, if you like, for two Puritan parents to burden the life of their poor innocent child with! Don't tell Mr Wood—or Florian if he wishes it; he'd make fun of it behind my back, I'm perfectly certain. I know his way. To him nothing, not even a woman's name, is sacred."

Will glanced at the word curiously. He couldn't forbear a quiet smile. "It's bad enough, I must admit," he answered, perforce. The Vision of Beauty had been christened Jerusha!

"But I make it Rue for short," she added, after a moment, with a deprecating smile.

Florian caught at the word, enraptured. "The very thing!" he cried, eagerly. "Capital, capital, capital! 'There's rue for you, and here's some for me: we may call it herb-o'-grace o' Sundays.' But Rue shall be your weekday name for the Brotherhood. Let's read the roll-call! Florian, Will, Rue, Ethel, Eva! Those are our names henceforth among ourselves. We scorn formalities! No mystery for us. We abolish the misters!"

And so indeed it was. As Will, Rue, and Florian, those three of the Elective House knew each other thereafter.

CHAPTER XIII

A FIRST NIGHT

'Twas with no little trepidation that Linnet arrayed herself that eventful night for her first appearance on this or any other public platform. When her hair was dressed and her costume complete, Philippina declared, with good-humoured admiration, she looked just lovely—for Philippina at least was never jealous of her. And Philippina was right: Linnet did look beautiful. She had tied her crossed kerchief very low about the neck, so as to leave her throat bare for the better display of Will Deverill's corals. They became her admirably. Andreas Hausberger inspected his prima donna with well-satisfied eye. The wise impresario had heard, of course, where the necklet came from; but that didn't in the least disturb his serenity. Will Deverill was gone, evaporated into space; and the coral at least was "good for trade," inasmuch as it enhanced and set off to the utmost the nut-brown alp-girl's almost gipsy-like beauty. For the sake of trade, Andreas could pardon much. And Will Deverill in England was no serious rival.

At eight o'clock sharp the concert was to begin at one of the big hotels. To the guests in the house it was just a matter of "some music, I hear, to-night, the usual thing, don't you know, Tyrolese singers with a zither in the salon." But to Linnet, oh, the difference! It was the most important musical event, the most momentous performance in the world's history. She trembled like a child at the thought of standing forth and singing her simple mountain songs alone, in a fine-furnished room, before all those grand well-dressed and well-fed Britons. She would have given thousands (in kreuzers), if only she had them, to forego that ordeal. But Andreas Hausberger said "You must," and she had to obey him. And the blessed Madonna, in Britannia metal, on an oval pendant, gave her courage for the trial.

By eight o'clock sharp, then, the troupe trooped in. Electric light, red velveted chairs, soft carpet on the floor, gilded mirrors by the mantelpiece and opposite console. So much grandeur and magnificence fairly took poor Linnet's breath away. 'Twas with difficulty she faltered across the open space to a chair by the table which was placed at one end of the room for the use of the performers. Then she raised her eyes timidly, to know the worst. Some twenty-five people, more or less listless all of them, composed the audience. Some leaned back in their chairs and crossed their hands resignedly, as who expects to be bored, and makes up his mind betimes to bear his boredom patiently. Some read the latest Times or the Vienna papers, hardly deigning to look up as the performers entered. 'Twas a lugubrious function; more chilling reception prima donna never met with. Linnet clutched the blessed Madonna in her pocket convulsively. One breath of mild applause alone reached her ears. "Pretty girl," one stout Briton observed aloud in his own tongue to his plentiful mate. Linnet looked down and blushed, for he was staring straight at her.

"Let's sit it out, here," Florian exclaimed in the smoking-room. The folding doors stood open, so that all might hear; but their group sat a little apart, Will, Rue, and he, in the farther corner, away from the draught, and out of sight of the musicians. "It's more comfortable so, just the family by itself; and besides, I've a theory of my own that one should hear the zither through an open door; it mitigates and modifies the metallic twang of the instrument."

Will and Rue were all acquiescence. Next to a tête-à-tête, a parti-à-trois is the pleasantest form of society. So they kept their seats still, in the rocking-chairs by the corner, and let the sound float idly in to them through the open portal.

Linnet waited, all trembling. Thank heaven, it wasn't her part to begin. Franz Lindner came first with a solo on the zither. Bold, confident, defiant, with his hat stuck a little on one side of his head, and his feather in his band, turned Robbler-wise, wrong way, quite as jaunty as ever, Franz faced his audience as if his life had been passed in first-class hotels, and an Edison light had been the lamp of his childhood. Nothing daunted or disconcerted by the novelty of the circumstances, he played his piece through with a certain reckless brilliancy, wholly in keeping with the keynote of the Tyrolese character. Florian observed outside, with connoiseur complacency, that the fellow had brio. But the audience went on unmoved with its Times and its Tagblatt. The audience was chilling; Franz Lindner, accustomed to his own mercurial and magnetic fellow-countrymen, could hardly understand it. His self-love was mortified. He had expected a triumph, a sudden burst of wild applause; he received instead a faint clap of the hands from Ethel and Eva, and an encouraging nod from the mercantile gentleman of nonconformist exterior.

Franz sat down, a smouldering and seething volcano.

Then came Linnet's turn. She rose, all tremulous, in her pretty costume, with her beautiful face and her shrinking timidity. Old gentlemen peeped askance over the edge of their papers at the good-looking girl; young ladies took stock of her abundant black hair and her dainty kerchief. "She's going to sing," Ethel whispered. "Isn't she pretty, Eva? And just look, how very odd, she's got a necklet exactly like the ones Mrs Palmer gave us!"

As they gazed and gurgled, Linnet opened her mouth, and began her song, quivering. She trembled violently, but her very trembling increased the nightingale effect of those beautiful trills which form so marked a feature in all Tyrolese singing. Her throat rose and fell; her clear voice flooded the room with bell-like music. At the very first line, the old gentlemen laid their Times contentedly on their laps, and beamed attention through their spectacles; the old ladies let the knitting-needles stand idle in their hands, and looked up with parted lips to listen. Andreas Hausberger was delighted. Never in her life had Linnet sung so before. Occasion had brought her out. And he could judge of her here more justly than at home; he was quite sure now he had found a treasure.

But at the very first sound of her well-known voice, Will started from his chair. He clapped his hands, fingers apart, to his cheeks in wonder, and stared hard at Florian. Florian in return opened his eyes very wide, leaned back in his seat with a sudden smile of recognition, and stared hard at Will, with a certain amused indulgence. Then both with one voice cried out all at once in surprise, "That's Linnet!"

After that, it was Florian who first broke the forced silence. "I see in this the finger of fate," he murmured slowly. But Will didn't want to see the finger of fate, or any other abstraction; what he wished to see, then and there, was his recovered Linnet. It was thoughtless, perhaps, to disturb her song; but young blood is thoughtless. Without a moment's hesitation, he walked unobtrusively but hastily into the room in front, and took a seat near the door, just opposite Linnet. Andreas Hausberger didn't notice him, his eyes were firmly fixed on Linnet's face, watching anxiously to see how his pupil would acquit herself in this her first great ordeal. But Linnet, Linnet saw him, and felt from head to foot a great thrill break over her, like a wave of fire, in long undulating movement. The wave rose from her feet and coursed hot through her limbs and body, till it came out as a crimson flush on her neck and chin and forehead; then it descended once more, thrilling through her as it went, in long undulating movement from her neck to her feet again. She felt it as distinctly as she could feel the blessed Madonna clenched hard in her little fist. And she knew now she loved him. Her Englishman was there, whom she thought she had lost; he had come to hear her sing her first song in public!

Strange to say, the interruption didn't impair her performance. For one second she faltered, as her eyes met his; for one second she paused, while the wave coursed through her. But almost before Andreas had time for anxiety, she had recovered at once her full self-possession. Nay, more; Will's presence seemed actually to encourage her. She sang now with extraordinary force and brilliancy; her voice welled from her soul; her notes wavered on the air as with a sensible quivering.

That was all Will knew at the time, or the rest of the audience either. They were only aware that a beautiful young woman in Tyrolese costume was rendering a mountain song for them as they never before in their lives had heard such simple melodies rendered. But to Linnet herself, a strange thing had happened. As her eyes met Will's, and that wave of fire ran resistlessly through her, she was conscious of a weird sense she had never felt before, a sudden failure of sound, a numb deadening of the music. It was all a vast blank to her. She heard not a note she herself was uttering. Her ears were as if stopped from without and within; she knew not how she sang, or whether she sang at all; all she knew was, that, come what might, for Will's dear sake, she must keep on singing. The little access of terror this weird seizure gave her in itself added much to the quality of her performance. Unable to correct herself and keep herself straight in her singing by the evidence of her ears, she devoted extravagant and incredible pains in her throat and bosom to the mere muscular effort of note-production and note-modulation. She sang her very best, for Will Deverill was there to listen and applaud her! Franz Lindner! Who talked of Franz Lindner now? She could pour out her whole soul in one dying swan-song, now she had found once more her dear, kind, lost Engländer!

Instinctively, as she sang, her hand toyed with the coral—her left, for with the right she still clasped Our Lady. A grand Frau had crept in just behind Will's back—a smiling, fair-haired Frau, all soft cheeks and dimpled chin, and aglow with diamonds. She had seated herself on a chair by Will Deverill's side. Herr Florian, too, had crept in at the same time, and taken the next place beside the fair-haired lady. They nodded and smiled and spoke low to one another. At the sight, Linnet clutched the coral necklace still harder. She was a very great lady—oh, the diamonds in her ears!—and she talked to Will Deverill with familiar carelessness!

And as Linnet clutched the necklet, a shade broke over Rue Palmer's face. With a quick little gasp, she leaned across to Will, growing paler as she recognised that familiar trinket. "Why, this is the girl," she whispered, "from the inn at St Valentin."

And Will whispered back, all unconscious, "Yes; this is the girl. And now you can see why I sent her the necklet!"

Through the rest of that song, there was breathless silence. At its end, the old gentlemen and ladies, after a short hushed stillness, broke into a sudden little burst of applause. There was a moment's interval, and then the demonstration renewed itself more vigorously than before. People turned to one another and said, "What a beautiful voice!" or, "She sings divinely!" By this time the loungers who held aloof in the smoking-room were crowding about the doorway. A third time they clapped their hands; and at each round of applause, Linnet, alternately pale and flushed with excitement, dropped a little mountain curtsey, and half cried, and half smiled at them. Her hearing had returned with the first symptom of clapping hands; she could catch the vague murmur of satisfied criticism; she could catch Andreas Hausberger's voice whispering low in an aside, "Very well sung, Linnet." But her eyes were fixed on Will, and on Will alone; and when Will framed his lips to one word of approbation, the hot blood rushed to her cheeks in a torrent of delight that at last she had justified her Engländer's praises.

Linnet was the heroine of that evening's performance. Andreas Hausberger sang "He was a jäger bold"; Philippina, looking arch, twanged the thankless zither. But the audience waited cold till 'twas Linnet's turn again. Then, as she rose, they signified their approval once more by another little storm of applause and encouragement. Linnet curtsied, and curtsied, and curtsied again, and stared straight at Will Deverill. This second time she sang in less fear and trembling; she could hear her own notes now, and Will's face encouraged her. She acquitted herself, on the whole, even better than before. Her rich pure voice, though comparatively untrained, exhibited itself at its best in that pathetic little ballad of her native hills, "The Alp-girl's Lover." She sang it most dramatically, with one hand pressed hard on her heaving bosom. At the end, the audience clapped till Linnet was covered with blushes. A mere scratch performance before some casual tourists in the drawing-room of an hotel; but to Linnet, it came home as appreciation and praise from the grandest of gentlefolk.

She sang three songs in all. Her hearers would gladly have made it six; but Andreas Hausberger knew his trade, and stuck firm to his programme. When all was finished, the foreign Herrschaft crowded round; Herr Florian shook Linnet's hand; Herr Will pressed it tenderly. The grand lady with the diamonds was graciousness itself. "With a voice like that, my child," she said, "you shouldn't be singing here; you should be training for the stage in some great musical centre." Many of the other guests, too, gathered round and congratulated her. It was noised abroad in the room that this was the pretty peasant girl's absolute début, and that Mr Deverill and Mr Wood had met her as a sennerin at an inn in the Zillerthal. More voices than one praised her voice enthusiastically. But Will Deverill whispered low, "You have done yourself justice. As I told you at St Valentin, so I tell you again—Heaven only knows how high that voice may carry you."

One thing Linnet noticed for herself, unprompted. That first appearance in operatic peasant dress as a musician in a troupe, had raised her at a bound in the scale of social precedence. At St Valentin, she was an alp-girl; at Innsbruck, all those fine-dressed ladies and gentlemen accepted her at first sight as a public singer. They spoke to her with a politeness to which she was hitherto unused. They bent forward towards her with a quiet sort of deference and equality which she felt instinctively the very same persons would never have shown to the sennerin in her châlet. Their curiosity was less frank; their questions were less blunt and better put than she was used to. It was partly the costume, no doubt, but partly also the function: she was a peasant girl in the Zillerthal; at Innsbruck she was a member of the musical profession.

She had only a second or two with Will that night. While the other guests crowded round her, uttering their compliments for the most part in rather doubtful German, which Linnet answered (by Andreas Hausberger's wise advice) in her pretty broken English, Will dropped but a few words of praise and congratulation. After all was over, however, and they were going away for the night to the Golden Eagle, he stood at the door, bare-headed, his hat in his hand, to say goodbye to her. Andreas Hausberger's keen eye watched their interview close. Will held Linnet's hand—that transfigured Linnet's, in her snow-white sleeves and her corset-laced bodice—held it lingering in his own with a mutual pressure, as he murmured, not too low for Andreas to overhear ('twas wisest so), "I'm pleased to see you wore my necklet."

And Linnet, half-afraid how she should answer him aright, with Andreas standing by and straining his ear for every word, replied in German, with a timid smile, raising her eyes to his shyly, "I'm so glad you were pleased. I wanted to wear it. It's a beautiful present. Thank you so very much for it."

That was all. She had no more talk than just that with her Engländer. But she went back to the Golden Eagle, and lay awake all night thinking of him. Of him, and of the fair-haired Frau who sat smiling by his side. That fair-haired Frau gave Linnet some pangs of pain. Not that she was jealous; that ugliest of all the demons that beset human nature had no place, thank Heaven, in Linnet's great heart. But she thought to herself with a sigh how much fitter for Will was that grand fair Frau than ever she herself could be. How could she expect him to make anything of her, when he could sit and talk all day long in great covered courts with grand ladies like that, his natural equals? He could think, after the Frau, no more of her, than she, after him, could think of Franz Lindner. And yet, and at that thought the billowy wave of fire broke over her once more from head to foot, he had left the grand lady in the room outside to come in and hear her song the moment he recognised her!

In the salon that same evening, when Linnet was gone, Rue stood talking for a minute by the fireside to Will Deverill. "She sings like an angel," the pretty American said, with unaffected admiration of the peasant girl's gifts. "What a glorious voice! Florian's quite right. It's a pity she doesn't get it properly trained at once. It's fit for anything."

"So I think," Will answered, looking her frankly in the face. "She needs teaching, of course, the very best teaching. But if only she gets it, I see no reason to doubt she might do what she likes with it."

"And she's beautiful, too," Rue went on, without one marring touch of any feminine but. "How queenly she'd look as a Mary Stuart or a Cleopatra! Your necklet suits her well." She paused, and reflected a second. "It's a pity," she went on, musingly, as if half to herself, "she shouldn't have the brooch and the earrings to match it!"

And next day, sure enough, at the Golden Eagle, about one o'clock, when Linnet went up to her own room after early dinner, she found on her dressing-table a small cardboard box containing some coral ornaments to go with the necklet, and this little inscription in a feminine hand inside it:—"For Linnet, from one who admired last night her beautiful singing."

Then Linnet knew at least that the fair-haired lady too had a great heart, and owed her no grudge for the possession of Will Deverill's necklet. For she divined by pure instinct what admirer had sent them.

CHAPTER XIV

AND IF FOR EVER

"It's no use wasting words," Florian observed, with decision. "As our old friend Homer justly remarks, 'Great is the power of words; wing'd words may make this way or that way.' I'm a practical man myself: I stick close to the facts; they're solid; they're tangible; they're not to be evaded. I won't allow myself to be argued out of a reasonable conviction. I put it like this: if it was right for you, as you admitted, to leave St Valentin, then, by parity of reasoning, it's right for you now to leave Innsbruck instantly. Mill, Whately, and Jevons would allow that that's logic. Why did we come here? Partly, no doubt, to instruct ourselves in the contents of this most interesting town; but mainly, I submit, to deliver you forthwith from your milkmaid's clutches. Why should we go away again? Partly because we've seen all that Innsbruck contains of historical or artistic; but largely, also, because the milkmaid insists upon pursuing us through the land and jingling her bells till she compels us to listen to her."

"She didn't know we were here," Will interjected, bristling up.

"She didn't know we were here, that's true; but she's followed us all the same, cow-bells and pails and all, and we must break away at once from her. I've said so to Rue, and Rue fully agrees with me. As I told you before, if you mean the girl harm, well and good; I don't meddle with you. But if you mean to go on shilly-shallying like this, saying goodbye for ever—and sending her coral necklets; meeting her again at hotels, and applauding her rapturously; saying goodbye once more, and letting it run, for aught I know to the contrary, to diamonds and rubies, why, what I say is this, I've seen the same thing tried on more than once before, and my experience is, the man who begins by meaning only to flirt with a girl, sinks down, down, down, by gradual degrees, till at last he loses every relic of self-respect, and ends by marrying her!"

Will fingered his under lip, and knit his brow reflectively. "At least," he said, "I must see her and tell her I'm going away again."

Stern justice once more embodied itself as Florian. "Certainly not," the little man answered, with an emphatic shake of the head. "If you say goodbye, she'll want to know where you're going. If she knows where you're going, she'll want, of course, to follow you. If you don't mean her harm, then, hang it all, my dear fellow, you must mean her good, which is far more dangerous. There are only two possible motifs in such an affair, ou le bon, ou le mauvais. You must mean the first, if you don't mean the second. I've talked it over with Rue, and Rue entirely supports me. For the poor girl's own sake, she says, it's your duty at once to run away from the spot, post haste, and leave her."

A little later in the day, on the slopes behind Mühlan, Will thrashed it out himself, tête-à-tête with Rue, seated close by her side on the grassy upland. "She's in love with you, poor thing," Rue said very seriously. "You mayn't see it yourself; sometimes, you know, Mr Deverill, I can't always say Will; it seems so forward, sometimes, you know, you men, even the best of you, are unkind to us poor women through pure excess of modesty. You don't realise how much a girl may really think of you. Your very want of self-conceit may make you blind to her feelings. But consider what you must seem to a child like Linnet. You're a gentleman, a poet, a man of the great world, wholly removed from her sphere in knowledge, position, culture. She looks up to you, vaguely and dimly no doubt, with a shrinking respect, as some one very grand and great and solemn. But your attentions flatter her. Florian has told me all about how you met her at St Valentin. Now, even a lady," and Rue looked down as she spoke, and half stifled a sigh, "even a lady might be pleased at attracting the notice of such a man as you; how much more then a peasant-girl! I watched her close last night when you first came into the room, and I saw such a red flush break over her throat and cheeks, like a wave surging upwards, as I never saw before on any woman's face, though long ago . . . myself . . . when I was very young . . . I think I may have felt it. And I knew what it meant at once; I said to myself as I looked, 'That girl loves Mr Deverill.'"

"I think she's fond of me," Will admitted modestly. "I didn't notice it so much myself, I confess, at St Valentin; but last night, I won't deny I watched her hard, and I could see she was really very pleased to meet me."

Rue looked grave. "Mr Deverill," she said in a serious voice, "a woman's heart is not a thing to trifle with, I'm an old married woman myself, you see, and I can speak to you plainly. You may think very little yourself, for I know you're not conceited, of the effect you're likely to produce on women. I've known cruel things done, before now, by very good men, just because they never realised how much store women set on their passing attentions. You've only to look at Linnet to see she has a deeply passionate nature. Now, I beg of you, don't play fast and loose with it any longer. If you don't mean anything, don't see her again. The more you see of her, the worse it will be for her."

Will listened, and ruminated. Rue's words had more effect on him by far than Florian's. For one thing, she was a woman, and she treated the matter earnestly, where Florian only treated it with the condescending flippancy of his native clubland. To Rue, in her true womanliness, an alp-girl's heart was still a sacred object; to Florian, 'twas a toy for the superior creature, man, as he said, "to play skittles with." But then, again, Florian had dwelt much to him on the chance of his finally marrying Linnet. To Will himself, that contingency seemed too remote to contemplate. As he sat by Rue's side on the grassy upland, and heard Rue speak so gently to him in her well-turned sentences, the distance between a refined and educated lady like that and a musical alp-girl appeared to his mind too profound to be bridged over. Was it likely, in a world which held such women as Rue, he ever could marry such a girl as Linnet? Now, Rue herself never spoke of marriage between Linnet and himself as even possible. She took it for granted the end must be either Linnet's ruin or Linnet's desertion. And all she urged him was not to break the poor child's heart for her. So, where Florian's worldly wisdom fell somewhat flat on his ears, Rue's feminine sympathy and tact produced a deep effect upon him.

"It'll make her very sad, I'm afraid, if she doesn't see me again," he said, looking down, with masculine shyness.

"I know it will," Rue answered, pushing her point with advantage. "I could see that last night. But all the more reason, then, you shouldn't let it go any further."

"Well, but must I never see her again?" Will inquired with an anxious air. For his own sake, even, that counsel of perfection was a very hard saying.

Rue's face grew still graver. "No; I think you must never see her again," she answered, seriously. "Remember what it involves. Remember what she is; how dazzled she must be by a gentleman's advances. The more you see of her, the more she'll think of it, the more she'll love you, confide in you, lean on you. That's only womanly. We all of us do it . . . with a man we admire and feel greater and better than us. And you and she, after all, are both of you human. Someday, perhaps, carried away by a moment of emotion—" She broke off quite suddenly, and let her silence say the rest. "And then," she went on, after a long pause, "when all's lost and all's done, you'll be sorry, poor child, you've spoilt and wrecked her whole life for her. . . ." She paused again, and grew crimson. "Mr Deverill—Will—" she said, faltering, "I wouldn't speak to you like this if I didn't feel I was doing it to save this poor child in the end from untold misery. It's not only the material consequences I'm thinking of now (though those are bad enough), but the girl's own heart—for I can see she has got one. If you don't go away, sooner or later you'll break it. What other end can there be to an affair like this between a poet like you and a Tyrolese peasant girl?"

What other end, indeed! Will knew it, and felt it. He saw she was right. And her words thrilled through him. When a beautiful woman discusses your personal affections in such a strain as this it isn't in human nature (in its male embodiment) not to tingle through and through in pure instinctive response with her. While Rue spoke like that, Will felt he must indeed see no more of Linnet. "But where must I go?" he asked, vaguely, just to distract the talk from his own potential misdeeds. Their original idea was Cortina and the Dolomites.

The innocent question fell in pat with Rue's plans. Already that morning she had talked it over with Florian; and Florian, for the furtherance of his own designs, had agreed it would be best for them to alter their route, as things stood, in favour of a new project which Rue suggested. She was going to Meran herself, for a month or six weeks of bright autumn weather, on her way down to Italy. Why shouldn't they come there, too, she asked, and keep the family together? Florian, not unmindful of her seven hundred thousand pounds, admitted at once the cogency of her reasoning. It would be quite delightful, he said—in point of fact, consummate. But would Will consent to it? Then Rue expounded to him her views about Will and his future in life—how he ought to retire to the wilderness for forty days, after the manner of the prophets, to meditate, and, if possible, to begin some great work, which should bring in the end name and fame and honour to him. Florian admitted, just to humour her, that if Will had the chance, and chose to buckle to, he might really produce something quite worth looking at. "Persuade him to it," he said, in his mellifluous tones. "To you, Rue, it comes so easy, you see, to be persuasive. One word from your lips is worth fifty from mine. Make him stop away for three months from that dear, delightful, distracting London, and begin some big thing that the world must listen to."

To inspire a great work is a mission in life for a woman—to be some Petrarch's Laura, some Dante's Beatrice. So, when Will asked plaintively, "Where must I go?" that afternoon, Rue answered with prompt decision, "Why, of course, to Meran. I'm going there myself. You must come with us and stop there."

"What for?" Will inquired, not wholly untouched in soul—for proximity counts for much, and they were sitting close together—that the pretty American should so desire his company.

Then Rue began to explain, to persuade, to reason. And reason from those lips was profoundly conclusive. No syllogism on earth could have failed to convince from them. Meran was the prettiest place in South Tyrol, she said; the pleasantest climate for the autumn months, the loveliest scenery. The sun always shone, and the birds always sang there. Though it froze underfoot, you could bask on the hill-tops. But that wasn't all;—and she leaned forward confidentially—she wanted to speak to him again about that subject she had broached the other day on the Lanser Kopf. When a pretty woman interests herself in your private concerns, she's always charming; when she pays you the delicate flattery of stimulating you to use "your own highest powers"—that's the proper phrase—she's quite irresistible. So Will Deverill found Rue. Why, she asked, should he go back so soon to London? This devotion to mere journalism was penny-wise and pound-foolish. Could he afford to stay away for six weeks at Meran, just barely afford it, and settle himself down at a quiet hotel to some really big work that would make him famous?

Will, drawing a deep breath, and looking wistfully into her eyes, admitted his funds in hand would permit him, with care, such a hard-working holiday.

Then Rue pressed him close. She brought ghee to his vanity. She was convinced if he stopped in this keen mountain air, among these glorious Alps, fresh inspired from Nature, he could turn out a poem, a play, a romance, some great thing of its kind, that the world must listen to. He had it in him, she felt sure, to make his name famous. Nothing venture, nothing have. If he didn't believe in himself enough to risk six weeks of his precious time on the effort to sketch out something really worthy of him, then all she could say was, and she flooded him as she spoke with the light of her lustrous eyes, he believed in himself far less, oh, so far, far less, than his friends believed in him. Florian had told her Will held no regular staff-appointment on any London paper; he was an occasional journalist, unattached, earning a precarious livelihood, in fear and trembling, by reviews and poems and descriptive articles in half-a-dozen assorted dailies and weeklies. Why shouldn't he give them up for awhile, then, and play boldly and manfully for some larger stake, some stake such as she knew he could well attain to? And she quoted Queen Elizabeth, or was it Walter Raleigh?—

"He either fears his fate too much,
Or his desert is small,
Who will not put it to the touch

To lose, or win it all."

Now, this line of argument, as it happened, exactly fell in, for a special reason of his own, with Will's mood for the moment. A holiday, we all know, especially in the pure and stimulating air of the mountains, has always a most invigorating and enlivening effect upon the jaded intellect. And Will's holiday in the Zillerthal had inspired him by degrees with fresh ideas and scenes for a Tyrolese drama. It was a drama of the hills, with some poeticised version of Linnet for its heroine—a half-musical sketch, a little mountain operetta, the songs in which were to be all of his own composing. Hitherto, he had never taken himself quite seriously as a composer; but Linnet and Andreas Hausberger had praised the few pieces he played over for them at St Valentin, and Rue had thought well of the stray snatches from his notes he had given them, under protest, on the very untuneful hotel piano. Now the idea occurred to him to write and compose a little play of his own, while the picture of Linnet was still fresh in his brain; and this holiday Rue dangled so temptingly before him would just suffice to get the first scaffolding of his piece together. The filling in he could manage at his leisure in London. So Rue won her point; but 'twas Linnet who won it for her.

"Yes; I'll go to Meran," he said at last, after a long break in their talk, "and I'll settle down to work there, and I won't even wait to say goodbye to Linnet."

Poets are weak, however, where a woman is concerned. In this respect, it may be allowed, Apollo's sons closely resemble the rest of the children of Adam. Will left Innsbruck, indeed, without bidding Linnet goodbye, but he couldn't refrain from just dropping her a line before he went, to say he must leave her. "To meet you once more," he wrote, "would be only to part again. I must say farewell, and this time for ever. But, Linnet, it makes my heart ache to do it!" You see, he was a poet.

CHAPTER XV

A CRITICAL EVENING

Florian and Rue, as it happened, were very ill-informed as to the Tyrolese minstrel market, otherwise they would certainly never have chosen Meran as a place of refuge for Will Deverill against the pressing temptations of his acquaintance with Linnet. They chose it because it was a delightful and frequented autumn resort; because the climate was charming and the sunshine unfailing; because the grape-cure was then on in full swing in the valley; and because everybody else at Innsbruck that moment was going there. For those very reasons, the wisdom of the serpent might have taught them to avoid it: 'twas the innocence of the dove that led them to fly right into it. In point of fact, Meran is crowded in October and November. High well-born Graf and consumptive plebeian disport themselves all day long on the leafy promenades, eating grapes as they go, beside the band and the Kurhaus. It stands to the world of Berlin and Vienna as Cannes and Mentone to the world of London. That was precisely why Andreas Hausberger had marked it out long since, as the next southward point on their way Riviera-wards.

"Are there many hotels there?" Franz Lindner asked dubiously, much crestfallen at his own comparative failure with the public of Innsbruck. A little of his jauntiness had been washed for the moment out of Franz Lindner's figure; he looked limper in the back and not so stiff in the neck, nay, even his hat stood cocked on his head at a less aggressive angle.

"There isn't anything else," Andreas Hausberger answered in his Western style. "Meran and Obermais are one enormous gasthaus. If Linnet does as well as she has done at Innsbruck, it'll take us take three weeks or a month, at least, to get right through with them. We took a good bit, considering all things, the other evening. I think she draws; I noticed old gentlemen slipped their florins under their palms into the plate unobtrusively. Besides, in a Kurort, she'll soon get talked about. People at one hotel or pension will speak of us at another—'Seen this Tyrolese troupe going about in the place? Pretty girl; sings sweetly.' I take it there can't be less than thirty houses in Meran where we could get an audience. That carries us well on to the end of November. By that time, San Remo and Bordighera'll be filling up fast, and from there we can go on to Cannes, Nice, Mentone."

So three days later saw them safe at Meran. To Linnet, that journey from north to south, across the great ridge of the Alps, seemed like transplantation into an earthly fairyland. She had never seen the luscious wealth of vineclad lands before; for North and South Tyrol are two different countries, one cold, bleak, Germanic, the other soft, warm, Italian. Meran itself appeared to her ardent imagination more beautiful than anything eye hath seen or mind conceived of. And, indeed, it is beautiful. Whoever knows it loves it. A brawling little mountain stream, the Passer, rushes headlong from the glaciers of the Otzthaler Alps through a wild upland glen, to join in due time the broader stream of the Adige, which threads the bleak Vintschgau on its precipitous course from the lofty snow-fields of the Ortler and the Wild-Spitze. Near the point where the two unite, on a long tongue of land, the little town of Meran nestles close among its vines, under shelter of the rounded ice-worn Küchelberg. It clings with its ancient walls, its steeples, its watch-towers, as if glued to the lower slopes of the basking mountain. Linnet gazed at it, delighted. For here, on the south side of the Alps, looking down the broad valley to sunny Italy, the vegetation differed greatly, both in richness and in character, from anything she had ever seen in her native Zillerthal. Indeed, even Italy itself, parched as it often is with excessive heat, seldom shows such wild luxuriance of foliage and fruit as these green and well-watered South Tyrolese valleys. There is a bowery, flowery lavishness and lushness about it all that defies description. The vines that trail loose across their trellised archways; the gourds that hang pendent from their wooden frails; the great yellow pumpkins that lean temptingly over every terraced wall; the lizards that bask blinking on the sun-smitten rock-face; the crimson sprays of Virginia creeper that droop in festoons from the brown verandah wood-work of coquettish châlets, mingled with the pine-clad slopes and bare snow-sprinkled peaks of the upper background, make a charming hybrid between Switzerland and Lombardy. Imagine for yourself an ancient German town, with mouldering walls and high turrets, like Boppard or Andernach, and crenellated castles of quaint mediæval architecture, but with arcaded streets and Italian loggias, plumped down incongruously in the midst of this half-Alpine, half-southern scenery, and you get a very fair bird's-eye view indeed, in its way, of the main traits of Meran.

On the very first morning of her arrival in the town, Linnet took her way out with Franz Lindner and Philippina along the brawling stream that forms the centre and rallying point of the gay little watering-place. Meran is all parade, winter-garden, and band, and they walked through its midst to see and be seen of the lounging Herrschaft. They were dressed in full costume; 'twas a form of advertisement Andreas greatly believed in. Franz held himself erect, with his feather still stuck Robbler-wise, and his defiant air, as he strode through the crowd that lined the promenade—the gayest, most varied, and most fashionable throng Linnet had ever set eyes on. He and Philippina stared hard at the world that displayed itself before them. German Jews from Frankfort, great Viennese bankers, the round-faced, engaging Bavarian fräuleins, the tall and tailor-made English lawn-tennis misses. Linnet gazed at them, too, but cast her eyes now and then from the people and the shops to the great cleft mountain peaks that soared everywhere high and clear-cut into the sky above them.

In the lower part of their walk the river was smooth, and the roadway was bordered by fantastic pensions and quaint Tyrolese buildings; but in the upper part, which they reached beyond a single bold arch of stone-work that spanned the Passer, precipitous rocks began to hem it in, the river assumed the guise of a foaming torrent, and the ruined fortress of the Zenoburg, with its Romanesque portal, frowned down from high above them on a water-worn gorge where the stream forced its way in a dashing cataract. A little platform overhangs the very edge of the cascade. Linnet stood there long, leaning over the iron rail, and gazing with delight at the white foam beneath, and the placid deep green of the calm rock-basin that received the mountain stream as it leapt from the precipice.

Franz and Philippina wouldn't let her remain there, however. With the restlessness of their kind, they were eager to explore this new world more fully. They strolled through the town, and up the hills behind, where all seemed fresh and southern and romantic to Linnet. Through green alleys of vines, trained like bowers over their heads, they mounted at last by a cloven ravine to the chestnut-covered slopes, where they looked down like a map on the vast garden of the Etschthal. It was a wonderful view. Linnet drank it in eagerly. In front crouched the town with its huddling red roofs wedged in between the hill and the scurrying river; beyond lay a wide plain of such luxuriant tilth as Linnet till then had never dreamt of. Villages and churches clustered thick by the dozen on slope and hill-top; but what added the last touch of charm to the strange scene in Linnet's eyes was the extraordinary number and variety of its feudal châteaux. Every height was crowned by its castellated Schloss, ivy-clad Planta, huge sun-smitten Labers, the terraced front of Rametz, the frowning bastions of Fragsburg: Franz Lindner, with his keen eyes, could count no less than forty-three of them. The exhilaration of the fresh scene, and of the southern trees and creepers, so different from the stunted pines of their own chilly Zillerthal, filled Linnet with a certain vague and indefinable delight: had but her Engländer been there, she would have been perfectly happy.

Andreas Hausberger had taken charge of the health of his troupe, in strict accordance with his own favourite theories. The two girls were to walk on the hills for three hours every morning. They were to dine thus and thus. They were to do or avoid this, that, or the other thing. He himself had gone off meanwhile to one of the smaller hotels to make arrangements beforehand for that evening's concert. One of the smaller hotels, bien entendu, for Andreas knew well the money value of mere gossip as a means of advertisement. Not till he had seen what impression Linnet made on the public of the lesser houses would he launch her on the Meranhof or the Erzherzog Johann. That ensured him the full benefit of the talk of the town. A shrewd man, Andreas Hausberger! By the time he reached those larger and richer houses in his nightly rounds, he didn't doubt the world of Meran would have heard and tattled much of his new-found singer; people would say to one another, "Don't miss the Tyrolese troupe that's coming to us to-night; they say there's one girl in it worth seeing and hearing." For Andreas was above all things a man of the world; he never threw away the chance of earning an extra gulden.

That evening, in due course, their concert came off at the Austria at Obermais. You know the Austria?—a small but select and aristocratic pension, much affected by the Von So-and-so's of Berlin and Vienna. The result (in net cash) surpassed the prudent Andreas's highest expectations. Though no Will Deverill was there to inspire her efforts, Linnet sang divinely. Indeed, to say the truth, though she had met him and lost him once more at Innsbruck, that meeting and losing, instead of dashing her hopes to the ground, as Rue and Florian expected, had only produced on her simple little mind a general impression that now, by the blessed Madonna's aid, her Engländer might turn up any day, anywhere. In that innocent hope, born of the age of faith, she sang her best with a will, and charmed her audience, looking hard at the door all the while, to see if, peradventure, her Engländer would enter. And when no Engländer came, she comforted her soul with the thought that Andreas had said there were twenty-nine other hotels in Meran and Obermais—at any one of which, no doubt, that dear friend might be stopping. Her heart wasn't crushed, not the least bit of it, and her trust in the blessed Madonna on the Britannia metal pendant that hung round her neck was as vivid and as childishly unquestioning as ever. Our Dear Frau had brought her her lover at Innsbruck; Our Dear Frau could bring him her just as well at Meran here.

She sang three times. Each time the audience applauded vociferously. The Austria, you see, is mainly frequented by Germans. Now, your German is musical; he has little reserve; he loves a good noise; and he's never afraid of displaying his feelings. Moreover, the little party in the salon that night was largely composed of Viennese or Bavarians; they understood the zither and the Tyrolese songs; they were to the manner born, good judges of execution. Franz Lindner's feather curled once more, quite as perkily as ever, when they applauded the bravado of his facile playing. Philippina smiled and bobbed, a wicked twinkle in her eye, when they cried "Bis!" to the loudest and sauciest of her jodels. But at each of Linnet's songs, her hearers grew silent, then burst as she ceased into uproarious approbation. She was the heroine of the night, the black swan of the party; not often had they heard such a voice as hers at so humble a performance.

When all was finished, 'twas Linnet's task to hand round the plate and make the little collection. She hated the work, but 'tis always imposed, and with sound commercial reason, on the prettiest girl of the troupe, so it naturally devolved upon Linnet to perform it. Even good-humoured Philippina admitted without dispute her claim to the function. Hot in the face, and ill at ease, Linnet walked round the room in a maze of confusion, with her little silver salver. She offered it first to the rich Jew banker from Frankfort-on-the Main, with the diamond pin, and the seals on his watch-chain. Now, your pretty face is a mighty opener of your purse-strings. The rich Jew banker, holding out one fat thumb and forefinger gingerly, after a second's hesitation (for 'tis hard to part with so much money at once) dropped a ten-florin piece in good Austrian gold, plump into the middle of the silver salver. It fell with a ring. His example was contagious. Christian Freiherrs could not stand being beaten in their appreciation of vocal art by Jewish financiers from Frankfort. People who meant to give one florin now gave two; people who meant to put off on their wives the duty of dispensing the family bounty now drew out their purses and became their own almoners. Linnet had never seen a gold piece in her life before; when she finished her round, bowing low, that night, there were three of them on the salver.

Andreas Hausberger eyed the plate with a carefully-suppressed smile of subdued satisfaction. His mouth never moved; only the corners of his eyes betrayed his emotion. But that evening's haul had far-reaching consequences, for him and for Linnet. He saw in a moment he had found indeed, as he thought, a treasure. He didn't need the assurances of the rich Jew banker, and the lady amateur with the tortoise-shell eyeglasses who came from Berlin, that Linnet should be placed at once for instruction in a proper conservatorium. He saw for himself, from the effect she produced on the audience that night, she would yet do wonders. As Linnet left the Austria, Andreas held her cloak for her. But it wasn't mere gallantry. "Wrap your throat round well, Linnet," he said, with much zealous care. "For Heaven's sake don't take cold. The air on the hills in the daytime won't hurt you; but after sitting in these crowded, over-heated rooms, the night fogs are so bad for you."

The goose that lays the golden eggs deserves to be well tended.

CHAPTER XVI

SCHLOSS TYROL

"Where shall we go to-day?" Will inquired next morning, as they sipped their early coffee at the Erzherzog Johann. He was already hard at work on his projected operetta, but 'twas a fad of his to compose in the open air; he went out for a long stroll every morning with Florian, and sat on the hillsides, jotting his thoughts down with a pencil, exactly as they occurred, face to face with Nature.

"Rue won't meet us to-day, she says," his friend answered with a yawn. "Her nerves are tired after her walk of yesterday. So, for my part, I vote we go and see Schloss Tyrol. It inspires me, that place," Florian went on, warming up, for he had been reading his guide-book. "It has the interest of a germ, a nucleus, a growing point. I like to think that here we stand before the embryo of a State, the very heart and core of the evolving Tyrol. We watch its development, so to speak, from its central cell. It's the evolution of law, of order, of authority. The robber chiefs of that high stronghold perched aloft on the hills"—and Florian extended one small white hand, as was his wont when he perorated—"are the centre round which clusters by successive degrees the whole Tyrolese and Austrian history. I see them pushing their power in concentric rings from their eagle's eyrie on the crags above the valley of the Adige, to Botzen and the Brenner, the basin of the Inn, the Bavarian March, the entire Eastern Alps, from the Engadine to the Dolomites. Their Schloss there is the original and only genuine Tyrol. By successful robbery, which is the basis of all the divine rights of governments, they become the masters and lords of a mighty province; they dictate peace and justice to obedient villagers; they stand out in course of time as an earthly providence. But what were they at first? Why, a den of thieves! There you have the whole evolution of morality in a nutshell—the rule of the strong, established and maintained by continued aggression. So I will see Schloss Tyrol; I will be a pilgrim at the shrine; I will refresh myself at the fount of law and order as it exists and envisages itself for these innocent mountains."

"It's an interesting place," Will replied, taking no notice of Florian's gush, "and it's well worth visiting. I've seen it before. I'll sit on the rocks outside and write, while you go in and look at it."

So after breakfast they started up the narrow old road, paved in places with cobble-stones, and overarched in its lower slopes by graceful festoons of trellised vines, that leads from Meran along a shoulder of the hills to the earliest home of the counts of Tyrol. 'Twas a true South Tyrolese November morning. It froze hard through the night, and the ice still lay thick on the pools by the wayside; but in that keen, crisp air, and with that cloudless sky, the sun overhead blazed as warm as summer. Up the Passer valley to their right, as they mounted, the villages and churches on the slopes of the Ifinger stood out in dazzling white against their dark green background. The little mountain path, bordered as usual by countless petty crucifixes and whitewashed shrines, wound in continuous zig-zags up the face of the Küchelberg, a wedge of rounded rock that overlooks the town, draped with vineyards on its sides, and worn smooth on its summits by the titanic ice mills of the glacial epoch. The chapels in particular excited Florian's interest. "There's more religion to the square mile in the Tyrol," he said, "than in any other country I ever visited!"

They rose by slow degrees till they reached the long hog's back which separated the wild Passer glen from the wider and more luxuriant Adige valley. Florian stood still to gaze. Tier upon tier of vines, in endless galleries, roofed the southern slope as with one leafy arbour; the long shoulder itself on whose top they now stood was green with pastures, and watered by plashing artificial leats which had worn themselves deep beds like natural streamlets. The music of falling water accompanied them all the way; the cow-bells tinkled pleasantly from the fields on either hand; and the views, as they walked along the crest of the ridge, looking down into the two valleys with their villages and klosters, their castles and towers, seemed infinite in the variety of their beauty and interest. Above soared the bare peaks of the Muthspitze and the Tschigatspitze; to the east rose the fissured summits of the cloven Dolomites; the white mass of the Lanser Ferner closed the glen to westward.

After nearly an hour's walk, as they approached the little village of Dorf Tyrol on the hill-top, they passed a huddled heap of wayside boulders, over whose ledge the stream that had accompanied them so far on their road tumbled from a small sluice in a bickering cataract. Two girls were seated on the brink of the torrent with their backs turned towards them. As the young men approached, one of the girls looked round, and gave a start of surprise. "Why, Linnet," she cried in German, "here he is again!—your Engländer!"

Linnet turned, with a crimson flush on her nut-brown face, to think that Philippina should speak so openly of Will, as of some one that belonged to her. But her cheek, to say the truth, was hardly redder than Will's own, as he heard himself so described by the laughing sennerin as Linnet's Engländer. He couldn't conceal from himself, however, the fact that he was glad to meet Linnet under whatever circumstances. With a wondering heart, he went up and took her hand. "Why, when did you come here?" he asked, all astonished.

"The day before yesterday," Linnet answered, tingling.

"And she sang last night at the Austria," Philippina put in, with her good-humoured smile, "and made a great success, too, I can tell you that; and took, oh, ever and ever so much money. Herr Andreas is so pleased. He goes chuckling to himself. I think he thinks Linnet will make his fortune."

"And how long do you stop here?" Will inquired, half-anxiously, half-eagerly.

"About a month," Linnet answered, looking deep into his eyes, and keeping down the rising tears as well as she could in her own. "And you, Herr Will? how long do you mean to remain here?"

"A month or six weeks," Will replied with a thrill. Then he added, gazing hard at her, in spite of Florian, "so I hope we may still have many chances of meeting?"

Florian flung his fragile form at full length on the heap of stones by their side, and began to laugh unrestrainedly. "Well, it's no use fighting against fate," he cried, looking up at the blushing pair, with philosophic indulgence for the errors and foibles of youth and beauty and the poetic temperament. "You must go your own way, I suppose. I retire from the contest. I've done my very best, dear boy, to preserve you from yourself; but the stars in their courses seem to fight against Sisera." He extended both his small hands with paternal unction. "Bless you, my children," he cried, theatrically. "Be happy. Be happy."

"Which way are you walking?" Will asked in German, to cover his confusion.

"Well, we were going towards the Schloss," Philippina replied, smiling. "But the climb's rather stiff, so we sat down for awhile by these stones, just to rest on the hill-top."

"The finger of fate again!" Florian cried, much amused, raising his hands deprecatingly. "Well, Will, there's no help for it; I see they must go with us. It's useless trying to keep you and your Oread apart any longer, so I won't attempt it. Two's company, three's none. The only thing left for a wise man like me—is just to walk on in front and take a German lesson from Fräulein Philippina."

Fortunately for Florian, too, Philippina proved to be one of those gay and easy-going young ladies with whom the want of a common tongue wherein to express one's thoughts forms a very slight barrier to the course of conversation. Already at her châlet he had guessed as much; and now on the hill-top, they walked along side by side, chatting and laughing as they went, with expressive eyes, and making themselves mutually understood as much by nods and becks and wreathèd smiles, so Florian poetically phrased it in his silent soul, as by any articulate form of the German language. Before they had reached the Schloss they stood already on excellent terms with one another, and

Florian even consoled himself for the enforced loss of Linnet's society with the reflection that Philippina was, after all, in many ways "a great deal more practical."

But Linnet, walking behind, was in the seventh heavens. She had found her Engländer once more, and that alone would have been enough for her. But that wasn't all; this second chance meeting, perfectly natural as it was, for Andreas had but followed the stream of tourists southward, impressed her simple mind with the general idea that the world, after all, wasn't as big as she had supposed it, and that she'd be liable now to meet the gnädige Herr wherever she went, quite casually and accidentally. Not, indeed, that she troubled her head much just then about the future in any way: with Will by her side, she lived wholly in the present. She didn't even ask him why he had gone away from Innsbruck without coming to say goodbye to her in person; she didn't utter a single word of reproach or complaint; she accepted all that; she took it all for granted. Will never could marry her; she didn't expect him to marry her: a gentleman like him couldn't marry a peasant-girl; a Catholic like herself couldn't marry a heretic who scarcely bowed the knee to Our Blessed Lady. But she loved him for all that, and she was happy if he would but let her walk beside him. And in this she was purely and simply womanly. True love doesn't ask any end beyond itself: it is amply satisfied with being loved and loving.

And Will? Well, Will had a poet's nature, and the poet lives in the passing emotion. Only a man of moods can set moods before us. Like Linnet herself, Will thought little of the future when Linnet was beside him. He meant her no harm, as he said truly to Florian; but he meant her no good either: he meant nothing at all but to walk by her side, and hold her hand in his, and feel his heart beat hard, and her finger-touch thrill through him. Walking thus as in a mist, they passed Dorf Tyrol; and the road at once grew wilder and more romantic. It grew also more sequestered, with deeper bends and nooks, as it turned the corners of little ravines and gulleys, where they could look at one another more frankly with the eager eyes of young love; and once, Will raised his hand to Linnet's nut-brown cheek, and pressed it tenderly. Linnet said nothing, but the hot blood rushed to her face with mingled shame and pleasure; and who was so glad as she that Will Deverill should touch her!

The path wound round a deep gorge, overhanging a torrent, with Schloss Tyrol itself frowning beyond on its isolated crag, a picturesque and half-ruinous mediæval fortress, almost isolated on a peninsular mass of crumbling mud-cliff, interspersed with the ice-worn débris of pre-historic glaciers. 'Tis a beautiful spot. Pretty Alpine rills, tearing headlong down the sides, have carved out for themselves steep ravines which all but island the castle; their banks rise up sheer as straight walls of cliff, displaying on their faces the grey mud of the moraine, from which the ice-worn boulders project boldly here and there, or tumble from time to time to encumber the littered beds of the streams that dislodged them. But what struck Florian most of all, as he paused and looked, was the curious effect produced where a single large boulder has resisted the denuding action of the streams and the rainfall, so as to protect the tapering column of hardened mud beneath it. Each big rock thus stood paradoxically perched on the summit of a conical pillar, called locally an earth-pyramid, and forming, Florian thought, the most singular element in this singular landscape. Close to its end the track bends round an elbow to skirt the ravine, and then plunges for a hundred yards or more into a dark and narrow underground passage through the isthmus of moraine stuff, before drawing up at the portcullis of the dismantled fortress. A more romantically mysterious way of approaching a mediæval stronghold Florian could hardly imagine: it reminded him of Ivanhoe or the Castle of Otranto.

But as Florian and Philippina disappeared under the shadow of the darkling archway, Will found himself alone for one moment with Linnet, screened from observation by the thick trellis-work of the vineyards. They were walking close together, whispering in one another's ears those eternal nothings which lovers have whispered in the self-same tones, but in a hundred tongues, for ten thousand ages. Occasion favoured them. Will glanced round for a moment; then with a rapid movement he drew the trembling girl to himself, half unresisted. Her cheek was flushed, partly with joy, partly with fear, that he should dare to lay hands on her. His boldness thrilled her through with a delicious thrill, the true womanly joy in being masterfully handled. "No, no," she cried in a faint voice; "you mustn't, you mustn't." But she said it shyly, as one who half-wishes her words to fail of their effect: and Will never heeded her "no"—and oh, how glad she was that Will never heeded it! He held her face up to his, and bent his own down tenderly. Linnet tried to draw back, yet pursed up her lips at the same time and let him kiss her when he tried; but she made him try first, though when at last he succeeded, she felt the kiss course trembling through her inmost being.

It was but a moment, yet that moment to her was worth many eternities. For a second of time she nestled against him confidingly, for now he was hers, and she was his forever. Their lips had sealed it. But before he could steal another, she had broken away from him again, and stood half-penitent, half-overjoyed, by the roadside, a little way from him. "No more now!" she said, gravely, lifting one finger in command; "we must follow Herr Florian." And with that, they plunged at once into the gloom of the tunnel.

What happened by the way, no one knows save themselves; but, two minutes later, with blushing cheeks, they rejoined their companions by the gateway of the castle. Even flushed as she was, Linnet couldn't help admiring it. It was beautiful, wonderful. The ancient wealth and dignity of the first counts of Schloss Tyrol remain well reflected to this day in the rude magnificence of their Romanesque residence. Linnet looked up with wonder at the round-arched portal of the principal doorway, richly carved with quaint squat figures of grotesque fancy, naïve, not to say childish and uncouth, in design, but admirable and exquisite in execution. "Tenth-century workmanship!" Florian said, with a bland smile, as he looked up at it, condescendingly; and Will, pulling himself together again, explained to the two girls in detail the various meanings of the queer little figures. Here were Adam and Eve; here Jonah and the whale; here saints revelled in Heaven; here, lost souls rolled in torment. Linnet gazed, and admired the beauty of the door—but still more, Will's learning. If only she could understand such things as that! But there!—he was so wise, and she so ignorant!

They passed into the hall, that stately old Rittersaal, adorned with marble carvings of the same infantile type, and looked sheer down from the windows a thousand feet on to the valley below, with the falls of the Adige behind, and a sea of tumultuous porphyritic mountains surging and rolling in the farther background. 'Twas a beautiful view in itself, rendered more beautiful still by its picturesque setting of semi-circular arches, divided and supported by slender shafts of polished alabaster. To an untutored girl of Linnet's native artistic temperament, it was delightful to pass through those lordly halls and into that exquisite chapel with its quaint old frescoes, in company with somebody who could explain their whole meaning to her simple intelligence so well as Will Deverill. Though she felt her own ignorance, felt it acutely, sensitively, she felt at the same time how fast she could learn from such a teacher; and as she dropped on her knees before the twelfth-century Madonna in the spangled shrine of that antiquated chantry, it was not for herself alone that she murmured below her breath, in very tremulous tones, an Ave Maria.

Will and Florian talked, too, of the Schloss and its history. Linnet listened with all her ears, though she hardly understood half the English words they used to describe it—how it commanded the whole vast plain of Meran and Botzen, the widest and most populous in the Eastern Alps, one basking garden of vines and Indian corn and fruit-trees, thickly dotted with hamlets, churches, and castles. "You can see why the counts who lived here spread their power and their name by slow degrees over the whole of this country," Will said, as they gazed down on it. And then he went on to talk of how the Counts of Tyrol gradually absorbed Meran and Botzen, and in course of time, by their possession of the Brenner route, the great mediæval highway from Italy to Germany, acquired the over-lordship of the whole wide tract which is now called after them. Oh, what grand words he used! Linnet listened, and wondered at them. She caught, from time to time, the name of Margaret Maultasch—that Meg of the Pocket-Mouth who made over her dominions to the house of Austria—and learned from stray hints how the Counts of the new line moved their capital northward from Meran to Innsbruck. It was marvellous how Herr Will, who was a stranger from England, should know so much more about her people's history than she herself did! But there! what did she say? Herr Will knew everything.

Florian and Philippina went off by themselves after awhile among the ruins of the ramparts. Linnet was left alone with Will again by the windows of the Rittersaal. All this historical talk had inflamed her eager mind with vague hopes and possibilities. Why should not she too know? Why should not she too be fit for him, like the fair-haired lady? "Herr Will," she said at last, turning round to him with a shy look in her shrinking eyes, "How I wish you could teach me! How I wish you could tell me how to learn such things! We shall be here for a month. Why shouldn't I begin? Why shouldn't I learn now? We may see each other often."

"Will you be on the hill behind the town to-morrow?" Will asked, half-ashamed of himself for these endless breakings-off, and these fresh re-commencements.

"Perhaps," Linnet answered timidly, in her accustomed phrase; "if Philippina will come . . . and if she doesn't tell Andreas."

"Where will you be?" Will inquired, taking her hand in his own once more and holding it.

Linnet looked down and paused. "I might be near the cross at the turn of the road by the second oratory, about ten o'clock," she said very low, "if Our Lady permits me."

Will pressed her hand hard. "And where do you sing to-night?" he asked, with a little smile of pleasure. "I must come and hear you."

To his immense surprise Linnet drew back at once, red as a rose, and fixed her eyes on him pleadingly. "Oh, no, don't," she cried, much distressed. "Don't, don't, I beg of you."

Will, in turn, lifted his head, astonished, and looked hard at her. He couldn't understand this strange freak of feeling. "Then don't you like me to hear you?" he cried, regretfully. "It's such a pleasure to me. I thought you wanted me to hear. And I thought I encouraged you."

"So you do," Linnet answered with a burst, half-sidling towards him, half-shrinking. "I love you to hear me. And I'll sing for you whenever you like. I'll sing for you till I'm hoarse. But don't come to the hotels. Oh, don't come, I implore you!"

"Why not, my child?" Will cried, drawing her close to him once more.

Linnet's cheeks burnt crimson. She looked down and stammered. Then, with a sudden impulse she hid her face on his bosom, and yielded up her whole soul to him. "Because," she whispered, all aglow with maiden shame at having confessed the truth, "if Andreas Hausberger sees you, he'll know you're in Meran—and then he won't allow me to come out on the hills to meet you."

CHAPTER XVII

That avowal of Linnet's that she didn't want Andreas Hausberger to know of Will's presence in the town put Will's relations towards her during the next few weeks on a different, and to some extent compromising, footing. It introduced into their meetings a certain shadowy element of clandestine love-making which was in many ways distasteful to Will's frank and manly nature, though it was at the same time, as Florian felt, a hundred times more "dangerous" for him than any open acquaintance. For Andreas, after all, was Linnet's ostensible guardian and nearest male protector. To meet Linnet on the hills, without his knowledge or consent, was to place oneself in the position of an unrecognised lover. Will knew it was a mistake. And yet—he did it. We, who have made no mistakes of any sort in all our lives, but have steadily followed the beaten track all through, with sheep-like persistence, can afford to disapprove of him.

So, day after day, during the next few weeks, Will went up on the hills to walk and talk with Linnet. Rue Palmer was delighted. She thought, poor soul, her scheme was succeeding admirably. Will was out every morning on the mountains alone, working hard at his magnum opus, which was to astonish the world, and with which she had inspired him. It was glorious, glorious! And, indeed, in spite of the time wasted in talking with Linnet, though the best spent time, as everybody knows, is the time we waste, Will did really succeed in writing and composing at odd moments and in the night watches no small part of his graceful and beautiful little operetta, "The Chamois Hunter's Daughter." But alas for poor Rue, it was not she who inspired it.

On these morning expeditions up the surrounding hills to some appointed trysting-place, Florian sometimes accompanied him, and sometimes not. But, in any case, he abstained from mentioning their object to Rue; as he put it himself, never should it be said that Florian Wood could split upon two ill-advised but confiding young people. It suited Florian's book now, indeed, that Will's attention should be distracted from Rue to Linnet. He wanted to make the running for himself with the American heiress, and he was by no means sorry that so dangerous and important a rival as the author of "Voices from the Hills" should be otherwise occupied. So he kept his own counsel about Will and Linnet; he had abdicated by this time his self-appointed function of moral censor; and seeing they would go to the devil in any case, he was inclined to let them go their own headlong way, into the jaws of matrimony, without preliminary haggling. He that will to Cupar, maun to Cupar. Deverill would marry his cow-girl in the end—of that Florian felt certain; and when a man's quite determined to make a fool of himself, you know, why, you only earn his dislike, instead of his esteem, by endeavouring to win him back again to the ways of wisdom.

And Will? Well, Will himself had as yet no very fixed ideas of his own as to whither he was tending. Being only a poet, he was content to drift with the wind and tide, and watch on what shoals or shores they might finally cast him. Most probably, if things had been allowed to go their own way, he would sooner or later have justified Florian's pessimistic prophecies by marrying Linnet. He would have gone on and on, falling more and more deeply in love with the pretty peasant every day, and letting her fall every day more and more deeply in love with him, till at last conventional differences sank to nothing in his eyes, and he remembered only that heart answereth to heart, be it poet's or alp-girl's. At present, however, he troubled himself little with any of these things. He was satisfied for the moment, Florian said, to bask in the sunshine of that basilisk's smile, without care for the morrow. Sooner or later, he felt sure, in so small a town, either Florian or he must run up unawares against Andreas Hausberger. Whenever that happened, no doubt, there must be some sort of change or new departure. Meanwhile, he religiously avoided the Promenade, where he was likeliest to come suddenly on the wise impresario. So he stuck to the hills, with or without Linnet.

The very next morning, indeed, after this their chance meeting, he went up the Küchelberg once more, impressed with an ardent desire to aid and abet Linnet's laudable wish for self-education. He brought a book up with him to read to the two girls under the bright blue sky, as they sat on the hillside. He chose a pleasant spot, in the full eye of the autumn sun, on a rounded boss of rock, whose crumbling clefts were still starred with wild pinks and rich yellow tormentils. Florian had contributed to the feast of reason and the flow of soul a kilogram of grapes—they cost but threepence-halfpenny a pound in the vintage season—unknown luxuries till then to Philippina and Linnet. Philippina found the grapes delicious, but the book rather dry; its style was stilted, and it appeared to narrate the story of a certain Doctor Faust, his transactions with a gentleman of most doubtful shape (who caused Philippina to look round in some fear), and his wicked designs against the moral happiness of a young girl called Gretchen. Philippina yawned; it was a tedious performance. Florian, having reduced his share of the grapes to their skins alone, yawned in concert with the lady, and began to play with his eyeglass. As his German didn't suffice to understand the lines, even when aided by Will's dramatic delivery and clear enunciation, he found the play slow, and the reader a nuisance. So he was very well pleased when Philippina suggested, at a break in the first act, they should go off for a walk by themselves alone, and continue their course of oral instruction in the German language. Florian liked Philippina; there was no silly nonsense about her. After all, in a woman, if all you want is a walk on the Küchelberg, the total absence of silly nonsense, you must at once admit, is a great recommendation.

But Linnet sat on. She sat on, and listened. She drank it in, open-eyed, and with parted lips—every line and every word of it. Dear Herr Will read so well, and made her feel and understand every point so dramatically; and the book—the book itself was so profoundly interesting. Never in her life before had Linnet heard anything the least bit like it. It was grand, it was beautiful! She didn't know till then the world contained such books; her reading had been confined to her alphabet and grammar at the parish folk-school, supplemented by the good little tracts on purgatory and the holy saints, distributed by the Herr Vicar and the sisters at the nunnery. Theological literature was the sole form yet known to her. This weird tale about Gretchen and the transformed philosopher opened out to her new vistas of a world of possibilities. Long after, when she sang in great opera-houses, as Marguerite in Gounod's "Faust," she remembered with a thrill how she had first heard that tale, in Goethe's deathless words, from Will Deverill's lips, on the green slopes of the Küchelberg.

She sat there for an hour or two, never heeding the time, but listening, all entranced, to that beautiful story. Now and again Will broke off, and held her hand for a moment, and gazed deep into her eyes, and said some sweet words of his own to her. He was a poet, Herr Will, in his own tongue and land; she knew now what that meant—he could make up such lovely things as he read from the book to her. "Tell me some of your own, Herr Will. Tell me some of your own verses," she said, sighing, at last. "I should love to hear them."

But Will shook his head. "The English is too hard. You wouldn't understand them, Linnet," he answered.

"Let me try," Linnet pleaded, with such a winning look that Will couldn't resist her. And to humour her whim, he repeated the simplest of the laughing little love-songs from his book of "Voices."

The ring of it was pretty, very sweet and musical. Linnet half understood, no more; for the words were too hard for her. But it spurred her on to further effort. "You must lend me some books like that in English," she said, simply. "I want to be wise, like you and Herr Florian."

So Will brought her next day from the book-shop in the town the dainty little "Poetry Book of Modern Poets," in the Tauchnitz edition. He wrote her name in it too; and Linnet took it home, and hid it deep in her box in a white silk handkerchief, and read bits of it by night, very stealthily in her own room, spelling out what it meant with Andreas Hausberger's dictionary. Long after, she had that precious volume bound in white Florentine vellum, with a crimson fleur-de-lys on the cover, at a house just opposite the Duomo at Florence. But at present she read it in its paper covers. She read other books, too, German books which Will chose for her; not instructive books which were over her head, but poetry and romance and imaginative literature, such as her ardent Tyrolese nature could easily assimilate. Day after day, Will read her aloud something fresh—Undine, the Maid of Orleans, Uhland's Ballads, Paul Heyse's short stories—but of all the things he read to her, the one she liked best was a German translation of an English play—a beautiful play by another English poet, whose name was also Will, but who died long ago—a play about two luckless and devoted lovers, called Romeo and Juliet. Linnet cried over that sad story, and Will kissed her tears away; and a little later, when Andreas Hausberger took her to Verona on their way south to Milan, Linnet went of her own accord to see Juliet's tomb in a courtyard in the town, and wasted much excellent sympathy and sentiment over the shameless imposture of that bare Roman sarcophagus. But she meant very well; and she believed in Juliet even more firmly than she believed in Siegfried and Chriemhild and all the other fine folks to whom Will introduced her.

So three weeks passed away, three glorious golden weeks, and day after day, on those lovely hillsides, Linnet saw her lover. At the end of a fortnight, Rue heard, from various friends at other hotels, of a wonderful singer in a Tyrolese troupe, then performing nightly in the various salons. "Why, that must surely be Linnet!" she said before Will, to the first friend who mentioned it.

"Yes; Linnet—that's her name," Rue's friend assented.

"I knew she was in the town," Will admitted somewhat sheepishly; for he felt as if he were somehow deceiving Rue, though it never would have entered his good, modest head to suppose she herself could care anything about him, except as a poet in whose work she was kind enough to take a friendly interest.

"Ah, I should love to hear her again!" Rue cried, enthusiastically. "She sings like a nightingale—such a splendid soprano! Let's find out where she'll be to-night, and go round in a body to the hotel to hear her!"

But Will demurred strongly. He'd rather not go, he said; he'd stop at home by himself and get on with his operetta. At that, Rue was secretly pleased in her own heart; she felt it throb sensibly. After all, then, her poet didn't really and truly care for the pretty alp-girl. He knew she was in the town—and, in spite of that knowledge, had spent every evening all the time with herself at the Erzherzog Johann! Nor would Florian go either; he invented some excuse to account for his reluctance. So Rue went with two new girls she had picked up at the hotel, in succession to the giggling inarticulates at Innsbruck. Linnet recognised her in the crowd, for the room was crowded—'twas a nightly ovation now, wherever Linnet sang—and knew her at once as the fair-haired lady. But Florian and Will weren't with her to-night! That made Linnet's heart glad. She had come without him! After all, her Engländer didn't always dance attendance, it seemed, on the fair-haired Frau with the many diamonds!

So easily had Will made two women's hearts happy, by stopping at home at his hotel that evening! For women think much more of men than men imagine—their poor little breasts live for the most part in a perpetual flutter of love and expectancy.

As the weeks wore away, however, it began to strike Franz Lindner as a singular fact, that Philippina and Linnet severed themselves so much every day from the rest of the troupe, and went up on the hills all alone for exercise. That fierce young Robbler was a true Tyrolese in his treatment of his women. Though he never abated one jot or tittle of his attentions to Linnet, it hardly occurred to him as forming any part of a lover's duty to accompany his mädchen in her morning rambles. Franz was too much engaged himself, indeed, with the young men of the place in the cafés and beer-gardens, to find much time hanging idle on his hands for female society. He had made many friends in the gay little town. His hat and his feather were well known by this time to half the gilded youth in the Meran restaurants. Andreas Hausberger had turned out the young women on the hills; and there they might stop, so far as Franz Lindner was concerned to prevent them. Andreas Hausberger had been wondrous careful of Linnet's health of late, since he saw he was likely to make pots of money from her. He had bound them all down by a three years' engagement, and he knew now that Linnet was worth at least five times the sum he had bargained to pay her. But Franz Lindner's health might take care of itself; and Franz didn't think much, personally, of the air of the mountains. He'd had enough of all that in his jäger days; now the chrysalis had burst, and let loose the butterfly; his wander-years had come, and he meant to sip the sweets of advanced civilisation. And he sipped them in the second-rate bars and billiard-rooms of a small town in South Tyrol.

On this particular morning, however, it occurred to his Robblership to inquire in his own mind why the womenkind loved to walk so much by themselves on the mountains. Philippina hadn't told him, to be sure; Philippina had an eye to Andreas Hausberger herself—was he not the wirth, and the master of the troupe?—and she was therefore by no means averse to any little device which might distract poor Linnet from that most desirable admirer. Still, Franz had his suspicions. Women are so deep, a man can never fathom them! He mounted the Küchelberg by the zig-zag path, and turning to the left by the third Madonna, came at last to a little knoll of bare porphyry rock, looking down on the wide vale and the long falls of the Adige.

A very small and dainty, not to say effeminate, young man, in a knickerbocker suit of most Britannic aspect, was strolling some distance off, with his arm encircling a woman's plump waist, which suspiciously reminded Franz of his friend Philippina's. The Robbler could hardly believe his eyes; could that be Herr Florian? Oh no; for they had left the foreign Herrschaft at the hotel at Innsbruck. But here, close by, behind the shadow of some junipers—stranger sight still!—stretched at length on the ground, and reading aloud in German to some unseen person, lay another young man in another tourist suit, with a voice that most strikingly and exactly recalled the other Engländer's at St Valentin. Franz drew a deep breath, and strode a long step forward. At sound of his foot, the unseen person sprang back where she sat with a quick, small scream. Black as night in his wrath, Franz peered round and faced them. It was undoubtedly Will; quite as undoubtedly Linnet!

The Robbler spoke angrily. "You again!" he cried, clenching his fist, and knitting his brow hard, with bullet head held forward. "Are you following us in hiding? What do you mean by this trick? You daren't show your face, coward, at our inn in the town! You steal up here and skulk! What do you mean with the mädchen?"

At that imputation of secrecy, and still worse of cowardice, Will sprang up and confronted him. "I dare show my face anywhere you like," he answered in hot blood. "I have not followed this lady; I came here before her, and met her at Meran by the purest accident. But I refuse to be questioned about her by you or by anyone. What right have you to ask? She is no mädchen of yours. Who gave you any power or authority over her?"

For a moment the Robbler instinct rose fierce and hot in Franz Lindner's breast. He drew back half a pace, as if making ready to spring at him. In a few angry words he repeated his cutting taunts, and spoke savagely to Linnet. "Go home, go home, girl; you are here for no good! What can this Engländer want, save one thing, with a sennerin?"

He laid his hand roughly on Linnet's shoulder. Will couldn't stand that sight; he clutched the man's arm fiercely, twisted it round in the socket, and pushed him back like a child, in the white heat of his anger. Franz saw the interloper was strong, far stronger than he supposed. "If you dare to lay your hand on this lady again," Will cried, standing in front of her like a living buckler, "I give you due warning, you do it at your peril. Your life is at stake. I won't permit you to behave with brutality before me."

In his native valley the Robbler would have flown at Will's throat on those words, and fought him, strong as he was, to the death, for his mädchen. But since he came to Meran he had learned some new ways: such were not, he now knew, the manners of civilisation. Will's resolute attitude even produced a calming effect upon the young barbarian. He felt in his heart he had a better plan than that. To beat Will in fair fight would, after all, be useless; the mädchen wouldn't abide, as mädchen ought, by the wager of battle. But he could wound him far worse. He could go down to the town, and tell Andreas Hausberger how his ward spent her mornings on the slopes of the Küchelberg!

Already he was learning the ways of the world. With a sarcastic smile, he raised his hat ceremoniously, turned feather and all, in mock politeness. "Good morning, mein Herr," he drawled out, with a fine north German accent, picked up in the billiard-rooms. "Good morning, sennerin." And without another word he strode away down the mountain.

But as soon as he was gone Linnet burst into tears. "Ah, I know what he'll do!" she cried, sobbing and trembling. "He'll go down to the town and tell Andreas Hausberger. He'll go down to the town and tell how he met us here. And, of course, after this, Andreas will put the very worst face upon it."

CHAPTER XVIII

TAKEN BY SURPRISE

Andreas Hausberger was a wise and prudent man. He felt convinced by this time that Linnet, as he said to himself, though to no one else, for to confess it would have been foolish, was a perfect gold mine, if only a man knew how to work her properly. And in exploiting this mine, like a sensible capitalist that he was, he determined to spare neither time nor pains nor money. Night after night, as the audiences at the hotels grew more and more enthusiastic, the truth forced itself upon his wise and prudent mind that what they said was right: Linnet was a singer fit for the highest undertakings. She must be trained and instructed for the operatic stage; and on the operatic stage, with that voice and that presence, she'd be worth her weight in gold if she was worth a penny.

So, ever since the first day when he left the Zillerthal, Andreas's views and ideas about his troupe and his tour had been undergoing a considerable and constant modification. It would cost a good deal, of course, to abandon his first plan, and instead of proceeding to the Riviera as he originally intended, take Linnet to be trained at Milan and Florence. But it was worth the money. You must throw a sprat to catch a herring. And it must be Italy, too, not Munich or Dresden. He wouldn't put her precious life in jeopardy, now, in those cold northern towns, during the winter months, for he had grown wonderfully careful of Linnet's health since he saw how her voice conjured florins into the plate for him; and though he believed as much as ever in the virtues of fresh air and a Spartan diet, he feared to expose the throat that uttered such golden notes to the rigours and changes of a Bavarian or Saxon December. So Milan and Florence it must be, though he had Franz Lindner and Philippina and the others on his hands to pay and care for. And in those great settled towns, where theatres and amusements were regularly organised, he couldn't hope his little troupe, deprived of its chief ornament, could compete, save at a loss, with more showy establishments. Still, to one thing he had made up his mind: Linnet should never utter another note in public, after they moved from Meran, until she could blaze forth, a full-fledged star, armed and equipped at every point with all that art could do for her, on the operatic stage of London, Paris, or Petersburg. He must put up with present loss for the sake of future gain; he must pay for his little troupe and for Linnet's training, though he spent by the way his bottom dollar.

Not that the wise impresario was moved in this affair by any mere philanthropic desire to benefit a favourite pupil. As a prior condition to any expenditure on fitting and preparing Linnet for the operatic stage, Andreas proposed to obtain a clear hold on her future earnings by the simple little business preliminary of marrying her. And he proposed this plan to himself in the same simple-hearted and entirely dictatorial way in which he would have proposed some arrangement about his cows or his horses. That Linnet could possibly object to his designs for her advancement in life was an idea that hardly so much as even occurred to him. He was her master, and, if he ordered her, she could scarcely say him nay. That would be plain contumacy. Besides, the match would be one so much to her own advantage! Not a girl in St Valentin but would be overjoyed to catch him. Philippina, he knew, would give her eyes for such a chance; but Philippina's high notes were shrill, a great deal too shrill, while Linnet's were the purest and clearest and most silvery ever uttered by woman. He was a husband any girl might well be proud of, and though Linnet would be worth money, too, if properly trained, yet without his capital to back her up and give her that needful training, she could never use her voice to full (mercantile) advantage. She'd be a fool, indeed, if she refused his offer. And if she did, well, she was bound to him for three years at any rate; he could use up her voice pretty well in those three years, as he used up his horses, on commercial principles, and make a very fair profit out of her meanwhile in the process.

Thinking which things to himself during his stay in Meran, Andreas, who was by nature a taciturn person, had been in no hurry to communicate his ideas on the point prematurely to Linnet. He didn't want to puff her up with too much vanity beforehand, by disclosing to her over-soon the high honour in store for her. She had received more than enough homage already from the audiences at their concerts; it would turn her head outright if she knew all at once she was also to be promoted to marry her master. He would make all the legal preparations for the wedding in due time, without consulting Linnet; then, when everything was finished, and the day had come for them to leave Meran, he would break to her all at once the good fortune he designed for her. Not only was she to marry a man of substance, and a man of weight, and a Land-amt of the parish, but she was to be trained and fitted by him with sedulous care as a special star of the operatic profession.

When Franz Lindner burst in upon him, however, at his old-fashioned inn, in the street that is called Unter den Lauben, all indignant with the news how he had lighted upon Linnet and the Herr Engländer together on the slopes of the Küchelberg, and how he believed they had been meeting there secretly for many mornings at a stretch, Andreas saw at once this was no laughing matter. It was serious rivalry. For Franz Lindner himself, as a possible suitor of Linnet's, he didn't care a button. He could afford to despise the self-assertive Robbler. But Will Deverill, ah, that was quite another matter! Will Deverill was dangerous; he saw so much at a glance; and all the more dangerous in that he made his advances to the girl clandestinely. Poaching on those preserves must be severely repressed. Andreas didn't for a moment suppose the Engländer intended or wanted to marry the child; that was hardly likely: but he might upset her feelings, and, lead her into trouble, and unsettle her heart, and what was worse still, stuff her head all full of silly romantic nonsense.

Still, being always a prudent man, Andreas said little at the time. He was content with assuring Franz, in a very confident tone, that he'd put a stop at once to this folly of Linnet's. He acquiesced for the present, it being his nature to temporise, in Franz's little pretension to treat the girl as his acknowledged mädchen. He acquiesced, and smiled, though he hadn't the slightest intention of relinquishing his own hold on a future prima donna. Meanwhile, he pushed on all the legal formalities for marrying Linnet himself, as soon as he thought it well to disclose his matured plans to her.

So when Will went up to their stated meeting-place on the slopes of the Küchelberg, the morning after that stormy interview at the knoll with Franz Lindner, hardly daring to expect Linnet would be there to receive him, he was astonished to find her awaiting him much as usual at the accustomed seat, undeterred by either the wirth or the redoubtable Robbler. "I can't understand it myself," she said, holding his hand, and half crying. "It's awfully curious. I thought he'd be angry with me, and scold me so hard, and perhaps shut me up in the house for a week, or, at any rate, not let me come out any more to meet you. But, instead of that, he never said a word; he hasn't even spoken to me at all about the matter. Perhaps Franz hasn't told him yet; but I think he must have, and so does Philippina. It almost seems as if he didn't mind my coming out at all. We can only wait and see. That's all I can make of it."

Thus, for the next few days, Linnet and Will lived on in a real fool's paradise. Andreas never said a word about the meetings on the hill; Franz Lindner looked wise, and bided his time in silence. At the end of the week, however, Will found himself reluctantly compelled to fulfil a long-standing engagement with Rue and Florian, entered into before Linnet's arrival at Meran, to go for a three days' tour among the Botzen Dolomites. Will had put it off and put it off, not to miss one morning of Linnet's time in the town, till Rue declared in her imperious little American way she wouldn't wait a single day longer for anyone. And, indeed, it was getting full late in the season, even south of the Alps, for a mountain excursion. Rue had ordered her carriage, and settled her day to start. Will must go or stop behind, she said; and to do the last would be to confess all to Rue; so with a pang at his heart and no small misgivings in his brain, for Linnet by this time had grown wonderfully dear to him, he made up his mind to absent himself for three days, and to miss three precious mornings on the hills with his lady-love. It would freshen up the operetta, Rue declared, with deep conviction; there's nothing like change of scene to inspire one with the germs of poetry and music. But Will, for his part, knew something better, and he got it every day on the slopes of the Küchelberg.

"You won't go away while I'm gone?" he asked eagerly of Linnet, on the day before he left for those hateful Dolomites. "You're sure Andreas means to stop longer in the town. You'll be here when I come back again?"

"Oh yes; quite certain," Linnet answered, confidently. "He's not going away yet. We've engagements at hotels for nearly another fortnight."

Will held her hand long. It was only for three days, yet he found it hard to part from her. "One last kiss!" he said, drawing her close to him behind the sheltering gourd-vines. And Linnet let him take it without struggling for it now. In after years, Will felt those words were a kind of omen. It was far more of a last kiss than ever he dreamed at the time. And Linnet, well, Linnet was glad in her heart, when she came to look back on it, she had allowed him to take that last kiss so easily.

Next morning Will left. Andreas knew he had gone. Not many things escaped the wise Andreas's notice. From the moment he first heard of Will's meetings with Linnet on the hill behind the town, that cool-headed wirth had been waiting for his chance; and now the chance had come of its own accord to him. That day, after dinner, he went into the parlour of their little inn, and called Linnet to speak to him. Linnet came, all trembling. In a few short sentences, concise, curt, business-like, Andreas unfolded to his tremulous ward the notable scheme he had devised for her advancement.

He would make her his wife. But that wasn't all; he would make her a great lady, a star of the first magnitude. If she did as he bid, crowds would hang on her lips; silver and gold would be hers; she should dress in silk robes, diamonds dangling at her ears, pearls in strings on her bosom. But he said never a word about her heretic lover. Still, he said never a word about himself any more. He never mentioned love, her heart, her feelings. He laid before her, like a man of the world as he was, a simple proposal for an arrangement between them, in much the same spirit as he might have laid before Franz Lindner an agreement for a partnership. And he took it for granted Linnet would instantly jump at him. Why shouldn't she, indeed? She had every reason. Not a girl in St Valentin but would be proud if she could get him.

Yet he wasn't the least surprised when Linnet, growing pale, and with quivering lips, hid her face in her hands at last and began to cry bitterly. These girls are so silly!

"You agree to it?" Andreas asked, laying his palm on her neck behind with what tenderness he could muster.

Linnet shook it away angrily. "Never, never!" she cried, "never!"

Andreas bore with her patiently. He knew the ways of women. They were all little idiots! And this Engländer on the hill had filled her poor head with sentimental rubbish. With infinite forbearance, like a business man, he began to explain, to expostulate, to admonish her. He pointed out to her how rare a chance in life it was for a girl in her position to get an offer of marriage from a man in his; how his capital would enable her to train herself for the stage; how, without it, she must remain for ever just what she was now; how, with it, she might rise to the very crown and head of an admired profession. And, besides, she was bound to him for three years in any case. In those three years, of course, he could do as he liked with her.

But Linnet, weeping passionately, with her face in her hands, and every nerve in her body quivering with emotion, only sobbed out now and again in a heart-broken voice, "No; never, never!"

At last, after one such convulsive outburst, even fiercer than before, Andreas put the question point blank, "Is it because of this Engländer?"

And Linnet, raising her head, and clasping her hands in despair, made answer, obliquely, in one wild burst of speech, "Oh, I love him, I love him!"

At those words, Andreas smiled a peculiar cold smile, and began once more. He kept his head cool; he explained, he reasoned. The Engländer, of course, never meant to marry her. Marriage in such a case was out of the question. She must know what that meant; why go off on such side-issues? . . . . And, besides, she must never forget, the man was a heretic!

Still, Linnet, unflinching, looked up and clasped her hands. "I don't care for that," she cried wildly. "I love him! I love him!"

"Then you refuse, point blank?" Andreas asked, stepping a little aside, and holding the knob of the bedroom door in his hand, half-irresolute.

"I utterly refuse!" Linnet answered, very firm, but sobbing.

With an air of cruel triumph, Andreas opened wide the door. "Come in, Herr Vicar!" he cried, with real theatrical effect. And even as he spoke, the Herr Vicar entered.

Linnet gazed at him, dumb with awe, surprise, and amazement. How had he ever got here? It was her own parish priest, her confessor from St Valentin!

CHAPTER XIX

SPIRITUAL WEAPONS

The Herr Vicar in Meran! It was wonderful, miraculous!

For a minute or two, Linnet was so utterly taken aback at this unexpected portent that she hardly knew how to comport herself under such novel circumstances. Now, that was exactly the result Andreas Hausberger had counted upon. Andreas loved not the Church, to be sure, but, like all sound strategists, political or social, he knew how to make use of it for his own wise purposes. As soon as ever he learned from Franz Lindner how things were going on between Linnet and her Engländer, and had ascertained by private inquiry from the Herr Oberkellner at the Erzherzog Johann that Herr Will was going away for a few days' tour among the Botzen Dolomites, why, taking opportunity by the forelock, he telegraphed at once to the Herr Vicar at St Valentin to come on by the first train, all expenses paid, over the Brenner to Meran, on purpose to save the soul of an erring member of his flock, in imminent danger of faith and morals, from a heretic Englishman. And the Herr Vicar, in return, though he loved not Andreas—for the wirth was a Liberal, an enemy of the "Blacks," and reputed to be even not far short of a freethinker—the Herr Vicar, for his part, was by no means averse to a pleasant holiday in a fashionable watering-place south of the Alps at that delightful season, especially if someone else was to pay the piper. It is well to combine the salvation of souls with an agreeable excursion. The Herr Vicar was prepared to make free use of the Mammon of Unrighteousness—in the Church's service; a good pastor employs it without stint or compunction to secure the eternal bliss of the particular flock committed to his guidance.

Not that the astute priest began at once with the matter in hand, on which Herr Andreas had already most amply coached him. He was far too wise and politic a fisher of souls for so clumsy a procedure. He angled gently. He started on his task by striking, first, all the familiar home chords of St Valentin. The moment he entered the room, indeed, Linnet rushed up and seized his hand—she had known him from her childhood, and taken the mass from him often; she had confessed to him her sins, and received time and again his paternal blessing. At such a moment as that any old friend from St Valentin would have been a welcome counsellor: how much more then the Herr Vicar, who had taught her the Credo, and the Vater Unser, and the Ave; who had prepared her lisping lips for First Communion; who had absolved her from her sins from her babyhood onward! And he had seen that dear mother only the day before! How she flooded him with questions as to everyone at St Valentin!

The Herr Vicar, in reply, folding two plump hands over his capacious waistband, sank back in an easy-chair, and answered her at full length as to all that had happened since she left the village. The good mother was well, very well indeed, seldom better in November; some holy oil rubbed on night and morning, had proved highly effectual against her threatened rheumatism. Oh yes; she had duly received the five florins that Linnet sent her, thanks very much for them, and had expended two of them, as Linnet would no doubt herself have wished, in the performance of a mass for the deliverance of the dear father's soul from purgatory. She knew the Herr Vicar was coming to Meran, and would see her daughter, and she had sent many messages (all detailed at full length)—how the cow with the crooked horn was giving no milk, and how the cat had five kittens, and how pleased they all were to hear at St Valentin there was talk Linnet was to make such a brilliant marriage.

Then poor Linnet faltered out, half-sobbing again, when the Herr Vicar spoke of that mass for the repose of her father's soul, how great a trial it had been to her to be away from St Valentin for the first time in her life on All Souls Day, the Feast of the Dead, when it had always been her custom to lay a little wreath, and burn four small tapers on her father's grave in the village churchyard. She was afraid that dear spirit in its present home would feel itself neglected by the duty unperformed in due season.

But the Herr Vicar, with a benign smile, was happy he should be able to reassure her as to this matter. The candles and the wreath had been forthcoming as usual; he had seen to them himself, at Herr Andreas's request, who had written to him on the subject from Meran most thoughtfully.

That was kind, Linnet thought, far kinder than she ever could have expected from Andreas. But that wasn't all. He had provided in many ways, or intended to provide, for the good mother's comfort. Then the Herr Vicar went on to speak still more of Andreas, who slipped out as he spoke, leaving priest and penitent alone together. So Herr Andreas, it seemed, was going to marry her! For a girl like her, that was a very great honour. And the sooner the better, indeed; the sooner the better! These were grave and painful rumours now afloat in St Valentin, and the Herr Vicar shook his head in solemn warning, grave and painful rumours, how Linnet had been seen on the hillsides more than once, with an English heretic. And he had followed her to Innsbruck! and then to Meran! and now, Heaven knew what he was trying to do with her! 'Twas a dangerous thing, a compromising thing (the Herr Vicar thought) for a girl to get involved in an affair like that with a man so much above herself in position and station. But Herr Andreas was so kind, and consented to overlook it; there were very few men who in a similar case would act like Herr Andreas. In other matters the Herr Vicar had withstood him to his face, because he was to be blamed; but in this, he had behaved like a generous gentleman.

To all which, poor Linnet, hiding her face in her hands, only made answer once more, "I can never marry Andreas Hausberger."

"Why not?" the priest asked, sharply.

And Linnet, hardly knowing how to answer him for fear and shame, yet murmured very low, "Because I don't love him."

Then the Herr Vicar, thus aroused, went off at a tangent into a clerical exhortation on the nature, duties, and inducements of matrimony. We must remember that, in these matters, the wishes of the flesh were not alone or even chiefly to be consulted. They were of minor importance. There was her duty as a daughter, for example: Herr Andreas was rich; how much might he not do to lighten her mother's old age? how much to release her poor father's soul from the flames of purgatory? There was her duty as a woman, and a child of the Church; how much might not Herr Andreas's money enable her to accomplish for the good of the world and for the souls of her people? She was still a giddy girl. What temptations such a marriage would enable her to avoid; what a brilliant future in the end it might open out before her! And then these floating rumours had disturbed him much; on his way from Jenbach, if she would only believe him, he had said prayers on her behalf to Our Lady, to preserve her honour.

But Linnet, raising her head, and looking him straight in the eyes, made answer at last in these wicked, rebellious words, "I love the Engländer! Ah, I love the Engländer! If ever I marry at all, I'll marry the Engländer!"

The Herr Vicar grew grave. This was a case, indeed, not for humouring and coaxing, but for the sternest admonition. And he administered it without stint. With the simple directness of the Tyrolese priest, accustomed to deal with coarse, straightforward natures, he spoke the plain truth; he brought her future sin home to her with homely force and unvarnished language. In the first place, this young man clearly meant no good by her. That was obvious to everyone. Now, if he were one of her own sort, a faithful son of the Church, and a Tyrolese jäger, well, the Herr Vicar might, in that case, have been disposed, no doubt, to be somewhat more lenient. He admitted, while he deplored, the temptations and difficulties of a sennerin's life, and was never too hard on them. And besides, in such circumstances, the young man might mean in the end to marry her. But this Engländer assuredly meant nothing of the kind; and, what was worse, even if he did, the Herr Vicar could by no means approve of such a union. The Holy See, acting as ever on the Apostolic advice, "Be not unequally yoked together with unbelievers," disallowed and discouraged the union of Catholics with Jews, heretics, infidels, and other schismatics, under one or other of which unholy categories (and the Herr Vicar frowned) he must needs place her Engländer. True, the Holy Father was sometimes pleased, on good cause duly shown, to grant certain persons an exceptional dispensation. But even if the Engländer desired to marry her, which was scarcely likely, and even if he consented to invoke such aid, which was still more improbable, how could he, the Herr Vicar, knowing the young man's circumstances, back up such a request?—how consign a lamb of his flock to the keeping of an infidel? Every sentiment of gratitude should bind her to Herr Andreas. Every feeling of a Catholic should turn her instinctively away from the false wiles of a schismatic.

To all which theological argument, Linnet, raising her head, and wringing her hands, only answered once more, in a wildly despairing voice, "But I love him, I love him!"

The priest saw at once this was a case for strong measures. Unless he adopted them, a lamb might slip from his pastoral grasp, a doubtful soul might stray for ever from the fold of true believers. He put on at once the set tone and manner of the confessional. It was no longer a question now of merely meeting Herr Andreas's wishes, though Herr Andreas's aid would be most useful indeed in the affairs of the parish; it was a question of preserving this poor sheep of his flock from everlasting perdition. What are a few fleeting years, with this lover or that, compared with an eternity of unceasing torment? The Herr Vicar was an honest and conscientious man, according to his lights; this poor girl was in deadly danger of her immortal soul, and that window for the chancel, which Herr Andreas vowed, would be a work of piety most pleasing to their holy patron saint, the blessed Valentin.

So, with all the strength of imagery he possessed at his command, the priest began to play of deliberate design upon the chords of poor Linnet's superstitious terror. In horribly vivid and realistic language, such as only a Tyrolese tongue could command, he conjured up before her mind that familiar picture of dead souls in purgatory, lost souls in torment. He poured out upon her trembling head all the thunders of the Church against unholy love, or, what came to the same thing, against an uncatholic union. Linnet listened, and cowered. To you and me, this would just have been a well-meaning but ignorant parish priest; to Linnet, he was the embodied voice of all Catholic Christendom. She had sat upon his knees; she had learnt prayers from his lips; she had looked upon him for years as the mouthpiece of whatever was right and just and holy. And now, he was bringing all the weight of his authority to bear against the dictates of her poor hot heart; he was terrifying her with his words; he was denouncing upon her the horrible woes of apostasy. Whether the man meant to marry her or not, all was equally sin; she was bent on the downward path; she was flying in the face of God and His priest, to her own destruction. She might marry Andreas or not, that was a question of inclination; but if she persisted in her relations with an infidel, who could mean her no good, she was hurrying straight to the devil and all his angels. And the devil and all his angels were very real and very near indeed to Linnet; the flames of purgatory were as familiar to her eyes as the fire on the hearth; the tortures of hell were as solid and as material as she had seen them pictured on every roadside oratory.

And the effect? Ah, well, only those who know the profound religious faith of the Tyrolese peasantry can fully understand the appalling effect this pastoral exhortation produced upon Linnet. It was no new discovery, indeed. All along, amid the tremulous delight of her first great love, she had known in her heart this thing she was doing, though sweet, too sweet, was unspeakably wicked. She was paltering with sin, giving her heart to a heretic. She herself had seen him pass many a wayside crucifix, many a shrine of Our Dear Lady, without raising his hat or letting his knee do obeisance, as was right, before them. He was good, he was kind; in a purely human sort of way he sympathised with her, and understood her as no one else in the world had ever yet done; but still, he was a heretic. She had known that all along; she had known the danger she ran, and the end, the horrible end, it must finally lead her to. And now, when her parish priest, her earliest friend, her own tried confessor, pointed out her sin to her, she quivered and crouched before him in bodily terror and abject submission. The flames of hell seemed to rise up and take hold of her. And the more frightened she grew, the more vehement and fierce grew the priest's denunciation. He saw his opportunity, and made the best use of it. What were the few short years of this life to an eternity of pain? What a dream of brief love to fiery floods for ever?

At last, appalled and horrified, Linnet, bowing her frightened head, held up her bloodless hands, and begged convulsively for mercy. "Give me absolution," she cried; "Father! O Father, forgive me!"

Her confessor seized the occasion, for her soul's benefit. "Not unless you abandon him!" he answered, in a very stern voice. "While you remain in your sin, how can God's priest absolve you?"

Linnet wrung her hands for a moment in silent agony. She couldn't give him up! Oh, no; she couldn't! "Father," she cried at last with a despairing burst, "what shall I do to be saved? Guide me! Save me!"

The priest snatched at the chance. "Will you come back to St Valentin to-morrow?" he asked, with two uplifted fingers poised half-doubtful in air, as if waiting to bless her. "Will you come back to St Valentin, and marry Andreas Hausberger?"

In an agony of abject religious terror, Linnet bowed her head. "Is there no other way?" she cried, trembling, "No other way of salvation?"

The priest pressed his advantage. "If you died to-night," he answered, in a very solemn voice, "you would die in your sin, and hell's mouth would yawn wide for you. Accept the escape an honourable man offers you, and be clear of your heretic!"

Linnet flung herself on her knees, and clasped her hands before him. The horrors of eternity and of the offended Church made her shake in every limb. She was half-dumb with terror.

"I'll do as you wish, Father," she moaned, in a voice of hushed awe, "if you'll only bless me. I'll go back to St Valentin and marry Andreas Hausberger!"

CHAPTER XX

FLORIAN ON MATRIMONY

In spite of the lateness of the season, and Will's preoccupation, that visit to the Dolomites turned out a complete success. Rue was in excellent spirits; Florian was in fine form; Nature smiled compliance, as he consummately phrased it, in other words, the weather was lovely, the mountains clear of cloud, the horses fresh, and the roads (for Austria) in very good order. Their capacious carriage held its party of five comfortably, for Rue, with her wonted wisdom, had consulted Mrs Grundy's feelings by inviting an old Indian colonel and his wife, whose acquaintance she had picked up at the Erzherzog Johann, to accompany them on their trip, and chaperon the expedition. Rue herself enjoyed those four days immensely. She had lots of long talks with Will on the hillsides, and she noticed Will spoke much, though always in an abstract and highly impersonal way, of the human heart, its doubts and its difficulties. He was thinking of Linnet, who engaged his thoughts much during that enforced absence; but Rue imagined he was thinking of himself and her, and was glad accordingly. She was growing very fond of her English poet. She hoped and half-believed he in turn was growing fond of her.

As for Will, now he was away from Linnet for awhile, he began to think much more seriously than he had ever thought before of the nature of his relations with her, and the end to which they were inevitably leading him. As long as Linnet was near, as long as he could hold her hand in his, and look deep into her eyes, and hear that wonderful voice of hers carolling out some sweet song for his ear alone among the clambering vineyards, why, he could think of nothing else but the passing joy and delight of her immediate presence. Imperceptibly, and half-unconsciously to himself, she had grown very dear to him. But now that he was away from her, and alone with Rue, he began to realise how much he longed to be once more by her side—how little he was prepared to do without her, how deeply she had entwined herself into his inmost being. Again and again the question presented itself to his mind, "When I go back to Meran, on what footing shall I stand with her? If I find it so hard to run away for four days, how shall I ever run away from her for ever and ever?"

Besides, during those few happy weeks at Meran, Linnet had begun to reveal herself to him as another person. He was catching faint glimpses now of the profounder depths of that deeply artistic, though as yet almost wholly undeveloped, character. The books he had read to her she understood so fast; the things he had told her she caught at so readily; the change to new scenes seemed so soon to quicken and stimulate all her latent faculties. Had not Nature said of her, as of Wordsworth's country lass, "She shall be mine and I will make A lady of my own"? For that she was a lady indeed had been forcing itself every day more and more plainly upon Will's mind, as he walked and talked with her. At Innsbruck, he had thought more than once to himself, "How could one dream in a world where there are women like Rue, of tying oneself for life to this sweet-voiced alp-girl?" Among the Dolomites, three weeks later, he asked himself rather, "How could one ever be content with mere brightness and sunniness like that charming Rue's, in a world which holds women so tender, so true, and so passionate as Linnet?"

Slowly, bit by bit, he began to wonder how he could muster up courage to tear himself away again— and, if he did, for how long he could manage to keep away from her? And then, as he debated, there arose in his mind the profounder question of justice or injustice to Linnet. Was it right of him so deeply to engage her affections, unless he meant by it something real, something sure, something definite? She loved him so well that to leave her now would surely break her heart for her. What end could there be to this serious complication save the end he had so strenuously denied to Florian?

On the very last evening of their drive through those great bare unearthly peaks that look down upon Botzen, Florian came into Will's room for an evening gossip. They sat up long over the smouldering embers of a fragrant pinewood fire. There's nothing more confidential than young men's confabulations over a smouldering hearth in the small hours of the morning. The two friends talked, and talked, and talked, and talked, till at last Will was moved to make a clean breast of his feelings in the matter to Florian. He put his dilemma neatly. He acknowledged he was going just where Florian had said he would go. "I pointed out the noose to you," the epicurean philosopher observed, with bland self-satisfaction, "and you've run your neck right into it. Instead of playing with her like a doll as a sensible man would have done, you've simply gone ahead and lost your heart outright to her. Foolish, foolish, exceedingly foolish; but, just what I expected from you. I said from the very first, 'Now mark my words, Deverill, as sure as eggs is eggs, you'll end by marrying her.'"

"I don't say I'll marry her now," Will replied, somewhat sheepishly. "How can I, indeed? I've got nothing to marry on. I find it hard enough work to keep body and soul together for myself in London, without thinking of an engagement to keep somebody else's into the bargain."

"Then what do you mean to do?" Florian inquired, with sound common-sense. "If you don't mean to marry her, and you don't mean to harm her, and you can't go away from her, and you can't afford to stop with her, why, what possible new term are you going to introduce into human relations and the English language to cover your ways with her?"

"That's just it. I don't know," Will answered, in a somewhat hopeless and helpless voice, piling the embers together in the centre as he spoke, just to keep them alight for some minutes longer. "There's the rub. I admit it. Nobody feels it more than I do. But I don't see any possible kind of way out of it. I've been thinking to myself, or perhaps half-thinking, I might manage it like this, if Linnet would assent to it. We might get married first—"

Florian raised one warning hand, and nodded his shapely head up and down two or three times solemnly. "I told you so," he interposed, in a tone of most mitigated and mournful triumph. "There we get at it at last. You have said the word. I was sure 'twould come to that. Marry, marry, marry!"

"And then," Will went on, with a very shamefaced air, never heeding his comment, "what's enough for one's enough for two, they say—or very nearly. I thought we might live in lodgings quite quietly for awhile, somewhere cheap, in London—"

"Not live," Florian corrected gravely, with another sage nod of that sapient head; "lurk, linger, vegetate. A very sad end! A most dismal downfall! I see it all: Surrey side, thirty shillings a week; cold mutton for dinner; bread and cheese for lunch; an ill-furnished parlour, a sloppy-faced slavey! I know the sort of thing. Pah! My gorge rises at it!"

"And then, I could get Linnet's voice trained and prepared for the stage," Will continued, perusing his boots, "and work very hard myself to keep us both alive till she could come out in public. In a year or two, I feel sure, if I watched her close and saw her capabilities, I could write and compose some good piece of my own to suit her exactly. With me to make the songs, and Linnet to interpret them, I believe, sooner or later, we ought easily to earn a very good livelihood. But it'd be a hard pull first; I don't conceal that from myself. We'd have a struggle for life, though in the end, I feel sure, we'd live it down and conquer."

Florian lighted a cigarette and watched the thin blue smoke curl upward, languidly. "Love's young dream!" he mused to himself with a placid smile of superior wisdom. "I know the style of old. Bread and cheese and kisses! Very charming, very charming! Chorus hymeneal of the most approved pattern. So odd, so interesting! I've often asked myself what it is in the world that leads otherwise sensible and intelligent fellows to make wrecks of their lives in this incredible way—and all for the sake of somebody else's daughter! Why this insane desire to relieve some other man of his natural responsibilities? I account for it in my own mind on evolutionary principles. Marriage, it seems to me, is an irrational and incomprehensible civilised instinct, by which the individual sacrifices himself on the shrine of duty for the benefit of the species. Have you ever heard of the lemmings?"

"The lemmings!" Will repeated, unable to conceive the connection in Florian's mind between two such totally dissimilar and unrelated subjects. "Not those little brown animals like rats or marmots they have in Norway?"

"Precisely," Florian answered, waving his cigarette airily. "Those little brown animals like rats or marmots they have in Norway. You put it like a dictionary. Well, every year or two, you know, an irresistible desire seizes on many myriads of those misguided rodents at once, to march straight to the sea in a body together, plunge boldly into the water, and swim out in a straight line, without rhyme or reason, till they can swim no farther but drown themselves by cartloads. What's the origin of this swarmery? It's only an instinct which keeps down the number of the lemmings, and so acts as a check against over-population. A beautiful and ingenious provision of Nature they call it!" and Florian smiled sweetly. "I've always thought," he went on, puffing a contemptuous ring of smoke from his pursed-up lips, "that marriage among mankind was a very similar instinct. It's death to the individual—mental and moral death; but it ensures at least a due continuance of the species. The wise man doesn't marry; he knows too well for that; he stands by and looks on; but he leaves no descendants, and his wisdom dies with him. Whereas the foolish burden themselves with a wife and family, and become thereby the perpetuators of their race in future. It's a wonderful dispensation; I admire it—at a distance!"

"But you said you'd marry yourself," Will objected, "if you met the right person; and, to tell you the truth, Florian, I fancied you'd been rather markedly attentive to Rue for the last few weeks or so."

Florian stroked a smooth small chin with five meditative fingers. "That's quite another matter," he answered, in a self-satisfied tone. "Circumstances, it has been well remarked by an anonymous thinker, alter cases. If an Oriental potentate in all his glory were to order me to flop down on my marrow-bones before him and kiss his imperial foot as an act of pure homage, I should take my proud stand as a British subject, and promptly decline so degrading a ceremony. But if he offered me a thousand pounds down to comply with his wishes, I would give the polite request my most earnest consideration. If he made it ten thousand, I would almost certainly accede; and if he went to half-a-million, which is a fortune for life, well, no gentleman on earth could dream of disputing the question any further with him. Just so, I say, with marriage. If a lady desires me, without due cause assigned, to become her abject slave, and serve her alone for a lifetime, I will politely but firmly answer, 'No, thank you.' If she confers upon me, incidentally, a modest competence, I shall perpend for a moment, and murmur, 'Well, possibly.' But if she renders me independent and comfortable for life, with a chance of surrounding myself with books, pictures, music, without a moment's hesitation I shall answer, 'Like a bird,' to her. Slavery, in short, though in itself disagreeable, may be mitigated or altogether outweighed by concomitant advantages."

"Florian," Will said, earnestly, "I don't know what you mean. You speak a foreign language to me. If I felt like that, I could never bring myself to marry any woman. If I married at all, I must do it for the sake of the girl I loved—and to make her happy."

Florian gazed at him compassionately. "Quixotic," he answered low, shaking his sculpturesque head once or twice with a face of solemn warning. "Quixotic, exceedingly! The pure lemming instinct; they will rush into it! It's the moth and the candle again: dazzle, buzz, and flutter, and pom! pom! pom!— in a second, you're caught, and sizzled hot in the flame, and reduced to ashes. That's how it'll be with you, my dear fellow: you'll go back to Meran and, by Jingo, to-morrow, you'll go straight up the hill, and ask the cow-girl to marry you."

"I think I will," the poet answered, taking up his candlestick with a sigh to leave the room. "I think I will, Florian. I'll fight it out to the bitter end, sloppy slavey and all, on your threatened south side, in those dingy lodgings." And he took himself off with a hurried nod to his bland companion.

Florian rose, and closed the door behind the poet softly. He had played his cards well, remarkably well, that evening. If he wanted to drive Will into proposing to Linnet, he had gone the right way to effect his object. "And I," he thought to himself with a contented smile, "will stand a fair chance with Rue, without fear of a rival, when once he's gone off and got well married to his cow-girl. It'll be interesting to ask them to a nice little dinner, from their Surrey side garret, at our snug small den in Park Lane or South Kensington. Park Lane's the most fashionable, but South Kensington's the pleasantest:

In Cromwell Road did Florian Wood,
A stately pleasure dome decree.

Such a palace of art as it will be, too! I can see it now, in my mind's eye, Horatio!—Botticellis, Della Robbias, Elzevirs, Stradivariuses! William Morris on the floor! Lewis Day on the ceiling! It rises like an exhalation, all beautiful to behold! Such things might I do—with Rue's seven hundred thousand!"

CHAPTER XXI

FORTUNE'S WHEEL

It was with no little trepidation that Will mounted the Küchelberg on the morning after his return to Meran from the Dolomites. Would Linnet be there, he wondered, or would he somehow miss her? He didn't know why, but a certain vague foreboding of possible evil possessed his soul. He was dimly conscious to himself of danger ahead. He couldn't feel reassured till he stood once more face to face with Linnet.

When he arrived at the appointed place, however, by the Station of the Cross which represented the Comforting of the Daughters of Jerusalem, a cold shudder of alarm came over him suddenly. No Linnet there! Not a sign of her to be seen! And hitherto she had always kept her tryst before him. He took out his watch and looked. Ha, a moment's respite! In his eagerness, he had arrived five minutes early. But Linnet was usually, even so, five minutes ahead of him. He couldn't make it out; this was ominous, very!

With heart standing still, he waited a quarter of an hour, half-an-hour, three-quarters. And still no Linnet came!—And still he watched eagerly. He paced up and down, looking again and again at his watch with impatience. Could she have mistaken the place? Yet he told her plain enough! On the bare chance of some error, he would try the other stations. He went to them all, one by one, from the Crown of Thorns to the Calvary. The same luck still! No Linnet at any of them! Then he mounted the great boss of ice-worn rock with the bench on its top, that commands far and wide the whole expanse of the Küchelberg. Gazing down on every side upon the long, low hog's back, he saw nobody all around save the women in the fields, watching their cows at pasture, and the men with the carts urging overtasked oxen to drag too heavy a load up the cobble-paved hill-track.

Thoroughly alarmed by this time, and uncertain how to act, Will determined to take a very bold measure. He descended the hill once more, and, passing under the archway of the old town gate, and through the narrow streets, and past the high-towered parish church, he made his way straight to Andreas Hausberger's inn in the street that is called Unter den Lauben. At the doorway, Franz Lindner, all on fire, was standing. Wrath smouldered in his face; his hat was cocked fiercely; his feather, turned Robblerwise, looked angrier, more defiant, more aggressive than ever. But to Will's immense surprise, the village champion, instead of scowling challenge at him, or receding under the arch, stepped forward with outstretched palm to meet him. He grasped Will's hand hard. His pressure struck some note of a common misfortune.

"You've come to look for Linnet?" he said, holding his head very haughtily. "She wasn't on the hill? She'd promised to meet you there? Well, we're both in the same box, it seems. He's done two of us at once. This is indeed a dirty trick Andreas Hausberger has played upon us!"

"What do you mean?" Will cried, aghast, clapping his hand to his head. "Where's Linnet? I want to see her."

"You won't see her ever again as Lina Telser, that's sure," the Robbler answered aloud, with an indignant gesture. His wrath against Andreas had wholly swallowed up all memory of his little quarrel on the hills with Will Deverill. It was common cause now. Andreas had outwitted both of them.

"You can't mean to tell me—" Will cried, drawing back in horror.

Franz took him up sharply. "Yes; I do mean to tell you just what I say," he answered, knitting his brows. "Andreas Hausberger has gone off with her . . . to St Valentin . . . to marry her."

It was a bolt from the blue—an unforeseen thunder-stroke. Will raised his hat from his brow, and held his hand on his stunned and astonished forehead. "To marry her!" he repeated, half-dazed at the bare thought. "Andreas Hausberger to marry her!—to marry Linnet! Oh no; it can't be true; you never can mean it!"

Franz stared at him doggedly. "He gave me the slip on Wednesday morning," he answered, with a resounding German oath. "He went off quite secretly. May the Evil One requite him! He knew if he told me beforehand I'd have planted my good knife to the handle in his heart. So he said never a word, but went off unexpectedly, with Linnet and Philippina, leaving the rest of us here stranded, but cancelling all engagements for the next three evenings. The white-livered cur! He'll never dare to come back again! He knows if I meet him now—it'll be this in his black heart!" And Franz tapped significantly the short hunting knife that stuck out from his leather belt in true jäger fashion.

"And you haven't followed him?" Will exclaimed, taken aback at the man's inaction. "You know all this, and you haven't gone after him to prevent the wedding!" In an emergency like the present one, with Linnet's happiness at stake, he was only too ready to accept as an ally even the village bully.

Franz shrugged his broad shoulders. "How could I?" he asked, helplessly. "Have I money at command? Have I wealth like the wirth, to pay my fare all the way from Meran to Jenbach?"

Will drew back with a deep sigh. He had never thought of that difficulty. It's so natural to us all to have money in our pockets, or at least at our command, for any great emergency, that we seldom realise how insuperable a barrier a bare hundred miles may often seem to men of other classes. It was as impossible for Franz Lindner to get from Meran to St Valentin at a day's notice as for most of us to buy up the house of Rothschild.

"Come with me!" Will cried, starting up. "The man has cheated us vilely. Come with me to St Valentin, Herr Franz, forget our differences, and before he has time to get through with the legal formalities, help me, help me, to prevent this nefarious wedding!"

"It's too late to prevent it now!" Franz answered, shaking his head, with a settled gloom on his countenance. "It's all over by this. She's his wife already. They were married on Friday."

At those words Will felt his heart stand still within him. He gasped for breath. He steadied himself mechanically. Never till that moment had he known how much he loved the Tyrolese singer-girl, and now the blow had come, he couldn't even believe it. "Married!" he faltered out in a broken voice; "what, married already! Linnet married to that man! Oh, impossible! Impossible!"

"But it's true, all the same," Franz answered sturdily. "Philippina was there, and she saw them married. She came back last night to collect their things and pack up for Italy. She's to meet them to-morrow by the mid-day train, at a place called Verona."

"But how did he do it in the time?" Will exclaimed still incredulous, and clinging still to the last straw with a drowning man's instinct. "Your Austrian law has so many formalities. Perhaps it's a story the man has made up on purpose to deceive us. He may have told Philippina, and she may be in league with him."

Franz shook his head with gloomy determination. "No, no," he said; "it won't do; don't flatter your soul with that; there's no doubt at all in the world about it. He's as deep as a well, and as false as a fox, and he'd laid all his plans very cunningly beforehand. He made the arrangements and swore to the Civil Act without consulting Linnet. He and the priest were in league, and the priest helped him out with it. At the very last moment, Andreas carried her off, and before she could say nay, he went straight through and married her."

Will's brain reeled round; his mind seemed to fail him. The sense of his loss, his irreparable loss, deadened for the moment every other feeling. Linnet gone from him for ever! Linnet married to somebody else!—and that somebody else so cold, so calculating, so cruel a man as Andreas Hausberger! It was terrible to contemplate. "He must have forced her to do it!" the Englishman cried in his distress. "But how could she ever consent? How could she ever submit? I can't believe it! I can't even understand it!"

"He didn't exactly force her," Franz answered, tilting his hat still more angrily on one side of his head. "But he brought the Herr Vicar from St Valentin to persuade her; and you know what priests are, and you know what women! The Herr Vicar just turned on purgatory and all the rest of it to frighten the poor child—so Philippina says. She was crying all the time. She cried in the train, and she cried on the road, and she cried in the church, and she cried at the altar! She cried worst of all when Herr Andreas took her home to the Wirthshaus to supper. . . . But I'll be even with him yet." And Franz tapped his knife once more. "When I meet him again—ten thousand devils!—this goes right up to the hilt in the base black heart of him!"

"Can I see Philippina?" Will gasped out, white as death.

"Yes; certainly you can see her," the Robbler answered with a burst, leading him in through the dark archway to the sunless courtyard. "Come this way into the parlour. She's upstairs just now, but I'll bring her down to speak to you."

In a minute or two more, sure enough, Philippina appeared in her very best dress, looking bright and smiling. She was garrulous as usual, and most gay and lively. "Oh yes; they had been to St Valentin, and no mistake, the Herr Vicar going with them, no scandal of any sort, and 'twas a very grand affair; never anything like it! Andreas Hausberger had spared no expense or trouble; red wine at the supper, and fiddlers for the dance, and all the world of the valley bidden to the feast on the night of the wedding! Linnet had cried a good deal; ach, yes, she had cried, how she had cried—but cried!— mein Gott, it was wonderful! But there, girls always will cry when they're going to be married; and you know, Herr Will," archly, "she was very, very fond of you." For herself, Philippina couldn't think what the child had to cry about—except, of course, what you call her feelings; but all she could say was, she'd be very glad herself to make such a match as Lina Telser was making. Why, would the gnädige Herr believe it? Herr Andreas was going to take her to a place called Mailand, away off in Italy, to train her for the stage, the operatic stage, and make in the end a real grand lady of her!

Will sat down on a wooden chair by the rough little table, held his face in his hands, and listened all aghast to Philippina's artless outpourings. The sennerin, unheeding his obvious distress, went on to describe in her most glowing terms the magnificence of the wedding, and of the wirth's entertainment. St Valentin hardly knew itself. Andreas had had a wedding-dress, oh, a beautiful wedding-dress, made beforehand, as a surprise, at Meran for Linnet, a white silk wedding-dress from a Vienna clothes-maker's on the Promenade, by the Stephanie Garten; it was cut to measure from an old bodice of Linnet's, which he abstracted all unknown from her box on purpose; and it fitted her like a glove, and she was ever so much admired in it. And all the young men thought Andreas the luckiest dog in the whole Tyrol; and cousin Fridolin had almost wanted to fight him for his bride; but Linnet intervened, and wouldn't let them have it out for her. "And on the morning after the marriage," Philippina concluded, with wide open eyes, "there wasn't a cradle at the door, though Linnet was a sennerin, not one single cradle."

"Of course not!" Franz Lindner cried, bridling up at the bare suggestion, and frowning native wrath at her.

"But perhaps if you'd been there, Franz—" Philippina put in saucily, and then broke off short, like a discreet maiden.

The Robbler rose above himself in his generous indignation that anyone should dare even to hint such things about their peerless Linnet. He clenched his fist hard. "If a man had said that, my girl," he cried, fingering his knife involuntarily, "though she's Andreas Hausberger's wife, he'd have paid with his blood for it."

Philippina for a moment stood silent and overawed. Then, recovering herself at once, with a sudden little recollection, she thrust her hand into her bosom and drew out a small note, which she passed to Will openly. "Oh, I forgot," she exclaimed; "I was to give you this, Herr Will. Linnet asked me to take it to you on the morning of her marriage."

Will opened it, and read. It was written in a shaky round hand like a servant's, and its German orthography was not wholly above criticism. But it went to Will's heart like a dagger for all that.

"Dear Herr Will," it began, simply, "I write to you to-night, the last night that I may, on the eve of my wedding; for to-morrow I may not. When Andreas asked me first, it seemed to me impossible. But the Herr Vicar told me it was sin to love a heretic; you did not mean to marry me, and if you did, you would drag my soul down to eternal perdition. And then, the good Mother, and the dear Father in purgatory! So between them they made me do it, and I dared not refuse. It is hard to refuse when one's priest commands one. Yet, dear Herr Will, I loved you; ah, how I loved you! and I know it is sin;

but, may Our Dear Frau forgive me, as long as I live, I shall always love you! Though I never must see you again.—Your heart-broken LINNET."

Will folded it reverently, and slipped it into the pocket just over his heart. "And tell her, Philippina," he said, "when you see her at Verona, I had come back to-day to ask her to marry me."

CHAPTER XXII

A WOMAN'S STRATAGEM

For the next three years, Will heard and saw nothing more of Linnet. Not that he failed to make indirect inquiries, as time went on, from every likely source, as to her passing whereabouts; once Linnet was lost to him, he realised to himself how deeply he had loved her, how much he had admired her. But, for her happiness' sake, he felt it would be wrong of him to write to her direct, or attempt in any way to put himself into personal communication with her. She was Andreas Hausberger's wife now, and there he must leave her. He knew himself too well, he knew Linnet too well, too, to cheat himself with false ideas of mere friendship in future. A woman with so passionate a nature as hers, married against her will to a man she could never love, and meeting once more the man whom she loved, the man who really loved her, must find such friendship a dangerous pitfall. So, for the very love's sake he bore her, he refrained from attempting to communicate with her directly; and all indirect inquiries failed to elicit anything more than the bare fact, already known to him, that Linnet was being musically educated for the stage, in Germany and Italy.

Three years, however, must be got through somehow, no matter how drearily; and during those next three years many things of many sorts happened to Will Deverill. To begin with, he was steadily growing in name and fame, in the stage-world of London, as a composer and playwright. That was mainly Rue's doing; for Rue, having once taken her Englishman up, was by no means disposed to lay him down again easily. Not twice in her life, indeed, does even a pretty American with money at her back stand her solid chance of booming a poet. And Rue boomed Will steadily, after the manner of her countrymen. It didn't escape her quick womanly eye, indeed, that Linnet's sudden marriage and hasty flight to Italy had produced a deep effect on Will's spirits for the moment. But it was only for the moment, she hoped and believed—a mere passing whim, a poet's fancy; impossible that a man who thought and wrote like Will Deverill—a bard of lofty aim and exquisite imaginings, one who on honey-dew had fed and drunk the milk of Paradise—should be permanently enslaved by a Tyrolese cow-girl. Surely, in the end, common-sense and good taste and right feeling must prevail; he must come back at last—well—to a woman worthy of him!

So, very shortly after Will's return to London, Rue decided on a complete change in her plans for the winter, and made up her mind, instead of going on as she had intended to Rome and Naples, to take a house for the season in Mayfair or South Kensington. But Florian would hear of no such temporary expedients; she must have a home of her own in London, he said, in the world's metropolis, and he himself would choose it for her. So he found her a shelter in Hans Place, Chelsea, and fitted it up beforehand with becoming magnificence—just such a palace of art as he had dreamed of among the Dolomites; though, to be sure, his own chance of inhabiting it now seemed considerably lessened, since the failure of his scheme for putting off Will Deverill on his musical sennerin. Still, Florian furnished it, all the same, with a strictly business eye to his own tastes and fancies—in case of contingencies. There was a drawing-room for Rue, of course quite utterly Hellenic; there was a dining-room for Society, not grim and gloomy, after the common superstition of all British dining-rooms, but gay and bright and airy, like Florian himself: for Florian held that the cult of the sacred dinner bell, though important enough in the wise man's scheme of life, should be a blithe and joyous, not a solemn and stolid one; there was a smoking-room, for which Rue herself had certainly no need, but which Florian insisted might be useful in the future, as events demanded. "For, you see," he said, pointedly, "we're not in Bombay. You may yet choose a new friend to light his cigars in it." All was decorated throughout in the most modern taste; incandescent wires shed tempered beams through Venetian glass globes on Liberty brocades and Morris wall-papers. 'Twas a triumph of ornamental art on a very small scale—an Aladdin's palace in Hans Place, and Florian took good care that paragraphs should get into the Society papers, both describing the house, and attributing its glories to his own superintendence.

However, he took good care, too, that due prominence should be given on every hand to Rue's own personal claims to social distinction. He was a first-rate wire-puller. Little notes about the beauty, the wealth, the cleverness, and the fine taste of the pretty American widow cropped up spasmodically in Truth and the Pall Mall. Even the Spectator itself, that high-and-dry organ of intellectual life, deigned to recognise her existence. It was Florian's intention, in short, to float his new protégée. Now, all the world admitted that Florian, if he chose, could float almost anybody; while Rue, for her part, was without doubt exceptionally easy of flotation. Seven hundred thousand pounds, to say the truth, would have buoyed up a far heavier social subject than the pretty and clever New Yorker. Americans are the fashion; for a woman, at least, the mere fact that she comes from beyond the mill-pond is in itself just at present a passport to the best society. But Rue had also money; and money in these days will admit anyone anywhere. Furthermore, she had good looks, taking manners, much culture, real cleverness. She was well informed and well read; Society itself, that collective critic, could find nothing to criticise or to carp at in her conversation. So, introduced by Florian on one side, and His Excellency the American Minister on the other, Rue made that spring a perfect triumphal progress through the London drawing-rooms. She was the fact of the season; she entertained in her own pretty rooms in Hans Place, where Florian exhibited his decorative skill with bland satisfaction to dowager-marchionesses, "I edited it," was his pet phrase—while Will Deverill hung modestly in the background by the door, talking, as was his wont, to those neglected souls who seemed to him most in need of encouragement and companionship.

Before two months were out, everybody was talking of Rue as "our new acquisition." It was Mrs Palmer this, and Mrs Palmer that. "We understand Mrs Palmer will not be present at the Duchess of Thingumabob's dance on Tuesday." "Among the guests on the Terrace, we noticed Lord So-and-so, Lady What's-her-name of Ware, and Mrs Palmer of New York, whose pretty house in Hans Place is fast becoming a rallying point for all that is most interesting in London Society." Old Miss Beard, indeed, when she arrived at the Langham Hotel early in May, and found Rue in quiet possession of the Very Best Houses, was positively scandalised. She declared, with a little sneer, it was perfectly disgraceful the way That Woman had forced herself by pure brass on the English Aristocracy. The widow of a dry-goodsman to give herself such airs!—but there, Miss Beard had begun to despair before now of the future of Europe! The Nobility and Gentry of England had degringolated. For true blue blood, she was perfectly convinced, you could only look nowadays to the heirs of the Puritans, the Knickerbockers, and the Virginians.

The very first use Rue made of her new-found friends and position in London was to push Will Deverill's claims with theatrical managers. Will had sent the manuscript score of his pretty little open-air operetta, "Honeysuckle," to Wildon Blades of the Duke of Edinburgh's Theatre. And, before Mr Blades had had time to consider the work submitted to him, backed up as it was by Florian Wood's powerful recommendation, Rue's new victoria drew up one day at the door of the manager's house in St John's Wood, and Rue herself, in her most becoming and bewitching costume, stepped out, with her blameless footman's aid, to interview him.

The pretty little American looked prettier and more charming than ever that morning. A dainty blush rose readily to her peach-blossom cheeks; her eyes were cast down; an unwonted tinge of flutter in voice and manner became her even better than her accustomed serenity. Mr Blades bowed and smiled as he scanned her card; he was a bullet-headed man with shifty grey eyes, a dubious mouth, and a sledge-hammer manner. He knew her name well; Florian had already sung the American's praises to the astute manager. They sat down and talked. With many indirect little feminine twists and turns, Rue gradually got round to the real subject of her visit. She didn't approach it straight, of course—what woman ever does?—by stray hints and roundabout roads she let Mr Blades understand in dim outline she was to some extent interested, platonically interested, in the success of Will Deverill's Tyrolese operetta. Mr Deverill, she explained, was merely a young poet of musical tastes, whom she had met last year at an hotel in the Tyrol—a friend of their mutual friend's, Mr Wood. The manager smiled wisely with that dubious mouth. Rue saw he drew his own inference—and drew it wrong; he thought it was Florian in whom her interest centred, not the unknown poet. Indeed, Florian himself had done his very best already to produce that impression; if you want to marry a rich woman, it's not a bad plan to let her friends and the world at large believe the matter's as good as settled already between you. So the manager smiled, and looked intensely wise. "Anything I can do for any friend of our friend Florian's," he said, politely, "I'm sure will give me the very greatest pleasure."

Rue was not wholly unwilling he should make this mistake; she could ask the more easily the favour she had to beg on behalf of Will Deverill. With many further circumlocutions, and many womanly wiles, she gradually let the bullet-headed manager see she was very anxious "Honeysuckle" should be duly produced at an early date at the Duke of Edinburgh's. But Mr Blades, for his part, like a man of the world that he was, was proof against all the smiles and blandishments of the pretty enchantress. A beautiful woman is thrown away, to say the truth, upon a theatrical manager; they are his stock-in-trade; he's accustomed to bargaining with them, bullying them, quarrelling with them. He regards them merely as a class of exceptionally exacting and irritating persons, who presume upon their good looks and their popularity with the public to excuse the infinite trouble and annoyance they give in their business relations. So Mr Blades smiled again, this time a hard little mercantile smile, as of a man unimpressed, and answered briefly, in his sledge-hammer style, "Now, let's be frank with one another, at once, Mrs Palmer. I run this theatre, not for the sake of high art, nor to oblige a lady, but on the vulgarest and commonest commercial grounds, just to make my living, and get a fair percentage on the capital I invest in it. I judge by returns, not by literary merit or artistic value. If Mr Deverill's little piece seems likely to pay, why, of course, I'll produce it. If it don't, why, I won't. That's the long and the short of it!"

Rue seized her cue at once with American quickness. "Just so," she replied, catching him up very sharp, and going straight to the point; "that's exactly why I've come here. I want you to read this play very soon, and to say as a candid business man what you think of it. Then I want you to tell me what you'll take, money down, to produce it at once, and to run it on your boards till you see whether it's likely to succeed or fail, if I give you a guarantee, secured against bonds, to reimburse you in full for any loss you may sustain, say, by giving it the chance of a fortnight's production."

It was a curious offer. The manager's shifty grey eyes ran her over with a sharp little stare of astonishment. Her directness amused him. "Well now," he said, "that's odd; but it's business-like, for a woman."

"You understand," Rue said, blushing crimson, and letting her eyelids drop once more, "I make this suggestion in strict confidence; I don't want it talked about."

"Certainly, certainly," Mr Blades replied, with a scrutinising glance. "Not even to our friend Florian?" And he eyed her quizzingly.

Rue's face flushed deeper still. "Above all, not to him," she answered firmly. "But what do you say to my offer? Is it business or not? Does it seem to you possible?"

The manager hesitated, and drummed with his finger on the desk before him. "Well, to tell you the truth, my dear lady," he answered, evasively, "I couldn't very well give you any opinion, good, bad, or indifferent, till I've read the manuscript, and considered it carefully. You see, a play's not quite like a book or picture; a deal of capital's involved in its production; and, besides, its success or its failure don't stand quite alone; they mean so much in the end to the theatre. It won't do for me to reckon only how many hundreds or thousands I may possibly lose on this or that particular venture if it turns out badly; there's the indirect loss as well to take into consideration. Every success in a house means success in future; every failure in a house means gradual increase in the public coldness. It wouldn't pay me, you understand, if you were merely to offer me a big lump sum down to produce a piece with no chance of a run in it. I never produce anything for anybody on earth unless I believe myself there's really money in it. But I'll tell you what I'll do," and he brightened up most amiably; "I'll read it this very day; and then, if I think it won't prejudice the Duke's to bring it out at once, why, . . . I'll consider whether or not I can accept your offer."

"Oh, thank you!" Rue cried, very gratefully indeed; for she was a simple soul, in spite of her thousands.

The manager drew himself up, and looked stonily grave. He shook his bullet-head. This charge was most painful. It hurt his feelings as a business man that a pretty woman should even for one moment suppose he meant to make a concession to her.

"You've nothing to thank me for," he answered, truthfully; and indeed she hadn't; for his answer, after all, amounted merely to this: that if he thought the play likely to prove a success, he would generously permit the rich American to indemnify him beforehand against the off-chance of a failure. In other words, if it turned out well, he stood to win all; while if it turned out ill, it was Rue who stood to lose whatever was lost upon it.

Nevertheless, after a few more preliminary arrangements, Rue drove off, not ill-satisfied with her partial success, leaving behind her many injunctions of profoundest secrecy with the blandly-smiling manager. As she disappeared down the road, Mr Blades chuckled inwardly. Was he likely to tell any one else in the world, indeed, that he had even entertained so unequal a bargain? He would keep to himself his own clever compact with the American heiress. But two days later, Rue's heart was made glad, when she came down to breakfast, by a letter from the manager, couched in politest terms, informing her that he had read Mr Deverill's manuscript; that he thought on the whole there was possibly money in it; and that he would be pleased to talk over the question of its production on the basis of the arrangement she had herself proposed at their recent interview. Rue read it, overjoyed. In the innocence of her heart, she agreed to promise whatever the astute Mr Blades demanded. Moreover, this being a strictly confidential matter, she couldn't even submit it to her lawyer for advice; she was obliged to act for once on her own initiative. She longed to rush off the very moment it was settled and tell Will the good news; but prudence and womanly reserve prevented her. However, she had her reward none the less next day, when Will hurried round immediately after breakfast to announce the splendid tidings which had come by that morning's post, that Blades had accepted "Honeysuckle," without any reserve, and intended to put it in rehearsal forthwith at the Duke of Edinburgh's. His face beamed with delight; Rue smiled contentment. She was pleased he should burst in upon her first of all the world in London with news of his good fortune; that really looked as if he rather liked her! And then, how sweet it was to feel she had managed it all herself, and he didn't know it. It was such a delightful secret that, womanlike, she longed to tell it to him outright, only that, of course, to divulge it would be to spoil the whole point of it. So she merely smiled a tranquil smile, to her own proud heart, and felt as happy as a queen about it. 'Tis delicious to do something for the man you love, and to know he doesn't even suspect you of doing it. . . . Some day, perhaps, she would be able to tell him. But not till he'd made a great name for himself. Then she might say to him with pride, at some tender moment, "Before the world found you out, Will, I knew what you were, and, all unknown to yourself, it was I who stretched out the first helping hand to your fortunes!"

CHAPTER XXIII

A PROPHET INDEED!

While Will Deverill's operetta was still in rehearsal at the Duke of Edinburgh's, a little episode occurred at Rue's house in Hans Place, which was not without a certain weird influence of its own on the after-life of herself and her companions.

Rue gave an At Home one night early in March, to which Florian and Will Deverill were invited. Will brought his sister with him, the sister who was married to an East End curate, and who had called upon Rue at her brother's bidding.

"Well, what do you think of her to-night, Maud?" Will asked a little anxiously as they stood alone for a minute or two in the middle of the evening.

Mrs Sartoris curled her lip. "Oh, she's pretty enough," she answered; "pretty enough, after her fashion. I could see that the first time; and she's got nice manners. She lights up well, too; women of her age always do light up well. They look better by night, even in the searching glare of these electric lamps, than in full broad sunshine. But, of course, she hasn't got quite the tone of our set; you couldn't expect it. A faded air of drapery clings about her to the end. That's the way with these people; they may be ever so rich, they may be ever so fascinating, but a discriminating nose still scents trade in them somewhere."

Will smiled a quiet smile of suppressed amusement. He didn't care to answer her. Rue's father, he knew, had been an episcopal clergyman in New York, and she herself, though she married a dry-goodsman, had been every bit as well brought up as Will and his sister. But 'tis a sisterly way to say these disparaging things about women whom one's brother might be suspected of marrying. Will didn't mean to marry Rue, it is true; but Maud thought he might; and that idea alone was more than enough to give a caustic tone to her critical comments.

The feature of the evening, it seemed, was to be a peculiar séance of a new American phenomenon, who had come over to Europe with a wonderful reputation for thought-reading, hypnotism, and what he was pleased to style "magnetic influences." Like most of her countrymen and countrywomen, Rue had a sneaking regard, in the background of her soul, for mesmerism, spiritualism, psychic force, electro-biology, and the occult and mysterious in human nature generally. She was one of those impressionable women, in short, who fall a ready prey to plausible impostors with voluble talk about ethereal vibrations, telepathic energy, the odic fluid, and the rest of such rubbish, unless strong-minded male friends intervene to prevent them. The medium on this occasion, it appeared, was one Joaquin Holmes, otherwise known as the Colorado Seer, who professed to read the inmost thoughts of man or woman by direct brainwaves, without contact of any sort. The guests that night had been specially invited to meet Mr Holmes on this his first appearance at a séance in London; so about ten o'clock, all the world trooped down to the dining-room, which Florian had cunningly arranged as a temporary lecture-hall, with seats in long rows, and an elevated platform at one end for the medium.

"What an odd-looking man!" Mrs Sartoris exclaimed, as the Colorado Seer, in full evening dress, bowed a graceful bow from his place on the platform. "He's handsome, though, isn't he? Such wonderful eyes! Just look! And such a Spanish complexion!"

"A Hidalgo, every inch!" Florian assented gravely, nodding his head, and looking at him as he would have looked at a Velasquez. "That olive-brown skin points back straight to Andalusia. It doesn't want his name to tell one at a glance that if his father was an American of English descent, his mother's folk must have emigrated from Cordova or Granada. I see a Moslem tinge in cheek and eye; those dusky thin fingers are the Moor all over!"

"For Moor, read blackamoor," Colonel Quackenboss, the military attaché to the American Legation, murmured half under his breath to his next-door neighbour.

And they were each of them right, in his own way and fashion. The Colorado Seer was a very handsome man, somewhat swarthier than is usual with pure-blooded Europeans. His eyes were large and dark and brilliant; his abundant black hair fell loose over his brow with a graceful southern curl; a heavy moustache fringed his upper lip; he looked to the unsophisticated European eye like a pleasing cross between Buffalo Bill and a Castilian poet. But his Christian name of Joaquin and his southern skin had descended to him, not from Andalusian Hidalgos, but from a mother who was partly Spanish and partly negress, with a delicate under-current of Red Indian ancestry. As he stood there on the platform, however, in his becoming evening dress, and flooded them with the light of his lustrous dark eyes—'twas a trick of the trade he had learned in Colorado, every woman in the room felt instinctively to herself he was a superb creature, while every man admitted with a grudging smile that the fellow had at least the outward air of a gentleman.

The Seer, stepping forward with a genial smile, entertained them at first with some common little tricks of so-called thought-reading, familiar enough to all those who have ever attempted to watch the ways of that simple exhibition. He found pins concealed in ladies' skirts, and guessed the numbers of bank-notes in financiers' pockets. Florian's mouth curled incredulity; why, these were just the same futile old games as ever, the well-known and innocent little conjuring dodges of the Bishops and the Stuart Cumberlands! But after awhile, Mr Joaquin Holmes, waking up all at once, proceeded to try something newer and more original. A pack of cards was produced. To avoid all suspicion of collusion or trickery, 'twas a brand-new pack, observe, there's no deception, bought by Rue herself that afternoon in Bond Street. With much air of serious mystery, the Colorado Seer pulled off the stamped cover before their very eyes, gave the cards themselves to Will to shuffle, and then proceeded to offer them to every member of the company one by one in order. Each drew a card, looked at it, and replaced it in the pack. Instantly, the Seer in a very loud voice, without one moment's hesitation, announced it correctly as ten of spades, ace of clubs, five of hearts, or queen of diamonds. It was an excellent trick, and the performer could do it equally well with open eyes or blindfolded; he could offer the cards behind his back, after the pack had been shuffled and handed him unseen; he could even succeed in the dark, he said, if the lights were lowered, and each person in the company took his own card out to inspect it in the passage.

"That looks like genuine thought-reading," Will was compelled to admit, thinking it over in his own mind; "but perhaps he forces his cards. One knows conjurers can do such wonderful things in the way of forcing."

Instantly the Seer turned upon him with an air of injured innocence. "If you think there's any conjuring about this performance," he exclaimed, with much dignity, drawing himself up to his full height of six feet two, "you can offer them yourself, and allow each lady and gentleman in the room to pick as they choose for themselves among them. I'll take each card, blindfold, as fast as they pick, hold it up behind my back, with my hands tied, without seeing it myself, and read off for you what it is by direct thought-transference."

Will accepted the test, a fairly severe one; and, sure enough, the Seer was right. Carefully blindfolded with one of those moulded wraps, invented for the purpose, which prevent all possibility of looking down through the chinks, he yet took each card behind his back in one hand, held it up before their eyes without moving his head, and gave out its name distinctly and instantly. The audience was impressed. There was a touch of magic in it. But the Seer smiled blandly.

"Oh, that's nothing," he murmured aloud, with a deprecating little laugh; "a mere matter of choosing between fifty-two alternatives, which, after all, is easy. With Mrs Palmer's consent," and he turned in a gracefully deferential attitude to Rue, "I can show you something a great deal more remarkable. Here are pencils and papers. Each lady or gentleman will please take a sheet as I hand them round. Write anything you like, in English, French, German or Spanish, on the piece of paper. Then fold it up, so, and put it into one of these envelopes gummed down and fastened. After that, as this experiment requires very great concentration of thought"—he knitted his brows, and assumed an expression of the intensest internal effort—"with Mrs Palmer's kind leave, we will turn out the electric light, which confuses and distracts one by revealing to the eye so many surrounding visible objects. And then, without breaking the envelopes in which you have enclosed the pieces of paper, I will read out to you, in the dark, what each of you has written."

He spoke deliberately, with slow western American distinctness, though with a pleasing accent. That accent, superimposed on his native negro dialect, had cost him no small effort. The guests, half-incredulous, took the sheets of paper he distributed to them one by one, and wrote down a sentence or two, according to taste, after a little interval of whispered consultation. Then, by the Seer's direction, they folded the slips in two and placed them in their envelopes, each bearing outside the name of the person who wrote it. Florian collected the papers, all carefully gummed down, and handed them to the Seer, who stood ready to receive them at his place on the platform. Without one moment's delay, the lights were turned out. It was the instantaneousness, indeed, and the utter absence of the usual hocus-pocus, that distinguished Mr Joaquin Holmes's unique performance from the ordinary style of spiritualist conjuring. In a second, the Seer's voice rang out clear from his place: "First envelope, Mrs Palmer, containing inscription in French—very prettily written:

'La vie est brève:
Un peu d'amour,
Un peu de rêve,
Et puis—bonjour.

La vie est vaine:
Un peu d'espoir,
Un peu de haine,
Et puis—bonsoir.'

"Extremely graceful verses; I don't know the author. However, no matter! . . . Second envelope, Colonel Marchmont, containing inscription in English, 'The general immediately ordered an advance, and the gallant 21st, regardless of danger, charged for the battery in magnificent style, sabring the enemy's gunners in a wild outburst of military enthusiasm.' Very characteristic! A most soldierly choice. And boldly written. . . . Third envelope, Mrs Sartoris, stop, please! the lady's thoughts are wandering; kindly fix your attention for a moment, Madam, on the words you have given me. Ah, so; that's better.—'The curfew tolls the knell of parting day; The lowing herd winds slowly o'er the lea; The ploughman homeward wends'—wends? wends? it should have been 'plods'; but 'wends' is what you thought—'The ploughman homeward wends his weary way, And leaves the world to darkness and to me.' Very appropriate; it's dark enough here! And I am the only speaker. Bend your minds to what you have written, please, or I may have to hesitate. Each think of your own. . . . Fourth envelope, Mr Florian Wood, containing inscription:

'We struggle fain to enlarge
Our bounded physical recipiency,
Increase our power, supply fresh oil to life,
Repair the waste of age and sickness: no,
It skills not! life's inadequate to joy,
As the soul sees joy, tempting life to take.'

An exceedingly appropriate quotation! I forget where it comes from. Try to concentrate your mind, Mr Wood. Ah, now I know!—from Browning's Cleon."

Florian's mellifluous voice broke the silence in the auditory. "This is wonderful!" he said, in his impressive tone, "most wonderful! miraculous! I never heard anything in my life to equal it."

The Seer, noting his advantage, didn't pause for a moment to answer the interruption, but, smiling a self-satisfied though invisible smile, which could be heard in his voice in spite of the dense darkness, went on still more rapidly, "Fifth envelope, Lady Martindale, a familiar quotation, 'A thing of beauty is a joy for ever.' Somewhat hackneyed that, but easy enough to read on her brain for that very reason. . . . Sixth envelope, Sir Henry Martindale—I regret to say, a confirmed sceptic; Sir Henry didn't believe I could read his thoughts, so he wrote down these rude words: 'The performance is a sham, and the man's a humbug.' But the performance is not a sham, and the man's a thought-reader. Sir Henry also wrote three words below in the Russian character, which he learnt in the Crimea. Now, I don't know Russian, and I can't pretend to read thoughts in languages I don't understand, any more than I could pretend to repeat a conversation I happened to overhear on top of an omnibus in Japanese or Hottentot. But I can tell Sir Henry what he thought in English as he wrote those words; he thought to himself, 'That's a puzzler for him, that is; I'll bet five quid that'll beat the fellow.'"

The audience laughed at this unexpected sally. Sir Henry felt uncomfortable. But the Seer, unabashed, went on as before, without an instant's pause, to the succeeding envelopes. He ran through them all in the same rapid manner, till he reached the last, "Miss Violet Farrar, kindly concentrate your thoughts on the subject, Señorita, Miss Farrar wrote a couple of lines from Swinburne:

'Thou hast forgotten, O summer swallow,
But the world shall end when I forget.'

That's the last I received!" He drew a deep sigh. Then without one instant interposed, "Turn up the lights, please," he said. "To show all's fair, I'll return you your envelopes."

Will turned the light on again in a turmoil of surprise. He had never before seen anything that looked so like a genuine miracle. There stood the Seer, erect and smiling, with all the envelopes in a huddled heap on the little round table on the platform beside him. With a quiet air of triumph, he stepped down to the floor, and reading out the names as he walked along the rows, replaced in each outstretched hand—its own envelope, unopened. The visitors tore the covers off before his eyes, and found inside—their own manuscript, exactly as they had written it. It was a most convincing trick, and the Colorado Seer had good cause to be proud of the astounded way in which his company received it.

A buzz of voices ran humming round the room for some minutes together as the Seer concluded. Everybody hazarded some conjecture of his own, more or less inept, as to how the man did it. The younger ladies were mostly of opinion that he "must have a confederate"—though how a confederate could help him with this particular trick, they didn't deign to explain, not having, indeed, any clear picture of their own in their sapient heads as to the nature of the confederacy. They merely threw out the hint in the self-same expansive and generous spirit in which they are wont to opine that "it's done by electricity," or, that "the thing has springs in it." Mr Arthur Sartoris, the East End curate, and two old maids with amiable profiles in a back row, were inclined to set it down to "cerebral undulations in the ethereal medium"—which, of course, would be competent to explain almost anything, if they only existed. Lady Martindale leaned rather towards the extremer view that "the man had dealings with a familiar spirit," and objected to take any further part in such doubtful proceedings. Sir Henry, while not venturing to offer any direct explanation, was yet reminded at once of some very remarkable and surprising feats he had seen performed by a fakir in India, who had told him the name of his future wife, made a mango-tree grow and bear fruit before his eyes, and sent a boy to climb up a loose end of twine till he disappeared in space, whence he was precipitated in fragments a few minutes later, to get up and walk away one moment afterwards, at the first touch of the fakir's wand, as cool and unconcerned as if nothing had happened. Everybody had a theory which satisfied himself; and every theory alike seemed pure bosh to Will Deverill.

To everybody's surprise, however, Florian's melodious voice, after that one interruption, took no further part in the brisk discussion. The world rather expected that Florian would intervene with some abstruse hypothesis of telepathic action, or enlarge on the occult influence of soul upon soul, without the need for any gross and palpable link of material connection. But Florian held his peace. He had an idea of his own, and he wasn't going to impart it for nothing to anybody. Only once did he speak. "The man has eyes in the back of his head," a lady had cried after one trick in profound astonishment.

"Say, rather, the man has eyes in the tips of his fingers," Florian corrected gravely. For he was no fool, Florian.

The Seer heard him, and darted a strange glance at his face. This man Wood was too clever. The Seer must square him!

The evening wore away, and conjecture died down. The Seer mixed with the throng in his private capacity, told good stories to the men with a strong Western flavour, said pretty things to the women with Parisian grace, and flashed his expressive eyes into theirs to point them. Everybody allowed he was a most agreeable man, and everybody thought his performance "simply marvellous."

Florian waited on the door-step as the Seer was leaving. "I'll walk home with you," he said, with an air of quiet determination.

The Seer stared at him hard. "As you like," he answered, coldly; but it was clear from his tone he distrusted Florian.

They walked round the corner for some yards in silence. Then Florian spoke first. "There was only one thing I didn't quite understand," he began, with a confidential air, "and that was how the dickens you managed to get those gummed envelopes open."

The Seer stood still for a second, and fronted him. They were in a lonely street. "Now, you look here, Mr Florian Wood," the American said quietly, dropping back all at once into his native dialect and his native accent, "you lay low this evening. You thought you spotted it. I saw you lay low, and I knew pretty well you meant to come round and have it out some time with me. Well, sir, what do you mean by insinuating to a gentleman like me that I broke those there envelopes? That's an imputation on my honesty and honour; and out West, you know, we answer questions like that only one way . . . with a six-shooter."

He spoke with the menacing air of an angry bully. But Florian wasn't exactly the sort of man to be bullied; small as he was, he did not lack for courage. If Mr Joaquin Holmes was tall and big-built, why, Florian was backed up by all the strength of the police of London. The Englishman smiled. "Yes, you do, out West, I know," he answered, calmly; "but in London, that style's very much out of fashion. We keep a police force on purpose to prevent it. Now, don't let's be two fools. I lay low, as you say. If you want me to go on lying low in future, you'll answer me sensibly, like a man of the world, and trust my honour. If you want me to expose you, you'll tell lies and bluster. You've had twenty pounds down from my friend Mrs Palmer for this evening's entertainment. That's first-rate pay. You can't earn it again, if your system's blown upon."

The Coloradan darted a furtive side-glance at Florian. This sleek-faced, innocent-looking, high-flown little Englishman was more dangerous, after all, than the Westerner imagined. But he blustered still for a while about his honour and his honesty; he was ashamed to throw up the sponge so easily. Florian listened, unmoved. All this talk fell flat upon him. At last, when the Seer had exhausted his whole stock of available indignation, Florian interposed once more, bland and suave as ever: "It's a very good trick," the small man said, smiling, "and I don't know how you managed that part about the envelopes. . . . Besides, I never met such delicacy of touch in my life before—in a sighted person!"

At that word, Joaquin Holmes gave a perceptible start. He saw its implications. It is the term which the blind in asylums or the like invariably apply to the outside world with normal vision.

Florian noticed the little start, all involuntary as it was; and the Seer in turn observed that he noticed it. No man can play the thought-reading or spiritualist game unless endowed with exceptional quickness of perception.

"How did you know I'd ever been blind?" he asked, quickly, taken aback for a moment, and making just that once an unguarded admission.

"I didn't know it," Florian answered, with equal frankness. "I didn't even guess it. But I saw at once you'd at least been bred and brought up among the blind. My own grandfather was blind, you see, and my uncle as well; and I've inherited from them, myself, some germs of the same faculty. But you've got it stronger than anyone I ever saw in my life till now. . . . Besides, I want to know how you managed those envelopes. I hate being baffled. When I see a good trick, I like to understand it. Remember, I have influence in the press and in Society. I can serve your purpose. But I make it the price of my lying low in future that you tell me the way you managed about the envelopes."

The Seer seized his arm. "You're a durned smart chap," he said, with genuine admiration. "Nobody, even in America, ever guessed that trick; and we're smarter out there, I reckon, than the run of the old country. Come along to my rooms, and we'll talk this thing over."

"No thank you," Florian answered, with a quiet little smile. "My friends wouldn't know where I'd gone to-night. Your hint about six-shooters is quite too pregnant. But if you care to come home to my humble chambers in Grosvenor Gardens, and make terms of surrender, we can see this thing out over a whiskey and soda."

CHAPTER XXIV

THE ART OF PROPHESYING

They walked on, side by side, to the house in Grosvenor Gardens. Florian let himself in with a latch-key, and rang the bell for his servant. While he waited, he wrote a name on the back of a card, carelessly. "Look here, Barnes," the butterfly of Society said, as his eminently respectable man-of-all-work entered; "this is Mr Joaquin Holmes,"—and he handed him the card—"you can read the name there. He comes from America. I particularly desire you to remark Mr Joaquin Holmes's appearance and features. You may be called upon to identify him." Then he turned with his bland smile to the discomfited Seer, and observed, in that unfailingly honeyed voice of his, "You must excuse me, Mr Holmes, but as a gentleman from out West, addicted to the frequent use of the six-shooter, I'm sure you'll appreciate the delicacy of my motives for this little precaution. You can go now, Barnes. A mere matter of form, so that, in case your evidence should be needed in court, you'll be able to swear to Mr Holmes's identity, and give evidence that he was here, in my company, this evening."

Barnes glanced at the card, and retired to the door, discreetly. The Seer flung himself down in an easy-chair with true Western sangfroid. He knew he was detected; but he wasn't going to give up the game so soon, without seeing how much Florian really understood of his secret and his methods. Meanwhile, Florian produced a couple of pretty little old-fashioned stoneware jugs and some Venetian glasses from a dainty corner cupboard. A siphon stood on a Moorish tray at his side by the carved Bombay black-wood fireplace. "Caledonian or Hibernian?" Florian asked, turning to his visitor, with his most charming smile—"I mean, Scotch or Irish?"

"Thanks, Scotch," the Coloradan answered, relaxing his muscles a little, as he began to enter into the spirit of his entertainer's humour.

Florian poured it out gracefully, and touched the knob of the siphon. Then he handed it, foaming, still bland as ever, to the hesitating American. "Now, let's be frank with one another, Mr Holmes," he said, with cheerful promptitude. "I don't want to hurt you. You're a very smart man, and I admire your smartness. I lay low to-night, as you justly observed, and I'm game to lie low—if you'll take my terms—in future. I'm not going to blow upon you, and I'm not going to stand in the way of your success in life; but I just want to know—how did you manage those envelopes?"

"If you think it's a trick, why, the envelopes would be a long chalk the easiest part of it," the Seer responded, with a dry little cough. "The real difficulty, of course, would be to read in the dark what folks had written. And that's the part, I claim, that I do myself by pure force of thought—in short, by psychic transference."

He stared hard at his host. Their eyes met searchingly. It was seldom that Florian did a vulgar or ungraceful thing; but, as Mr Joaquin Holmes uttered those high-sounding words, and looked him straight in the face with great solemnity, Florian gravely winked at him. Then he raised that priceless Venetian glass goblet to his curling lips, took a long pull at the whiskey without speaking a word, and went over to a desk by the big front window. From it he took out a pack of cards, and returned with them in his hand. "Shuffle them," he said, briefly, to the uneasy Seer, in his own very tone. And the American shuffled them.

Florian picked one out at random, and held it before him, face down, for some seconds in silence. "Now, I can't do this trick like you," he said, in a very business-like voice; "but I can do it a little. Only, I'm obliged to feel the card all over with my fingers like this; and I'm often not right as to the names of the suits, though I can generally make a good shot at the pips and numbers. This is a three that I've drawn—I think, the three of spades; but it may be clubs—I don't feel quite certain."

He turned it up. Sure enough, it was a three, but of clubs not spades. "I'll try another," he said, unabashed. And he drew one and felt it.

"This is a nine of diamonds," he continued, more confidently, after a moment's pause. The American took it from him, without turning up its face, drew his forefinger almost imperceptibly over the unexposed side, and answered without hesitation, "Yes; you're right, that's it, the nine of diamonds."

Florian pulled out a third, and felt it again carefully with the tips of his fingers. "It's a picture card this time," he went on: "King, Queen, or Knave of Hearts, I'm not sure which. I'm no good at picture cards. They're all a blur to me. I can tell them only by the single pips in the corners."

The Seer took it from him, hardly touching it perceptibly. "That's not a heart!" he answered in a sharp voice, without a second's hesitation; "that's the Jack of Spades! You're right as to the general shape, but you've neglected the handle."

He turned it up as he spoke. The Knave of Spades indeed it was. Florian corrected him solemnly.

"In good English society," he murmured, still polite and still inscrutable, "we say Knave, not Jack. Remember that in future. To call it a Jack's an odious vulgarism. I merely mention this fact because I notice how cleverly you've managed to acquire the exact little tricks of accent and manner which are sure to take with an English audience. I should be sorry to think a man of your brains, and a man of your moral character, positive or negative, should be thought the less of in this town of London for so very unimportant a matter of detail."

"Thank you," the Seer responded quietly, with another searching look. "I believe, Mr Florian Wood, we two understand each other. But mind you"—and he looked very wise and cunning—"I didn't pass my finger over the cards at Mrs Palmer's."

"So I saw," Florian replied, with unabated good-humour. "But I looked at them close—and I noticed they were squeezers. What's more, I observed you took them always by the left-hand corner (which was the right hand, upside down) whenever they were passed to you. That gave me the clue. I saw you could read, with one touch of your finger, the number and suit marked small in the corner. I recognised how you did it, though I couldn't come near it myself. Your sense of touch must be something simply exquisite."

The American's mouth curled gently at the corners. Those words restored his confidence. He took up a casual book from the table at his side—'twas the first edition of Andrew Lang's "Ballades in Blue China"—for Florian, as a man of taste, adored first editions. "Look here," the Seer said, carelessly. He turned it face downwards and opened it at random. Then, passing one finger almost imperceptibly over the face of a page, he began to read, as fast as the human voice can go, the very first verses he chanced to light upon.

"BALLADE OF PRIMITIVE MAN."
 "He lived in a cave by the seas;
He lived upon oysters and foes;
But his list of forbidden degrees
An extensive morality shews.
Geological evidence goes
To prove he had never a pan,
But he shaved with a shell when he chose.
'Twas the manner of Primitive Man."

He read it like print. Florian leaned back in his chair, clasped his dainty hands on his small breast before him, and stared at the Seer in unaffected astonishment. "I knew you did it that way," he said, after a pause, nodding his head once or twice; "I felt sure that was the trick of it; but now I see you do it, why, it's more wonderful, almost, than if it were nothing more than a mere ordinary miracle. Miracles are cheap; but sleight of hand like this—well, it's priceless, priceless!"

"Now, you're a man of honour," the Seer said, leaning forward anxiously. "You've found me out, fair and square, and I don't deny it. But you're not going to round on me and spoil my business, are you? It's taken me years and years to work up this sense by constant practice; and if I thought you were going to cut in right now, and peach upon me—why, hanged if I don't think, witness or no witness, I'd settle this thing still, straight off, with a six-shooter. Yes, sir—r—r, I'd settle it straight off, I would, and let 'em scrag me if they would for it!"

Florian stirred the fire languidly with a contemplative poker (a poker's a very good weapon to fall back upon, one knows, in case of necessity). "That'd be a pity," he drawled out calmly, in an unconcerned voice. "I wouldn't like you to make such a nasty mess on my Damascus carpet. This is a real old Damascus, observe, and I paid fifty guineas for it. It's a nice one, isn't it? Good colour, good pattern! Besides, as you say, I'm a man of honour. And I've a fellow-feeling, too, being clever myself, for all other clever fellows. I've promised you not to peach, if only you'll tell me how you managed those envelopes. That's a mere bit of ordinary everyday conjuring; it's nothing to the skill and practice required to read, as you do, with the tips of your fingers."

The Seer drew a long breath, and passed his dark hand wearily across his high brown forehead.

"That's so!" he answered, with a sigh. "You may well say that." Then he dropped spontaneously into his own Western manner. "See here, stranger," he said, eyeing Florian hard, and laying one heavy hand on his entertainer's arm; "it's bred in the bone with me to some extent; but all the same, it's cost me fifteen years of practice to develop it. I come of a blind family, I do; father was blind, and mother as well; made their match up at the Indiana State Asylum. Grandfather was blind in mother's family, and two aunts in father's. I was born sighted; but at five year old I was taken with the cataract. They weren't any great shakes at the cataract in Colorado where I was raised; I was fifteen year old before they tried to couch it. So I learned to read first with embossed print on Grandfather's old blind Boston Bible. I learned to read first-rate; that was as easy as A.B.C., for the tips of my fingers were always sensitive. I learnt to make mats a bit, too, and to weave in colours. Weaving in colours develops the sensitiveness of the nerves in the hand; you get to distinguish the different strands by the feel, and to know whereabouts you're up to in the pattern."

"And at fifteen you recovered your sight?" Florian murmured reflectively, still grasping the poker.

"Yes, sir—r—r; at fifteen they took me to New York and got my eyes couched there. As soon as ever I could see, I began to learn more things still with the tips of my fingers; my eyes sort of helped me to interpret what I felt with them. Pretty soon I saw there was money in this thing. People in Colorado didn't care to play poker with me; they found out I'd a wonderful notion what was printed on a card by just drawing my finger, like this, over the face of it. I see you're a straight man, and haven't got many prejudices; so I don't mind telling you now my first idea was to go in for handling the cards as a profession. However, I soon caught on that that wasn't a good game; people in our section observed how I worked it, and it was apt to lead in the end to bowies and other unpleasantness. Several unpleasantnesses occurred, in fact, in Denver City, before I retired from that branch of the business. So then I began to reflect this thought-reading trick would come in more handy; one might do a bit at the cards now and again for a change; but if one tried it too often, it might land one at last in free quarters at the public expense; and the thought-reading's safer and more gentlemanly any way. So I worked at learning to read, as time afforded, till I could read a printed book as easy with my fingers as I could read it with my eyes. It took me ten years, I guess, to bring that trick to perfection."

"You made us write with a pencil, I noticed," Florian interposed, with a knowing smile. "That's easier to read, of course, for a pencil digs in so."

The Seer regarded him with no small admiration. "You're a smart man, and no mistake, sir," he answered, emphatically. "That's just how I do it. I read it from the back, where it's raised into furrows, in relief as it were, by the digging-in; I read it backwards. I gave 'em each a pad with the paper, you may have noticed. That pad supplies just the right amount of resistance. I had to stop once or twice to-night, where I couldn't read a sentence, and fill in the space meanwhile with a little bit of patter about concentrating their thoughts upon it, and that sort of nonsense. Mrs Sartoris's hand was precious hard to decipher, and there was one young lady who pressed so light, she almost licked me."

"And the envelopes?" Florian asked once more.

The Seer smiled disdainfully. "Why, that's nothing," he answered, with a contemptuous curl of the lip. "Any fool could do that; it's as easy as lying. The lower side-flap of the envelopes is hardly fastened at all, with just a pin's head of gum,"—he drew one from his pocket—"See here," he said; "it's got a bit left dry to wet and fasten afterwards. I draw out the paper, so, and read it with my finger; then I push it back, gum down again, and pull out the next one. It's the rapidity that tells, and it's that that takes so many years of practice."

"But Browning's Cleon?" Florian exclaimed. "And Sir Henry Martindale's having learnt the Russian character in the Crimea? He told me it was there he picked it up himself. How on earth did you get at those, now?"

The Seer stretched out his legs with a self-satisfied smirk, and took a pull at his whiskey. "See here, my dear sir," he said, stroking his smooth chin placidly; "a man don't succeed in these walks of life unless he's got some nous in him to start with. He's bound to observe, and remember, and infer, a good deal; he's bound to have an eye for character, and be a reader of faces. Now, it happens you wrote those self-same lines in Mrs Palmer's album; and I chanced to read them there while I waited for her in the drawing-room this very morning. A man's got to be smart, you bet, and look out for coincidences, if he's going to do much in occult science to astonish the public. Well, I've noticed every one has certain pet quotations of his own, which he uses frequently; and you'd be surprised to find how often the same quotation turns up, time after time, in these psychical experiments. 'The curfew tolls the knell,' or, 'Not a drum was heard,' are pretty sure to be given six times out of seven that one holds a séance. But yours was a new one; so I learnt it by heart, and observed you set it down to Browning's Cleon. As for the Russian character—well, where was an English officer likely to learn it except in the Crimea? That was risky, of course; I might have been mistaken; but one bad shot don't count against you, while a good one carries conviction straight off to the mind of your subject."

Florian paused, and considered. Before the end of the evening, indeed, he had learnt a good many things about the trade of prophet; and Mr Joaquin Holmes had taken, incidentally, every drop as much whiskey as was good for his constitution. When at last he rose to go, he clasped Florian's delicate hand hard. "You're a straight man, I believe, stranger," he said, significantly, "and I'm sure you're a smart one. But mind this from me, Mr Florian Wood, if ever you round on me, Colorado or London, the six-shooter'll settle it."

Florian smiled, and pressed his hand. "I don't care that for your six-shooter," he answered, calmly, with a resonant snap of his tiny left forefinger. "But I don't want to spoil a man's prospects in life, when he's taken fifteen years to make a consummate rogue of himself. You're perfect in your way, Mr Holmes, and I adore perfection. If ever I breathe a single word of this to my dearest friend—well, I give you free leave to whip out that six-shooter you're so fond of bragging about."

CHAPTER XXV

A DRAMATIC VENTURE

Among the minor successes of that London season, all the world reckoned the Colorado Seer's Psycho-physical Entertainment at the Assyrian Hall in Bond Street, and Will Deverill's dainty operetta, "Honeysuckle," at the Duke of Edinburgh's Theatre in Long Acre. The Seer, indeed, had been well advertised beforehand by the Morning Post and other London dailies, which gave puffs preliminary of his marvellous performance, "as privately exhibited to a select audience at Mrs Palmer's charming and hospitable residence in Hans Place, Chelsea." A well-known society writer, with a lingering love of the occult and the supernatural, saw in Mr Joaquin Holmes's abstruse gifts "a genuine case of Second Sight, and a curious modern parallel to the most famous feats of the Delphic oracle and the Indian Yogis." The Spectator suggested in a learned article that "Mahatmas were about"; the Daily News averred that "Nothing like Mr Holmes's extraordinary powers had been seen on earth since the Egyptian magicians impiously counterfeited the miracles of Moses and Aaron before the throne of Pharaoh." Every one of the accounts particularly insisted on the presence at the first trial of Mr Florian Wood, the distinguished musical and dramatic critic; whose inmost thoughts the Seer had read offhand like an open book, and whose quotations from little-known and unpopular sources he had instantly assigned to their proper origin. But when Florian himself was questioned on the subject, he shook his head with an air of esoteric knowledge, put two soft white fingers to his delicate lips, and smiled mysteriously. To say the truth, Florian loved a mystery. It flattered his sense of personal importance. Nay, he would almost have joined Mr Joaquin Holmes as a confederate in his little tricks for pure love of mystification, were it not for a wholesome and restraining dread that others might find them out as he himself had done. So the Seer, thus well and cheaply advertised by anticipation, made a hit for the moment, as dozens of such quacks have done before and since, from Home and Bishop to the Little Georgia Magnet.

As for Will Deverill's play, the first night was crowded. All London was there, in the sense that the Savage, the Garrick, and the Savile give to all London. Rue had taken tickets for stalls with reckless extravagance, and bestowed them right and left, as if on the author's behalf, to every influential soul among her fine acquaintance. Florian whipped up a fair number of first-nighters of the literary clique, and not a few great ladies from Belgravia drawing-rooms. The audience was distinctly and decidedly favourable. But not all the packed houses that ever were can save a bad play, if bad it is, from condign damnation. The incorruptible pit and the free and independent electors of the gallery are no respecters of persons, in their critical capacity. Fortunately, however, as it happened, Will's play was a good one. It didn't take the audience by storm at the first hearing, but it pleased and satisfied them. One or two of the melodies had a catchy ring; one or two of the scenes were both brilliant and pathetic. The house encored all the principal tunes; and when the curtain fell on virtue triumphant, in the person of Honeysuckle, vociferous cries arose on every side for "Author! Author!"

Will sat in a stage box, throughout the whole performance, with Florian, Rue, his sister, Mrs Sartoris, and her husband, the amiable East End curate. It was a three-act piece. As far as the end of the second act, Maud Sartoris was delighted; it was a distinct success, and Rue was very well pleased. Maud thought that was good; after all, whether she "smelt of drapery" or not, it's well for one's brother to produce a favourable impression on a woman with a fortune of seven hundred thousand. But the third act, she felt sure, was distinctly inferior to the two that preceded it. She said as much to Rue, while Will, trembling with excitement from head to foot, slipped off to make his expected bow before the curtain.

At those words of hers, Rue turned pale. She had thought so all through, though she would hardly acknowledge it, even to herself, and she feared in her own heart she knew the reason. Could Will have written the first two acts during those happy days when his head was stuffed full of Linnet at Meran, and gone on with the third in a London lodging after he learned of her marriage to Andreas Hausberger? Rue more than half-suspected that obvious explanation, for Honeysuckle was Linnet, and the thought disquieted her.

"You're quite right," Florian interposed, with his airy eloquence. "The first two acts are good, distinctly good. Will wrote them in the Tyrol. The third's a poor thing, mere fluff and feather: oh, what a falling off was there! It was written in London! But who can sing aright of Arcady in the mud of Mayfair? Who can sing of Zion by the willows of Babylon? Will drew his first inspiration from the sparkling air of Meran; it faded like a mist with the mists of the Channel."

"The audience doesn't seem to think so," Rue put in, somewhat anxiously, as a hearty round of applause greeted Will by the footlights. "They feel it's all right. They're evidently satisfied, on the whole, with the nature of the dénouement."

"If you look at the papers to-morrow morning," Florian answered, carelessly, "you'll find every candid critic disagrees with the audience and agrees with Mrs Sartoris. But what matter for that! It's a very good play, with some very good tunes in it; and the actors have made it. I really didn't think our dear friend Will could do anything so good—till I saw it interpreted. I call the reception, on the whole, most promising."

Rue felt positively annoyed that Florian should speak so condescendingly of Will's beautiful music. He damned it with faint praise, while Rue herself felt for it a genuine enthusiasm. For she knew it was good, all except that third act, and even there she saw touches of really fine composition.

In a minute or two more, Will came back to them, radiant. Florian boarded him at once. "Ten thousand congratulations, dear boy," he cried, affectedly. "We're all delighted. Laurel wreaths for the victor! Bays drape your lute. Everybody's been saying the first two acts are a triumphal progress, though the third, we agree, fails to sustain the attention—flags in interest somewhat."

Will coloured up to his eyes. Rue noted the blush; her heart sank at sight of it. "I knew it was weak myself," he admitted, a little shamefacedly. "The inspiration died down. Perhaps it was natural. You see, Maud," he went on, turning round to his sister as to a neutral person, and avoiding Rue's eye, "I wrote and composed the first two acts at Innsbruck and Meran, under the immediate influence of the Tyrolese air and the Tyrolese music; they welled up in me in the midst of peasant songs and cow-bells. The third act, I had to manufacture at my rooms in Craven Street. Surroundings, of course, make a deal of difference to this sort of thing. I was in the key there, and out of it in London. Pumped-up poetry and pumped-up music are poor substitutes after all for the spontaneous article."

He didn't dare to look at Rue as he spoke those words. He was conscious all the while, let him boggle as he might, that she knew the real reason for the failure of the dénoument. And he was conscious, too, though he was a modest man, that Rue would feel hurt at the effect Linnet's marriage had had upon his music. As for Rue herself, poor girl, her face was crimson. To think she should have done so much, and wronged her modesty so far with Mr Wildon Blades to get Will's operetta put on the stage that evening; to think she should have risked her own money to ensure its success, and then to find it owed its inspiration wholly and solely to the charms of her peasant rival, Linnet! Rue was more than merely vexed; she was shamed and humiliated. Will's triumph was turned for her into gall and bitterness. His heart, after all, was still fixed on his cow-girl!

They drove home together in Rue's luxurious brougham to Hans Place, Chelsea, Mr Sartoris and Florian following close in a hansom. The party were engaged to sup at Rue's. Florian had invited them, indeed, to a banquet at Romano's, as more strictly in keeping with the evening's entertainment; but Maud Sartoris had objected to such a plan as "improper," and likely to damage dear Arthur's prospects. So at Rue's they supped. But, in spite of Will's success, and his health which they drank in Rue's finest champagne, with musical honours, the party somehow lacked go and spirit. Will was dimly conscious in his own soul of having unwittingly behaved rather ill to Rue; Rue was dimly conscious of harbouring some deep-seated but indefinite resentment towards Will and Linnet. It was some consolation, at least, to know that the girl was now decently married and done for; sooner or later, for certain, such a man as Will Deverill was sure to get over a mere passing fancy for a handsome up-standing Tyrolese peasant-girl.

After supper, Will Deverill and the Sartorises went home in a party. But Florian lingered late. This was an excellent opportunity. Rue was annoyed with Will, and therefore all the more likely to accept another suitor. He gazed around the room, that little palace of art he had decorated with such care for his soul to dwell in. "Upon my word, Rue," he murmured at last, after some desultory talk, glancing around him complacently, "I'm proud of this place; I never knew before what a decorator I was. It's simply charming." He gazed at her fixedly. "It's the sweetest home in all London," he went on in a rapt voice, "and it's inhabited by the sweetest and brightest creature in the whole of Christendom. I sometimes think, Rue, as I gaze round this house, how happy I should be, if I too lived in it."

For a moment, Rue stared at him without quite understanding what he meant to convey by this singular intimation. Then all at once it flashed across her. In spite of her distress, a smile stole over her face. She held out her hand frankly. "Good night, Florian," she said, in a very decided tone. "Let me urge upon you to be content with your chambers in Pimlico. You're a delightful and always most amusing friend; I hope you're not going to make your friendship impossible for me. I like you very much, in your own sort of way; but if ever you re-open that subject again, . . . I'm afraid I could give you no further opportunity of admiring your own handicraft in this pretty little house of mine. That's why I say good-night to you now so plainly. It's best to be plain, best to understand one another, once for all, and for ever."

Two minutes later, a dejected creature named Florian Wood found himself walking disconsolate, with his umbrella up, on the sloppy wet flags of ill-lighted Sloane Street. He had sustained a loss of seven hundred thousand pounds on a turn of fortune's wheel, at an inauspicious moment. And Rue, with her face in her hands by the fire, was saying to herself with many tears and sighs that, Linnet or no Linnet, she never would and never could love anyone in the world except that dear Will Deverill.

CHAPTER XXVI

A WOMAN'S HEART

The papers next morning, with one accord, were almost unanimous in their praise of Honeysuckle. Will's operetta didn't set the Thames on fire, to be sure, a first work seldom does, but it secured such an amount of modest success as decided him to change his plans largely for the future. It was certain, now, that he might take himself seriously as a musical purveyor. So he began to drop off to some extent from the hack work of journalism, and devote his energies in earnest to his new task in life as a playwright and composer. Rue had nothing to pay for her guarantee of Honeysuckle; on the contrary, Will received a very solid sum for his royalties on the run through the remainder of that season. He never knew, indeed, how much he had been indebted to the pretty American's not wholly disinterested act of kindness; for Mr Blades kept his word; and, in spite of what he said, Rue's timely intervention had decided him not a little in accepting that first piece by an unknown author.

Thus, during the next few years, as things turned out, Will's position and prospects improved very rapidly. He was regarded as one of our most rising composers; critics spoke of him as the sole representative and restorer of the serious English poetical opera. Monetary troubles no longer oppressed his soul; he had leisure to write, and to write, if he would, the thing that pleased him. His position was secured, so much so, indeed, that judicious mammas gave him frequent invitations to their gayest At Homes and garden parties. But he successfully avoided all snares so set for him. Many people expressed no little surprise that so nice a young man, and a poet to boot, with a position like his, and such excellent Principles, should refrain from marriage. Society expects that every man will do his duty; it intends him to marry as soon as he has means to relieve it becomingly of one among its many superfluous daughters. But, in spite of Society, Will still remained single, and met all the casual feelers of interested acquaintances as to the reasons which induced him so to shirk his duty as a British citizen with a quiet smile of self-contained resolution.

Rue came to London now for each succeeding season. Will was much at her house, and a very real friendship existed between them. Busybodies wondered, indeed, that those two young people, who were so thick together, didn't stop scandal's mouth by marrying as they ought to do. The busybodies could see no just cause or impediment why they should not at once be joined together in holy matrimony. The young woman was rich; the young man was a genius. She was "mad for him," every one said, in every one's usual exaggerated phraseology; and as for him, though perhaps he wasn't quite so wildly in love, yet he liked her so well, and was so often in her company, that it would surely be better to avoid whispers at once by marrying her offhand, like the earl in the "Bab Ballads," "quite reg'lar, at St George's!" The busybodies were surprised he didn't see it so himself; it really was almost somebody's duty, they thought, to suggest the idea to him. But perhaps Mrs Palmer's money was strictly tied up; in which case, of course—Society broke off short, and shrugged its sapient shoulders.

To some extent, in fact, Will agreed with them himself. He almost fancied he would have proposed to Rue—if he wasn't so fond of her. As he sat with her one evening by the drawing-room fire at Hans Place, before the lights were turned on, during blind-man's holiday, he said to her suddenly, after a long, deep pause, "I daresay, Rue, you sometimes wonder why it is I've never tried to ask you to marry me."

Rue gave a little start of half-tremulous surprise. He could see how the colour mounted fast to her cheek by the glow of the firelight. She gave a faint gasp as she answered candidly, with American frankness, "Well, to tell you the truth, Will, I've fancied once or twice you were just going to do it."

Will looked across at her kindly. She was very charming. "I won't be cruel enough, Rue," he said, leaning forward to her like a brother, "to ask you what answer you meant to give, if I'd done as you expected. I hope you won't think me conceited if I say I half believe I know it already. And that's just why I want to tell you now the reason that has prevented me from ever asking you. If your nature were a little less deep, and a little less womanly than it really is, I might have asked you long ago. But, Rue, you know, I feel sure you know, how deeply I loved that other woman. I love her still, and I won't pretend to deny it. I've waited and wondered whether in time her image might fade out of my heart; but it never has faded. She's another man's wife, and probably I shall never see her again; yet I love her as dearly and regret her as much as I did on the day when I first heard she'd thrown herself away for life upon Andreas Hausberger."

"I've felt sure you did," Rue answered, with downcast eyes. "I've felt it, Will, and for that very reason, I've wondered all the less you didn't ask me."

Will looked across at her again. She was beautiful as she sat there with the glow of the fire on her pensive features. "Dear Rue," he said, softly, "you and I are no mere children. We know our own minds. We're grown man and woman. We can venture to talk freely to one another of these things, without the foolish, childish nonsense of false shame or false blushes. In spite of Linnet, I'd have asked you long ago to be my wife, if I hadn't respected and admired you so deeply. But I feel you're not a woman who could ever put up with half a man's heart, or half a man's confidence; and half my heart is all I could give you. I love Linnet still, and I shall always love her. I never shall cease to feel an undying regret that I didn't marry her, instead of that fellow Hausberger. Now, there are women not a few I might still have asked to marry me, in spite of that regret; but you're not one of them. I love you better than I ever have loved anyone else on this earth, anyone else, but Linnet; and, therefore, I don't ask you to marry a man who could give you a second place only in his affections."

The tears stood dim in Rue's swimming eyes. She looked at him steadily, and let them trickle one by one down her cheeks, unheeded. "Dear Will," she answered him back, with equal frankness, "it was kind of you to speak, and I'm glad you've spoken. It'll make our relations all the easier in future! I guessed how you felt; I guessed it all long ago; but I'm glad, all the same, to have heard from your own lips the actual facts of it. And, Will, you quite rightly interpret my feelings. I'm an American at heart, and, you know, we Americans are very exacting in matters of affection. Some savage strain of monopoly exists in us still. I can't help it. I acknowledge it. I won't deny to you"—and she stretched out her hand quite frankly, and let him hold it in his own for a few brief moments—"I won't deny that I'm very very fond indeed of you. If you could have given me your whole heart, I would have accepted it gratefully. I admired you with a deep admiration from the very first day I ever met you. I loved you from the time we sat together on the Lanser Kopf that afternoon at Innsbruck. I'm not ashamed to tell you so, nay, rather, dear, I'm proud of it; for, Will, you're a man any woman might be proud to waste her love upon. But much as I love you, much as I admire you, I never could accept you if you feel like that. As an American born, with my monopolist instincts, I must have a whole man to myself all alone, or I won't have any of him."

"I knew it," Will answered, caressing her hand with his fingers, and bending over it chivalrously. "And that's why I never have ventured to ask you. But I've loved you all the same, Rue, as one loves the woman who stands best of all . . . save one . . . in one's affections."

Rue withdrew her hand gently. Her tears were falling faster. "Well, now," she said, with a quiet sigh, "we can be friends in future, all the better, I hope, for this little explanation. I'm rich, of course, Will; and a great many men, circumstanced as you were, would have been glad to marry me for the sake of my money. I liked you all the more, I like you the more to-day, in that that has never counted for one moment with you. If you'd been a mercenary man, you'd have dissembled and pretended; you need never have let me see how much you loved that girl; or, if you had, you might have led me to suppose you had gradually forgotten her. . . . Dear friend"—and she turned to him once more with a sudden burst of uncontrollable feeling—"we are man and woman, as you say, not boy and girl; so why should I be ashamed to open my whole heart to you? You've told me the truth, like a man; why shouldn't I tell you the truth, in return, like a woman? I will. I can't help it. I have waited and watched and thought often to myself, 'In time, he must surely, surely get over it. He must cease to love her; he can never really have loved her so much as he imagines; he must turn at last to me, when he forgets all about her.' So I waited and watched, and, month after month, I thought at last you must surely begin to forget her. But, month after month, I have seen you loved her still; and while you loved her still, . . . Will, Will, dear Will, I didn't want you to ask me."

Will seized her hand once more, and kissed it tenderly. "Oh, how good you are!" he cried, in a very melting voice. "Rue, do you know, when you talk like that, you make me love you!"

"But not better than her?" Rue murmured, softly.

Will couldn't lie to her. "No; not better than her," he answered slowly, in a very low voice. "If it were otherwise, I'd have asked you this very minute, dear sister."

Rue rose and faced him. The firelight flickered red on her soft white dress; he could see by its bright glow the tears still trickling slow down those full round cheeks of hers. "After this, Will, I must go," she said. "Don't come again to-morrow. Next week, you may call if you like, some afternoon, casually; but for Heaven's sake, please, don't refer to this interview. I have only one thing to say, and when I've said it, I must run from you. Remember, I'm a woman; my pride is fighting hard against my love to-night—and, if I let love win, I should for ever despise myself. As long as you live, don't speak to me of this matter again, unless you speak to say, 'Rue, Rue, I've forgotten her.' If ever that day comes—" and she flushed rosy red—"you have my answer already; you know you can claim me."

She moved over to the door, with hurried step and beating heart, hardly able to trust herself. With a true sense of delicacy, Will abstained from opening it. He stood on the hearth-rug, irresolute, and just watched her depart; he felt, in the circumstances, that course was the more respectful.

With her fingers on the handle, Rue paused, and looked round again. "I wouldn't have said so much, even now," she faltered, "if it weren't for this—that I feel you're the one man I've ever met in my life to whom the question of my money was as dust in the balance. You speak the truth, and I know I can trust you. If ever you can say to me, 'I love you better now, Rue, than I ever loved anyone,' I am yours: then, take me! But till that day comes, if come it ever does, let us only be friends. Never speak to me again, for Heaven's sake, never speak, as we have spoken this evening."

She opened the door and passed out, all tremulous. Will waited a moment, and then, with a throbbing heart, went slowly down the stairs. As he did so, something moist fell suddenly on his hand that grasped the bannister. To his immense surprise, he found it was a tear from his own eyelids—for he too was crying. Poet that he was, he felt more than half-inclined, while he stood there, hesitating, to rush after her as she went, and seize her in his strong arms, and cover her with warm kisses that very minute. For a poet is a man even more than the rest of us. But could he tell her with truth he had quite forgotten Linnet? Oh, no, no, no; Linnet's image on his heart remained graven, even then, quite as deeply as ever. We men are built so.

CHAPTER XXVII

AULD LANG SYNE

A week or two later, one bright spring afternoon, Will was strolling by himself down the sunny side of Bond Street. All the world was there, for the world was in town, and the pavements were crowded. But Will moved through the stream of well-dressed dawdlers, seeing and hearing little. In the midst of all that idle throng, his head was full of melodies; he was working up rhymes to ready-made tunes, undisturbed by the hubbub and din of London. Of a sudden, somebody stopped and stood straight in front of him. "Mr Deverill, I believe!" a tuneful voice said, brusquely. Will's eyes returned at once from heaven to earth, and saw standing before them, a tall young man, of somewhat defiant aspect, dressed in the black frock coat and shiny silk hat of Metropolitan respectability.

Will paused, and surveyed him. He was a good-looking young man, with much swagger in his air, and a black moustache on his upper lip; but his face seemed somehow strangely familiar to Will, while his voice stirred at once some latent chord in the dim depths of his memory. But he wasn't one of Will's fine London acquaintances, the poet saw that much at once by the cheap pretentiousness of his coat and hat, the flaring blue of his made-up silk tie, the obtrusive glitter of the false diamond pin which adorned its centre. The stranger's get-up, indeed, was redolent of the music halls. Yet he was handsome for all that, with a certain strange air of native distinction, not wholly concealed by the vulgar tone of his costume and his solicitous jewellery. Will held out his hand with that dubitative air which we all of us display in the first moment of uncertainty towards half-recognised acquaintances.

"I see you have forgotten me, zen," the stranger said, in very decent English, drawing himself up with great dignity, and twirling his black moustache airily between one thumb and forefinger. "It is long, to be sure, since we met in ze Tyrol. And I have changed much since zen, no doubt: I have mixed with ze world; I have grown what you call in English cosmopolitan. But I see it comes back; I see you remember me now; my voice recalls it to you."

Will grasped his hand more cordially. "Yes, perfectly, when you speak," he said; "though you are very much changed indeed, as you say; but I see you're Franz Lindner."

"Yes; I'm Mr Franz Lindner," the stranger replied, half-imperceptibly correcting him, for it was indeed the Robbler. Will scanned him from head to foot, and took him in at a glance. He was a fiery young man still, and his mien, as of old, was part fierce, part saucy. But, oh, what a difference the change of dress had made in him! No conical hat, no blackcock's feather now, whether "turned" or otherwise. In his Tyrolese costume, with his rifle in his hand, and his cartridges at his side, Franz Lindner had looked and moved of yore a typical Alpine jäger. But, in black frock-coat and shiny tall hat, strolling like a civilised snob that he was down the flags of Bond Street, all the romance and poetry had faded utterly out of him. The glamour was gone. He looked and moved for all the world to-day like any other young man of the baser mock-swell sort, dressed up in his Sunday best to lounge and ogle and bandy vulgar chaff in Burlington Arcade with his predestined companions.

"Why, what has brought you to London, then?" Will asked, much astonished.

"Art, art," the transfigured Robbler responded, offhand, with inimitable swagger. "You must surely zen know my stage name, zough you don't seem to have heard me." He pulled out a printed card, and handed it to Will with a flourish. "I am ze Signor Francesco," he continued, "all ze world is talking about." And he threw back his chin and cocked his head on one side, looking, even as he spoke, more pretentious than ever.

"Oh, indeed!" Will answered with a bewildered little laugh. But it was the non-committing "Oh, indeed!" of mere polite acquiescence.

Franz Lindner caught the tinge of implied non-recognition in the Englishman's voice, and hastened to add, as if parenthetically, "I perform at ze Pavilion."

"What, the London Pavilion at the top of the Hay market?" Will exclaimed, beginning to realise.

Franz Lindner looked hurt. "I've seen your name often enough," he said, asserting himself still more vigorously as Will seemed to know less of him; "and I sought, as you were a pillar of ze profession yourself, you would certainly have seen mine, if it were only on ze posters. I'm advertised largely. All London rings wis me. Ze County Council has even taken notice of me. I'm a public character! And I have had ze intention more zan once of looking you up, as also Mr Florian. But zere, here in London our time is so occupied! You and I, who are public men, wis professional engagements, we are ever overtaxed; we know not how to find ze leisure or ze space for ze claims of friendship."

"Have you been long in London?" Will asked, turning down with him towards Piccadilly.

"More zan two years now," the Robbler answered briskly, lounging on at his own pace, with a cane in his gloved hand, and staring hard, as he passed, at every pretty girl he saw on foot or in the carriages. "After I leave you at Meran, I worked my way slowly, singing, singing, ever singing, by degrees to Paris. But Paris didn't suit me; zere is too much blague zere; zey go in for buffoons; zey laugh at a man of modest merit. I hate blague myself. So zen I came on pretty soon to London. At first I had to sing in common low music halls, sous side and zat; but talent, talent is sure to make its way in ze end. I rose very quick, and now, I am at ze head of my branch of ze profession."

"You sing, of course?" Will interposed, restraining a smile at the Robbler's delicious self-satisfaction. The man himself was the very same as ever, to be sure; but 'twas strange what a difference mere externals had made in him!

"Yes; I sing, and sometimes, too, I play ze zither. But mostly, I sing. It surprises me, indeed, you should not have heard of my singing."

"And what's the particular branch of which you're the acknowledged head?" Will asked, still amused at the Tyroler's complacency.

Franz Lindner held his head very high in the air, and gave a twirl to his cane, as he answered, with much importance, "My line is ze Mammoss Continental Comique; ze serio-comic foreigner; zey call me Frenchy. I sing ze well-known songs in broken English zat are in everybody's mous, 'Mossoo Robert is my name,' or 'Lay-ces-terre Squarre,' or 'Ze leetle black dawg,' or 'Zat lohvely Matilda.' I wonder you have not heard of me. 'Mossoo Robert' is all ze talk of London. Frank Wilkins writes songs especially for my voice. If you look in ze music shops, you will see on ze covers, 'Written expressly for Signor Francesco.' Signor Francesco, zat's me!" And he tapped his breast, and swelled himself visibly.

"I remember to have seen the name, I think," Will answered, with a slight internal shudder, well pleased, none the less, to give some tardy salve to his companion's wounded vanity. "I'm glad you've got on, and delighted to find you have such kindly recollections of me."

Franz Lindner laughed. "Oh, zat!" he said, snapping his fingers in the air very jauntily. "I was a hot young man zen; I knew little of ze world. You mustn't sink much of what a young man did in ze days before he knew how Society is managed. I owe you no grudge. We were bose of us younger. Besides, our friend Hausberger has wiped out our old scores. I have transferred to him, entire, all my feelings in ze matter."

"That's well," Will replied, anxious indeed to learn whether the Tyroler had heard anything fresh of late years about Linnet. "And Hausberger himself? What of him . . . and his wife? Have you ever knocked up against them?"

The Robbler's brow gathered; his hand clenched his cane hard. It was clear civilisation and cosmopolitanism, however neatly veneered, hadn't made much serious change in his underlying nature. "Zat rascal!" he exclaimed, bringing his stick down on the pavement with a noisy little thud; "zat rogue; zat liar! If ever I had come across him, it would be bad for his head. Sousand devils, what a man! . . . Here, we're close to ze Cri; will you come and have a drink? We can talk zis over afterward. I like to offer somesing to a friend new discovered."

"It's not much in my line," Will answered, smiling; "but still, for old times' sake, I'll go in and have a glass with you." To say the truth, he was so eager to find out what Franz might have to communicate that he stretched a point for once, and broke through his otherwise invariable rule never to drink anything anywhere except at meal times.

Franz stalked along Piccadilly, and strode airily into the Criterion like one who knew his way well about the London restaurants. "What'll you take?" he asked of Will in an assured tone, which showed the question in English was a very familiar one to him.

"Whatever you take yourself," Will answered, much amused, for the Tyroler was far more at home than himself in a London bar, and far more at his ease with the London barmaid.

"Two half porters and two small Scotch, miss," the Robbler cried briskly to the tousely-haired young woman who attended to his call. "You'll find it a very good mixture for zis time of day, Mr Deverill. I always take it myself. It softens ze organ."

The young woman fulfilled the order with unwonted alacrity, Franz was a favourite at the bar, and gave his commands leaning across it with the arch smile of an habitué, and Will then discovered that the mixture in question consisted of a glass of Dublin stout, well fortified with a thimbleful of Highland whisky. He also observed, what he had not at first sight noticed, that Franz Lindner's face, somewhat redder than of old, bore evidence, perhaps, of too frequent efforts for the softening of the organ. Franz nodded to the barmaid.

"Here's our meeting!" he said to Will. "Shall we step a little aside here? We can talk wisout overhearing."

They drew aside to a round table for their unfinished gossip. "You're not in town often, I suppose," the Tyroler began, scanning his companion from head to foot with a critical scrutiny.

"Why, I live here," Will answered, taken aback—"in Craven Street, Strand; I've always lived here."

"Oh, indeed," the Robbler responded, with a somewhat superior air; "I sought from your costume you'd just come up from ze country."

Will smiled good-humouredly. He was wearing, in point of fact, a soft slouch hat and a dusty brown suit of somewhat poetical cut, which contrasted in more ways than one with the music-hall singer's too elaborate parody of the glossy silk chimney-pot and regulation frock-coat of the orthodox Belgravian.

Then Franz came back at a bound to the subject he had quitted on the flags of Piccadilly. He explained, with much circumlocution and many needless expletives, how he had heard from time to time, through common friends at St Valentin, that Andreas Hausberger and his wife had fluctuated of late years between summer at Munich, Leipzig, Stuttgart, and winter at Milan, Florence, Naples, Venice. Linnet got on with him very well, oh, very well indeed, yes; Linnet, you know, was just the sort of girl to get on very well with pretty nearly anyone. No doubt by this time she'd settled down into tolerably amicable relations with Andreas Hausberger! Any children? Oh dear, no; Hausberger'd take care of that; a public singer's time is far too valuable to be wasted on the troubles of a growing young family. Had she come out yet? Well, yes; that is to say, from time to time she'd sung at concerts in Munich, Florence, and elsewhere. Successfully? Of course; she'd a very good voice, as voices go, for her sort, and training was sure to do something at least for it. Franz had heard rumours she was engaged next season for San Carlo at Naples; you might count upon Hausberger's doing his very best, now he'd invested his savings in preparing her for the stage, to make money out of his bargain.

Through all Franz said, however, there ran still, as of yore, one constant thread of undying hatred to the man who had outwitted him at Meran and St Valentin. "Then you haven't forgiven him yet?" Will inquired at last, after one such spiteful allusion to Andreas's meanness.

The Robbler's hand moved instinctively of itself to his left breast pocket. He had changed his coat, but not his customs. "I carry it here still," he answered, with the same old defiant air, just defining with finger and thumb the vague outline of the knife that bulged between them through the glossy broadcloth. "It's always ready for him. Ze day I meet him—" and he stopped short suddenly, with a face like a bulldog's.

"You Tyrolers have long memories," Will answered, with a little shudder. "It's very unfashionable you know, to stab a rival in London."

Franz showed his handsome teeth. "Unfashionable or not," he replied, with a shrug, "it is so I was born; it is so I live ever. As we say in ze song, I am made zat way. I cannot help it. I never forget an injury. . . . Zough, mind you," he continued, after a telling little pause, during which he drove many times an imaginary knife into an invisible enemy, "it isn't so much now zat I grudge him Linnet. Let him keep his fine Frau. Zere are better girls in ze world, you and I have found out, zan Lina Telser, to-day Frau Hausberger. We were younger zen; we are men of ze world now; we know higher sings, I sink, zan a Zillerthal sennerin. What I feel wis him at present is not so much zat he took away ze girl, as zat he played me so mean a trick to take her."

Will smiled to himself in silence. How strangely human feelings and ideas differ! He himself had never forgotten the beautiful alp-girl with the divine voice; in the midst of London drawing-rooms he never ceased to miss her; while Franz Lindner thought he had left Linnet far, far behind, since he became acquainted with those higher and nobler types, the music-hall stars of the London Pavilion! "There's no accounting for tastes," people say; oh, most inept of proverbs! surely it's easy for anyone to account for the reasons which made Linnet appear so different now in Franz Lindner's eyes and in her English poet's.

But before Franz and Will parted at the Circus that afternoon, they had made mutual promises, for old acquaintance's sake—Franz, that he would graciously accept a stall, on an off-night, at the Duke of Edinburgh's, to see Will's new piece, The Duchess of Modena; and Will, that he would betake himself to the London Pavilion one of these next few evenings, to hear Signor Francesco, alias the Frenchy, in his celebrated and universally encored impersonation of Mossoo Robert in Regent Street.

CHAPTER XXVIII

SIGNORA CASALMONTE

Three years and more had passed since Will's visit to the Tyrol. Events had moved fast for his fortunes meanwhile. He was a well-known man now in theatrical circles. Florian Wood went about, indeed, boasting in clubs and drawing-rooms that 'twas he who had discovered and brought out Will Deverill. "It's all very well to be a poet," he said, "and it's all very well to be born with a head full of rhymes and tunes, of crochets, clefs, and quavers; but what's the use of all that, I ask you my dear fellow, without a critic to push you? A Critic is a man with a fine eye for potentialities. Before the world sees, he sees; before the world hears, he listens. He sits by the world's wayside, as it were, with open eye or ear, and catches unawares the first faint lisping notes of undeveloped genius. He divines in the bud the exquisite aroma and perfect hue of the full-blown blossom. Long ago, I said to Deverill, 'You have the power within you to write a good opera!' He laughed me to scorn; but I said to him, 'Try!'—and the outcome was, Honeysuckle. He took up a battered fiddle one day at an old inn in the Zillerthal, when we two were rusticating on the emerald bosom of those charming unsophisticated Tyrolese valleys; he struck a few notes on it of his own composing; and I said to him, 'My dear Will, Sullivan trembles on his pedestal.' At the time he treated it as a mere passing joke; but I made him persevere; and what was the result?—why, those exquisite airs which found their way before long to the sheep-runs of Australia, and resounded from lumberers' camps in the backwoods of Canada! The Critic, I say, is the true prophet and sage of our modern world; he sees what is to be, and he helps to produce it."

But whether Florian was right in attributing Will's success to himself or not, it is certain, at least, that Will was rapidly successful. The world recognised in him a certain genuine poetical vein which has seldom been vouchsafed to the English librettist; it recognised in him, also, a certain depth and intensity of musical sense which has seldom been vouchsafed to the English dramatic composer.

One afternoon that spring, Will returned to town from a visit to the Provinces in connection with his new opera, The Lady of Llandudno, then about to be performed in several country theatres by Mr D'Arcy Clift's operatic company. He drove almost straight from the station to Rue's. Florian was there in great form; and Mr Joaquin Holmes, the Colorado Seer, had dropped in for afternoon tea at his fair disciple's. In spite of Will's ridicule, Rue continued to believe in Mr Holmes' thought-reading and other manifestations. For the Seer had added by this time a touch of spiritualism to the general attractions of his flagging entertainments at the Assyrian Hall; and it is a mysterious dispensation of Providence that wealthy Americans, especially widows, fall a natural prey to all forms of transcendentalism or spiritualistic quackery. It seems to be one of the strange devices which Providence adopts for putting excessive or monopolised wealth into circulation.

"Mr Holmes wants me to go to the Harmony to-night," Rue said, with a smile—"you know what it is—the new Harmony Theatre. He says there's a piece coming out there this evening I ought to see—a pretty new piece by an American composer. You're going to be crushed, Will. They've got a fresh tenor there, a very good man, whom Mr Holmes thinks a deal of. I've half a mind to go; will you join our party?"

"You ought to hear it," the Seer remarked, with his oracular air, turning to Will, and looking critical. "This new tenor's a person you should keep your eye upon; I heard him rehearse, and I said to myself at once, 'That fellow's the very man Mr Deverill will want to write a first part for; if he doesn't, I'll retire at once from the prophetic business.' He has a magnificent voice; you should get Blades to secure him next season for the Duke of Edinburgh's. He's worth fifty pounds a night, if he's worth a penny."

"Very good trade, a tenor's," Florian mused philosophically. "I often regret I wasn't brought up to it."

"What's his name?" Will asked with languid interest, for he had no great faith in the Seer's musical ear and critical acumen.

"His name? Heaven knows," the Seer answered, with a short laugh; "but he calls himself Papadopoli—Signor Romeo Papadopoli."

"There's a deal in a name, in spite of that vastly overrated man, Shakespeare," Florian murmured, musingly. "It's my belief, if the late lamented Lord Beaconsfield had only been christened Benjamin Jacobs, or even Benjamin Israels, he never would have lived to be Prime Minister of England. But as Benjamin Disraeli—ah, what poetry, what mystery, what Oriental depth, what Venetian suggestiveness! And Romeo's good, too; Signor Romeo Papadopoli! Why, 'twas of Romeo himself the Bard first asked, 'What's in a name? the rose,' etcætera. And in the fulness of time, this singer man crops up with that very name to confute him. 'Ah, Romeo, Romeo, wherefore art thou Romeo?' Why, because it looks so extremely romantic in a line of the playbill, and helps to attract the British public to your theatre! Papadopoli, indeed! and his real name's Jenkins. I don't doubt it's Jenkins. There's a Palazzo Papadopoli on the Grand Canal. But this fellow was born, you may take your oath, at Haggerston or Stepney!"

"Well, your own name has floated you in life, at any rate," Rue put in, a little mischievously.

Florian gazed at her hard—and changed the subject abruptly. "And there's a woman in the troupe who sings well, too, I'm told," he interposed, with airy grace, the airy grace of five feet, turning to

Joaquin Holmes. "I haven't heard her myself; I've been away from town, you know how engaged I am, visits, visits in the country, Lady Barnes; Lady Ingleborough. But they say she sings well; really, Will, you ought to come with us."

"Yes; she's not bad in her way," the Seer admitted, with a stifled yawn, stroking his long moustache, and assuming the air of a connoisseur in female voices. "She's got a fine rich organ, a little untrained, perhaps, but not bad for a débutante. A piquante little Italian; Signora Carlotta Casalmonte she calls herself. But Papadopoli's the man; you should come, Mr Deverill; my friend Mr Florian has secured us a box; I dine at Mrs Palmer's, and we all go together to the Harmony afterwards."

"I should like to go," Will replied with truth; for he hated to leave Rue undefended in that impostor's clutches; "but, unfortunately, I've invited my sister and her husband to dine with me to-night at my rooms in Craven Street."

"Well, wire to them at once to come on and dine here instead," Rue suggested, with American expansiveness; "and then we can all go in a party together, the more the merrier."

Will thought not badly of this idea; it was a capital compromise: the more so as he had asked nobody else to meet the Sartorises, and a family tête-à-tête with Maud and Arthur wasn't greatly to his liking. "I'll do it," he said, after a moment's reflection, "if they're at home and will answer me."

Rue sent out a servant to the nearest office with the telegram at once; and, in due time, an answer arrived by return that Arthur and Maud would be happy to accept Mrs Palmer's very kind invitation for this evening. It was most properly worded; Maud was nothing if not proper. Her husband had now been appointed incumbent of St Barnabas's, Marylebone; and her dignity had received an immense accession. Indeed, she debated for ten minutes with dear Arthur whether it was really quite right for them to go at all on such hasty notice; and she was annoyed that Will, after inviting her himself, should have ventured to put her off with a vicarious dinner-party. But she went all the same, partly because she thought it would be such a good thing for Will, "and for our own dear boys, Arthur, if Will were to marry that rich bourgeoise American," and partly because she remembered it would give her such an excellent opportunity of displaying her pretty new turquoise-blue dinner-dress among the best company, in a box at the Harmony. Besides, a first night is a thing never to be despised by the wise man or woman; it looks so well to see next day in the Society papers, "Mrs Palmer's box contained, amongst others, Mr Florian Wood, Mr W. Deverill, his sister, Mrs Sartoris, and her husband, the incumbent of St Barnabas's, Marylebone."

So, at half-past seven, Maud Sartoris sailed in, torquoise-blue and all, and, holding out her hand with a forgiving smile, murmured gushingly to her hostess, "We thought it so friendly of you, dear Mrs Palmer, to invite us like that at a moment's notice, as soon as you knew we were engaged to Will, and that Will couldn't possibly go unless he took us with him! We want to see this new piece at the Harmony so much; a first night to us quiet clerical folks, you know, is always such a treat. We're immensely obliged to you."

Dinner went off well, as it usually did where Florian was of the party. To give Florian his due, he bubbled and sparkled, like the Apollinaris spring, with unfailing effervescence. That evening, too, he was in specially fine form; it amused him to hear Mr Joaquin Holmes discourse with an air of profound conviction on his own prophetic art, and then watch him glancing across the table under his long dark eyelashes to see between whiles how Florian took it. The follies and foibles of mankind were nuts to Florian. It gave the epicurean philosopher a calm sense of pleasure in his own superiority to see Rue and Arthur Sartoris drinking in open-mouthed the mysterious hints and self-glorificatory nonsense of the man whom he knew by his own confession to be a cheat and a humbug. Their eyes seldom met; Joaquin Holmes avoided such disconcerting experiences; but whenever they did, Florian's were brimful of suppressed amusement, while the Seer's had a furtive hang-dog air as of one who at once would deprecate exposure and beseech indulgence.

After dinner, the Seer kept them laughing so long at his admirable stories of the Far West of his childhood (which Arthur Sartoris received with the conventional "Ah really, now, Mr Holmes!" of forced clerical disapprobation) that they were barely in time for the beginning of the opera. As they entered, the tenor held possession of the stage. Will didn't think so much of him; Florian, his head on one side in a critical attitude, observed oracularly, at the end of his first song, that the Papadopoli was perhaps not wholly without capabilities. That's the sort of criticism that Florian loved best; it enables a man to hedge in accordance with the event. If the fellow turns out well in the near future, you can say you declared from the very first he had capabilities; if the public doesn't catch on, you can remark with justice that he hasn't developed what little promise he once showed, and that from the beginning you never felt inclined to say much for him.

Presently, from the rear of the stage, down the mimic rocks that formed the background of the scenery, a beautiful woman, entering almost unobserved, sprang lightly from boulder to boulder of the torrent bed, with the true elastic step of a mountain-bred maiden. She had a fine ripe figure, very lithe and vigorous-looking; her features were full, but extremely regular; her mouth, though large and somewhat rich in the lips, was yet rosy and attractive. Eyes full of fire, and a rounded throat, with a waxy softness of outline that recalled a nightingale's, gave point to her beauty. She was exquisitely dressed in a pale cream bodice, with what passes on the stage for a peasant kirtle, and round her rich brown neck she wore a drooping circlet of half-barbaric-looking lance-like red coral pendants. Before she opened her mouth, her mere form and grace of movement took the house by surprise. A little storm of applause burst spontaneous at once from stalls, boxes, and gallery. The singer paused, and curtsied. She looked lovelier still as she flushed up with excitement. Every eye in the house was instinctively fixed upon her.

Will had been gazing round the boxes as the actress entered, to see what friends of his they might contain, and to nod recognition. The burst of applause recalled him suddenly to what was passing on the stage. He looked round and stared at her. For a moment he saw only a very beautiful girl, in the prime of her days, gracefully clad for her part, and most supple in her movements. At the self-same instant, before he had time to note more, the singer opened her mouth, and began to pour forth on his ear lavish floods of liquid music. Will started with surprise; in a flash of recognition, voice and face came back to him. He seized Florian by the arm. "Great God!" he cried, "it's Linnet!"

Florian struck a little attitude. "Oh, unexpected felicity! Oh, great gain!" he murmured, in his supremest manner. "You're right! So it is! A most undoubted Linnet!"

And Linnet it was; dressed in the impossible peasant costume of theatrical fancy; grown fuller and more beautiful about the neck and throat; with her delicate voice highly trained and developed by all that Italian or Bavarian masters could suggest to improve it; but Linnet still for all that, the same beautiful, simple, sweet Linnet as ever.

Joaquin Holmes glanced at the programme. "And this," he murmured low, "is Signora Carlotta Casalmonte that I spoke about."

Florian's eyes opened wide. "Why, of course!" he exclaimed with a start. "I wonder we didn't see it. It's a mere translation: Casalmonte—Hausberger: Carlotta—Carolina—Lina—Linnet; there you have it!" And he turned, self-applausive of his own cleverness, to Rue, who sat beside him.

As for Rue, her first feeling was a sudden flush of pain; so this girl had come back to keep Will still apart from her! One moment later that feeling gave place with lightning speed to another; would he care for this peasant woman so much, and regret her so deeply, if he saw her here in England, another man's wife, and an actress on the stage, dressed up in all the vulgar tinsel gew-gaws, surrounded by all the sordid disenchanting realities of theatrical existence?

But Will himself knew two things, and two things alone. That was Linnet who stood singing there— and she wore the necklet he had sent her from Innsbruck.

CHAPTER XXIX

FROM LINNET'S STANDPOINT

Yes; it was Linnet indeed! The natural chances of Will's profession had thrown them together almost inevitably on the very first night of her appearance in London.

Linnet had looked forward to that night; she had always expected it. During those three long years that had passed since they parted, she had never yet ceased to hope and believe that Andreas would some day take her to England. And if to England, then to London, and Will Deverill. But much had happened meanwhile. She was the self-same Linnet still, in heart and in soul, yet, oh! how greatly changed in externals of every sort. Those three years and a half had made a new woman of her in art, in knowledge, in culture, in intellect. She had left the Tyrol a mere ignorant peasant-girl; she came to London now an educated lady, an accomplished vocalist, a powerful actress, a finished woman of society.

And it was Will Deverill who had first put into her head and heart the idea and the desire of attaining such perfect mastery in her chosen vocation. The capacity, the potentiality, the impulse, the instinct, were all there beforehand; no polish on earth can ever possibly turn a common stone into a gem of the first water: the beauty of colour, the delicacy of grain must be inherent from the outset, only waiting for the art of the skilful lapidary to bring them visibly out and make them publicly manifest. So Linnet had been a lady in fibre from the very first, inheriting the profound Tyrolese capacity for artistic receptiveness and artistic effort; everything that was beautiful in external Nature or human handicraft spoke straight to her heart with an immediate message—spoke so clear that Linnet could not choose but listen. Still, it was Will Deverill's words and Will Deverill's example that first set her soul upon the true path of development. It was he who had read her Goethe's Faust on the Küchelberg; it was he who had explained to her the rude Romanesque designs on the portal of the Rittersaal. She had treasured up those first lessons in her inmost heart: they were the key that unlocked for her the front door of culture.

Andreas Hausberger, for his part, could never have taught her so. He had taken her straight from Meran to Verona and Milan. But his soul was bounded by the one idea of music. Even in the first poignant sorrow of that hateful honeymoon, however, Linnet had found time to gaze in wonder at the great amphitheatre, still haunted by the spectral form of the legendary Dietrich; to cry like a child over the narrow tomb where Juliet never lay; to tread with silent awe the vast aisles and solemn crypt of San Zeno Maggiore. At Milan, they loitered long; Andreas set her to work at once under a famous local teacher, and took her often in the evening to hear celebrated singers on the stage of La Scala. Such elements in an artistic education he thoroughly understood, but it never would have occurred to his mind as any part of a soprano's training to make her examine the Luinis and Borgognones of the Brera, or do homage before the exquisite Botticellis and Peruginos of the

Museo Poldi-Pezzoli. To the Wirth of St Valentin such excursions into the sister arts would have seemed mere waste of valuable time, for Andreas regarded music as a branch of trade, and had not that higher wisdom which understands instinctively how every form of art reflects its influence indirectly on the musician's mind and the musician's inspiration. That wisdom Linnet possessed, and Andreas, after a few ineffectual remonstrances, let her go her own way and live her own artistic life unchecked to the top of her bent—the more so as he perceived she sang best and most vigorously when least thwarted or worried. Moreover, many well-advised friends assured him in private it was desirable for an actress to know as much as possible of costume, of colour, of posture, and of grouping, which could best be learned by studying the works of the great early painters.

So Linnet went her way, undeterred by her husband, and educated herself in general culture at the same time that she received her strict musical training. She knew Raphael's Sposalizio as intimately after a while as she knew her own châlet; she gazed on the flowing lines of Luini's frescoes till they grew familiar to her eyes as the Stations of the Cross in the old church at St Valentin. She drank in the cathedral with an endless joy; she loved its innumerable pinnacles, its thousand statues in the marble niches: she admired the gloomy antiquity of mouldering Sant' Ambrogio, the dim religious aisles of Santa Maria delle Grazie. Amid surroundings like these, her artistic nature expanded by degrees as naturally as a bud opens out into a flower before the summer sunshine. She revelled in the architecture, the pictures, the statuary: Milan stood to the soul of the peasant-singer as a veritable university.

It was the first time, too, that Linnet had ever found herself in a bustling, business-like, modern city. The hurry and scurry were as new as the art to her. The throng of men and women in the crowded streets, the Piazza, brilliant with the flare of glowing lamps, the great glass-roofed gallery where the gilded Lombard youth promenaded by night in twos and threes, or sipped absinthe before the doors of dazzling cafés: all these were quite fresh, and all these were, in their way, too, an element of education. There are many who can see no more in Milan than this: they know it only as the most go-ahead and modernised of Italian cities. Linnet knew better. To her it was the town of Leonardo and his disciples, of the great marble pile whose infinite detail escapes and eludes the most observant eye, of the vast and stately opera house where Otello and Carmen first unfolded their wonders of sight and sound to her ecstatic senses. Wiser in her generation, she accepted it aright as the vestibule and ante-chamber of artistic Italy.

From Milan they went on in due time to Florence. There they stopped less long, for opportunities of learning were not by any means so good as at Milan and Naples. But those few short weeks in the City of the Soul were to Linnet as a dream of some artistic Paradise; they made her half forget, for the moment at least, her lost English lover—and her husband's presence. The Duomo, the Palazzo Vecchio, the Loggia, the Piazza, the old bridge across the Arno, the enchanted market-place; Michael Angelo's tomb, Giotto's crusted campanile! What hours she spent, entranced, in the endless halls of the Uffizi and the Pitti; what moments of hushed awe and rapt silence of soul before the pallid Fra Angelicos in the dim cells of San Marco. Ach, Gott, it was beautiful! Linnet gazed with the intense delight of her mountain nature at Raphael's Madonnas and Andrea's Holy Families; she stood spellbound before the exquisite young David of the Academia; she wandered with a strange thrill among the marvellous della Robbias and Donatellos of the Bargello. The Tyrolese temperament is before all things artistic. A new sense seemed quickened within Linnet's soul as she trod those glorious palaces instinct with memories of the Medici and their compeers. A great thirst for knowledge possessed her heart. She read as she had never known how to read before. That Florentine time was as her freshman year in the splendid quadrangles of this Italian Oxford.

Then Rome—the Vatican, the Colosseum, the monuments, St Peter's, the loud organs, the singing boys, the incense, the purple robes and mitres, the great guttering candles! All that could awake in unison every chord of religion and its sister art, in that simple religious artistic nature, was there to gratify her! It was glorious! it was wonderful! So her winter passed away, her first winter with Andreas; she was learning fast, both with eye and with ear, all that Italy and its masters could possibly teach her.

As spring returned, they went northward through Lombardy and the Brenner once more on their way to Munich. Her own Tyrol looked more beautiful than ever as they passed, with its unmelted snows lying thick on the mountains. But, save for a night at Innsbruck, they might not stop there. Yet, even after that short lapse of time in southern cities, oh, how different, how altered little Innsbruck seemed to her! She had thought it before such a grand big town; she thought it now so much shrunken, so old-world, so quaint, so homely. And then, no Will Deverill was there, as before, to brighten it. The mountains gazed down as of old from their precipitous crags upon the nestling town; they were Tyrolese and home-like; and therefore she loved them. But everything had a smaller and meaner air than six months earlier; the queer old High Street was just odd, not magnificent; the Anna Säule was dwarfed, the Rathhaus had grown smaller. She had only seen Milan, Florence, Rome, meanwhile; but Milan, Florence, Rome, made Innsbruck sink at once to its proper place as a mere provincial capital. While they waited for the Munich train next morning, she strolled into the Hofkirche, to see once more Maximilian's tomb with its attendant figures. She started at the sight. After the Venus and the Laocoon it surprised her to think she could so lately have stood awestruck before those naïf bronze abortions!

That summer they spent in Germany, almost wholly at Munich. There Linnet went through a course of musical training under a well-known teacher, and there, too, she had ample opportunities, at the same time, of cultivating to the full her general artistic faculties. Next winter, back to Italy—this time to Venice, Rome, and Naples. Linnet learnt much once more; it was all so glorious; the Grand Canal, St Mark's, the Academy, the Frari, Sorrento, Capri, Pozzuoli, the great operas at San Carlo. So she stored her brain all the time with fresh experiences of men, women, and things; with pictures of places, of architecture, of sculpture, of scenery. Everywhere her quick mind assimilated at once all that was best and most valuable in what she saw or listened to; by eye and by ear alike, she was half-unconsciously educating herself.

But that wasn't all. She had ideas as well of still higher education. Will Deverill had given her the first key to books—and books are the gateways of the deepest knowledge. Partly to escape from the monotony of Andreas Hausberger's conversation, partly also quite definitely to fit herself for the place in the world she was hereafter to fill, when she went to England, Linnet turned to books as new friends and companions. German literature first of all, and especially the dramatic. Andreas was wise enough in his generation to approve of that; he was aware that acquaintance with plays and with romantic works in general forms no small integral part of an opera-singer's equipment. German literature, then, first—Goethe, Schiller, Lessing, Richter, Paul Heyse, Freiligrath—German literature first, but after it English. Andreas approved of that, too, for was there not much money to be made out of England and America? It was well Linnet should enlarge her English vocabulary; well, too, she should know the plays and novels on which Romeo e Giulietta, and Lucia di Lammermoor, and I Puritani were founded. But Linnet herself had other reasons of her own for wishing to study English. Though she looked upon Will Deverill as something utterly lost to her, a bright element in her life now faded away for ever, she yet cherished the memory of that one real love episode so deep in her heart that, for her Englishman's sake, she loved England and English. She looked forward to the time when she should go to England; not so much because she thought she should ever meet Will Deverill there—Naples and Munich had taught her vaguely to appreciate the probable vastness of London— but because it was the country where Will Deverill lived, and it spoke the tongue Will had made so dear to her. So she read every English book she could easily obtain—Shakespeare, Milton, Scott,

Dickens, Thackeray—and she took oral lessons in conversational English, which as Andreas justly remarked, would improve her accent, and enable her to sing better in English opera.

Thus three years passed away, and Linnet in their course saw much of the Continent. They got as far north and west at times as Leipzig, Brussels, and even Paris. But they always spent their winters in Italy; it was best for Linnet's throat, Andreas thought; it gave her abundance of fresh air and sunshine; and besides, the Italian style of teaching was better suited, he felt sure, to her ardent, excitable Tyrolese temperament, than the colder and more learned Bavarian method.

'Twas at Naples, accordingly, that Linnet came out first as Signora Casalmonte. But after a short season there, Andreas was quite sufficiently assured of ultimate success to venture upon taking his prize at once to England. He would sell his goods, like a prudent merchant that he was, in the dearest market. When Linnet first learned she was to go to London, a certain strange thrill of joy and hope and fear coursed through her irresistibly. London! that was the place where Will Deverill lived! London! that was the place where she soon might meet him!

She clasped the little metal Madonna that still hung from her neck, convulsively. "Our Dear Frau, oh, protect me! Save me, oh, save me from the thoughts of my own heart! Help me to think of him less! Help me to try and forget him!"

She was Andreas Hausberger's wife now, and she meant to be true to him. Love him she never could, but she could at least be true to him. Not in deed alone, but in thought and in word, as Our Dear Frau knew, she strove hard to be faithful.

Then came the first fluttering excitement and disappointment of London—that dingy Eldorado, so rich, so miserable—the dim, dank streets, the glare, the gloom, the opulence, the squalor of our fog-bound metropolis! For a week or two, thank Heaven, Linnet was too busy at arrangements and rehearsals to think of surroundings. They were the weeks during which Will was away in the Provinces, or he must almost certainly have heard of and attended the preliminary performances of the forthcoming opera. The final day arrived, and Linnet, all tremulous at the greatness of the stake, had to make her first appearance before that stolid sea of unsympathetic, hide-bound English faces. She had peeped at them from the wings before the curtain rose; oh, how her heart sank within her. The respectable sobriety of stalls and boxes, the square-jawed brutality of pit and gallery, the cynical aspect of the gentlemen of the press, in their faultless evening clothes and unruffled shirt-fronts—all contrasted so painfully with the vivid excitement and frank expectancy of the Neapolitan audiences to which alone she had hitherto been accustomed. One brighter thought, and only one, sustained her—Dear Lady, forgive her that she should think of it now! these were all Herr Will's people, and they spoke Herr Will's tongue; as Herr Will was kind, would not they too be kind to her?

So, plucking up heart of grace, though trembling all over, she tripped down the stage rocks with her free gait of a sennerin. To her joy and surprise, a burst of applause rose responsive at once from those seemingly irresponsive dress-coated stalls, those stolidly brutal and square-faced pittites. Her mere beauty stirred them. Even the gentlemen of the press, smiling cynically still, drummed their fingers gently on the flat tops of their opera-hats. Thus encouraged, Linnet opened her mouth and sang. Her throat rose and fell in a rhythmical tide. She rendered the first stanza of her first song almost faultlessly. She knew, herself, she had never sung better. Then came a brief pause before she went on to the second. During that pause, she raised her eyes to a box of the first tier. The Blessed Madonna in Britannia metal on the oval pendant, ever faithful at a pinch, almost crumpled in her grasp as she looked and started. It was Will she saw there, Will, Will, her dear Englishman; and Herr Florian by his elbow, and the grand foreign Frau, the fair-haired Frau, the Frau with the diamonds, ever still beside them!

In a second, Linnet felt from head to foot a great thrill break over her. It broke like a wave of fire, in long, undulating movement, as she had felt it at Innsbruck. The wave rose from her feet, as before, and coursed hot through her limbs, and burnt bright in her body, till it came out as a crimson flush on neck and chin and forehead. Then it descended once more, thrilling through her as it went, in long, undulating movement, from her neck to her feet again. She felt it as distinctly as she could feel Our Blessed Lady clenched hard in her little fist. Her Englishman was there, whom she thought she had lost; as at Innsbruck, so in London, he had come to hear her sing her first song in public!

All at once, yet again, the same strange seizure came over her. As her eyes met Will's, and that wave of fire ran resistlessly through her, she was conscious of a weird sense she had known but once in all her life before—a sudden failure of sound, a numb deadening of the orchestra. Not a note struck her ear. It was all a vast blank to her. Instinctively, as she sang, her right hand toyed with Will's coral necklet, but her left, with all its might, still gripped and clasped Our Lady with trembling fingers. She heard not a word she herself was uttering; she knew not how she sang, or whether she sang at all; in an agony of terror, of remorse, of shame, she kept her eyes fixed on the conductor's bâton. By its aid alone she kept true to her accompaniment. But her heart went up silently in one great prayer to Our Lady. When she felt this at Innsbruck she knew it was love. If it meant love still—Andreas Hausberger's wife—Oh! Blessed Mother, help! Oh! Dear Lady, protect her!

CHAPTER XXX

AN UNEXPECTED VISITOR

How she got through that song, how she got through that scene, Linnet never knew. She was conscious of but two things—Will Deverill's presence and the Blessed Madonna. Remorse and shame almost choked her utterance. But mechanically she went on, and sang her part out to the end—sang it exquisitely, superbly. Have you ever noticed that what we do most automatically, we often do best? It was so that night at the Harmony with Linnet. She knew her music well; she had studied it carefully; and the very absence of self-consciousness which this recognition gave her, made her sing it more artlessly, yet more perfectly than ever. She forgot the actress and the singer in the woman. That suited her best of all. Her mental existence was divided, as it were, into two distinct halves; one conscious and personal, absorbed with Will Deverill and Our Dear Lady in Britannia metal; the other unconscious and automatic, pouring forth with a full throat the notes and words it was wound up to utter. And the automatic self did its work to perfection. The audience hung entranced; Andreas Hausberger, watching them narrowly from a box at the side, hugged his sordid soul in rapture at the thought that Linnet had captured them on this her first night in that golden England.

She sang on and on. The audience sat enthralled. Gradually, by slow stages, the sense of hearing came back to her. But she had done as well, or even better without it. The act went off splendidly. Andreas Hausberger was in transports. At the first interval between the scenes, Rue debated in her own soul what to do about Linnet; but, being a wise woman in her way, she determined to wait till the end of the piece before deciding on action. Act the Second, Act the Third, Act the Fourth followed fast; in Act the Fifth when Linnet, no longer a peasant girl, but the bride of the Grand Duke, came on in her beautiful pale primrose brocade, cut square in the bodice like a picture of Titian's, the audience cheered again with a vociferous outburst. Linnet blushed and bowed; a glow of conscious triumph suffused her face; then she raised her eyes timidly to the box on the first tier. Her victory was complete. She could see by his face Will Deverill was satisfied—and the grand lady with the diamonds was sincerely applauding her.

Was the grand lady his wife? Why not? Why not? What could it matter to her now? She was Andreas Hausberger's. And Will—why, Will was but an old Zillerthal acquaintance.

Yet she clutched Our Blessed Frau tighter than ever in her grasp, at that painful thought, and somehow hoped illogically Our Blessed Frau would protect her from the chance of the grand lady being really married to Will Deverill. Not even the gods, says Aristotle, in his philosophic calm, can make the past not have been as it was. But Linnet thought otherwise.

The curtain fell to a storm of clapping hands. After that a moment's lull; then loud cries of "Casalmonte!" The whole theatre rang with them. The Papadopoli, revived by magic from his open-air deathbed on the blood-stained grass, came forward before the curtain, alive and well, his wounds all healed, leading Linnet on his right, and bowing their joint acknowledgments. At sight of the soprano, even the cynical critics yielded spontaneous homage. It was a great success; a very great success. Linnet panted, and bowed low. Surely she had much to be grateful for that night; surely the Blessed Madonna in heaven above had stood by her well through that trying ordeal!

But in Rue Palmer's box, after all was over, Florian's voice rose loud in praise of this new star in our musical firmament. "When first she swam into my ken," he said, "on her Tyrolese hillside, you remember it, Deverill, I said to myself, 'Behold a singer indeed! Some day, we may be sure, we shall welcome her in London.' And now, could any mortal mixture of earth's mould breathe purer music or more innate poesy?"

For it was Florian's cue, as things stood, to make much of Linnet, for many reasons. In the first place, it would reflect credit and glory on his insight as a critic that he should have spotted this flaming comet of a season while as yet it loomed no larger than the eleventh magnitude. Indeed, he had gone down among the other critics between the acts, and buttonholed each of them in the lobby, separately. "A discovery of my own, I can assure you. I found her out as a peasant-girl in a Tyrolese valley, and advised her friends to have her trained and educated." Then, again, his praise of Linnet no doubt piqued Rue; and Florian, in spite of rebuffs, had still one eye vaguely fixed in reserve on Rue's seven hundred thousand. Faint heart, he well knew, never won fair lady. Besides, Florian felt it was a good thing Will's cow-girl should have come back to him in London thus transformed and transfigured; for he recognised in Will his one dangerous rival for Rue's affections, and he was bent as of old on getting rid of Will by diverting him, if possible, upon poor helpless Linnet. The mere fact of her being married mattered little to a philosopher. So he murmured more than once, as Linnet bowed deeper and deeper, "What a beautiful creature she is, to be sure! You remember, Will, what I said of her when we met her first in the Zillerthal?"

Even poets are human. There was a malicious little twinkle in the corner of Will's eye as he answered briskly, "Oh yes; I remember it word for word, my dear fellow. You said, you thought with time and training, she ought to serve Andreas Hausberger's purpose well enough for popular entertainments. Her voice, though undeveloped, was not wholly without some natural compass."

Will had treasured up those words. Florian winced at them a little, they were not quite as enthusiastic as he could have wished just now; but he recovered himself dexterously. "And I told Hausberger," he went on, "it was a sin and a shame to waste a throat like that on a Tyrolese troupe; and, happily, he took my advice at once, and had her prepared for the stage by the very best teachers in Italy and Germany. I'm proud of her success. It's insight, after all, insight, insight alone, that makes and marks the Heaven-born Critic."

Rue was writing meanwhile a hurried little note in pencil on the back of a programme. She had debated with herself during the course of the piece whether or not to send down and ask Linnet to visit them. Her true woman's nature took naturally at last the most generous course, which was also the safest one. She folded the piece of paper into a three-cornered twist, and handed it with one of her sunny smiles to the Seer. It was addressed "Herr Hausberger." "Will you take that down for me, Mr Holmes?" she asked, with a little tremor, "and tell one of the waiting-girls to give it at once to Madame Casalmonte's husband."

The Seer accepted the commission with delighted alacrity. In a moment he had spied game; his quick eye, intuitive as a woman's, had read at a glance conflicting emotions on Rue's face, and Will's and Florian's. Whatever else it might mean, it meant grist for the mill; he would make his market of it. A suspicion of intrigue is the thought-reader's opportunity.

Linnet was standing at the wings in a flutter of excitement, all tremulous from her triumph, and wondering whether or not Will would come down to ask for her, when Andreas Hausberger bustled up, much interested, evidently, with some pleasurable emotion. He had seen his wife between the acts already, and assured her of his satisfaction at so fortunate an event for the family exchequer. But now he came forward, brimming over with fresh pleasure, and waving a note in his hand, as he said to her briskly in German, "Don't wait to change, Linnet. This is really most lucky. Mrs Palmer, the lady we met at Innsbruck, you know, wants to see you in her box. She's immensely rich, I'm told; and Florian Wood's up there with her. The manager assures me he's one of the most influential critics in London. Come along, just as you are, and mind you speak nicely to her."

The lights were left burning long in the passages, as is often the case on first nights in London. Andreas led the way; Linnet followed him like one blindfolded. Oh, Blessed Madonna, how strangely you order things on this earth of yours sometimes! It was her husband himself, then, of all men in the world, who was taking her to the box where Will Deverill was waiting for her!

As for Andreas Hausberger, he stalked on before, elated, hardly thinking of Will, as indeed he had no cause to do. The rich woman of the world and the influential critic monopolised his attention. Tyrolese though he was, he was by no means jealous; greed of gain had swallowed up in him all the available passions of that phlegmatic nature. Linnet was his chattel now; he had married her and trained her; her earnings were his own, doubly mortgaged to him for life, and no poet on earth, be he ever so seductive, could charm them away from him.

He opened the box door with stately dignity. At St Valentin or in London, he was a person of importance. Linnet entered, quivering. She still wore her primrose brocade, as all through the last act, and she looked in it, even yet, a very great lady. Not Rue herself looked so great or so grand, charming, smiling Rue, as she rose to greet her. They stood and faced each other. One second Rue paused; then a womanly instinct all at once overcame her. Leaning forward with the impulse, she kissed the beautiful, stately creature on both cheeks with effusion, in unfeigned enthusiasm.

"Why, Linnet," she said, simply, as if she had always known her; "we're so glad to see you, to be the very first to congratulate you on your success this evening!"

A flood of genuine passion rushed hot into Linnet's face. Her warm southern nature responded at once to the pressure of Rue's hand. She seized her new friend by either arm, and returned her double kiss in a transport of gratitude. "Dear lady," she said, with fervour, in her still imperfect English, "how sweet that you receive me so! How kind and good you English are to me!"

Andreas Hausberger's white shirt-front swelled with expansive joy. This all meant money. They were really making wonderful strides in England.

Will held his hand out timidly. "Have you forgotten me, Frau Hausberger?" he asked her in German.

Linnet's face flushed a still deeper crimson than before, as she answered frankly, "Forgotten you, Herr Will. Ach, lieber Gott, no! How kind of you . . . to come and hear my first performance!"

"Nor me either, Linnet, I hope," Florian interposed more familiarly, in his native tongue; for he had caught at the meaning of that brief Teutonic interlude. "I shall always feel proud, Herr Andreas, to think it was I who first discovered this charming song-bird's voice among its native mountains."

But Will found no such words. He only gazed at his recovered peasant-love with profound admiration. Fine feathers make fine birds, and it was wonderful how much more of a personage Linnet looked as she stood there to-night in her primrose brocade, than she had looked nearly four years since in her bodice and kirtle on the slopes of the Zillerthal. She was beautiful then, but she was queenly now, and it was not dress alone, either, that made all the difference. Since leaving the Tyrol, Linnet had blossomed out fast into dignified womanhood. All that she had learnt and seen meanwhile had impressed itself vividly on her face and features. So they sat for awhile in blissful converse, and talked of what had happened to each in the interval. Rue sent Florian down with a message to ask their friend the manager not to turn his gas off while the party remained there. The manager, bland and smiling, and delighted at his prima donna's excellent reception, joined the group in the box, and insisted that they should all accompany him to supper. To this, the Sartorises demurred, on the whispered ground of dear Arthur's position. Dear Arthur himself, indeed, resisted but feebly; it was Maud who was firm; but Maud was firm as a rock about it. Let dear Arthur go to supper with a theatrical manager, to meet a bedizened young woman from a playhouse like that, and him a beneficed clergyman with an eye to a canonry! Maud simply put her foot down.

So the Sartorises went home in a discreet four-wheeler; but the rest lingered on, and gossipped of old times in the Tyrol together, and heard each others' tales with the deepest interest.

"And your mother?" Will asked at last; he was the first who had thought of her.

Linnet's face fell fast. She clasped her dark hands tight. "Ah, that dear mother," she said, with a deep-drawn sigh, and a mute prayer to Our Lady. "She died last winter, when I was away from home, away down in Venice. I couldn't get back to her. 'Twas the Herr Vicar's fault. He never wrote she was ill till the dear God had taken her. It was too late then. I couldn't even go home to say a pater noster over her."

"So now you're alone in the world," Will murmured, gazing hard at her.

"Yes; now I'm alone in the world," Linnet echoed, sadly.

"But you have your husband, of course," Florian put in, with a wicked smile, and a side glance at Andreas, who for his part was engaged in paying court most assiduously to the rich young widow.

Linnet looked up with parted lips. "Ah, yes; I have my husband," she answered, as by an afterthought, in a very subdued tone, which sent a pang and a thrill through Will's heart at once, so much did it tell him. He knew from those few words she wasn't happy in her married life. How could she be, indeed, such a soul as hers, with such a man as Andreas?

Their first gossip was over, and they were just getting ready to start for supper, when one of the box-keepers knocked at the door with a card in his hand, which he passed to Andreas Hausberger. "There's a gentleman here who's been waiting outside for some time to see you," he said; "and he asked me to give you this card at once, if you'll kindly step down to him, sir."

Andreas took it with a smile, and gazed at it unconcernedly. But a dash of colour mounted suddenly into those pale brown cheeks, as his eye caught the words neatly engraved on the card, "Mr Franz Lindner," and below in the corner, "Signor Francesco, The London Pavilion."

CHAPTER XXXI

WHEN GREEK MEETS GREEK

Andreas handed the card to Will with a sardonic smile. "That wild fellow again," he muttered. "I didn't know he was in England. I suppose I must go down to the door to see him."

But Will glanced at the name in profound dismay. It was an awkward moment. Heaven knew what might come of it. As he gazed and paused, all that Franz had said to him at the Criterion bar a year before recurred to his mind vividly. He seized Hausberger's arm with a nervous clutch, and drew him a little aside. "Take care of this man Lindner," he said in a warning whisper. "He doesn't love you. He is not to be trusted. If I were you, I wouldn't see him alone. He owes you a grudge. Ask him up here, and talk with him before us all and the ladies."

"Did you know he was in London?" Andreas inquired, scarcely flinching.

"Yes; I met him by accident in Bond Street a year ago. I've been to hear him sing at the music hall where he works, and he came with Mr Wood and myself to the Duke of Edinburgh's to see Sweet Maisie, one of my pieces. But he was breathing forth fire and slaughter against you, even then, for leaving him in the lurch that time at Meran. To tell you the truth, he's a dangerous man in a dangerous mood; I can't answer for what may happen if you go down alone to him."

"Let me go down and fetch him," Florian suggested, blandly. "The job would just suit me. I'm warranted to disarm the most truculent fool in Christendom with a smile and a word or two."

To this middle course Andreas consented somewhat doubtfully. He knew Franz's temper and his Tyrolese impetuosity; but, as a Tyroler himself, hot-hearted at core for all his apparent phlegm, he didn't feel inclined to parley through an ambassador with a pretentious Robbler. However, a scene on the first night would be bad business. That touched a tender point. So he gave way ungraciously. Florian departed, full of importance at his post of envoy, and returned in a minute or two with the Robbler's ultimatum. "He's been drinking, I fancy," he said, "and he's very wild and excited; Montepulciano in his eye, Lacrima Christi in his gait, Falernian in his utterance. But he'll come up if you like; only I thought, Rue, as it's your box, I'd better ask you first whether you'd care to see him."

"He isn't drunk, is he?" Rue asked, shrinking back. "We couldn't have a drunken man shown up into the box here."

"Not more drunk than a gentleman should be," Florian answered, airily. "He can walk and talk, and I think he can behave himself. But he's a good deal flushed, and somewhat flustered, and he expresses a burning desire for Herr Hausberger's heart-blood, in a guttural bass, with quite unbecoming ferocity."

Rue shrank away with a frightened face. "Oh, don't bring him up here!" she cried. "Please, Florian, don't bring him up here. I'm so afraid of tipsy men; and you don't really think he wants to murder Herr Hausberger?"

"Well, not exactly to murder him, perhaps," Florian replied, with a tolerant and expansive smile; "that would be positively vulgar; but to fight him, no doubt; and, if possible, to put an end to him. The duel in one form or another, you see, is a most polite institution. We don't call it murder in good Society. Lindner feels himself aggrieved—there's a lady in the case—" and he gave an expressive side-glance over his shoulder towards Linnet, "so he desires to bury his knife to the hilt in the gentleman's body whom, rightly or wrongly, he conceives to have acted ill towards him. Nothing vulgar in that you'll allow: a most natural sentiment. Only, as Herr Hausberger's friends in this little affair, we must strive our best to see that all things are done, as the apostle advises, decently and in order."

Linnet drew back with a convulsive gasp. Was this bloodshed they contemplated, and were talking of so calmly? Will laid his hand on Rue's arm. Even in the heat of the moment, Linnet noticed that simple action, and, she knew not why, her heart sank within her.

"If I were you, Rue," Will put in very hurriedly, "I'd let this man come in; drunk or sober, I'd see him. It's better he should speak with Herr Hausberger here than anywhere else. Try to sink your own feelings and put up with him for a minute or two. If you don't, I'm afraid I can't answer for the consequences."

He spoke very seriously. Rue drew back, still shrinking. Her face was pale but her voice was firm. "Very well, Will," she answered, without another word of demur. "I hate a tipsy man; but if you wish it, I'll see him here."

Linnet noticed the lingering stress of her voice on the you, and the obvious familiarity that subsisted between them; and she thought to herself once more, what did it matter to her?—she was Andreas Hausberger's wife now. Blessed Madonna, protect her!

Florian disappeared a second time, buoyant as usual, and came back in a minute—bringing Franz Lindner with him. The Seer had left the box some moments earlier; Linnet and Rue stood forward towards the door, as if to break the attack, with Andreas in the background, between Will and the manager. Florian flung the door open with his customary flourish. "Mr Franz Lindner!" he said, introducing him with a wave of his dainty small hand, "whose charming performance on the zither we had the pleasure of hearing, you will recollect, Rue, with Signora Casalmonte, some years ago at Innsbruck."

The Robbler stepped into the box, erect, haughty, defiant. His handsome face was flushed and flown with drink; but his manner was alert, self-respecting, angry. He glared about him with fierce eyes. His left hand, held to his bosom, just defined between finger and thumb the vague shape of the bowie in his breast coat pocket; his right was disengaged with a tremulous quiver, as if in readiness to spring at Andreas Hausberger and throttle him.

With unexpected presence of mind, Rue extended her pretty gloved hand towards the Robbler, cordially, as if she fancied he had come on the most ordinary errand. "We're so glad to see you, Mr Lindner," she cried, in a natural voice, and with apparent frankness—though that was a fearful feminine fib; "I remember so well your delightful jodels! You were a member of Herr Hausberger's company then, I recollect. How charmingly his wife has been singing here this evening!"

The Robbler gazed about him, a little disconcerted at so different a welcome from the one he had expected. However, as things stood, the acquired instincts of civilisation compelled him to hold in check for a moment the more deeply ingrained impulses of his mountain nature. Besides, Rue's words appealed at once to his personal vanity. To think that this beautiful and exquisitely-dressed lady, with the diamonds on her white neck, and the dainty pale gloves on her tapering fingers, should receive him in her box like a gentleman and an equal! How could he jump at his enemy's throat then and there before her eyes? How remain insensible to so much grace, so much tact, so much elegance? Moreover, he was taken aback by the number of persons in the box, the unexpected brilliancy, the imposing evening dress, Linnet's stately costume, Rue's dazzling jewellery. He had come up there, meaning to rush at his antagonist the very moment he saw him, and plunge a knife into his heart, like a true Tyrolese Robbler, even here in London. Instead of that, he paused irresolute, took the gloved hand in his, bent over it with the native dignity and courtesy of his race, and faltered, in broken English, some inarticulate words of genuine gratification that Mrs Palmer should deign to remember so kindly his poor performances on the zither at Innsbruck.

Then Will came forward in turn, seized the Robbler's right hand, wrang it hard and long, just to occupy the time, and prevent possible mischief, and poured forth hurried remarks, one after another, hastily, about Linnet's first appearance, and the success of her singing. It was a friendly meeting. The manager chimed in, with Florian in his most ecstatic mood for chorus. Franz Lindner's blood boiled; dazed and startled as he was, more than ever now he felt in his heart of how great a prize Andreas Hausberger had defrauded him. By trickery and stealth that sordid wretch had defrauded him. The ladies at the London Pavilion, indeed! Why, Linnet on those boards, Linnet in that dress, Linnet in her transformed and transfigured beauty, she was worth the whole troupe of them! Yet what could he do? Linnet held out her frank hand; Franz grasped it fervently. Her beauty surprised him. She was no longer, he saw well, the mere musical peasant girl; she had risen to the situation; she was now a great artist, a great lady, a queen of the theatre.

Primitive natures are quick. Their emotions are few, but strong and overpowering. Mood succeeds mood with something of the rapidity and successive effacement we see in children. Franz Lindner had entered that box, full of rage and anger, thirsting only for blood, eager to wreak his vengeance on the man who had offended him. He had no thought of love for Linnet then; only a fierce, keen sense of deadly resentment towards Andreas. Now, in a moment, as Linnet let her soft hand lie passive in his, like an old friend recovered, another set of feelings rushed over him irresistibly. His heart leaped up into his mouth at her pressure. Why, Linnet was beautiful; Linnet was exquisite; Linnet was a prize worth any man's winning. If he stabbed Andreas then and there before his wife's very eyes, he might glut his revenge, to be sure, but what would that avail him? Why go and be hanged for killing Linnet's husband, and leave Linnet herself for some other man to woo, and win, and be happy with? Herr Will, there, would thank him, no doubt, for that chance; for he could plainly see by his eyes Herr Will was still deeply in love with Linnet. No, no, hot heart; down, down for the present! Keep your hands off Andreas's throat; wait for sweeter vengeance! To win away his wife from him, to steal her by force, to seduce her by soft words, to wile her by blandishment—that were a better revenge in the end than to stick a knife in him now—though to stick a knife, too, is very good requital! Sooner or later, Franz meant to have Andreas Hausberger's blood. But not to be hanged for it. He would rather live on . . . to kill Hausberger first, and enjoy his wife afterwards.

All this, quick as lightning, not thought but felt in an indivisible flash of time, darted fast through Franz Lindner's seething brain, at touch of Linnet's fingers. She spoke a few words to him of friendly reminiscence. Then Andreas, stepping forward, held out his hand in turn. It was a critical moment.

Linnet's heart stood still. Franz lifted his arm, half hesitating, towards his breast coat pocket. Should he stab him—or wring his hand? The surroundings settled it. It's a thousand times harder to plunge your knife into your man before the eyes of ladies and dramatic critics, in a box of a London theatre, than among the quarrelsome hinds on a Tyrolese hillside. Surlily and grudgingly, Franz lifted his right—extended it with an effort, and shook hands with his enemy. Rue and Linnet looked on in an agony of suspense. Once the grasp was over, every member of the party drew a deep breath involuntarily. The tension was relieved. Conversation ran on as if nothing had happened. The whole little episode occupied no more than two fleeting minutes. At its end they were all chatting with apparent unconcern about old times at Meran and old friends at St Valentin.

Franz was sobered by the conflict of emotion within him. The manager, with great tact and presence of mind, invited him promptly to join them at supper. Franz accepted with a good grace, uncertain yet how he stood with them, and became before long almost boisterously merry. He kept himself within due bounds, indeed, before the faces of the ladies, and drank his share of champagne with surprising moderation. But he talked unceasingly, for the most part to Linnet, Rue, and Florian; very little to Will; hardly at all to Andreas Hausberger. They sat late and long. They had all much to say, and Will, in particular, wished to notice with care the nature of the relations between Linnet and Andreas. At last they rose to go. Will saw Franz sedulously to the door of the supper-rooms. He wanted to make sure the man was really gone. Franz paused for a minute on the threshold of the steps, and gazed out with vague eyes on the slippery Strand. "Zat's a fine woman," he said, slowly; "a very fine woman. Andreas Hausberger took her from me. You saved his life zis night. But she's mine by ze right, and some day I shall claim her!"

Will took Rue home; she dismissed Florian early. In the brougham, as they drove, for some time neither spoke of the subject that was nearest both their hearts; an indescribable shyness possessed and silenced them. At last, Will said, tentatively, in a very timid voice, striking off at a tangent, "She's more beautiful than ever, and she sang to-night divinely. These years have done much for her, Rue. She returns to us still the same; and yet, oh, how altered!"

"Yes; she is beautiful," Rue answered, in a very low tone—"more beautiful than ever. And such a perfect lady, too—so charming and so graceful, one can't help loving her. I don't wonder at you men, Will, when even we women feel it."

They drove on for another minute or two, each musing silently. Then Will spoke again. "Do you think," he inquired, in a very anxious voice, "she's . . . she's happy with her husband?"

"No!" Rue answered, decisively. It was the short, sharp, extremely explosive "No" that closes a subject.

"I thought not, myself," Will went on, with still greater constraint. "I was afraid she wasn't. But . . . I thought . . . I might be prejudiced."

Rue lifted her eyes, and met his, by the gloom of the gas-lamps. "She's very unhappy with him," she burst out all at once with a woman's instinct. "She does not love him, and has never loved him. How could she, that block of ice, that lump of marble. She tries to do everything that's right and good towards him, because he's her husband, and she ought to behave so to him. She's a good woman, I'm sure, a pure, good woman; her soul's in her art, and she tries not to think too much of her unhappiness. But she loves somebody else best, and she knows she loves him. I saw it in her eyes, and I couldn't be deceived about it."

"You think so?" Will cried, eagerly. Her words were balm to him. Rue drew a deep sigh. "I don't think it; I know it," she answered, sadly.

"O Rue, how good you are," Will murmured, with a feeling very much like remorse. "What other woman on earth but yourself would tell me so?"

Rue sighed a second time. "I saw it in her eyes," she went on, looking hard at him still, "when first she noticed you; I saw it still more when that dreadful man Lindner came up into the box, and she waited trembling, to see what was going to happen. I watched her face; it was full of terror. But it wasn't the loving terror of a woman who thinks the husband she adores is just about to be attacked; it was the mere physical terror of a shrinking soul at the sight of a crime, a quarrel, a scuffle. You saved that man's life, Will; whether you know it or not, you saved it; for the other was a quarrelsome, revengeful fellow, who came there fully prepared, as Florian told us, to stab his rival. You saved his life; and when I looked at yourself, and Linnet standing by, I thought at the time what a bad turn you had done—"

"For her?" Will suggested, in a very low tone.

"Oh no," Rue answered aloud; "not for her alone, but for you as well, for you and her, for both of you."

CHAPTER XXXII

WEDDED FELICITY

Signora Casalmonte scored a distinct success. She was the great dramatic and musical reality of that London season. All the world flocked to hear her; her voice made the fortune of the Harmony Theatre. She was invited everywhere—"You must have the Casalmonte," Florian laid down the law in his dictatorial way to Belgravian hostesses—and Andreas Hausberger went always in charge, wherever she moved, to guard his splendid operatic property. And what care Andreas took of her! It was beautiful, beautiful! Unobservant people thought him a most devoted husband. He lingered always by the Signora's side; he supplied wraps and shawls on the remotest threat of a coming chill; he watched what she ate and drank with the composite eye of a lynx and a physician; he guarded her health from the faintest suspicion of danger in any way. On off-nights, he would seldom allow her to dine out or attend evening parties; on Sundays, he took her down for change of scene and fresh air to the sea or the country. Ozone was his hobby. Every day, the prima donna drove out in the Park, and then walked for exercise a full hour in Kensington Gardens. Unobservant people set all this down to the account of the domestic affections; Will Deverill noticed rather that Andreas guarded his wife as a racing man guards the rising hope of his stables. Andreas was far too sensible a man of the world to run any needless risks with the throat of the woman who made his fortune. He had staked a great deal on her, and he meant to be repaid with compound interest.

As for London itself, it went wild about Linnet. 'Twas the Casalmonte here, the Casalmonte there; the diva will sing at Lady Smith's to-night; the diva will go with Sir Thomas Brown and party to supper. Linnet's head was half-turned with so much admiration; if she hadn't been Linnet, indeed, it would have been turned altogether. But that simple childlike nature, though artistically developed and intellectually expanded, remained in emotion as straightforward and unaffected and confiding as ever. Still, that season did the best it knew to spoil her. She was queen of the situation. It rained choice flowers; diamond bracelets and painted fans showered down upon her plentifully. Linnet accepted all this homage, hardly realising its money worth; she was pleased if she gave pleasure; what others gave in return, she took as her right, quite simply and naturally. This charm of her simplicity surprised and delighted all who grew to know her; she had none of the affected airs and graces of the everyday great singer; she sang because she must; at heart she was, as always, the mountain-bred peasant-girl.

Will Deverill saw but little of her. 'Twas better so, he knew, and kinder so for Linnet. Once or twice that year, however, he supped after the theatre in the Strand with "the Hausbergers," as he had learned to call them. On all these occasions, he noticed, Andreas watched his wife close. "One glass of champagne, Linnet; you remember, last time, when you dined at the Mowbrays', you took two glasses, and you sang next day very much less well for it"; or else—"If I were you, Linnet, I wouldn't touch that lobster. It disagreed with you once, and I noticed in the evening one or two of your high notes were decidedly not so clear or so sharp as usual."

"But, Andreas," Linnet answered, on one such occasion, "I'm sure it doesn't hurt me. I must take something. I've hardly eaten a single mouthful yet, and to-night I'm so hungry."

"It does you no harm to be hungry," Andreas answered, philosophically. "Nobody ever reproached himself afterwards for having eaten too little. A taste of something to eat, after playing a trying part like Melinda, before you go to bed, helps you to sleep sound, and keeps you well and healthy; but a square meal at this hour can't be good for anybody. It interferes with rest; and what interferes with rest, tells, of course, upon the voice—which is very serious. You may have a bit of that sweetbread, if you like—no; that's a great deal too much; half that quantity, if you please, Mr Florian. Pull your woollen thing over your shoulder, so, Linnet; there's a draught from that door! I can't have you getting as hoarse as a frog to-night, with the Prince and Princess coming to hear you on Monday!"

"Why on earth does she stand it?" Florian asked of Will afterwards, as they walked home together down the unpeopled Strand. "I can't make it out. There she's earning Heaven only knows how much a night, and filling the treasury; yet she allows this fellow to bully her and badger her like this; to dictate to her how much she's to eat and to drink; to make her whole life one perpetual torment to her. Why doesn't she rise and strike for freedom, I wonder? He'd have to come to terms; she's too useful to him, you see, for him to risk a quarrel with her."

"She's too good—that's where it is," Will responded, with a tinge of stifled sadness in his voice; "and, besides, she doesn't care for him."

"Of course she doesn't," Florian answered, airily. "How could she, indeed!—a mass of selfishness like him!—so mean, so sordid! But that only makes it all the stranger she should ever put up with it. If she doesn't love him, why on earth does she permit him to dictate to her as he does—to order her and domineer over her?"

"Ah, that's how it looks to you," Will answered, with a sigh; "but Linnet—well, Linnet sees things otherwise. You must remember, Florian, above all things, she's a Catholic. She doesn't love that man, but she's entered with him into the sacrament of marriage. To her, it has all a religious significance. The less she loves Andreas, the more does she feel she must honour and obey him, and be a good true wife to him. If she loved him, she might perhaps sometimes rebel a little; because she doesn't love him, she has become a mere slave to do his bidding."

"I suppose that's it," Florian answered, swinging his stick in his hand, and stepping along gingerly. "Drôle de croyance, isn't it? Still, I call it disgraceful. An exquisite creature like that, a divinely-inspired singer, a supply-moulded form of Hellenic sculpture, whom the Gods above have given us as a precious gift for the common delight and the common enjoyment, to be thwarted and pulled up short at every twist and turn, and by whom, I'd like to know? Why, by a Tyrolese innkeeper, a mere village host, who arrogates to himself the right of monopolising what Heaven meant for us all—Ach! I call it detestable, just simply detestable. He hardly allows her enough to eat and drink. She might just as well be a sennerin on her hillside again, for any pleasure or delight she gets out of her success, tied and hampered as she is with this creature Hausberger."

"That's quite true," Will replied. "She was happier in the Zillerthal. She has money, and fine dresses, and jewellery, and applause; but, for any good they can do her, she might as well be without them. Hausberger treats her as a mere machine for making money for him. He's careful to see the machine works thoroughly well, and doesn't get out of order—absurdly careful, in fact, for he's by nature over-cautious; but as for allowing her to enjoy anything of what she earns herself, in any reasonable way—why, it never even occurs to him."

"Do you think he's unkind to her?" Florian asked, somewhat carelessly. "I mean, do you think he ill-treats her—keeps her short, and so forth?"

"He doesn't actively ill-treat her, I'm sure," Will answered with confidence; "he has far too great a sense of the value of her health to do anything to injure it. And I don't suppose he even keeps her actually short; she's always beautifully dressed, of course, that's part of the advertisement; and he takes her about as much as he can, without risk to her voice, and lavishes a certain sort of wooden care upon her. But I don't think he ever regards her as a human being at all; he regards her as a delicate musical instrument in which he has invested money, and out of which, during a given number of years, he has to recoup himself and make his fortune. As to sympathy between them, why, naturally, that's quite out of the question; he's a harsh, stern man who hardly knows how to be kind, I should say, to anyone."

Florian brought down his stick on the pavement with a bang. "It's atrocious," he said, snorting; "I declare, quite atrocious. Here's this exquisite creature, a banquet fit for the Gods, with her superb voice and her queenly beauty; a creature almost too ethereal for ordinary humanity to touch or handle; one that should be reserved by common consent for the delectation of the very pink and pick of the species"—and he drew himself up to his five feet nothing with a full consciousness of his own claim to be duly enrolled in that select category—"here's this exquisite creature, who should be held in trust, as it were, for the noblest and truest and best of our kind, a Koh-i-noor among women, flung away upon a solid, stolid, three-per-cent. investing, money-grubbing, German-speaking beerhouse-keeper. Pah! It makes me sick! This Danae to a Satyr! How a Greek would have writhed at it!"

"And yet I thought," Will murmured, reflectively, with a quiet little smile, "you considered her a cow-girl, and looked upon her as just fit for gentlemen to play skittles with!"

It took a great deal to abash Florian. He paused for a second, then he answered with warmth, "Now, there, Deverill! that's just like you. You want me to be consistent! But the philosophic mind, as Herbert Spencer remarks, is always open to modification by circumstances. Consistency is the virtue of the Philistine intellect; it means, inability to march abreast with events, to readjust one's ideas, one's sympathies, one's sentiments, to the ever-changing face of circumambient nature. When we saw Linnet first in the Tyrol, long ago, why, the girl was a cow-girl; a cow-girl she was, and a cow-girl I called her. I frankly recognised the facts of life as I found them, though I saw even then, with a voice like that, there was no perilous pinnacle of name or fame to which fate might not summon her. Now that she reappears in London once more, a flaming meteor of song, the cynosure of neighbouring eyes, a flashing diamond of the purest water, I recognise equally the altered facts. I allow that training, education, travel, the society of cultivated men and women, have practically made a brand-new Linnet of her. It's that brand-new Linnet I admire and adore, that queen of the stage, not the Tyrolese cow-girl."

Will turned sharp down Craven Street "And I," he said, with a Parthian shot, "I admire and adore the real woman herself, the same Linnet still that we knew in the Zillerthal."

Meanwhile, Andreas Hausberger, lighting a big cigar, had taken his wife down to a cab outside the supper-room.

"O Andreas!" Linnet cried, in German, "you've called a hansom. I can't bear those things, you know. I wanted a four-wheeler."

Andreas looked at her fixedly. "Get in!" he said, with curt decision. "Don't stand and talk like that out here in the cold street, opening your throat in this foggy air after those over-heated rooms. It's simply ridiculous. And mind you don't knock your dress against that muddy wheel! Pick it up, I say! pick it up! You are so careless!"

"But, Andreas!" Linnet exclaimed, in an imploring tone, "I hate these hansoms so. Whenever I go in one, the horse invariably either kicks or jibs. I wish, just this once, you'd let me have a four-wheeler."

She spoke almost coaxingly. Andreas turned to her with an angry German oath. "Didn't I tell you to get in at once?" he cried. "Pull that thing over your shoulder. Don't stand here chattering and catching cold all night. Jump in when I bid you. A pretty sort of thing, indeed, if you're going to stop and discuss in a dress like that on an English evening upon these muddy pavements!" He helped her up the step, guarding her skirt with one hand, and jumped after her sulkily. "Avenue Road, St John's Wood!" he called out through the flap to the attentive cabman. "Half-past twelve! Ach, donner-wetter! How late we've stayed! We'll have to pay double fare! Have you got your purse with you?"

"Yes," Linnet half sobbed out; "but I've hardly any money, not enough for the cab in it. You gave me half-a-sovereign, you know, and I paid for those gloves, and got a new bottle of that mixture at the chemist's."

"Only three shillings left!" Andreas exclaimed, opening the purse, and screwing his mouth up curiously. "Only three shillings left, out of a whole half-sovereign! So! London's the dearest town for everything on earth I ever lived in. Only three shillings left! Well, that's enough for the cab; it's a one-and-sixpenny fare, and I rather think they double it at midnight."

"Mayn't I have sixpence over for trinkgeld?" Linnet ventured to inquire, in a timid voice. "When they go so far at this time of night, they always expect something."

"No; certainly not," Andreas answered; "why on earth should you give it to them? If you or I expect something, do other people make that any reason for giving it us? Three shillings is the legal fare; if he doesn't like that, there's no compulsion, he needn't be a cabman. Three-and-sixpence indeed! why you talk as if it was water! Three-and-sixpence is a lot to spend on oneself in a single evening."

"I should have thought so at St Valentin," Linnet answered, softly; "but I earn so much, now. You must save a great deal, Andreas."

"And I spent a great deal in getting you trained and educated," Andreas retorted with a sneer. "But that's all forgotten. You never think about that. You talk as though it was you yourself by your unaided skill who earned all the money. How could you ever have earned it, I should like to know, if I hadn't put you in the way of getting a thorough musical training? You were a sennerin when I married you, and now you're a lady, Signora. Besides, there's your dress; remember, that swallows up a good third of what we earn. I say we advisedly, for the capital invested earns its share of the total just as truly as you do."

"But, Andreas, I only want sixpence," Linnet pleaded, earnestly. "For the poor cold cabman! I'm sure I don't spend much, not compared with what I get; and the man looks old and cold and tired. I ought to have a shilling or two a week for pocket money. It's like a child to have to ask you for every penny I'm spending."

Andreas pulled out half-a-crown, which he handed her grudgingly. "There, take that, and hold your tongue," he said. "It's no use speaking to you. I told you before not to talk in this misty air. If you don't care yourself whether it hurts you or not, you owe it to me, at least, after all I've done for you."

Linnet leant back in her place, and began to cry silently. She let the tears trickle one by one down her cheeks. As Andreas grew richer, she thought, he grew harder and harder to her. For some minutes, however, her husband didn't seem even to notice her tears. Then he turned upon her suddenly. "If you're going to do like that," he said, "your eyes'll be too red and swollen to appear at all on Monday, and what'll happen then, I'd like to know, Signora. Dry them up; dry them up at once, I tell you. Haven't I given you the money?"

Linnet dried her eyes as she was bid; she always obeyed him. But she thought involuntarily of how kind Will had been, and how nicely he had spoken to her. And then, oh, then, she clasped the little Madonna hard in her fist once more, and prayed low to be given strength to endure her burden!

CHAPTER XXXIII

PLAYING WITH FIRE

And yet, Linnet was happier that first season in London than ever before since her marriage with Andreas. She knew well why. In fear and trembling, with many a qualm of conscience, she nevertheless confessed to herself the simple truth; it was that Will was near, and she felt at all times dimly conscious of his nearness. Not that she saw much of him; both she and Will sedulously avoided that pitfall; but from time to time they met, for the most part by accident; and even when they didn't, she knew instinctively Will was watching over her unseen, and guarding her. She was no longer alone in the great outer world; she had some one to love her, to care for her, to observe her. Often, as she sang, her eyes fell on his face upturned in the stalls towards her; her heart gave a throb; she faltered and half-paused, then went on again all the happier. Often, too, as she walked in Kensington Gardens with Andreas, Will would happen to pass by—so natural for a man who lives in Craven Street, Strand, to be strolling of an afternoon in Kensington Gardens!—and whenever he passed, he stopped and spoke a few words to her, which Linnet answered in her pretty, hardly foreign English.

"How well you speak now!" Will exclaimed, one such day, as she described to him in glowing terms some duchess's house she had lately visited.

The delicate glow that rose so readily to that rich brown cheek flushed Linnet's face once more as she answered, well pleased, "Oh yes; I had so many reasons, you see, Herr Will, for learning it!"—she called him Herr Will even in English still—it was a familiar sound, and for old times' sake she loved it;—then she added, half-shamefacedly, "Andreas always said it was wiser so; I should make my best fortunes in England and America."

Will nodded, and passed on, pretending not to catch at her half-suppressed meaning; but he knew in his own heart what her chief reason was for taking so much pains to improve her English.

They saw but little of one another, to be sure, and that little by chance; though Andreas Hausberger, at least, made no effort to keep them apart. On the contrary, if ever they met by appointment at all, 'twas at Andreas's own special desire or invitation. The wise Wirth of St Valentin was too prudent a man to give way, like Franz Lindner, to pettish freaks of pure personal jealousy. He noted, indeed, that Linnet was happiest when she saw most of Will Deverill; not many things escaped that keen observer's vision. But when Linnet was happiest she always sang best. Therefore, Andreas, being a wise and prudent man, rather threw them together now and again than otherwise. That cool head of his never allowed anything to interfere with the course of business; he was too sure of Linnet to be afraid of losing her. It was a voice he had married, not a living, breathing woman—an exquisite voice, with all its glorious potentialities of wealth untold, now beginning to flow in upon him that season in London.

But to Linnet herself, struggling hard in her own soul with the love she could not repress, and would never acknowledge, it was a very great comfort that she could salve her conscience with that thought: she seldom saw Will save at Andreas's invitation!

The next three years of the new singer's life were years of rapid rise to fame, wealth, and honour. Signora Casalmonte grew quickly to be a universal favourite, not in London alone, but also in Berlin, Vienna, Paris. 'Twas a wonderful change, indeed, from the old days in the Zillerthal. Her name was noised abroad; crowned heads bowed down to her; Serene Highnesses whispered love; Archdukes brought compliments and diamond necklaces. No one mounts so fast to fame as the successful singer. She must make her reputation while she is young and beautiful. She may come from nowhere, but she steps almost at once into the front rank of society. It is so with all of them; it was so with Linnet. But to Will she was always the same old Linnet still; he thought no more of her, and he thought no less, than he had thought in those brief days of first love in the Tyrol.

At the end of Linnet's first London season, after some weeks in Paris, when August came round, Andreas took his wife for her yearly villeggiatura to a hill-top in Switzerland. He was for ozone still; he believed as much as ever in the restorative value of mountain air and simple life for a vocalist. It gave tone to the larynx, he said, and tightened the vocal chords: for he had taken the trouble to read up the mechanism of voice production. So he carried off Linnet to an upland village perched high on the slopes behind the Lake of Thun—not to a great hotel or crowded pension, where she would breathe bad air, eat made French dishes, drink doubtful wine, keep very late hours, and mix with exciting company, but to a châlet nestling high beneath a clambering pinewood, among Alpine pastures thick with orchids and globe-flowers, where she might live as free and inhale as pure and unpolluted an atmosphere as in their own green Zillerthal. For reasons of his own, indeed, Andreas wouldn't take her to St Valentin, lest the homesickness of the mountaineer should come over her too strong when she returned once more to London or Berlin. But he chose this lofty Bernese hamlet as the next best thing to their native vale to be found in Europe. There, for six happy weeks, Linnet drank in once more the fresh mountain breeze, blowing cool from the glaciers, climbed, as of old, among alp and crag and rock and larch forest—felt the soft fresh turf rise elastic under her light foot as she sprang from tussock to tussock of firmer grass among the peaty sward of the hillside.

Before leaving town that summer, she had lunched once with Will at Florian's chambers and mentioned to him casually in the course of talk the name and position of their Bernese village. Will bore it well in mind. A week or two later, as Linnet strolled by herself in a simple tweed frock and a light straw hat among the upland pastures, she saw to her surprise a very familiar figure in a grey knickerbocker suit, winding slowly along the path from the direction of Beatenberg. Her heart leapt up within her with joy at the sight. Ach, himmel! what was this? It was her Engländer, her poet! Then he had remembered where she was going; he had come after her to meet her!

Next moment, she reproached herself with a bitter reproach. The little oval Madonna, which kept its place still round her neck amid all her new magnificence, felt another hard grip on its sorely tried margin. Oh, Dear Lady, pardon her, that her heart should so jump for a stranger and a heretic—which never jumped at all for her wedded husband.

The Church knew best! The Church knew best! For her soul's sake, no doubt, the Herr Vicar was right—and dear Herr Will was a heretic. But if only they had wedded her to Herr Will instead, her heart gave a great thump—oh, how she would have loved him!

Though now, as things stood, of course, she could never care for him.

And with that wise resolve in her heart, and Our Lady clasped hard in her trembling hand, she stepped forth with beaming eyes and parted lips to greet him.

Will came up, a little embarrassed. He had no intention, when he set out, of meeting Linnet thus casually. It was his design to call in due form at the châlet and ask decorously for Andreas; it made him feel like a thief in the night to have lighted, thus unawares, upon Linnet alone, without her husband's knowledge. However, awkward circumstances will arise now and again, and we have all of us to face them. Will took her hand, a trifle abashed, but still none the less cordially. "What, Frau Hausberger!" he cried in German—and Linnet winced at the formal name, though of course it was what he now always called her; "I didn't expect to see you here, though I was coming to ask after . . . your husband in the village," and he glanced down at his feet with a little nervous confusion.

"I saw you coming," Linnet answered, in English, for she loved best to speak with her Engländer in his own language; "and I knew that it was you, so I came on to meet you. Isn't it lovely here? Just like my own dear Fatherland!"

Will was hot and dusty with his long tramp from Interlaken. It was a broiling day. He sat down by Linnet's side on the grassy slope that looks across towards the lake and the great snow-clad giants of the Bernese Oberland. That was the very first time he had been quite alone with her since she married Andreas. The very first time since those delicious mornings on the vine-draped Küchelberg. They sat there long and talked, Linnet picking tall grasses all the while with her twitching fingers, and pulling them into joints, and throwing them away bit by bit, with her eyes fixed hard on them. After a time as they sat, and grew more at home with one another, they fell naturally into talk of the old days at St Valentin. They were both of them timid, and both self-conscious; yet in the open air, out there on that Alpine hillside, it all seemed so familiar, so homely, so simple—so like those lost hours long ago in the Zillerthal—that by degrees their shyness and reserve wore off, and they fell to talking more easily and unrestrainedly. Once or twice Will even called her "Linnet," tout court, without noticing it; but Linnet noticed it herself, and felt a thrill of strange joy, followed fast by a pang of intense remorse, course through her as she sat there.

By-and-by, their talk got round by slow degrees to London. Linnet had seen one of Will's pieces at the Duke of Edinburgh's, in June, and admired it immensely. "How I should love to sing in something of your composing, Herr Will," she exclaimed, with fervour. "Just for old times' sake, you know—when neither of us was well-known, and when we met at St Valentin."

Will looked down a little nervously. "I've often thought," he said, with a stifled sigh; "I should love to write something on purpose for you, Linnet. I know your voice and its capabilities so well, I've watched you so close—for your career has interested me; and I think it would inspire one, both in the lines and in the music, to know one was working for a person one—well . . . one knew and liked, and . . . had met before, under other circumstances."

He looked away, and hesitated. Linnet clasped her hands in front of her between her knees, on her simple tweed frock, and stared studiously at the mountains. "Oh, that would be lovely!" she cried, pressing her fingers ecstatically. "That would be charming! that would be beautiful! I should love that I should sing in something you'd written, and, above all, in something you'd written for me, Will. I'm sure it would inspire me too—it would inspire both of us. I do not think you could write for anybody, or I could sing for anybody, as we could write and sing, each one of us, for one another. We should do ourselves justice then. Why don't you try it?"

She looked deep into his eyes. Will quailed, and felt his heart stand still within him. "There are difficulties in the way, my child," he answered, deliberating. "You're more or less bound to the Harmony, I think; and I'm more or less bound to the Duke of Edinburgh's. And then, there's Herr Hausberger to consider as well. Even if we could arrange things with our respective managers, do you think he'd be likely to fall in with our arrangements?"

Linnet seized his arm impulsively. With these warm southern natures, such acts are natural, and mean less than with us northerners. "Oh, do try, dear Herr Will!" she exclaimed, bending forward in earnest entreaty. "Do try if we can't manage it. Never mind about Andreas. I'm sure he would consent, if he saw it was a good piece, and I could sing in it with spirit. And I would sing in it—ach, lieber Gott, how well I would sing in it! You would see what I could do, then! It would be splendid, splendid!"

"But I'm afraid Willdon Blades—"

Linnet cut him short impatiently, jerking her little curled forefinger with a contemptuous gesture. "What matter about Willdon Blades!" she cried. "We can easily settle him. If you and I decide to work this play together, the manager must give in: we can arrange it somehow." And she looked at him with more conscious dignity and beauty than usual; for, simple peasant-girl as she was, and a child still at heart, she knew by this time she was also a queen of the opera. How the gommeux had crowded her salon in her Paris hotel; how great ladies had fought for stalls at her triumphant première!

"I might think about it," Will answered, after a brief pause, half-alarmed at her eagerness. Was it not too dangerous?

But Linnet, quite sure in her own soul she was urging him from purely artistic motives, had no such scruples. "Do try," she cried, laying her hand impulsively on his arm once more. "Now, promise me you'll try! Begin to-day! I should love to see what sort of a part you'd write for me."

Will stammered, and hesitated. "Well, to tell you the truth, I've begun already, Linnet," he answered, fingering the pencil-case that hung from his watch chain with ill-concealed agitation. "I've been walking about for a fortnight through the mountains alone—Florian wanted to come, but I wouldn't bring him with me, that I might have time for thinking; and everything I saw seemed somehow to recall . . . well, why shouldn't I confess it?—those days on the Küchelberg. I thought of you a great deal—I mean of your voice and the sort of words and chords that would be likely to suit you. I always compose best in the open air. The breeze whispers bars to me. And I've begun a few songs—just your part in the play, you know—words and airs together, Wagner-wise—that's how I always do it. The country I passed through brought the music of itself; it all spoke to me direct—and I thought it would be something new to bring this breezy Alpine air to freshen the stuffy atmosphere of a London theatre."

"Have you got what you've done with you?" Linnet inquired, with deep interest.

"It's here in my knapsack," Will answered, half reluctant.

"Ah, do let me see it!" And she pressed one hand to her breast with native southern vehemence.

"It's only in pencil, roughly scratched on bits of paper over rocks or things anyhow," Will replied, apologetically. "I don't suppose you'll be able to read one word of it. But, if you like, you can try," and he pulled it forth and opened it.

For twenty minutes or more of terrestrial time Linnet sat entranced in the seventh heavens. She tried over parts of the songs, half to herself, half to Will, with many an "Oh" and an "Ach, Gott," and was charmed and delighted with them. They were written straight at her—not a doubt in the world about that; and they suited her voice and manner admirably. It's so innocent for a singer to sit on the grassy mountain sides like this, with a poet and composer close at hand to consult and talk over the work they mean to produce together. This was art, pure art; the sternest moralist could surely find nothing to object to in it Linnet didn't even feel bound to give another hard squeeze to the poor much-battered, and hardly-used Madonna. She only sat and sang, with Will smiling by her side, there in the delicate mountain air, among the whispering pines, gazing across at the stainless peaks, and thrilling through to the finger tips.

"O Herr Will," she cried at last, "how lovely it is out here, how high, how soft, how pure, how much lovelier than in London! I've never enjoyed anything in my life so much, since," . . . her voice sank low—"since those days on the Küchelberg."

Will leant over towards her for a moment. His heart beat hard. He laid one palm on the ground and rested on it as he looked at her. He was trembling all over. Surely, surely he must give way! For a moment he paused and debated; then he rose to his feet suddenly. "I think, Linnet," he said, in a very serious voice, "for your sake—I think—we ought to go on and find your husband."

CHAPTER XXXIV

AN OLD ACQUAINTANCE

When Will, with fear and trembling, explained his plan half-an-hour later at the châlet to Andreas Hausberger, that wise man of business, instead of flouting the idea, entered into his suggestion with the utmost alacrity. He knew Linnet was still very fond of Will Deverill and, being a practical man, he was perfectly ready to make capital out of her fondness. It was good for trade; and whatever was good for trade appealed at once to Andreas on the tenderest point of his nature. He had perfect confidence in Linnet's honour, as well, indeed, he might have; but if she chose to cherish an innocent sentimental attachment of the German sort, in point of fact, a schwärmerei, towards a young man she had known and liked before her marriage, that was no business of his; or, rather, it was just so much his business as it might help him to make a little more money out of her. Andreas Hausberger was a proud and self-respecting person, but his pride and his self-respect were neither of them touched by a purely romantic feeling on his young wife's part towards a rising poet-composer who was anxious to write and score an opera to suit her. Indeed, he rather congratulated himself than otherwise on the thought that very few husbands of theatrical favourites had such very small cause for jealousy as he had.

So he listened to Will's humming and hawing apology with a quiet face of subdued amusement. What a bother about nothing! If Will wrote a piece for Linnet, why, of course, he'd write it excellently, and write it with most intimate knowledge of her voice, as well as with close sympathy for all its shades of feeling. Will knew her exact compass, her range, her capabilities; he knew also her weak points, her limitations, her dramatic failings. And Linnet, for her part, was sure to sing well whatever Will wrote for her, both because it was Will's, and because it was suited to her voice and character. The idea was an excellent one; how absurd to make a fuss about it!

"And he has some of it scored already, he says," Linnet put in, half-trembling.

"Let me see it," Andreas exclaimed, in his authoritative way; and he skimmed it over carefully. "H'm, h'm . . . that's not bad," he muttered from time to time as he went along . . . "suits her style very well . . . not at all a weak close; fine opportunity for that clear upper G of hers; excellently considered piece, have you tried it over, Linnet? I should think it ought to do very nicely indeed for you."

"I just sang it a bit at sight," Linnet answered, "on the hillside. When I met Herr Will first, we sat down and talked, because Herr Will was tired; and he showed me his score, and I tried part of it over a bit. But it was not that which you would quite call fairly trying it, for I had not seen it before, and had no time to study it. Still, I thought it very good, oh, exquisite, perfect!—and I should like so much the chance to sing in it."

"Try it now!" Andreas said, in his dictatorial tone.

And Linnet, without any affected hesitation, or professional airs, opened her rich mouth naturally, and trilled forth upon Will's delighted ear in a raptured flood her native first reading of his own graceful music.

"That'll do!" Andreas said, with decision, as soon as she'd finished. "That'll do, Linnet. We'll arrange for it."

And Will, leaning across to her over the plain deal table, as she stood blushing in front of him, exclaimed with delight, "Why, Linnet, Frau Hausberger, I mean, that's charming, charming! I couldn't have believed how pretty my own song was, till I heard you sing it!"

So that very day the whole matter was settled, as far, at least, as those three could settle it. It was decided and contracted that Will should definitely write an opera for Linnet; that he should offer it first to Mr Wells, the manager of the Harmony; and that if Wells refused it, it should go next to the Duke of Edinburgh's, on condition that Linnet was engaged for the title-role. Before evening, Will had shouldered his knapsack once more (though Andreas would fain have constrained him to stay the night at their inn), and, with a timorous farewell to Linnet at the châlet door, had gone on his way rejoicing, to descend towards Oberwesel.

That interview gave him courage. During the course of the autumn he completed his piece, for he was a man of inspirations, and he worked very rapidly when the fit was upon him. The greater part of his opera he wrote and composed in the open air, beneath the singing larks, on those green Swiss hillsides. And the larks themselves did not sing more spontaneous, with heart elate, for pure joy of singing. That one short tête-à-tête with Linnet at her châlet had filled his teeming brain with new chords and great fancies. Words and notes seemed to come of themselves, and to suggest one another; moods seemed to mirror themselves in becoming music. Besides, Will thought with no little pleasure, this new venture would bring him, for a time at least, into closer personal connection with Linnet. While rehearsals and other preliminary arrangements went on, he must be thrown a great deal perforce into Linnet's company. And how delightful to think they would be working together for a common end; that success, if achieved, would be due in part and in equal degrees to each of them.

Will didn't return to London till the end of October. He had spent the time meanwhile partly in the Bernese Oberland, and partly, later, on the south side of the Alps, among the valleys and waterfalls of the Canton Ticino. But when he arrived at Charing Cross, it was not empty-handed; he carried in his portmanteau the almost complete manuscript of Cophetua's Adventure, that exquisite romance of no particular time and place, with its fanciful theme and its curious episodes, which proved at last that poetry is not stone-dead on our English stage, and that exquisite verse wedded to exquisite harmonies has still its fair chance of a hearing in England. He had only to polish it at his rooms in Craven Street, before submitting it to the opinion of the manager of the Harmony.

Linnet came later. She had a two months' engagement first to fulfil in Paris, where Will read, with a little pang of regret, in the Figaro how she had turned the heads and captured the hearts (if any) of ten thousand boulevardiers. Her very innocence and simplicity at once delighted and surprised the profoundly sophisticated Parisian mind. All the world of the foyer unanimously voted her tout ce qu'il-y-a de plus enfantin. "She has afforded us," said a famous lady-killer of the Avenue Victor Hugo, "the rare pleasure of a persistent and unreasoning refusal." So all Paris was charmed, as all Paris always is at any new sensation. An opera-singer insensible to the persuasiveness of diamonds and the eloquence of bank-notes, all Paris shugged its shoulders in incredulous astonishment. "Incroyable!" it muttered: "mais enfin, elle est jeune, cette petite, ça viendra!"

So it was March before Linnet was in London once more. Andreas, ever business-like, had preceded her by a week or two, to conclude the needful arrangements with the people at the Harmony. By the time the prima donna herself arrived, everything was already well in train for the rehearsals. Linnet had studied her part, indeed, in Paris beforehand, till she knew every line, every word, every note of it. She had never learnt anything so easily in her life before, though she would hardly admit, even to herself, the true reason, because Will had written it. They met at the Harmony the very next afternoon, to discuss the details. Andreas was there, of course, he never left his wife's side when business was in question; he must protect her interests: erect, inflexible, tall, powerful, big-built, with his resolute face and his determined mien, he was a man whom no theatrical manager on earth could afford to bully. He bargained hard with the Harmony for his wife's services in this new engagement; for, indeed, her late Parisian vogue had put up her price another twenty per cent, or so; and now he stood there, triumphant, self-conscious, jubilant, aware that he had done a good stroke of business for himself, and ready to do battle again on his wife's behalf with all and sundry. So satisfied was he, indeed, with their rising fortunes, that he had presented Linnet spontaneously with a five-pound note, all pocket-money of her own to do as she liked with, on their way to the theatre.

Linnet stood a little behind. Will grasped her hand eagerly. She took his in return without the faintest pressure, for Our Dear Lady knew well how wisely and circumspectly she meant to behave now towards him. The circumstances were dangerous: so much the more, Beloved Frau, would she strive to comport herself as becomes a good Catholic wife in the hour of temptation.

"You like your part, Signora?" Will asked of her, half-playfully, adopting her theatrical Italian style and title.

Linnet raised her big eyes. "I have never sung in anything I liked half so well," she answered, simply.

The company assembled by degrees, and the usual preliminary discussion ensued forthwith as to parts, and cues, and costumes, and properties. Will's own ideas, conceived among the virgin snows and pure air of the high Alps, were a trifle too ethereal and a trifle too virginal for that practical manager. He modified them considerably. Various points had to be talked over with various persons. In the midst of them all, Will was surprised to feel of a sudden a sturdy gloved hand laid abruptly on his shoulder, and a powerful though musical feminine voice exclaiming volubly at his ear in very high German, "Ach mein Gott! it's Herr Will! So we meet again in London. Herr Andreas told me you had written this piece for Linnet; but one hardly knows you again, you've grown so much older, and better dressed, and richer! And, Dear Frau! in the Tyrol, you wore no beard and whiskers!"

Will turned in surprise. It was a minute, even so, before he quite recognised the stalwart speaker. It was Philippina, still good-humoured and buxom and garrulous as of old; but, oh, great heavens, how much changed from the brown-faced sennerin with the rough woollen petticoat who had offered them milk, all frothy from the cow, in the stoneware mug on the hillside at St Valentin! If Linnet was altered, Philippina was transmogrified. Her jolly round face was surmounted incongruously by the latest and airiest thing out in Parisian bonnets; her dress was the very glass and mirror of fashion; her delicate gloves looked as dainty as seven-and-a-halfs are ever likely to look upon feminine fingers. Civilisation, indeed, had done its worst for Philippina: it had transformed her outright from a simple and natural if somewhat coarse-fibred cow-girl into the jolly, bouncing, distinctly vulgar type of third-rate actress. With all the good-humoured coarseness of her original nature, she now possessed in addition all the airs and graces, all the coquettish affectations, all the noisy self-assertion of the theatrical utility.

"Why, I didn't know you were in England," Will exclaimed, taken aback at her unexpected salute, and surveying from head to foot with no very pleased eye the fly-away peculiarities of her over-trimmed costume. "Then you've taken to the stage!" He turned hastily to Linnet, and added in English, which Philippina did not understand when he last met her, "She isn't surely going to play in this piece of mine, is she?"

"So!" Philippina answered, in a very Teutonic voice, indeed, but in our native vernacular. "Ach, yes; I am going to play in it; Herr Andreas has arranched all zat wis ze manager. You are surbrized to zee zat I shall blay in your biece. But I haf blay pevore in many bieces in Paris."

Will glanced at Linnet, a mute glance of inquiry. He didn't know why, but Linnet's eyes fell, and a blush spread quick over that clear brown cheek of hers. It wasn't the familiar blush he was accustomed to see there; he noted at once some tinge of shame and personal humiliation in the look that accompanied it. But she answered quickly, "Oh yes; Philippina's to play. My husband and Mr Wells have settled all about it."

"What part?" Will inquired, with a slight sense of sinking; for he wasn't over-well pleased to hear those dainty lines of his were to be murdered by Philippina's coarse guttural utterance.

"Ze Brincess Berylla," Philippina replied, with glib promptitude and great self-satisfaction. "It's a very schmall part; bod I shall do my best in it."

Will gave a slight sigh of relief. The Princess Berylla would do at a pinch. If she must sing at all, it was well at least she should sing in so minor a character. Though, to be sure, he had his misgivings how his water-fairies' song would sound on the stage when delivered with her clumsy Teutonic pronunciation:

"They loved to dwell
In a pearly shell
And to deck their cell
With amber;
Or amid the caves
That the riplet laves
And the beryl paves
To clamber.

By the limpets' home
And the vaulted dome
Where the star-fish roam
They'd linger;
In the mackerel's jaw,
Or the lobster's claw,
They'd push and withdraw
A finger."

He trembled to think what sort of strange hash those thick lips of hers would make of his lilting versification.

However, for the moment, and for Linnet's sake, he said nothing against it. A little later in the afternoon, he had five minutes with the prima donna alone in one of the passages. "Look here, Linnet," he said hurriedly with a beseeching glance, "must we have Philippina?"

"There's no must at all in the matter, except the musts you make," Linnet answered, trembling. "If you say she must go, Mr Wells will cut her out, I suppose, to please you. Only—" and she hesitated.

"Only what?" Will cried, inquiringly.

"Only . . . I'm afraid Andreas wouldn't like it."

Her face flushed again. Will looked down at her and paused. A great many thoughts ran through his head in a second. Linnet scanned the floor, embarrassed. After awhile, Will spoke again in a very low tone. "I'd let anybody sing, Linnet," he said, "with a voice like a frog's, rather than allow, well, any trouble to crop up between myself and your husband."

"Thank you," Linnet answered simply. But she lifted her eyes and gave him one grateful look that was more than full recompense.

"How did Philippina learn English?" Will asked once more, hardly daring to press the subject.

"Oh, Andreas has always taken—well—a very great interest in her, you know," Linnet answered, with a faintly evasive air. "She went with us to Italy. He kept her on when he paid off the rest of his troupe at Meran; and he got her trained under agreement, and put her into a minor part when I sang at San Carlo. When we came to England first, she went for awhile to Paris; but he's always been getting her English lessons everywhere. He has a claim on her, he says, for money advanced to train her for the stage. . . . She's a very good-natured girl, and she's always been kind to me."

"I see," Will answered, with a suddenly sobered air. "Very well, then, Linnet," and he drew a deep sigh—though not for himself; "she shall sing the part of Princess Berylla."

"Thank you," Linnet said simply, with a sigh, once more.

But till then, he had never thought Linnet had that to put up with.

CHAPTER XXXV

GOLDEN HOPES

Mr Franz Lindner, alias Signor Francesco of the London Pavilion, laid down his morning paper at his lodgings in Soho, with unmistakable outward and visible signs of a very bad humour. Montepulciano and Lacrima-Christi, as Florian put it, had evidently disagreed with him. But that was not all. The subject which roused his undisguised discontent was the marked success of the woman he once loved, the woman he loved now even more than ever.

For this was what Franz had read, amid much else of the same cheap laudatory strain, in the theatrical column of the Daily Telephone.

"The first performance of Mr W. Deverill's new English opera, Cophetua's Adventure, at the Harmony last night marks an epoch in the renascence of the poetical drama in England. Never has the little house on the Embankment been so crowded before; never has an audience received a new play with more unanimous marks of profound enthusiasm. Both as a work of literature and as a musical composition, this charming piece recalls to mind the best days of the great Italian outburst of song at the beginning of the century." Franz snorted internally as he ran his eye in haste over the learned digression on the various characteristics of the various operas which Cophetua's Adventure suggested to the accomplished critic who works the drama for that leading newspaper. Then, skipping the gag, he read on once more with deeper interest, "It would be hard to decide whether the chief honours of the night belonged more unmistakably to Mr Deverill himself or to his charming exponent, Signora Casalmonte. The words of the songs, indeed, possessed to a rare degree high literary merit; the music, as might be expected from so accomplished a composer, was light and airy, yet with the genuine ring of artistic inspiration; but the ever-delightful soprano rendered her part so admirably that 'twas difficult to disentangle Mr Deverill's tunes from the delicious individualisation conferred upon them by Signora Casalmonte's voice and acting. The prima donna's first appearance on the stage as the Beggar Maid, lightly clad in a graceful though ostentatiously simple costume, was the signal for a burst of irrepressible applause from stalls, boxes, and gallery. In the second act, as Cophetua's Queen, the popular diva looked, if possible, even more enchantingly beautiful; while the exquisite naïveté with which she sang the dainty aria, 'Now all ye maidens, matrons, wives, and widows,' brought down the house in one prolonged outburst of unmixed appreciation. Our operatic stage has seldom boasted a lady so perfectly natural, in manner, gesture, and action, or one who allowed her great native gifts to degenerate so little into affectations or prettinesses."

Franz flung down the paper and sighed. He admitted it; he regretted it. What a fool he had been not to marry that girl, offhand, when he once had the chance, instead of dawdling and hanging about till Hausberger carried the prize off under his nose to St Valentin. It was disgusting, it was silly of him! And now it began to strike him very forcibly indeed that his chance, once gone, was gone for ever. A full year and more had passed since Linnet and her husband first came to London. During that year it had dawned slowly upon Franz's mind that Linnet had risen into a higher sphere, and could never by any possibility be his in future. He was dimly conscious by this time that he himself was a music-hall gentleman by nature and position, while Linnet was born to be a special star of the higher opera. Never could he recover the ground thus lost; the woman he loved once, and now loved again distractedly, had climbed to a higher plane, and was lost to his horizon.

What annoyed Franz more than anything, however, was his feeling of chagrin that he had let himself be cajoled, on the night of Linnet's first appearance in London, into abandoning his designs against her husband's person. He knew now he had done wrong; he ought to have stabbed Andreas Hausberger, then and there, as he intended. In a moment of culpable weakness, he had allowed himself to be beguiled from his fixed purpose by the blandishments of Linnet and the rich American widow. That would indeed have been the dramatic time to strike; he had let the psychological moment go by unheeded, and it would never return, or, at least, it would never return in so effectual a fashion. To have struck him then and there, on their very first meeting after Linnet's marriage, and on the night when Linnet made her earliest bow before an English audience, that would have been splendid, that would have been beautiful, that would have been romantic: all London would have rung with it. But now, during those past months, he had met Andreas twice or thrice, on neutral ground, as it were, and the relations between them, though distant and distinctly strained, had been nominally friendly. The Robbler felt he had committed a fatal error in accepting Mr Will's invitation to supper on that critical evening. It had compelled him to treat Andreas as an acquaintance once more; to turn round upon him now, and stab him in pure pique, would be feeble and self-stultifying. Franz wished he had had strength of mind to resist the women's wiles that first night at the Harmony, and to draw his rival's blood before their very eyes, as his own better judgment had told him he ought to do.

He had seen Linnet, too, and there came the unkindest cut of all; for he recognised at once that the girl he had described to Will Deverill as beneath his exalted notice since he rose to the front ranks of the profession at the London Pavilion, was now so much above him that she scarcely thought of him at all, and evidently regarded him only in the light of the man who had threatened her husband's life when they came to England.

Yes; Linnet thought nothing of him now; how could you expect it to be otherwise? She had money and rank and position at her feet; was it likely, being a woman, she would care greatly, when things were thus, for a music-hall singer who earned as much in six months as she herself could earn in one easy fortnight? And yet . . . Franz rose, and gazed abstractedly at his own face in the glass over the mantelpiece. No fault to find there! Many women did worse. He was excellently pleased with his black moustache, his flashing dark eyes, his well-turned figure; he even thought not ill of his blazing blue necktie. And Andreas was fifty if he was a day, Franz felt sure; old Andreas with his solid cut, his square-set shoulders, his steely-grey eyes, his heavy, unimpassioned, inexpressive countenance! Ach, if only he himself had the money to cut a dash, the mere wretched rhino, the miserable oof, for Franz had lived long enough in England now to have picked up a choice collection of best British slang, he might stand a chance still against that creature Andreas!

It was one o'clock by this time, though Franz had only just risen from his morning coffee. What would you have? A professional man must needs sing till late at night, and take his social pleasures at his café afterwards. So Franz was seldom in bed till two or three in the morning, recouping himself next day by sleeping on till mid-day. 'Twas the hour of the promenade. He went into his bedroom, doffed his flannel smoking-coat, and arrayed himself in the cheaply-fashionable broadcloth suit in which it was his wont to give the daily treat of seeing him to the girls in Bond Street. Then he lighted a bad cigar, and strolled out towards Piccadilly. At the Circus, he met a friend, an English betting man, who was a constant patron of the London Pavilion.

"Hello, Fred!" he cried, with a start, "how spruce you look to-day! Ze favourite must have lost. You have ze appearance of ze man who is flush of money. And yet, ze winter, is it not your off season?"

The bookmaker smiled a most self-contented smile. He certainly had the air of being in the very best of spirits. He was one of those over-fed, full-faced, knowing-eyed creatures who lurk round racecourses with a flower in their buttonholes, smoke the finest cigars, drink Heidsieck's Dry Monopole, and drop their H's over the grand stand with surprising unanimity. But his aspect just then was even more prosperous than usual. He seized Signor Francesco's arm with good-humoured effusiveness. "Flush!" he cried, with a bounce. "Well, my boy, I should rather think so. Wy, I ain't on the turf any longer, that's jest w'ere it is. I've retired from business. Jest you look 'ere, Frenchy; that's gold, that is; I've been over in your country for six weeks, I 'ave; and danged if I ain't come back with my pockets 'arf bust with furrineerin' money!"

"To my country! To Tyrol?" Franz put in, greatly astonished. "Zer ain't moch money going zere, I fancy. We're as poor as ze church mice. But, perhaps," he added, with an afterthought, "you mean Vienna."

"Vienna be 'anged!" the bookmaker responded, with a hearty slap on the Frenchy's back. To him, as to all his kind, the Continent was the Continent, one and indivisible. He made and encouraged no petty distinctions between France and Austria. "Vienna be 'anged. It's Monty Carlo I've been to. By George, sir, that's the place to rake the looees in! You puts down your cash on red or black or numbers, or ong cheval they calls it; wh'rr, wh'rr, goes the roolett, pop, out jumps the pea, 'Rooge gang!' sez the croopyer;—and you hauls in your money! I tell you, Frenchy, that's the place to make your pile in! Wy, I haven't been there more 'n jest six weeks—an' I come back last night with a cool twenty thou' in my britches pocket!"

"Twenty sousand francs?" Franz cried, fairly dazzled.

His companion's eyes gazed unutterable contempt "Twenty thousand francs! Francs be blowed!" he answered, briskly. "None o' your furrineerin' reckonin's for me, if you please, young man! I'm a true-born Briton, and I count in pounds sterlin'. No, no; twenty thousand pounds in good French bank-notes, a cool twenty thousand in my britches pocket. I've carried 'em home myself, all the way from Monty Carlo, for fear of bein' robbed, there's a lot o' shady people down there on the Literal, and I'm going down now to my banker's in the Strand, with the twenty thousand pound, to pay 'em in and invest 'em!"

"And you earned all zat lot in six weeks!" Franz cried, his mouth watering.

"Well, I didn't exactly earn it, old chap," the bookmaker replied, with a knowing wink; "though I've got a System. I just let it flow in, without doing anything pertickler myself to 'elp it, excep' it might be to rake in the rhino. But I mean to retire now, and do the toff in future, just runnin' down there again every two or three years, when I feel the shoe pinch, to replenish the exchequer."

"How much did you start wis?" Franz inquired, eagerly; for a Plan was rising up in indefinite outline before his mind's eye as they stood there.

"Oh, I took across five 'underd," the bookmaker replied, with easy confidence, as though five hundred pounds were to him the merest flea-bite. "I wouldn't advise anybody to try and work his luck on less than that. You want the capital, that's where it is; the fly 'uns know that; outsiders go smash through not startin' with the capital."

He took Franz's arm in his own. Luck makes men generous. They lunched together at Simpson's, at the winner's expense, after he had deposited his gains at the bank in the Strand. The lobster salad was good; the asparagus was fine; the iced champagne made glad the heart of the bookmaker. Expanding by degrees, he waxed warm in praise of his infallible System. It was fallacious, of course, all such Systems are; but its inventor, at any rate, implicitly believed in it. Little by little, with the aid of a pencil and paper, and a diagram of a roulette table, he explained to his eager listener the nature of his plan for securing a fortune offhand at Monte Carlo. Franz drank it in open-mouthed. This was really interesting! How could any man be such a fool as to sing for a miserable pittance six nights a week in smoky, grimy London, when a turn of fortune's wheel could bring him a hundred pounds every time the table spun in cloudless Monte Carlo? It was clear as mud how to win; the bookmaker was right; no fellow could fail to pull off five strokes out of nine with this infallible martingale! Visions of untold wealth floated vague before his eyes. He saw his way to be rich beyond the dreams of avarice.

But it wasn't avarice alone that inflamed Franz Lindner's desire; it was love, it was revenge, it was wounded vanity. At once the idea rose up clear in his mind that if he could go to Monte Carlo and win a fortune, as the bookmaker had done, he might come home and lay it all at Linnet's feet, with a very good chance of final acceptance. His experience at the London Pavilion had led him to believe that women in general, and theatrical stars in particular, had all their price, and might all be bought, if you only bid high enough. He didn't doubt that Linnet was like the rest of her kind in this matter. She didn't love Andreas; she couldn't love Andreas. If a good-looking man, with a very fine figure and a very black moustache, laid the untold gold of Monte Carlo at her feet, could Linnet resist? Would she care to resist him? Franz opined she would not. He didn't think it likely. There was only one thing needed to break the slender tie that bound her to Andreas. That one thing he would get, money, money, money!

So, from that day forth, Franz Lindner's life was changed. He began to work on quite a new basis. Hitherto, like most others of his trade and class, he had spent all he earned as fast as he got it. Now, he began to save and lay by for love, with the thrift of his countrymen. One great object in life swam clear before his eyes; he must manage to scrape together five hundred pounds, and take it to Monte Carlo, where he could make it by a stroke or two of that wonder-working roulette-table into twenty thousand. And, with twenty thousand pounds, he didn't for a moment doubt he'd be able to pay his suit once more to Linnet.

CHAPTER XXXVI

AN ECCLESIASTICAL QUESTION

While Cophetua's Adventure was running at the Harmony, Will necessarily saw a good deal of Linnet. Signora Casalmonte was now the talk of the town. Her name cropped up everywhere. Many men paid her most assiduous court. She was greatly in request for meets of the Four-in-hand Club, for Sundays at the Lyric, for picnics at Virginia Water, for little dinners at Richmond. To all of them Linnet went in her innocent way, that deeper-seated innocence that sees and knows much evil, yet passes unscathed through it; for the innocence that springs from mere ignorance alone is hardly worth counting. Andreas accompanied her everywhere with marital solicitude; the foolish were wont to say he was a jealous fellow; wiser heads saw well he was only making sure that the throat which uttered such valuable notes should take no hurt from night air or injudicious ices. It was the singer, not the woman, Andreas guarded so close, the singer herself, and the money she brought him.

For Will Deverill, however, as a special old friend, Andreas always made very great concessions. He knew it did Linnet good to see much of her Englishman; and what did Linnet good gave resonance to her voice, and increased by so much her nett money value. So Will was allowed every chance of meeting her. When the weather permitted it, the Hausbergers often went down by the first train on Sunday morning to Leith Hill, or Hind Head, or Surrey commons; and Florian, and Rue, and Will Deverill, and Philippina, were frequently of the company. On such occasions, Will noticed, he was often sent on, as if of set design, to walk in front with Linnet, while Florian paired in the middle distance with Rue, and Andreas Hausberger himself, being the heaviest of the six, brought up the rear with that strapping Philippina. More than once, indeed, it struck Will as odd how much the last couple lagged behind, and talked earnestly. He remembered that look Linnet had given him at the theatre while Cophetua was being arranged for. But, there, Philippina was always a flirt; and Andreas and she had been very old friends in the Tyrol together!

On one such excursion, as it chanced, when Rue was not of the party, Florian brought down his queer acquaintance, the Colorado Seer, and an American friend who had lately made a hit at a London theatre. This theatrical gentleman did the English Stage Yankee in drawing-room comedies to perfection by simply being himself, and was known in private life as Theodore Livingstone. He was tall and handsome, with peculiar brown eyes, brown hair and beard, and a brown tweed suit to match that exactly echoed them. Philippina had always been a susceptible creature, she was one of those women who take their loves lightly, a little and often, with no very great earnestness or steadfastness of purpose. She flirted desperately all that day with the handsome stranger. Andreas smiled sardonically; he himself was nowhere by Mr Theodore Livingstone's side, though he was generally a prime favourite; and even Florian himself, who had resumed at once in London the amicable relations broken off on the Küchelberg, felt his attentions slighted in favour of the new and good-looking American. Philippina, to say the truth, was all agog with excitement at her fresh acquaintance. When they lunched on the heather-clad slope of Holmbury, she sat by his side and drank out of the same cup with him; and when he left them at last to descend towards Guildford, while the rest made their way back on foot to Gomshall Station, she was momentarily disconsolate for the loss of her companion. Not till they had gone a full half-a-mile or more did she recover sufficiently to bandy words with Florian.

"Philippina has her moments," Andreas said, with his bitter smile, when Florian chaffed her a little on her evident captivation, for the brown eyes and beard of the handsome actor had quite taken her by storm. "Philippina has her moments. I've seen her so before, and I shall see her so again, I don't doubt, in future. She's always volage." And his lip curled curiously.

"Well, volatsch or not," Philippina replied, turning round to him sharply, with one of her arch little looks—Philippina was always famed for her archness—"volatsch or not, Herr Andreas, I haf always returnt to my olt frents at last, sooner or later, haf I not?"

"That's true," Florian answered, taking the remark to himself, in the Florianesque manner, and fingering his own smooth chin with his white hand, lovingly. "And I'm sure, Philippina, if it comes to that, your old friends have never forgotten you, either. In London or at Meran, they've always been the same—to you, and to everyone." As he spoke, he gave a side-long glance at Linnet; for though he had said in his haste, once, the grapes were sour, he had never ceased in his own heart to admire them greatly; and since Linnet had come forth from her chrysalis stage, a full-fledged butterfly of the cosmopolitan world, decked in brilliant hues, and much praised or desired of all beholders, he had paid her assiduous court with every device in his power. It was Franz Lindner's naïf belief that every woman must yield in the end to money or diamonds, if you only bid high enough; it was Florian's, equally naïf, though a trifle less gross, that every woman must yield in the end to flattery and address, if you only flatter long enough. So he pressed himself assiduously upon Linnet's attention, in season and out of season; and Linnet, who now regarded such compliments as part of the small change in which the world pays its successful entertainers, took very little heed of all his hints and innuendoes.

Andreas was wrong, however, in supposing this fancy of Philippina's for the brown-eyed American was merely one of the good-humoured Tyrolese girl's passing affections. For once, at last, Philippina was fairly caught in a genuine attachment "'Tis a scratch," Andreas said at first; "she'll soon get over it." But, as a matter of fact, Philippina didn't. On the contrary, the attack grew more and more serious. In a week or two, she was madly in love with Mr Theodore Livingstone; they had dropped insensibly into Christian names; it was Theodore this, and Theodore that, and Theodore the other thing, till Andreas, out of joint, was fairly sick and tired of it. What was odder still, the good-looking American on his side returned the feeling with interest. Philippina had always been a fine-built girl of the buxom beauty type, very large and vigorous; she was lively, and bright, and head over ears in love; and the American, though not unaccustomed to female admiration, was thoroughly taken with her. Before long, it was evident they meant to make a match of it. Andreas shrugged his shoulders; still, he was amused and yet piqued by it. Why any man should ever be minded to marry an actress at all, unless, indeed, there was money in her, fairly passed his comprehension; he felt sure there was no money in poor dear Philippina. For every other purpose, the ceremony in such a case is so absurdly superfluous. However, being a wise and prudent man, who trusted much to the mitigating effects of time, Andreas threw no obstacles in their way, and raised no objections. He only observed, in his dry fashion, more than once to Linnet, "She'll get tired of him soon; it's always the way with these hot first loves; like straw fires, they flare up fast, and cool down again quickly." The thought seemed to afford him much inward consolation.

But though Andreas saw no difficulties in the young people's way, Linnet, with her quicker feminine instinct, immediately spied one. "Is he a Catholic, Philippina?" she asked almost at once, somewhat doubtfully.

"Ah, no; he isn't a Catholic," Philippina answered in German, with a nonchalant air; "he belongs to some queer kind of American religion, I know not what. They have lots of assorted religions in America, I'm told, to suit all tastes. His they call in English a hard-shell Baptist. So, of course, when we marry, we'll have to get a dispensation."

The dispensation, however, proved a harder matter in the end than Philippina or her lover at all imagined. The Church was obdurate. Florian, who, as a friend of the house, had been called in to assist in this domestic difficulty, and who knew an Archbishop—Florian, in his easy-going Gallio mood, was of opinion that the problem might easily be solved by Mr Livingstone's immediate conversion and reception into the bosom of the Church; a course to which he, for his part, saw no possible objection. But, greatly to his surprise, the American stuck to his grotesque and quaintly-named creed with dogged persistence. Why any man should trouble to haggle about a faith when a woman was in question, Florian couldn't understand—he'd have turned Mahommedan himself, or Esoteric Buddhist, for that matter, with the greatest pleasure if it gave the lady one moment's satisfaction; and Mr Livingstone's own character hardly led him to expect any greater devotion on his part to the nice abstractions of dogmatic theology. But the American, though he dealt largely in fearsome Western oaths, and played poker with a will, and was not more particular in his domestic relations than most other members of his own uncensorious profession, yet stood firm as a rock on the question of recusancy. The Inquisition itself would never have moved him. He had no particular reason, indeed, for his dogged refusal, except an innate prejudice against Papistry, prelacy, and all forms of idolatry; he had no objection of any sort to marrying a Roman Catholic girl, and bringing up her future children, if any, in the Roman Catholic religion; but he stood out firm himself for his own personal Protestantism. "A hard-shell Baptist I was born," he said, with great persistence, "and a hard-shell Baptist I'll die, you bet. I was never a church member, nor even an inquirer, but a hard-shell Baptist I was and will be—and be durned to all Papists."

To Florian, such obstinacy on so unimportant a point seemed simply incomprehensible; if it had been a critical question, now, about Pacchiarotto or Baudelaire or Pater's prose style, he might perhaps have understood it: but infant baptism! theological quibbles! an obscure American sect! impossible! incredible! Still, the wise man has to take the world as he finds it, allowing for all existing follies and errors of other people's psychology. So Florian, who was really a good-natured fellow in a lazy sort of way, when things cost him no trouble, went to see his friend the Archbishop more than once about the dispensation. He found the Archbishop, however, even more impracticable on the subject than the hard-shell Baptist. Those two minds were built, indeed, on such opposite lines that 'twas impossible they should discuss anything, except at cross-questions. The Archbishop, tall, thin, ascetic, ecclesiastical, a churchman to the finger-tips, saw in this proposed marriage a breach of discipline, a relaxation of the Church's rules, a danger to a woman's immortal soul, and to heaven knows how many souls of her unborn children. Florian, short, dainty, easy-going, worldly-minded, tolerant, saw in it all only a question of obliging a jolly, good-looking, third-rate actress, whom marriage would perhaps reclaim for a few brief months from a shifting series of less regular attachments. But the mere fact that she was an actress told against her with the Archbishop. Why should he make exception in favour of a young woman of ill-regulated life and flippant conversation, who belonged to a profession already ill-seen by the Church, and who wished to enter into one of the most solemn sacraments of life with a professed unbeliever? The Archbishop interposed endless objections and vexatious delays. He must refer this matter to Rome, and that one to further personal deliberation. He must satisfy himself about the state of the young woman and the young man by actual interviews. Florian, like most others of his type, was patient of delays, and seldom lost his temper; but he almost lost it now with that grim, thin old man who could make such a strange and unnecessary fuss about allowing a third-rate playhouse singing-girl to contract marriage with a nondescript hard-shell Baptist!

Two or three weeks passed away in this undecided fashion, and still Florian called almost daily, and still the Archbishop hummed and hawed and shilly-shallied. Philippina, all the time, grew more and more visibly eager, and the hard-shell Baptist himself, unable to enter into his Eminence's ecclesiastical frame of mind, consigned the Archbishop and all his Church to eternal perdition ten times a day in sound round Western phrases. Florian heartily sympathised with him; it was absurd to treat so slight a matter so seriously. Why, Florian himself, if he'd been an Archbishop (which he might have been in the great age of Italian churchmanship), would have granted the girl dispensations enough in less than half the time to drive a round dozen of husbands abreast, if her fancy so dictated. His Eminence couldn't have asked more questions or insisted on more proof if he'd been buying a Leonardo for the National Gallery, instead of handing over the precarious possession of a Tyrolese cow-girl to a handsome but highly-flavoured Western-American mountebank.

At last, when Florian returned, much disturbed, from his sixth or seventh unsuccessful interview, to Linnet's house in Avenue Road, where he was to meet Philippina and her betrothed by special appointment, his hansom drew up at the door just as Philippina herself and Mr Theodore Livingstone, in their most Sunday array, disappeared into the vestibule. Florian followed them fast upstairs into Linnet's drawing-room. Andreas Hausberger was there, with Linnet by his side; Philippina and Mr Livingstone looked radiantly happy, and bursting with excitement.

"Well, the Archbishop still refuses," Florian exclaimed, with great disgust, dropping exhausted on a sofa. "I never in my life met such a stubborn old dromedary. I've tried him with reason, and I've tried him with ridicule, and I've tried him with authority, but nothing answers. He's impervious to any of 'em—a typical pachyderm. I don't believe, myself, if you gird at him for a year, you'll get anything out of him."

"It doesn't matter now," Philippina answered, glibly, withdrawing her light glove. "Teodore and I haf taken ze law into our own hands. He persuade me to it zis morning. I do not care by zis time, were it for twenty Archbishops."

"Oh dear, what do you mean?" Linnet cried, all aghast, regarding her friend with profound dismay.

Philippina held up her left hand significantly. "Just zat!" she cried, with a little air of petulant triumph, touching a plain gold ring on her third finger. Then she turned to Theodore. "My husband!" she said, smiling, as if to introduce him in his novel capacity.

"I'd arranged it all beforehand," the American explained, coming to her aid at once with a somewhat exulting air; "I'd got the licence, and put everything well in hand against the Archbishop's consent; and this morning I felt I wasn't going to wait knocking about for the blamed thing any longer. So I persuaded Philippina, and Philippina gave way; and we were married by twelve o'clock at a Baptist Chapel, by a minister of religion, as the Act directs, in the presence of the registrar. I expect that's about as binding as you make 'em in England; an Archbishop himself couldn't fix it up any firmer with a dozen dispensations."

"I congratulate you!" Florian cried, fanning his face with his hand. "You've done the right thing. Archbishops, I take it, are impracticable anachronisms. It's absurd to let these priests interfere with one's individuality in such a private matter."

But Linnet started back with an awestruck face. "O Philippina," she cried, "how dreadful! Why, a Catholic wouldn't think you were married at all! There's been no sacrament. From the Church's point of view, you might almost as well not have gone before the registrar."

Florian laughed down her scruples. The happy bridegroom, never doubting in his own soul the validity of his marriage, invited them all to dine with him that evening at the Criterion before the theatre. But a little later in the afternoon, when the women had left the room, Andreas Hausberger drew Florian mysteriously aside. "Linnet's quite right," he whispered in the philosopher's ear. "I know my countrywomen. Philippina'll be as happy as the day is long—for a matter of a week or two; and then, when she comes to think over what it is she's done, she'll never forgive herself. From the Catholic point of view, this is no marriage at all. Philippina must answer for it sooner or later to the priests: and they won't be too gentle to her."

CHAPTER XXXVII

Andreas Hausberger was right. Philippina's nemesis found her out all too quickly. Just six weeks later, Will Deverill had called round one afternoon at Florian's rooms in Grosvenor Gardens. They were engaged in discussing Florian's latest purchase—an etching of a wood-nymph after a new Dutch artist, very pure and precious—when Mr Barnes, that impeccable man-servant, opened the door with a flourish, and announced in his cut-and-dried official voice, "Signora Cazzlemonty; Mrs Theodore Livingstone!"

And Linnet and Philippina burst in upon them like a whirlwind.

Will rose hurriedly to greet them. In a moment, he saw something serious was amiss. Philippina's eyes were red and swollen with crying; Linnet's, though less bloodshot, looked weary and anxious. "Why, Madre de Dios, what's the matter?" Florian exclaimed in his affected way, rushing forward effusively in his brown velvet smoking-coat. "My dear Signora, to what happy star do I owe the honour of this unexpected visit? And all unbidden, too! Such good luck is too infrequent!"

"It's poor Philippina!" Linnet cried, half-inarticulate with sympathy. "She's in such a dreadful state. She really doesn't know what on earth to do about it."

Florian smiled the calm smile of superior wisdom. "What, already?" he exclaimed, raising one impressive hand. "So soon? So soon? A little rift within the lute, a little tiff with her Theodore? Well, well, dear Diva, we know these offences must needs come, in the best regulated families. They're part and parcel of our ridiculous marriage system. Will and I are wiser in our generation, you see; we keep well out of it."

"No, no; it is not zat!" Philippina cried, excitedly. Then turning to Will, she burst out in German, "I've been to see the priest and the bishop to-day, to ask for absolution, and it's all no use; they'll neither of them give it to me. I've been to ask them again and again these two weeks; but they're hard like rock; hard, hard, as that mantelpiece: they refuse to forgive me. They say it's no true marriage at all that I've made, but the lusts of the flesh—a sinful union. Ach! what shall I do, what ever shall I do? This is terrible, terrible!" And she wrung her hands hard. "It'll kill me," she cried; "it'll kill me."

Linnet turned in explanation to the bewildered Florian. "You see," she said simply, "she's living in sin now, and they won't absolve her. She may not take the mass, nor receive the sacraments of the Church in any form. She's like one excommunicated. If she died to-morrow, they would refuse her extreme unction; she would pass away in her sin, and must go at once, straight, straight to perdition."

"But surely," Florian ventured to observe, turning theologian for once, in these peculiar circumstances, "her present life—well, my dear Signora, without rudeness to the lady, we must all admit, it's—h'm, h'm—how shall I put it? It's at least quite as innocent as her previous habits."

Linnet made no false pretence of misunderstanding his plain meaning. This was a serious matter, and she felt its full seriousness herself so deeply that she sympathised with Philippina. "You don't understand," she answered, gasping; "you don't at all understand; you can't throw yourself into our standpoint. You're not a Catholic, you see, and you don't feel as we feel about it. To sin once, twice, three times, till seventy times seven, I care not how often—that is simply to sin: and if we repent in our hearts, God is faithful and just, the Church absolves us. But to live in open sin, to persist in one's wrong, to set the authority and discipline of the Church at defiance, ah! that to us is quite another matter. Philippina may have done wrong sometimes; we are all of us human; Heaven forbid I should judge her"—she spoke very earnestly; "but to continue in sin, to live her life without the sacraments and consolations of the Church, to remain with a man whom no Catholic can recognise as really her husband—that is too, too terrible. And, just think, if she were to die—" Linnet gazed up at him appealingly.

"But that can't be the Catholic doctrine!" Will exclaimed with great vehemence.

Florian was more practical. "I dare say not," he answered, with a shrug—"as the Catholic doctrine is understood by theologians, archbishops, and casuistical text-books. But that's nothing to the point. It is the Catholic doctrine as these women understand it, and it's sufficient to make them both supremely unhappy. That's enough for us. What we've got to ask is, how can we help them now out of this hole they've got into?"

The longer they talked about it, indeed, the clearer did this central fact come out to them. Philippina had married in haste, without the Church's consent; she was repenting at leisure now, in the effort to obtain it. And she sat there, cowering and quivering in bodily terror of those pains and penalties of fire and flame which were every whit as real to her to-day in London as they had been long ago by the wayside shrines at St Valentin. Either she must give up her husband, she said, or her hopes of salvation. It was evident that to her mind the little peccadilloes which the Church could absolve were as absolutely nothing; but to live with the husband whom the Church disowned, appalled and alarmed her. Her agonised terror was as genuine as though the danger she feared were actually confronting her. She saw and heard the hissing flames of purgatory. It made Will realise far more keenly than he had ever realised before the deep hold their creed keeps over these Tyrolese women. He couldn't help thinking how much Linnet would suffer, with her finer mould, and her profounder emotions, under similar circumstances, if even Philippina, that buxom, coarse-fibred girl, took so deeply to heart the Church's displeasure. He remembered it afterwards at a great crisis of their history; it was one of the events in life that most profoundly affected him.

Philippina, meanwhile, rocked herself up and down, moaning and trembling piteously. Will's heart was touched. He seized his friend by the arm. "Look here, Florian," he cried, all sympathy, "we must go at once and see the Archbishop."

"My dear fellow," Florian answered, shaking his head, "it isn't the slightest use. I've tried too long. The man's pure priest. Heart or pity he has none. The bowels of compassion have been all trained out of him. The simplest offence against ecclesiastical law is to him sheer heresy."

"Never mind," Will answered. "We can always try." It struck him, in fact, that the Archbishop might perhaps be more easily moved by himself than by Florian. "Philippina must go with us. We'll see whether or not we can move the Churchman."

They drove off together in a cab to Westminster; but Linnet went back by herself to St John's Wood.

When she reached her home, Andreas met her at the door with a little sneer on his face. Though they lived more simply than ever prima donna lived before, his avarice grew more marked as Linnet's earnings increased; and since Philippina's marriage he had been unkinder than ever to her. "What did you want with a cab?" he asked, "wasting your money like that. Wherever you've been, without my knowledge or consent, you might at least have come home by the Underground, I should fancy."

Linnet's face flushed hot. In her anxiety for her friend's soul, she had never thought of such trifles as the hire of a hansom. "It was for Philippina," she said, reproachfully, with a good home thrust: and Andreas, wincing, imagined he could detect a faintly personal stress upon Philippina's name which almost disconcerted him. "She came round here in such a terrible state of distress that I couldn't help going with her. She can't get her absolution; she's almost out of her mind with it."

Andreas' face set harder and sterner than ever. He eyed his wife narrowly. "Philippina can settle for her own cabs," he said with an ugly frown. "What's Philippina to us or we to Philippina, that we should waste our hard-earned money upon her? Let Philippina pay for the saving of her own precious soul, if she wants to save it. Don't spend a penny upon her that belongs to your husband."

An answer struggled hard for utterance upon Linnet's tongue; but with an effort she repressed it. Andreas hadn't always thought so little of Philippina, before she married the handsome brown-eyed American. However, Linnet refrained from answering him back as he himself would have answered her. The Blessed Madonna in her hand gave her strength to restrain herself. She merely said, with a little sigh, "I never thought about the cab; it was Florian who called it."

Andreas turned upon her sharply. "So so!" he exclaimed, with an air of discovery. "You've been round to Herr Florian's! And the other man was there, I suppose! You went by appointment to meet him!"

"Herr Will was there, if you mean him," Linnet answered, fiery red, but disdaining the weak subterfuge of a pretended ignorance. "I didn't go to meet him, though; I didn't know he was there. He's gone round with her, poor girl, to see the Archbishop."

Andreas drew himself up very stiff. He hadn't quite liked that stress Linnet put on Philippina's name, and he wasn't sorry accordingly for this stray chance of a diversion. "So Herr Will was there!" he repeated, with a meaning smile, "What a singular coincidence! You've been seeing too much altogether of Herr Will of late. I'm not a jealous man, but mind you, Linnet, I draw a line somewhere."

Linnet's face was crimson. "It's not you who have had cause to feel jealous," she answered, quietly. "Herr Will is too good a man to act . . . well, to act as you would do. You know what you say or what you hint at isn't true. You're put out because—"

"Because what?" Andreas asked, provokingly, as she broke off and hesitated.

But Linnet brushed past him, and went up to her own room without answering a word. She was too proud to finish the sentence she had begun, "Because Philippina has given you up and married the American."

She had known it all along—known it, and never minded. But she felt in her heart the reason why; she had never loved Andreas, so how could she be jealous of him? He had married her as a very sound investment; he had never pretended to care for her at all in herself; and she, in turn, had never pretended to care for him. But now, in an agony of remorse and terror, she flung herself on her bed and, with white hands clasped, besought Our Lady, with all the strength she possessed, to save her from despising and hating her husband. She had never loved him, to be sure; but to her, as a Catholic, marriage was a most holy sacrament of the Church, and she must try to live up to it. She prayed, too, for strength to love Will Deverill less—to forget him, to neglect him. Yet, even as she prayed, she thought to herself ten thousand times over how different it would all have been if she had married Will Deverill; how much she would have loved him; how true at heart she would have been to him. All heretic that he was, his image rose up between herself and Our Lady. She wiped her brimming eyes, and, with sobs and entreaties, begged hard to love him less, begged hard to be forgiven that she loved him now so dearly.

Yet, even in her own distress, Linnet thought of Philippina. She prayed hard, too, for Philippina. She begged Our Lady, with tears and sighs, to soften the obdurate Archbishop's heart, and make smooth for Philippina the path to Paradise. For, in a way, she really liked that big, bouncing alp-girl. Unlike as they were in mould, they both came from St Valentin; Philippina was to Linnet the one tie she still possessed that bound her in memory to the land of her birth, the land where her father and mother lay dead, awaiting their souls' return from the flames of purgatory.

That evening at the theatre, Philippina burst in upon her with a radiant face, as she dressed for her part in Cophetua's Adventure. "It's all right," she cried aloud in German, half-wild with joy. "Mr Deverill has managed it! He spoke to the Archbishop, and the Archbishop said Yes; and he gave me absolution then and there on the spot, and I went home for Theodore; and I'm to spend to-night at a lodging-house alone, and he'll marry us with all the rites of the Church to-morrow."

Linnet clasped her hand tight. "I'm so glad, dear," she answered. "I knew he'd give way if Herr Will only spoke to him. Herr Will's so kind and good, no mortal on earth can refuse him anything. He's a heretic, to be sure, but, O Philippina, there's no Catholic like him! . . . Besides," she added, after a pause, rearranging the folds in the Beggar Maid's dress with pretended pre-occupation, "I prayed Our Lady that she might soften the Archbishop's heart; and Our Lady heard my prayer; she always hears me."

As she spoke, a great pang passed suddenly through her bosom: Our Lady had answered that prayer; would she answer the other one? Would she grant Linnet's wish to love Will Deverill less? Staring before her in an agony, she sobbed at the bare thought. It was horrible, hateful! A flood of conflicting emotion came over her like a wave. Sinful as she felt it herself to be, she knew she never meant that prayer she had uttered. Love Will Deverill less? Forget him? Oh, impossible! She might be breaking every commandment in her heart at once, but she couldn't frame that prayer she must and would love him!

Oh, foolishness of men, who think they can bind the human heart with a vow! You may promise to do or leave undone what you will; but promise to feel or not to feel! The bare idea is preposterous!

CHAPTER XXXVIII

HUSBAND OR LOVER?

The Hausbergers spent that winter in Italy. Andreas thought the London air was beginning to tell upon Linnet's throat, and he took good care, accordingly, to get her an autumn engagement in Vienna, followed by a winter one at Rome and Naples. The money was less, to be sure, but in the end 'twould repay him. Linnet was an investment, and he managed his investment with consummate prudence. Before they went away, however, he and Linnet had another slight difference of opinion about Will Deverill. On the very morning of their departure, a bouquet arrived at the door in Avenue Road, with a neat little note attached, which Linnet opened and read with undisguised eagerness. Bouquets and notes were not infrequent arrivals at that house, indeed, and Andreas, as a rule, took little or no notice of them, unless accompanied by a holder of the precious metals. But Linnet flushed so with pleasure as she read this particular missive that Andreas leaned across and murmured casually, "What's up? Let me look at it."

"I'd, I'd rather not, if you don't mind," Linnet answered, colouring up, and half-trying to hide it.

Andreas snatched the paper unceremoniously from her trembling hands. He recognised the handwriting. "Ho, Will Deverill!" he cried, with a sneer. "Let's see what he says! It's poetry, is it, then? He drops into verse!" And he glanced at it angrily.

"TO LINNET."
"Fair fortune gild your southward track,
Dear bird of passage, taking wing.
For me, when April wafts you back,
Will not the spring be twice the spring?"

It was imprudent of Will, to be sure; but we are all of us a leetle imprudent at times (present company of course excepted); and some small licence in these matters is accorded by common consent to poets. But Andreas was angry, and more than merely angry; he was suspicious as well—beginning to be afraid, in fact, of his hold over Linnet. At first, when he came to England, the wise impresario was so sure of his wife—so sure of keeping her, and all the money she brought him, in his own hands—that he rather threw her designedly into Will's company than otherwise. He saw she sang better when she was much with Will; and for the sake of her singing, he lumped the little question of personal preference. But of late he had begun really to fear Will Deverill. It occurred to him at odd moments as just within the bounds of possibility, after all, that Will might some day rob him of his wife altogether, and to rob him of his wife was to rob him of his most serious and profitable property. Why, the sale of her presents alone, bracelets, bouquet-holders, rings, and such like trifles, was quite a small fortune to him. And, all Catholic that she was, and devout at that, a pure woman who valued her own purity high, quite unlike Philippina, Andreas felt none the less she might conceivably go off in the end with Will Deverill. The heart is always a very vulnerable point in women. He might attack her through the heart, or some such sentimental rubbish; and Linnet had a heart such a fellow as that could strike chords upon easily.

So Andreas looked at the flowers and simple little versicles with an angry eye. Then he said, in his curt way, "Pretty things to address to a married woman, indeed! Pack them up and send them back again!"

Linnet flushed, and flared up. For once in her life, her temper failed her. "I won't," she answered, firmly. "I shall keep them if I choose. There's nothing in them a poet mayn't rightly say to a married woman. If there was, you know quite well I wouldn't allow him to say it. . . . Besides," she went on, warmly, "you wouldn't have asked me to send them back if they'd been pearls or diamonds. You kept the duke's necklet." And she hid the note in her bosom before the very eyes of her husband.

Andreas was not a noisy man. He knew a more excellent way than that to carry his point in the end—by biding his time, and watching and waiting. So he said no more for the moment, except to mutter a resounding High German oath, as he flung the flowers, paper cover and all, into the dining-room fireplace. In half-an-hour more, they were at Charing Cross, on their way to Vienna. Linnet kept Will's verses inside the bosom of her dress, and close to her throbbing heart. Andreas asked no more about them just then, but, all that winter through, he meditated his plan of action for the future, in silence.

Their two months at Vienna were a great success, professionally. Linnet went on to Rome laden with the spoils of susceptible Austrians. For the first few weeks after their arrival in Italy, she noticed that Andreas received no letters in Philippina's handwriting; but, after that time, notes in a familiar dark-hued scrawl began to arrive for him—at first, once a fortnight or so, then, later, much more frequently. Andreas read them before Linnet's eyes, and burnt them cautiously, without note or comment. Linnet was too proud to allude to their arrival in any way.

Early in April, with the swallows and sand-martins, they returned to England. The spring was in the air, and Andreas thought the bracing north would suit Linnet's throat better now than that soft and relaxing Italian atmosphere. On the very day when they reached Avenue Road, Philippina came to see them. She greeted Andreas warmly; Linnet kissed her on both cheeks. "Well, dear," she said in German, clasping her friend's hand hard, "and how's your husband?"

"What! that dreadful man! Ach, lieber Gott, my dear, don't speak of him!" Philippina cried, holding up both her hands in holy horror. Linnet smiled a quiet smile. Florian's forecast was correct; Andreas's words had come true. Her hot first love had cooled down again as quickly as it had flared up, all aglow, like a straw fire in the first instance.

Then Philippina began, in her usual voluble style, to pour forth the full gravamen of her charges against Theodore. She was living with him still, oh yes, she was living with him, for appearance' sake, you understand; and then besides—Philippina dropped her eyes with a conventional smile, and glanced side-long at Andreas—there were contingencies . . . well . . . which made it necessary, don't you know, to keep in with him for the present. But he was a dreadful man, all the same, and she had quite seen through him. She wished to goodness she had taken Herr Hausberger's excellent advice at first, and never, never married him. "Though there! when once one's married to a man, like him or lump him, my dear, the best thing one can do is to drag along with him somehow, for the children's sake, of course"—and Philippina simpered once more like the veriest school-girl.

As soon as she had finished the recital of her troubles with that dreadful man, she went on to remark, in the most offhand way, that Will Deverill, presuming on his altered fortunes, had taken new and larger rooms in a street in St James's. They were beautiful rooms, oh yes, of course, and Herr Florian had furnished them, ach, so schön, so schön, was never anything like it. She saw Herr Florian often now; yes, he was always so kind, and sent her flowers weekly, such lovely flowers. Herr Will had heard that Linnet was coming back; and he was hoping to see her. He would be round there that very night, he had told her so himself just half-an-hour ago in Regent Street.

At those words, Andreas rose, without warning of any sort, and touched the electric bell. The servant entered.

"You remember Mr Deverill?" he said to the girl; "the tall, fair gentleman, with the light moustache, who called often last summer?"

"Oh yes, sir, I mind him well," the girl answered, promptly "him as brought the bokay for Mrs Hausberger the morning you was going away to the Continent last October."

It was an awkward reminiscence, though she didn't intend it so. Andreas frowned still more angrily than before at the suggestion. "That's the man!" he cried, savagely. "Now, Ellen, if he calls to-night and asks for your mistress, say she isn't at home, and won't be at home in future to Mr Deverill."

His voice was cold and stern. Linnet started from her chair. Her face flushed crimson. That Andreas should so shame her before Philippina and her own servant, it was hateful, it was intolerable! She turned to the girl with a tinge of unwonted imperiousness in her tone. "Say nothing of the sort, Ellen," she cried, in a very firm voice, standing forth and confronting her. "If Mr Deverill comes, show him up to the drawing-room."

Andreas stood still and glared at her. He said never a word, but he clenched his fists hard, and pressed his teeth together. The girl looked from one to the other in feeble indecision, and then began to whimper. "Which of you am I to take my orders from?" she burst out, with a little sob. "From you, or my mistress?"

"From me!" Linnet answered, in a very settled voice. "This house is mine, and you are my servant. I earn the money that keeps it all going. Mr Hausberger has no right to dictate to me here whom I may see or not in my own drawing-room."

The girl hesitated for a moment, and then left the room with evident reluctance. As soon as she was gone, Andreas turned fiercely to his wife. "This is open war," he said, with a scowl; "open war, Frau Hausberger. This is sheer rebellion. You are wrong in what you say. The house is mine, and all that's in it; I took it in my own name, I furnished it, I pay the rent of it. The money you earn is mine; I have your own signature to the document we drew up before I invested my hard cash in getting you trained and educated. I'm your husband, and if you disobey me, I'll take you where I choose. Now mind, my orders are, you don't receive Mr Deverill in this house this evening. Philippina, you are my witness. You hear what I say. If she does, all the world will know what to think of it. She'll receive him against my wish, and in my absence. Every civilised court puts only one construction on such an act of open disobedience."

He went out into the hall, fiery hot, and returned with his hat. "I'm going out," he said, curtly. "I don't want to coerce you. I leave it in your own hands whether you'll see this man alone against my will or not, Frau Hausberger. But, recollect, if you see him, I shall take my own course. I'll not be bearded like this before my own servants by a woman, a woman I've raised from the very dregs of the people, and put by my own act in a position she's unfit for."

Linnet's blood was up. "You can go, sir," she said, briefly. "If Mr Deverill calls, I shall see for myself whether or not I care to receive him."

Andreas strode out all on fire. As soon as he was gone, Linnet sank into a chair, buried her face in her hands, pressed her nails against her brow, and sobbed long and violently. The little Madonna in Britannia metal gave scant comfort to her soul. She rocked herself to and fro in unspeakable misery. Though she had spoken up so bravely to Andreas to his face, she knew well in her heart this was the end of everything. As a wife, as a Catholic, let him be ever so unworthy, let him be ever so unkind, her duty was plain. She must never, in his absence, receive Will Deverill!

Her strength was failing fast. She knew that well. Dear Lady, protect her! If she saw Will after this, Heaven knew what might happen—for, oh, in her heart, how she loved him, how she loved him! She had prayed to the Blessed Frau that she might love Will Deverill less; but she never meant it. The more she prayed, the better she loved him. And now, why, the Madonna was crumpled up almost double in her convulsive grasp. Philippina leant over her with a half-frightened air. Linnet rose and rang the bell. It was terrible, terrible. Though it broke her poor heart, she would obey the Church; she would obey her husband. "If Mr Deverill calls," she said, half-inaudibly, to the servant, once more, "you may tell him . . . I'm not at home."

The Church had conquered.

Then she sank back in her chair, sobbing and crying bitterly.

CHAPTER XXXIX

DOCUMENTARY EVIDENCE

Mr Joaquin Holmes was making a morning call one of those days on Mrs Theodore Livingstone—better known to the readers of these pages as Philippina—at her furnished apartments in Bury Street, Bloomsbury. Of late, Mr Joaquin Holmes had been down on his luck; and the weather in London that day was certainly not of a sort to propitiate the nerves of a man who had been raised on the cloudless skies of Southern Colorado. Though it was early April, a settled gloom, as of November, brooded impartially over city and suburbs. Mr Joaquin Holmes was by no means happy. Society in London had grown tired of his seership; the Psycho-physical Entertainment at the Assyrian Hall attracted every night an ever-dwindling audience; Maskelyne and Cooke had learnt to counterfeit all the best of his tricks; and things in general looked so black just then for the trade of prophet that the Seer was beginning to wonder in his own inmost soul whether he wouldn't be compelled before long to fall back for a while on his more lucrative but less reputable alternative profession of gambler and card-sharper. However, being a man of sentiment, he consoled himself meanwhile by a morning call on Mrs Theodore Livingstone.

Philippina was looking her very best that afternoon, attired in a coquettish costume, half peignoir, half tea-gown, especially designed for the reception of such casual visitors. And Mr Joaquin Holmes was one of Philippina's most devoted admirers. Florian had introduced him long ago to the good-natured singer, before her marriage, and the Seer had ever since been numbered among her most frequent and attentive callers. He could talk with her in German; for, as befits his trade, he was an excellent linguist; and Philippina was glad when she could relieve herself for a while from the constant strain of speaking English by an occasional return to the free tongue of her Fatherland. Theodore was out, she said, glibly, with her accustomed volubility; oh yes, he was out, and he wouldn't be back, she supposed, till dinner. No fear about that; the horrid man never came near her now, except at meal times, or to go down to the theatre. He was off, she had no doubt, with some of his hateful companions in some billiard-room or something, wasting the money that ought to go to the support of the household. If it weren't for herself, and for some very kind friends, Philippina really didn't know what on earth would become of them.

The Seer smiled sweetly. He was an engaging man, and when he flooded Philippina with the light of his great eyes she thought him really as nice as anybody on earth, except Herr Andreas. They sat there long, and chatted in that peculiar vein which Philippina affected when she found herself alone with one of her male admirers. She was a born flirt, Philippina, and though she was a matron now, with a distinct tendency to grow visibly stouter on good English fare, she had still all that archness and that liveliness of manner which had captivated Florian the first morning they met her on the hill-top at St Valentin.

As they sat there, exchanging a quiet fire of repartee, with many ach's and so's of very Teutonic playfulness, the lodging-house servant came up with a note, which Philippina tore open and read through somewhat eagerly. The Seer noticed that as she read it her colour deepened—such signs of feeling seldom escaped the eyes of that observant thought-reader. He noticed also that the envelope, though directed in English letters, bore evident traces of a German hand in the twists and twirls of the very peculiar manuscript. He could see from where he sat an unmistakable curl over the u of Bury Street. A curl like that could only have been produced by a person accustomed to German writing.

Philippina crumpled the envelope, and looked vacantly at the fireplace. The fire wasn't lighted, for the day, though damp and dark, was by no means chilly. The Seer noted that glance: so she wanted to burn it, then! Philippina, unheeding him, poked the envelope through the bars of the grate with the aid of the tongs, but laid the note itself on the table by her side, a little uneasily. The Seer, with that native quickness of perception which had made him into a thought-reader, divined at once what was passing through her mind; she must destroy that note before Theodore returned, and she was anxious in her own soul for a chance of destroying it.

Joaquin Holmes spotted a mystery—perhaps an intrigue; but, in any case, a mystery. Now little family affairs of this sort were part and parcel of his stock-in-trade; there was nothing so useful to him in life as possession of a secret. And Philippina was indeed an open book; he could read her as easily as he could read a pack of cards with the tips of his fingers. The longer he stopped, the more obviously and evidently Philippina fidgeted; the more she fidgeted, the longer he determined, as he phrased it to himself with Western frankness, "to stop and see the fun out." Philippina grew more and more silent as time went by; the Seer talked on and on with more unceasing persistence. Meanwhile, the fog without grew denser and denser. At last, of a sudden, it descended, pitch dark, with that surprising rapidity we all know so well in our smoky metropolis. Philippina yawned; she saw there was no help for it. It was a case for the gas. "Will you ring the bell, Mr Holmes?" she asked languidly, in German.

The Seer seized his chance, and rose briskly to obey her. As he brushed past her side, Philippina, in a quiver, put out her hand for her letter. The room was black as night. She fumbled for it in vain; a cold chill came over her. "Why, where's that paper?" she exclaimed, in a tone of most evident and undisguised dismay. "I wish I had a match. It was lying here a minute ago."

Mr Holmes stood calmly in the dark, with his hand upon the bell-handle. He was in no hurry to ring it. "You'll have to wait now," he said, in his very coolest manner, "till the servant comes up. Unfortunately, I don't happen to have a match about me."

"There are some upon the mantelpiece, perhaps," Philippina faltered, unwilling to rise and move away from the table that held that compromising letter.

"Oh, that's all right!" the Seer said quietly, in his slow Western drawl. "Don't trouble yourself about me. I can see very well in the dark without one." Then he began to read aloud, "Du liebste Philippina!"

Philippina made a wild dash across the room in his direction. This was horrible! He had abstracted it! But the Seer, unabashed, took a step or two backward with great deliberation. "That's all right!" he said again, in a languid tone of the blandest unconcern. "There's nothing fresh here; you needn't trouble yourself. It's only a little note from a very old friend, signed, 'Thy ever affectionate, Andreas Hausberger.'"

Philippina darted once more blindly in the direction of the voice; Joaquin Holmes heard her coming, and stepped aside noiselessly. He passed his practised finger-tips again over the lines of the writing. "Very pretty!" he said, smiling. "Very nice, indeed—for Signora Casalmonte! Why, I fancied you were her friend. This is charming, charming! And only to think so prudent a man as our dear friend Hausberger should have ventured to write such a compromising letter! 'At three o'clock to-morrow, at the usual place,' he says. Dear me, that's interesting! So you've met him there before! And what a fool the man must be to go and put it on paper!"

Philippina clasped her hands, and dashed wildly against the sofa. "Oh, give it back to me!" she cried, really alarmed. "What will Andreas ever say! How can you be so cruel? And my husband—my husband!"

The American, still wholly undisconcerted by her cries, popped the paper inside his breast-coat pocket, buttoned it up securely, drew a match-box from his waistcoat, and lighted the gas with a calm air of triumph. "Now, don't be a fool, Philippina," he said, taking hold of her by those plump round arms of hers, and pushing her back with conspicuous calmness into an easy-chair. "Compose yourself! Compose yourself! There's nothing new in all this; we all know what you are—Theodore Livingstone, I suppose, just as well as the rest of us. Why trouble to give yourself these airs of tragic virtue? To tell you the truth, my dear girl, they don't at all become you. Nobody expects miracles from an actress nowadays—not even her husband. Besides, I'm not going to make money out of you; you're a very nice girl, and you've always been kind to me; so why should I want to show this letter to Theodore? What's Theodore to me, or I to Theodore, that I should bother my head to uphold his domestic dignity? No, no, my child; that's not the game. I hold the letter as a threat over Andreas Hausberger. Hausberger's rich, don't you see, and his wife's his fortune. What's more, she hates him, and he keeps her always precious short of money. She'll be ready to pay anything for a letter like this; it's a handle against him; and he, for his part, well—he'll make any terms she likes rather than drive her away from him."

He took up his hat, and made a courtly bow. "Good-bye, Philippina," he said, smiling; "this'll never come out at all, as far as regards yourself and your husband. Hausberger'd pay me well to keep the thing out of court; but I shan't take it to him; I'll go and offer it direct, money down, to the Casalmonte."

He walked lightly to the door, leaving Philippina petrified. He turned into the street: the fog began to lift again. He walked briskly on in the direction of Portland Place. Before he crossed the Regent's Park, he had made up his mind to his plan of action. It was no use trying to blackmail a cool hand like Andreas; he must offer the letter, as he said, direct to Linnet. He didn't doubt she would gladly seize on the pretext for a divorce, or at least a rupture. It would give her a good excuse for going away from the man whom his observation and instinct had rightly taught him she despised and detested.

He rang at the door in Avenue Road. By a lucky chance, he found Linnet in—and alone: her husband, she said, was out; he had gone for the day, she thought, with a party down to Greenwich.

The Seer didn't mince matters. With American directness, he went straight to the root of things. "I'm glad of that," he said, coolly, "for I didn't want to see him. I wanted to see you alone. I've got something against him I want to sell you."

"Something against him?" Linnet cried, puzzled. "I don't know what you mean, Mr Holmes; and why on earth should you think I'd care to buy it?"

"Now, just you look here," the Seer went on, holding the letter, face downward, before him and fumbling it with his fingers; "why shouldn't we speak straight? What's the good of going beating about the bush like this? Let's talk fair and square. You hate your husband."

Linnet rose and faced him. She was flushed and angry. "You've no right to say that," she cried. "I never told you so."

The Seer smiled sweetly. "I wouldn't be a thought-reader," he answered, with unaffected frankness, "if I needed to be told a thing in order to know it. But that's neither here nor there. Don't let's quarrel about these trifles. The real thing's this. I have a letter in my hand here that may be of very great use to you, if you want to get away from this man, as you do, and to marry Mr Deverill."

Linnet's face was crimson with shame and indignation. "How dare you say such a thing, sir!" she cried, trying to move towards the door. "You know it isn't true. I never dreamt of marrying him."

By a quick flank movement, the Seer sprang in front of her and cut off her retreat. "That won't do," he said, sharply. "You can't deceive me like that. Remember, I can read your inmost thoughts as readily as I can read this letter in my hand. I'll read it to you now. It's to your friend Mrs Livingstone." And, without a passing tremor on that handsome face or a quiver in his voice, he read out with his fingers the short compromising note, from "Thou dearest Philippina" down to "Thy ever affectionate, Andreas Hausberger."

Linnet faced him, unmoved externally but with a throbbing heart. The Seer, as he finished it, darted a triumphant glance at her.

"Well?" Linnet said quietly, drawing herself up to her full height.

"Well, what'll you give me for that, in plain black and white?" the Seer asked, with a calm tone of unquestioned victory.

"Nothing!" Linnet answered, moving once more towards the door. "It's nothing fresh to me. I knew all that, oh, long ago."

"Knew it? Ah, yes, no doubt," the Seer answered, with a curl of those handsome lips. "There's nothing much in that. Of course we all knew it. But it's not enough knowing it. You want it written down in plain black and white, to put in evidence against him. You see he acknowledges—"

Linnet cut him short sharply. "To put it in evidence?" she repeated, staring at him with a bewildered look. "In evidence against whom? What on earth can you mean? To put in evidence where? I don't understand you."

"Now, don't let's waste useful time," the Seer interposed seriously. "This is a practical matter. There's no knowing how soon your husband may return. I just mean business. I want to hear, straight and short, what you'll give for this letter. We all know very well you've got enough already to prove the count of cruelty upon. You've only got to prove the other thing in order to get a regular divorce from him. And the proof of it's here, in plain black and white, under his own very hand, in this letter I've read to you. Now, what do you offer? If you name my figure, it's yours; if you don't— well, Philippina's a very good friend of mine; here goes—I'll burn it!"

He held it over the fire, which was burning in the grate, as he looked hard into her eyes. Linnet drew back a pace or two, and faced him proudly. "Mr Holmes," she said, in her very coldest voice, "you entirely misunderstand. You reckon without your host. You forget I'm a Catholic. Divorce to me means absolutely nothing. I'm Andreas Hausberger's wife before the eye of God, and all the law-courts on earth could never make me otherwise—could never set me free to be anyone else's. So your letter would be absolutely no use at all to me. I knew pretty well, long since, the main fact it implies; and it mattered very little to me. Andreas Hausberger is my husband—as such, I obey him, by the law of God—but he never had my heart; and I never had his. On no ground whatsoever do I value your document."

The Seer, in turn, drew back in incredulous amazement. Was she trying to cheapen him? He interpreted her words after his own psychology. "No; you don't mean that," he said, with an unbelieving air. "You'd get a divorce if you could, of course, like anyone else; and you'd marry that man Deverill. Don't think I'm such a fool as not to know how you feel to him. But you're seeming to hang back so as to knock down my price. You want to get it a bargain. You think you can best me. Now, don't let's lose time haggling. Make me an offer, money down, and I'll tell you at once whether or not I'll entertain it."

Linnet gazed at him in unspeakable scorn and contempt. "Do you think," she said, advancing a step, "I'd bargain with you to buy a wretched thing like that! If I wanted to leave my husband, I'd leave him outright, letter or no letter. I stop with him now, of my own free will, by the Church's command, and from a sense of duty."

So far as the Seer was concerned, this strange woman spoke a foreign language. Duty was a word that didn't enter into his vocabulary. He scanned her from head to foot, as one might scan some queer specimen of an unknown wild species. "You can't possibly mean that," he cried, with a discordant little laugh, for he was used to the free Western notions on these subjects. "Come now, buy it or not!" he went on, dangling the letter before her face, between finger and thumb. "It's going, going, going! Won't you make me a bid for it?"

He shook it temptingly, held it aloft; it was valuable evidence. As he did so, the paper slipped all of a sudden from his grasp, and fell fluttering at Linnet's feet. Mr Holmes was quick, but Linnet was quicker still. Before he could stoop to pick it up, she had darted down upon it and seized it. Then, with lightning haste, she thrust it inside her dress, in the shelter of her bosom. The baffled Seer seized her hand—too late to prevent her.

"Give it back to me!" he cried, twisting her wrist as he spoke. "How dare you take it? That's a dirty trick to play a man. It's mine, I say; give it back to me!"

Though he hurt her wrist and frightened her, Linnet stood her ground well. She was stronger than he thought—with all the stored-up strength of her mountain rearing. She pushed him back with a sudden burst of explosive energy. "You're wrong," she cried, indignantly. "It never was yours, though I don't know how you got it. You must have stolen it, no doubt, or intercepted it by some vile means, and then tried to make money out of it. I don't want it myself, but I won't give it back. It belongs to Philippina, and I mean to return it to her."

"That's a lie!" the Seer answered, catching her hands with a hasty dash, and trying to force her on her knees. "Damn your tricks; I'll have it back again!" And, in the heat of his rage, he tried to unfasten her dress and snatch it from her bosom.

She tore herself away. The Seer followed her, still struggling. It was a hand-to-hand grapple. He fought her for it wildly.

At that very moment, before Linnet had time to scream for help, the door opened suddenly, and— Andreas Hausberger entered.

CHAPTER XL

OPEN WAR

He glared at them for a moment before he fully took it in. The Seer, thus suddenly surprised, loosed his hold on Linnet, and drew back instinctively. But an awful feeling of doubt came over Linnet's mind. The position was most equivocal—nay, even compromising. Would Andreas misunderstand what this man was doing with her—one hand held on her wrist, and one clutching at her bosom?

But Andreas knew that simple loyal nature too well to doubt her relations with anyone—except Will Deverill. As he stood there and stared, he saw only that the American had been offering violence, personal violence, to Linnet. His hot Tyrolese blood boiled at once at that insult. He sprang forward and caught Joaquin Holmes by the throat. "You scoundrel!" he cried through his clenched teeth; "what are you doing to my wife? How dare you touch her like that? How dare you lay your blackguard hands upon her?"

The Coloradan freed himself with a jerk, and shook off his assailant, for he was a powerful man, too, though less sturdy than Andreas. He drew back half-a-pace, and faced the infuriated husband. His hand wandered half mechanically to the faithful six-shooter, which after all those years in civilised England old habit still made him carry always in his pocket. But he thought better of it after a moment, these Britishers have such a nasty insular way of stringing one up for the merest accident!—and answered instead, with an ugly smile, "It's her fault, not mine. She snatched a letter away from me. It's my own, and I want it back. She won't give it up to me."

Andreas Hausberger had his faults; but he had too much sense of dignity to bandy words with an intruder who had insulted his wife—above all, to bandy them in his wife's very presence. It mattered little to him just then what that question about the letter might really import. He stepped forward in his wrath once more, and caught the Seer by the shoulders. "You cur!" he cried, pushing him before him. "How dare you answer me like that?" And, with a sudden wrench, he flung the fellow against the door, bruising and hurting him violently.

The Coloradan rushed back on him. There was a short, sharp scuffle. Then Andreas, getting the better, opened the door with a dash, and dragged his opponent after him. At the head of the stairs, he paused, and gave him a sounding kick. The Coloradan writhed and squirmed, but, strong as he was, he found himself no match for the gigantic Tyroler. Besides, he was less used than his antagonist to these hand-to-hand struggles. Andreas, for his part, was quite in his element. "A Wirth who can't turn out a noisy or drunken guest, isn't worth his salt," he had said one day to Florian long ago in the Zillerthal; he was well used, indeed, of old to such impromptu encounters. The Seer on the contrary was more accustomed to the bowie and the six-shooter than to wrestling and scuffling. He yielded after a moment to Andreas's heavy hand, only stopping to shout back through the open drawing-room door, "Then you owe me fifty pounds, Signora, for that letter!"

Andreas hauled him down the stairs, dragged him, half-resisting, through the hall and vestibule, opened the front door with one free hand, hastily, and kicked his man down the steps with a volley of angry oaths in his native German. Then he slammed the door in the face of the discomfited Seer (who had rushed back again to assault him), and went upstairs once more, as outwardly cool as he could, but hot in the face and hotter at heart, to Linnet.

Linnet was really grateful to him. The man had frightened her. For the first time in her life, she admired her husband. The natural admiration that all her sex feel for physical strength and prowess in men was exceptionally marked in her, as in most other women of primitive communities. "Thank you," she said simply, as Andreas strolled in, trying to look unconcerned, with his hands in his pockets, and confronted her stonily. "The man hurt my wrist. If you hadn't come in, I don't know what on earth he might ever have done to me."

Andreas stared at her in silence with close-knit brows for half-a-minute. Then he said in an insolent tone, "Now, tell me, what's all this fuss he was making about some letter?"

His question brought Linnet back to herself with a sudden revulsion of feeling. In the tremulousness of those two scuffles, she had almost forgotten for the moment all about the first cause of them. But now, she looked her husband back straight in the face, and, without flinching or hesitating, she answered him in a scarcely audible voice, "He brought me the last letter you wrote to Philippina. The one making an appointment at the usual place for three to-morrow. I don't know how he got it, but he wanted to sell it to me."

Andreas never moved a muscle of that impassive face, but his colour came and went, and his breath stopped short, as he stood still and stared at her. "My last letter to Philippina!" he repeated, with a glow of shame. "And that fellow dared to show it to you! I'd have choked him if I'd known! The mean scoundrelly eavesdropper!"

Linnet folded her hands in front of her where she sat on her low chair. Her air was resigned. She hardly seemed to notice him. "You needn't be afraid," she said. "It's no matter to me. I guessed all that long ago. I didn't want your letters, or hers either, to prove it to me. I told him as much. To me, at least, it's no matter."

"And he offered to sell it you?" Andreas cried, growing in wrath. "He tried to make money of it! What did he want you to buy it for?"

"He said I could get a divorce with it," Linnet answered simply.

"A divorce!" Andreas shouted, losing control of himself for once. That word went straight home to all the deepest chords in his sordid nature. "He wanted to egg you on, then, to try and get a divorce from me! He wanted to cheat me of all I've worked and toiled for!" He flung himself into a chair, and clenched his fists, and ground his teeth. "The damned rogue!" he cried once more. "When I get at him, oh, I'll throttle him!"

He sat for a minute or two revolving many things angrily in his own burning soul. He had not only Linnet to think of now, but Philippina, too, and her husband. Heaven only knew what harm that man might do him in revenge for his drubbing—what scandal he might raise, what devils he might let loose upon him. If Linnet left him now, all the world would say she was amply justified. And the English law would allow her a divorce! No; not without cruelty! and he had never been cruel to her. There was comfort in that: he consoled himself in part with it. He had spoken harshly to her at times, perhaps, and taken care of her money for her—women are so reckless that a man must needs look after them. But cruel! oh no, no; she could never prove that against him!

"Divorce!" he said slowly, knitting his brows, and leaning forward. "He talked to you of divorce, Linnet! That's all pure gammon. There's no divorce for a woman, by English law, without cruelty or desertion. I've never been cruel to you, and I'm not likely to desert you. You can't get a divorce, I say. You can't get a divorce! You surely didn't promise him fifty pounds for that letter!"

"No; I didn't," Linnet answered. "I told him I didn't want it. Divorce would be no use in the world to me. I'm a Catholic, as you know, and I believe my religion."

Andreas stared at her hard. He fingered his chin thoughtfully. She had struck the right chord. How foolish of him in his haste not to have thought of that by pure instinct! Divorce, indeed! Why, of course, the Church wouldn't hear of it. To think that a Tyrolese woman would accept the verdict of a mere earthly court to dissolve a holy sacrament! "You're quite right," he muttered slowly, nodding his head once or twice; "divorce is pure sacrilege. There's no such thing known in the Catholic Church; there's no such thing known in the Austrian Empire."

He subsided for a moment. Then, all at once, with a bound, another emotion got the better of him. He must go out without delay and inquire how all this bother got abroad from Philippina. And yet— 'twas hard to know how he could govern himself aright. Not for worlds would he let Will Deverill come to the house in his absence now, after all that had happened. Linnet hadn't seen him yet since her return from Italy. If he came in, as things stood, and found her in her present mood, Andreas felt he himself couldn't answer for the consequences.

He paused, and reflected. For Philippina's sake, for his own, nay, even for Linnet's, he knew he must go out without one minute's delay, to prevent further mischief with Theodore Livingstone. But still— it was dangerous to go away from Linnet. Yet he must make up his mind one way or the other; and he made it up quickly. "I'm going out," he said in his curt tone, turning sharply to his wife, without one word of apology or explanation; "but before I go, I've a message to give the housemaid."

"Go when you like," Linnet answered coldly. Little as she cared for him now, little as she ever cared for him, it hurt her feelings none the less that he shouldn't even try to explain or to excuse himself. His very silence was insolent. She felt it keenly.

Andreas rang the bell, and then crossed his arms in a sullen fashion. That attitude alone seemed to exasperate Linnet. The housemaid answered the bell. He looked up at her with a scowl. "Ellen," he said, in a very slow and deliberate voice, "If Mr Will Deverill should call while I'm out, will you tell him the Signora's not at home to-day? She's never at home to him, you may say, except when I'm present."

Linnet's blood was boiling. These perpetual insults before her own servants' eyes were driving her fast into open rebellion. She answered not a word, but rose with dignity, and went over like a queen to her davenport in the corner. "Stop, Ellen," she said calmly, restraining herself with an effort. "I've a note I want you to post. Stand there, and wait till I've written it." She turned to her husband, whose hand was on the door-handle. "Don't go, Andreas," she said in her most authoritative voice. "I wish you to read it before I have it posted."

She sat down and wrote hastily. Then she directed an envelope. She was prepared for a scene; but if a scene arose, she was determined it should be before a friendly witness Ellen stood by, demure, in her cap and apron. Linnet spoke in English, that she might know what happened.

"I've written to Mr Deverill," she said, as calmly as she could manage, though her voice trembled somewhat. "We haven't seen him yet since we came back to London. And this is what I've said: I hope you'll approve of it:—

"'MY DEAR MR DEVERILL, It will give my husband and myself great pleasure if you'll lunch with us here at two next Thursday. We want to talk over our Italian experiences.—

Yours sincerely,
LINNET HAUSBERGER.'"

Andreas darted at her, livid with rage and jealousy. "You shall not send that note!" he exclaimed, in German. "I forbid him the house. He shall not come near you."

Linnet darted aside, for her part, and held the note out to Ellen. The girl, terrified at such a scene, and at her master's loud voice, drew back, not daring to interpose or to take it. Linnet held it at arm's-length. Andreas seized her arm and wrenched it. "You shan't send it," he cried once more, clutching her wrist with his hand till his nails drew blood from it. He tried to seize the note again, but Linnet was strong and resisted him. He flung her violently to the ground; but still she held it out, crying, "Here, post it, Ellen!" Andreas was beside himself now with rage and fury. He struck her several times; he hit her wildly with his fist; he caught her by the hair and shook her angrily like a bulldog. The marks of his hands showed red through her thin dress upon her neck and shoulders. At last he seized the note, and tore it into shreds, flung the tatters into her face, and struck her again heavily. Linnet bent down and let him strike. Her blood was up now. She was angry too. And she also had inherited the hot heart of the Tyrol.

At last, Andreas's passion cooled down of pure fatigue, and, with a final oath or two, he turned on his heel and left her. As he quitted the room, he stood for a second with his hand on the door, looking round at the startled and horrified maid-servant. "Mind, Ellen," he said, huskily, "post no letters for your mistress this afternoon; and if the man Deverill calls, she isn't at home to him."

But, as the front door closed with a snap behind him, it came back to him all at once, that wise and prudent man, that he had played into her rebellious hands all unawares; he had given her the one plea she still needed for a divorce—the plea of cruelty.

CHAPTER XLI

GOD'S LAW—OR MAN'S?

Linnet took less than one minute to make up her mind. Not twice in his life should Andreas treat her so before her own servants. She was too proud to cry; but as soon as her husband had left the room she picked herself up from the floor where he had brutally flung her, wiped the blood from her arm, smoothed her hair with her hand, and motioned silently to Ellen to follow her into her bedroom. She motioned to her, because she couldn't trust herself to speak without crying, and never now should she allow that hateful man to wring a single tear from her. In those few brief moments, she had decided once for all what she meant to do. After all that had passed just now, she must leave him instantly. The crisis had come; Andreas Hausberger should suffer for it.

Hastily, with Ellen's aid, she packed a few things into her little portmanteau. She put in just what she would most need for some evenings' stay; she put in also her diamonds and the rest of her jewellery, not omitting the coral necklet Will Deverill gave her long ago in the Tyrol. Luckily, she had in her desk the week's money for the housekeeping. She took it out, it was her own, and turned more calmly to Ellen. "My child," she said, laying two sovereigns in her hand, "will you come with me where I go? Remember, Mr Hausberger says you're his servant."

And the girl, looking up at her with a burst of compassion and enthusiastic affection, made answer at once: "I'd go with you, Signora, if they was to cut off my head for it. How dare he ever treat you so, such a man as him, and you a lady anyone 'ud love to die for!"

"Thank you, dear," Linnet said, much touched; for to her, even her servants were perfectly human. "Then run up and put your things on as fast as you can, and ask Maria to call a hansom."

When it came to the door, she stepped in, and Ellen after her. "Where shall I drive, Mum?" the cabman asked. And Linnet, through the flap, made answer boldly, "To Duke Street, St James's."

"That's where Mr Deverill lives, ma'am, isn't it?" Ellen interposed, somewhat tremulously.

"Yes, child," Linnet answered, with a choking voice, but very firmly still, for she had quite made her mind up. "Mr Deverill lives there, and I'm going to Mr Deverill's. I've no right to go, but I'm going, all the same. If you'd rather not come, you can leave me at the door. You know what it means. Perhaps it would be better."

The girl glanced back at her, all flushed. "I don't care a pin whether it's right or whether it's wrong," she answered warmly. "I'll go with you to the world's end. I'll go with you anywhere. I'd go with you if you was going to the worst house in London."

Linnet answered nothing. She was red with shame, the very words appalled her, but she meant to go through with it. Too long had she trampled her own heart under foot; now her heart would have its way, and she meant to allow it. Her fiery Southern blood had got the better of her. She would fly from the man who had married her only for what he could make of her, to the man she had always truly loved, the man who had always truly loved her.

"Is Mr Deverill in?" she asked with a beating heart of the servant at the lodgings. And when the man answered, "Yes, ma'am," in an unconcerned tone, her heart rose like a lump in her throat within her.

But she kept her exterior coolness. "Bring in the portmanteau, Ellen," she said, with a quiet air of command; and the girl obeyed her. "Now, sit there in the hall till I come down again and call you."

She trod the stairs like a queen. Will Deverill was seated at his desk at work, when the servant flung open the door with a flourish, and announced, in his most grandiose tone, "Signora Casalmonte!"

Will looked up in surprise, and saw Linnet before him.

Her face, which had been flushed five minutes earlier, was now pale and bloodless with intense excitement. Marks of fingers stood out on her neck and wrists; a slight bruise scarred the surface of her smooth left temple. But she was beautiful still, in spite of all such accidents, very beautiful and winning. She stood a second and gazed at him. At sight of her one true love, her bosom rose and fell; that strange wave of delight she had felt at Innsbruck, and again at the Harmony, thrilled once more through and through her. Of a sudden, as she paused, her face flushed rosy red again, her eyes grew bright, her full throat heaved and panted. She spread out her arms towards him with a hasty little quiver. "O Will, Will, Will," she cried, in a voice of complete and intense self-surrender; "at last, I have come to you!"

Will rose in surprise and moved across to her, trembling. He seized her two hands in his and gazed at her longingly. "Linnet, dear Linnet," he cried, drawing a very deep breath; "what has brought you here to-day? What on earth do you mean by it?"

But Linnet had flung away all artificial restraints and conventions now. She abandoned herself to her love with the perfect abandonment of a pure and good woman, when once she has made up her mind to repress nature no longer. With a wild impulse of delight, she flung herself bodily into her lover's arms. She flung herself into Will's arms, and buried her head confidingly on his tender shoulder. Then she broke into a storm of deep-drawn sobs. "It means," she cried, between little bursts, "I've left him for ever. That man I never loved, I've left him for ever. And I've come home at last where I ought to have come to nestle long ago. Will, Will, dear Will, will you take me? May I stop with you?"

In a transport of joy, Will clasped her to his bosom. Not to have done so, indeed, would have been more, or less, than human. No man can even pretend to be otherwise than overjoyed when the woman he loves flings herself into his arms for the first time in a fierce access of passion. He clasped her long and hard, breast pressed against heaving breast, and lips meeting lips in a sharp shower of kisses. For some minutes they neither knew, nor felt, nor remembered, nor thought of anything else on earth save their present intoxication. But surely those minutes were in themselves worth living for! What mattered so many years of cruel and unnatural repression beside that one fierce draught at the hot wine of passion?

After a while, however, Will woke up to a true sense of the situation. Man though he was, and therefore aggressive, it was his duty first of all to think of protecting Linnet. He must protect her, if need were, even against her own impulses. He must learn what she meant, and what could have led her so suddenly to this strange decision, so unlike herself, so untrue, as it seemed, to her whole past history.

He unwound his arms gently, and placed the poor sobbing, throbbing girl, half-unresisted, in an arm-chair by the fireplace. Then he drew up a seat for himself very close by her side, took her hand in his, and soothed it gently with his other one. "He's been cruel to you, Linnet, I can see," he murmured softly at her ear. "Now, what has led you to this? Tell me all he has done to you."

Thereat, Linnet, holding his hand hard, and looking deep into his eyes, yet crimson for very shame, began in her own tongue the story of their interview. She hid nothing from Will, and extenuated nothing. She told him in full how Joaquin Holmes had brought her Andreas's letter to Philippina and offered it for sale; how she had refused to buy it, or have anything to do with it; how he had dropped it by accident and she had picked it up before him, intending to restore it to its rightful owner; how a scuffle had ensued, in the midst of which Andreas had unexpectedly entered; how in his wrath at being discovered, he had fairly lost his temper, and provoked her for once to an act of rebellion; and how in his rage at her note he had turned upon her bodily, and inflicted the marks Will could see so plainly now upon her person. Only the question of divorce she never touched on; a certain feminine delicacy made her shrink from alluding to it. Will listened to every word with profound attention, letting her tell her own tale her own way, unquestioned, but stroking her hand from time to time very gently with his own, or smoothing her fiery cheeks with the tips of his fingers in silent sympathy.

At last she ceased, and looked hard at Will, inquiringly.

"So I've come to you, Will," she said, in her simple way, with childlike confidence; "and, now I've come, may I stop with you always? May I never go away again?"

Will's heart beat high. Her loving trust, her perfect self-surrender, could not fail to touch him. Yet he gazed at her ruefully. "My darling," he said with a burst, belying his words as he spoke by laying her soft head once more in the hollow of his shoulder; "you shouldn't have come to me. You've done very very wrong, very foolishly I mean. I'm the exact last person on earth you should have come to."

Linnet nestled to him close. "But I love you," she cried, pleadingly. "You're the only living soul I'd have cared to come to."

"Yes, yes; I know," Will answered hastily. "I didn't mean that, of course. You're mine, mine, mine! Sooner or later, now, you must certainly come to me. But for the present, darling, I mean, it's so unwise, so foolish. It'll prejudice your case, if it ever comes to be heard of. We must take you somewhere else, somewhere free from all blame, don't you see, for the immediate future."

"Prejudice my case!" Linnet exclaimed, looking up at him in amazement, and growing more shamefaced still with awe at her own boldness. "You must take me somewhere else! Ah, Will, I don't understand you. No, no; I must stop here, I must stop here with you for ever. I've broken away from him now; I've broken away from everything. I can never, never go back. I'm yours, and yours only."

"No; you can never go back, Linnet," Will answered decisively. "You're mine, darling, mine, mine, mine only"; and he kissed her again fervently. "But we must be prudent, of course, if we're to make this thing straight before the eyes of the world; and for your sake, dearest, you must see yourself how absolutely necessary it is that we should make it so."

Linnet gazed at him once more in childlike astonishment. She failed utterly to comprehend him. "What do you mean, Will?" she faltered out. "You don't mean to say I'm not to stop with you?"

Her eyes filled fast with tears, and her face looked up at his, full of wistful pleading. She clung to him so tight, in her love and her terror, that Will bent over her yet again and covered her with kisses. "Yes, darling; you're to stop with me," he cried; "to stop with me all your life, but not just at present. We must make this thing straight in the regular way first. Meanwhile, you must stay with some friend, some lady whose name is above suspicion. All must be carefully arranged. Even to have come here to-night may be positively fatal. We must play our cards cautiously. You've kept the letter?"

Linnet drew it, much crumpled, from the folds of her bosom, and handed it to him at once, without a moment's hesitation. What he meant, she couldn't imagine. Will ran his eye over it hastily. Then he glanced at the deep red marks on her neck, and her half-bared arm—for she had rolled back her sleeve like a child to show him. "This is conclusive," he said slowly. "Prudent man as he is, he has cut his own throat. And you had a witness, too—a friendly witness; that's lucky. We must take you to a doctor, and let him see you to-night, as soon as ever we've arranged where you can sleep this evening. The evidence of cruelty—and of the other thing—is more than sufficient. No court in England would refuse you a divorce upon such conduct."

Linnet started at the word. "Divorce!" she cried, growing redder and still redder with shame. "Oh, Will, not that, not that! You don't understand me. Divorce would be no use in the world to me. I'm a Catholic, you must remember, and I could never, never marry you. If I did, it would only be a mockery and a snare. It would be worse than sin; it would be open rebellion. I want no divorce; I want only to be allowed to stop here with you for ever."

She laid her hand on his arm, as if to draw him to herself in some natural symbolism. Her face was flushed with her womanly modesty. She hid it once more like a shy child on his shoulder. Will looked at her, sore puzzled. How strange that this pure and passionate nature should see things in a light that to him was so unfamiliar! But he remembered what she had said to him in Philippina's trouble, and began to understand now in what manner she regarded it.

"Well, but, Linnet," he cried eagerly lifting her head from where she put it, and laying her cheek against his own, "you must see for yourself how much better it would be, if only from the mere worldly point of view, to arrange this matter as the world would arrange it. Granting even that a marriage after an English divorce would mean to you, from the strictly religious standpoint, simply nothing—why, surely, even then, it must be no small matter to set oneself right with the world, to be received and acknowledged as an honest woman, and my wife, in ordinary English society. If we get a divorce, we can do all that; and to get a divorce, we must act now circumspectly. But if we don't get one, and if you try to stop here with me without it—remember, dear, the penalty; you lose position at once, and become for society an utter outcast."

Linnet flung herself upon him once more in a perfect fervour of abandonment. Her love and her shame were fighting hard within her. Her passionate Southern nature overcame her entirely. "Will, Will, dear Will," she cried, hiding her face from him yet again, "you don't understand; you can't fathom the depth of the sacrifice I would make for you. I come to you to-day bringing my life in my hand—my eternal life, my soul, my future; I offer you all I have, all I am, all I will be. For you I give up my good name, my faith, my hopes of salvation. For you I will endure the worst tortures of purgatory. I've tried to keep away—I've tried hard to keep away—Our Dear Lady knows how hard— all these months, all these years—but I can keep away no longer. Two great powers seemed to pull different ways within me. My Church said to me plainly, 'You must never think of him; you must stop with Andreas.' My heart said to me no less plainly, but a thousand times more persuasively, 'You must fly from that man's side; you must go to Will Deverill.' I knew, if I followed my heart, the fires of hell would rise up and take hold of me. I haven't minded for that; I've dared the fires of hell; the two have fought it out, the Church and my heart, and, my heart has conquered."

She paused, and drew a great sigh. "Dear Will," she went on softly, burying her head yet deeper in that tender bosom, "if I got a divorce, the divorce would be nothing to me, a mere waste paper. What people think of me matters little, very little in my mind, compared to what God and my Church will say of me. If I stop with you here, I shall be living in open sin; but I shall be living with the man my heart loves best; I shall have at least my own heart's unmixed approval. While I lived with Andreas, the Church and God approved; but my own heart told me, every night of my life, I was living in sin, unspeakable sin against human nature and my own body. Oh, Will, I don't know why, but it somehow seems as if God and our hearts were at open war; you must live by one or you must live by the other. If I stop with you, I'm living by my own heart's law; I will take the sin upon me; I will pay the penalty. If God punishes me for it at last, well, I will take my punishment and bear it bravely; I won't flinch from pain; I won't shrink from the fires of hell or purgatory. But, at least, I do it all with my eyes wide open. I know I'm disobeying God's law for the law of my own heart. I won't profane God's holy sacrament of marriage by asking a heretical and un-Catholic Church to bless a union which is all my own, my own heart's making, not God's ordinance, God's sacrament. I love you so well, darling, I can never leave you. Let me stop with you, Will; let me stop with you! Let me live with you; let me die with you; let me burn in hell-fire for you!"

A man is a man. And the man within Will Deverill drove him on irresistibly. He clasped her hard once more to his straining bosom. "As you wish," he said, quivering. "Your will is law, Linnet."

"No, no," she cried, nestling against him, with a satisfied sigh of delight. "My law is Will." And she looked up and smiled at her own little conceit. "You shall do as you wish with me."

CHAPTER XLII

PRUDENCE

It was a trying position for Will. He hardly knew what to do. Duty and love pulled him one way, chivalry and the hot blood of youth the other. When a beautiful woman makes one an offer like that, it would be scarcely human, scarcely virile to resist it. And Will was not only a man but also a poet, for a poet is a man with whom moods and impulses are stronger than with most of us. As poet, he cared little for mere conventional rules; it was the consequences to Linnet herself he had most to think about. But he saw it was no use talking to her from the standpoint he would have adopted with most ordinary Englishwomen. It was no use pointing out to her what he himself realised most distinctly, that her union with Andreas was in its very essence an unholy one, an insult to her own body, a treason against all that was truest and best in her being. It ran counter from the very first to the dictates of her own heart, which are the voice of Nature and of God within us. But to Linnet, those plain truths would have seemed but the veriest human sophisms. She looked upon her marriage with Andreas as a holy sacrament of the Church; and any attempt to set aside that sacrament by an earthly court, and to substitute for it a verbal marriage that was no marriage at all to her, but a profound mockery, would have seemed to her soul ten thousand times worse than avowed desertion and unconcealed wickedness. Better live in open sin, she thought, though she paid for it with her body, than insult her God by pretending to invoke his aid and blessing on an adulterous union.

Will argued feebly with her for a while, but it was all to no purpose. The teachings of her youth had too firm a hold upon her. He saw she was quite fixed in her own mind upon one thing; she might stop with him or she might go back, but she was Andreas Hausberger's wife by the Church's act, and no earthly power could make anything else of her. So Will gave up the attempt to convince her, as all in vain, at least for the present. He saw what he had to do first was to provide at once for the immediate future. Linnet couldn't remain in his rooms alone with him that night; to him, at least, so much was certain. For her own dear sake, he must save her from herself; he must throw at least some decent veil for the moment over the relations between them.

For Linnet herself, long before this, the die was cast. She felt she had already deserted her husband; she had sinned in her heart the unspeakable sin; all the rest was in her eyes mere detail and convention. But she realised gratefully none the less Will's goodness and kindness to her. "You are better to me far than I've been to myself," she cried, clinging hard to him still; "I've wrecked my own soul, and you would try to save my poor earthly body." And yet, in the mere intoxication of being near him and touching him, she more than half-forgot all else on earth; her warm Southern nature rejoiced in the light of her poet's presence. She cared for nothing now; she thought of nothing, feared nothing; with Will by her side, she would gladly give her soul to burn for ever in nethermost hell, for the sake of those precious, those fleeting moments.

"I must find some place for you to spend the night in, Linnet," Will said at last seriously. "Even if it were only to save scandal for the immediate future, I should have to do that; by to-morrow, all the world in London would be talking of it. But I hope, after a while, when I've reasoned this thing out with you, you may see it all differently, you may come round to my point of view; and then, you'll be glad I arranged things now so as to leave the last loophole of divorce and re-marriage still open before you."

Linnet shook her head firmly. "I'm a Catholic," she said, with a sigh, "and to me, dear Will, religion means simply the Catholic faith and the Catholic practice. If I gave up that, I should give up everything. Either marriage is a sacrament, or it's nothing at all. It's to the sacrament alone that I attach importance. But if you wish me to go, I'll go anywhere you take me; though, if I obeyed my own heart, I'd never move away from your dear side again, my darling, my darling!"

She clung to him with passionate force. Will felt it was hard to drive her from him against her will, how hard, perhaps, no woman could ever tell; for with women, the aggressiveness of love is a thing unknown; but for the love's sake he bore her, he kept down his longing for her. "Have you brought any luggage with you?" he asked at last, drawing himself suddenly back, and descending all at once to the level of the practical.

"A little portmanteau, and—all I need for the night," Linnet answered with a deep blush, still clinging hard to him. "My maid's in the passage."

"But how about the theatre this evening?" Will inquired with a little start. "You know, this was to have been your first appearance this season."

Linnet opened her palms outward with a speaking gesture. "The theatre!" she cried, half-scornfully. "What do I care for the theatre? Now I've come to you, Will, what do I care for anything? If I had my own way, I'd stop here with you for ever and ever. The theatre, well, the theatre might do as best it could without me!"

Will paused, and reflected. He saw he must absolutely take measures to protect this hot passionate creature against the social consequences of her own hot passion. "You've got an understudy, I suppose," he said; "someone who could fill the part pretty decently in your enforced absence? They don't depend altogether upon you, I hope, for to-night's performance."

"Yes; I've got an understudy," Linnet answered, in a very careless voice, clasping his hand tight in hers, and gripping it hard now and again, as though understudies were a matter of the supremest indifference to her. "She doesn't know her part very well, and I'm the soul of the piece; but I daresay they could get along with her very tolerably enough somehow. Besides," she added, in a little afterthought, looking down at her wounded arm, "after what Andreas has done to me, I'm too ill and too shaken to appear to-night, whatever might have happened. Even if I'd stopped at home, instead of coming here, I couldn't possibly have undertaken to sing in public this evening."

"Very well, then," Will replied, making up his mind at once. "We must act accordingly. If that's the case, the best thing I can do is to go out and telegraph to the management, without delay, that Signora Casalmonte is seriously indisposed, and won't be able to appear in Carmen this evening."

"To go out!" Linnet cried, clutching his arm in dismay. "Oh, dear Will, don't do that! Don't leave me for a moment. Suppose Andreas were to come, and to find me here alone? What on earth could I do? What on earth could I say to him?"

Will stroked her cheek once more, that beautiful soft cheek that he loved so dearly, as he answered in a grave and very serious tone, "Now, Linnet, you must be brave; and, above all, you must be practical. This is a crisis in our lives. A great deal depends upon it. If you love me, you must do as I advise you in this emergency. You have done quite right to come away from Andreas, instantly, the very moment you discovered this letter, the very moment he offered you such unmanly violence. In that, you were true woman. You're in the right now, and if you behave circumspectly, all the world will admit it; all the world will say so. But you mustn't stop here one second longer than is absolutely necessary. You must spend the night with some friend whom we know, some lady of position and unblemished reputation; and the world must think you went straight from your husband's roof to hers, when all these things happened."

Linnet drew back, all aghast. "What, go from you!" she cried: "this first night of our love. O Will, dear Will! Go, go right away from you!"

"Yes," Will answered firmly. "For the moment, the one thing needful is to find such a shelter for you. If you took refuge in a hotel or private lodging to-night, people would whisper and hint, you know what they would hint; we must stop their hateful whisperings! Now, darling, you mustn't say no; you must act as I advise. I'm going out at once to find that lady. I shall ask my sister first, she's a clergyman's wife, and nothing looks so well as a clergyman's wife in England. But if she objects, I must try some other woman. You're agitated to-night, and I should be doing you a gross wrong if I took advantage now of your love and your agitation. Though it isn't you and myself I'm thinking of at all; you and I know, you and I understand one another. Let me not to the marriage of true minds admit impediment; it isn't that that I trouble for, it's the hateful prying eyes and lying tongues of other people. For myself, darling, my creed is quite other than your priests'; I hold that, here to-night, you are mine, and I am yours; God and Nature have joined us, by the witness of our own hearts"; his voice sank solemnly, "and whom God hath joined together," he added, in a very grave tone, "let not man put asunder." He paused and hesitated. "But, for to-night," he went on, "we must make some temporary arrangement; to-morrow and afterwards, we may settle for the future with one another at our leisure. When you look at it more calmly, dearest, you may change your mind about the matter of the divorce; till then, we must be cautious, and, in any case, we must take care to give the wicked world no handle against you."

Linnet clutched him tight still. "But if you go," she cried, all eagerness, "you won't leave me; I may go with you."

Her voice was so pleading, it cut Will to the quick to be obliged to refuse her. He leant over her tenderly. "My Linnet," he cried, caressing her with one strong hand as he spoke, "I'd give worlds to be able to say yes; I can't bear to say no to you. But for your own dear sake, once more, I must, I must. I can't possibly let you go with me. Just consider this; how foolish it would be for me to let you be seen with me, to-night, on foot or in a cab, in the streets of London. All the world would say, with truth, you'd run away from your husband, and rushed straight into the arms of your lover. You and I know you've done perfectly right in that. But the world, the world would never know it. We must never let them have the chance of saying what, after their kind, we feel sure they would say about it."

He rose from his chair. She clung to him, passionately. "Oh, take me with you, Will!" she cried, in a perfect fever of love. "Suppose Andreas was to come! Suppose he was to try and carry me off by force against my will! Oh, take me, take me with you!—don't leave me here, alone, to Andreas!"

Sadly against his wish, Will disengaged her arms and untwined her fingers. He did it very tenderly but with perfect firmness. "No, darling," he said, in a quiet tone of command; "let go! I must leave you here alone; it's imperative. And it's wisest so; it's right; it's the best thing to do for you. You are mine in future, you were always mine, and we shall have plenty of time to love one another as we will, hereafter. But to-night I must see you suffer no harm by this first false step of yours. My servant knows your husband well. He shall wait in the hall; and, if Andreas comes, deny us both to him. Your maid can come up here with you. I'll take care no evil happens to you in any way in my absence. Trust me, trust me for this, Linnet; you needn't be afraid of me."

With a sudden change of front, Linnet held up her face to him. "I can always trust you, dear Will," she cried. "I have always trusted you. All these long, long years I've known and seen how you yearned for one kiss, and would never take it. All these long, long years, I've known how you hungered and thirsted for my love, and kept down your own heart, letting only your eyes tell me a little, a very little, while your lips kept silence. The other men asked me many things, and asked me often, you know a singer's life, what it is, and what rich people think of us, that they have but to offer us gold, and we will yield them anything. I never gave to one of them what I was keeping for you, my darling; I said to myself, 'I am Andreas's by the sacrament of the Church; but Will's, Will's, Will's, by my own heart, and by the law of my nature!' I trusted you then; I'll trust you always. Good-bye, dear heart; go quick: come back again quick to me!"

She held the ripe red flower of her lips pursed upward towards his face. Will printed one hard kiss on that rich full mouth of hers. Then, sorely against his will, he tore himself away, and, in a tumult of warring impulses, descended the staircase.

CHAPTER XLIII

LINNET'S RIVAL

Will hailed a cab in St James's Street, and drove straight to his sister's, only pausing by the way to despatch a hasty telegram to the management of the Harmony: "Signora Casalmonte seriously indisposed. Quite unable to sing this evening. Must fill up her place for to-night, at least, and probably for to-morrow as well, by understudy."

Then he went on to Maud's. "Mrs Sartoris at home?"

"Yes, sir; but she's just this minute gone up to dress for dinner."

"Tell her I must see her at once," Will exclaimed with decision, "on important business. Let her come down just as she is. If she's not presentable, ask her to throw a dressing-gown round her, or anything, to save time, and run down without delay, as I must speak with her immediately on a most pressing matter."

The maid, smiling incredulity, ran upstairs with his message. Will, with heart on fire, much perturbed on Linnet's account, walked alone into the drawing-room, to await his sister's coming. He was too anxious to sit still; he paced up and down the room, with hands behind his back, and eyes fixed on the carpet. A minute . . . two minutes . . . four, five, ten passed, and yet no Maud. It seemed almost as if she meant to keep him waiting on purpose. He chafed at it inwardly; at so critical a juncture, surely she might hurry herself after such an urgent message.

At last, Maud descended—ostentatiously half-dressed. She wore an evening skirt—very rich and handsome; but, in place of a bodice, she had thrown loosely around her a becoming blue bedroom jacket, trimmed with dainty brown facings. Arthur Sartoris, in full clerical evening costume and spotless white tie, followed close behind her. Maud burst into the room with a stately sweep of implied remonstrance. "This is very inconvenient, Will," she said in her chilliest tone, holding up one cheek as she spoke in a frigid way for a fraternal salute, and pulling her jacket together symbolically—"very, very inconvenient. We've the Dean and his wife coming to dine, as you know, in a quarter of an hour—and the Jenkinses, and the Macgregors, and those people from St Christopher's. Fortunately, I happened to go up early to dress, and had got pretty well through with my hair when your name was announced, or I'm sure I don't know how I could ever have come down to you. Oh, Arthur, you're ready, run and get me the maiden-hair and the geranium from my room; I can be sticking them in before the glass, while Will's talking to me about this sudden and mysterious business of his. They're in the tumbler on the wash-hand-stand, behind the little red pot; and, wait a moment, of course I shall want some hairpins, the thin twisted American ones. You know where I keep them—in the silver-topped box. Go quick, there's a dear. Well, Will, what do you want me for?"

This was a discouraging reception, to be sure, and boded small good for his important errand. Will knew well on a dinner night the single emotion of a British matron! Church, crown, and constitution might fall apart piecemeal before Maud Sartoris's eyes, and she would take no notice of them. Still at least he must try, for Linnet's sake he must try; and he began accordingly. In as brief words as he could find, he explained hastily to Maud the nature and gravity of the existing situation. Signora Casalmonte, that beautiful, graceful singer who had made the success of Cophetua's Adventure— Signora Casalmonte (he never spoke of her as "Linnet" to Maud, of course,) had long suffered terribly at the hands of her husband, whose physical cruelty, not to mention other things, had driven her to-day to leave his house hurriedly, without hope of return again. Flying in haste from his violence, and not knowing where to look for aid in her trouble, she had taken refuge for the moment—Will eyed his sister close, it was an error of judgment, no more, at his rooms in St James's. "You recollect," he said apologetically, "we were very old friends; I had known her in the Tyrol, and had so much to do with her while she was singing in my opera."

Maud nodded assent, and went on unconcerned, with a quiet smile on her calm face, arranging the geranium and maiden-hair in a neat little spray at one side of her much frizzed locks, with the profoundest attention.

"Well?" she said inquiringly at last, as Will, floundering on, paused for a moment and glanced at her. "So the lady with many names—Casalmonte, Hausberger, Linnet, Carlotta, and so forth—is this moment at your rooms and I suppose is going to sup there. A queer proceeding, isn't it? It's no business of mine, of course, but I certainly must say I should have thought your own sister was the last person in the world even you would dream of coming to tell about this nice little escapade of yours."

"Maud," Will said, very seriously, "let's be grave; this is no laughing matter." Then, in brief words once more, he went on to explain the difficulty he felt as to Linnet's arrangements for the immediate future. He said nothing about the divorce, of course; nothing about his love and devotion towards Linnet. Those chords could have struck no answering string in the British matron's severely proper nature. He merely pointed out that Linnet was a friend in distress, whose good name he wished to save against unjust aspersions. Having left her husband she ought to go somewhere to a responsible married woman—"And I've come to ask you, Maud," he concluded, "as an act of Christian charity to a sister in distress, will you take her in, for to-night at least, till I can see with greater clearness what to do with her in future?"

Maud stared at him in blank horror. "My dear boy," she cried, "are you mad? What a proposal to make to me! How on earth can you ever think I could possibly do it?"

"And it would be such a splendid chance, too," Will cried, carried away by his enthusiasm—"the Dean coming to dinner and all! in a clergyman's house, with such people to vouch for her! Why, with backers like that, scandal itself couldn't venture to wag its vile tongue at her!"

Maud looked at him with a faint quiver in her clear-cut nostrils. "That's just it!" she answered promptly. "But there, Will, you're a heathen! You'll never understand! You have quite a congenital incapacity for appreciating and entering into the clerical situation. Isn't that so, dear Arthur? You belong to another world, the theatrical world, where morals and religion are all topsy-turvy, anyhow! How could you suppose for a moment a clergyman's wife could receive into her house, on such a night as this, an opera-singing woman with three aliases to her name, who's just run away in a fit of pique from her lawful husband! Whether she's right or wrong, she's not a person one could associate with! To mix oneself up like that with a playhouse scandal! and the Dean coming to dine, whose influence for a canonry's so important to us all! The dear, good Dean! Now Arthur, isn't Will just too ridiculous for anything?"

"It certainly would seem extremely inconsistent," Arthur Sartoris replied, fingering that clerical face dubiously; "extremely inconsistent." But he added after a pause, with a professional afterthought, "Though, of course, Maud, if she's leaving him on sufficient grounds, compelled to it, in fact, not through any fault of her own, but through the man's misconduct, and if she thinks it would be wrong to put up with him any longer, yet feels anxious to avoid all appearance of evil, why, naturally, as Christians, we sympathise with her most deeply. But as to taking her into our house, now really, Will, you must see, I put it to you personally, would you do it yourself if you were in our position?"

Maud for her part, being a woman, was more frankly worldly. "And it'd get into the papers, too!" she cried. "Labby'd put it in the papers. . . . Just imagine it in Truth, Arthur!—'I'm also told, on very good authority, that the erring soul, having drifted from her anchorage, went straight from her husband's house to Mrs Arthur Sartoris's. Now, Mrs Arthur Sartoris, it may be necessary to inform the innocent reader, is Mr Deverill's sister; and Mr Deverill is the well-known author and composer of Cophetua's Adventure, in which capacity he must doubtless have enjoyed, for many months, abundant opportunities for making the best of the Signora's society. Verbum sap.—but I would advise the Reverend Arthur to remember in future the Apostle's injunctions on the duty of ruling his own house well, and having his children in subjection with all gravity.' That's just about what Labby would say of it!"

Will's face burned bright red. If his own sister spoke thus, what things could he expect the outer world to say of his stainless Linnet. "You forget," he said, a little angrily, "the Apostle advises, too, in the self-same passage, that a bishop should be given to hospitality; and that his wife should be grave; not a slanderer; sober and faithful in all things. I came to you to-night hoping you would extend that hospitality to an injured wife who desires to take refuge blamelessly from an unworthy husband. If you refuse her such aid, you are helping in so far to drive her into evil courses. I asked you as my sister; I'm sorry you've refused me."

"But, my dear boy," Maud began, "you must see for yourself that for a clergyman's wife to have her name mixed up, oh, good gracious, there's the bell! They're coming, Will, I'm sure. I must rush up this very moment, and put on my bodice at once. Thank goodness, Arthur, you're dressed, or what ever should I do? Stop down here and receive them."

"Then you absolutely refuse?" Will cried, as she fled, scuffling, woman-wise, to the door.

"I absolutely refuse!" Maud answered from the landing. "I'm surprised that you should even dream of asking your sister to take into her house, under circumstances like these, a runaway actress-woman!" And, with a glance towards the hall, she scurried hastily upstairs, with the shuffling gait of a woman surprised, to her own bedroom.

Mechanically, Will shook hands with that irreproachable Arthur Sartoris, passed the Dean, all wrinkled smiles, in the vestibule below, and returned again with a hot heart to his waiting hansom. "Hans Place, Chelsea!" he cried through the flap: and the cabman drove him straight to Rue's miniature palace.

Mrs Palmer was at home; yes, sir; but she was dressing for dinner. "Say I must see her at once!" Will cried with a burst. And in less than half-a-minute Rue descended, looking sweet, to him.

She had thrown a light tea-gown rapidly around her to come down; her hair was just knotted in a natural coil on top; she was hardly presentable, she said, with an apologetic smile, and a quick glance at the glass; but Will thought he had never seen her look prettier or more charming in all his life than she looked that moment.

"I wouldn't keep you waiting, Will," she cried, seizing both his hands in hers. "I knew if you called at this unusual hour, you must want to see me about something serious."

"It is serious," Will answered, with a very grave face. "Rue, I've something to tell you that may surprise you much. That wretch Hausberger has been very, very cruel to Linnet. He's offered her bodily violence to-day. And that's not all;—she has proof, written proof of his intimacy with Philippina. He's thrown her on the floor, and struck her and bruised her. So she's left him at once—and she's now at my chambers."

A sudden shade came over Rue's face. The shock was a terrible one. This news was different, very different indeed from what she expected to hear. Could Will have found out, she asked herself with a flutter, as she put on her tea-gown, that he loved her at last, better even than Linnet? Linnet had been away one whole long winter; and when he dined here last week, he was so kind and attentive! So she came down with a throbbing heart, all expectant of results. That was why Will had never seen her look so pretty before. And now, to find out it was all for Linnet he had come! All for Linnet, not for her! Ah me, the pity of it!

Yet she bore up bravely, all the same, though her lips quivered quick, and her eyelids blinked hard to suppress the rising moisture. "At your chambers!" she cried, with a jump of her heart. "O Will, she mustn't stop there!"

She sank into a chair, and looked across at him piteously. Will, dimly perceptive, seized her hands once more, and held them in his own with a gentle pressure. Then he went on to explain, in very different words from those he had used to Maud, all that had happened that day to himself and to Linnet. He didn't even hide from Rue the question of divorce, or the story of Linnet's complete self-surrender. He knew Rue would understand; he knew Linnet herself would not be afraid of Rue's violating her confidence. He said everything out, exactly as he felt it. Last of all, he explained how he had been round to Maud's, what he had asked of Maud, and what answer Maud had made to him.

He had got so far when Rue rose and faced him. Her cheeks were very white, and she trembled violently. But she spoke out like a woman, with a true woman's heart. "She must come here at once, Will," she cried. "There's not a moment to lose. She must come here at once. Go quick home and fetch her."

"You're quite sure you can take her in, Rue?" Will asked, with a very guilty feeling, seizing her hands once more. "I can't bear to ask you; but since you offer it of your own accord—"

Rue held his hands tremulously in her own for awhile, and gazed at him hard with a wistful countenance. "Dear Will," she faltered out in a half-articulate voice, "I invite her here myself; I beg of you to bring her. Though it breaks my own heart—it breaks my heart. Yet I ask you all the same—bring her here, oh, bring her!"

Heart-broken she looked, indeed. Will leant forward automatically. "Dear Rue," he cried, "you're too good—too good and kind for anything; I never knew till this moment how very good and kind you were. And I love you so much!" He held forward his face. "Only once!" he murmured, drawing her towards him with one arm. "Just this once! It's so good of you!"

Rue held up her face in return, and answered him back in a choking voice, "Yes, yes; just this once, O Will, my Will—before I feel you're Linnet's for ever!"

He clasped her tight in his arms. Rue let him embrace her unresistingly. She kissed him long and hard, and nestled there tenderly. For fifty whole seconds she was in heaven indeed. At last, with a little start, she broke away and left him. "Now go," she said, standing a yard or two off, and gazing at him, tearfully. "Go at once and fetch her. Every moment she stops in your rooms is compromising. . . . Go, go; goodbye! . . . You're mine no longer. But, Will, don't be afraid I shall be sad when she comes! I'll have my good cry out in my own room first; and, by the time she arrives, I'll be smiling to receive her!"

CHAPTER XLIV

AND WILL'S

At Will's chambers, meanwhile, Linnet sat and waited, her flushed face in her hands, her hot ears tingling. She had plenty of time in Will's absence to reflect and to ruminate. Horror and shame for her own outspokenness began to overcome her. If Will had accepted her sacrifice, indeed, as frankly as she offered it, that profound emotional nature would have felt nothing of the kind: her passion would have hallowed and sanctified her love in her own eyes—not as the Church could have done, to be sure; not from the religious side at all; but still, from the alternative point of view of the human heart, which to her was almost equally sacred in its way, 'twould have hallowed and sanctified it. Linnet would have regarded her union with Will as sinful and wrong, but not as impure or unholy; she wouldn't have attempted to justify it, but she would never have felt ashamed of it. She recognised it as the union imposed upon her by the laws of her own highest nature; the laws of God, as she understood them, might forbid it and punish it—they never could make it anything else for her than pure and beautiful and true and ennobling.

But Will's refusal, for her own sake, to accept her self-surrender, filled her soul with shame for her slighted womanhood. She understood Will's reasons; she saw how unselfish and kind were his motives; but still, the sense remained that she had debased herself before him, all to no purpose. She had offered him the most precious gift a woman can offer to any man, and he, he had rejected it. Linnet bowed down her head in intense humiliation. On her own scheme of life, she would have been far less dishonoured by Will's accepting her then and there, in a hot flood of passion, than by his proposal to wait till she could get a purely meaningless and invalid release from her sacrament with Andreas. Having once made up her mind to desert her husband and follow her own heart, in spite of ultimate consequences, it seemed to her almost foolish that Will should shrink on her account from the verdict of the world, when she herself did not shrink, so great was her love, from the wrath of heaven and eternal punishment.

But, as she sat there and ruminated, it began gradually to dawn upon her that in some ways Will was right; even if she sinned boldly and openly, as she was prepared to sin, before Our Lady and the Saints, it might be well for her immediate comfort and happiness to keep up appearances before English society. Perhaps it was desirable for the next few days, till the talk blew over, to go, as Will said, under some married woman's protection. But what married woman? Not that calmly terrible Mrs Sartoris, at any rate. She dreaded Will's sister, more even than she dreaded the average middle-aged British matron. She knew how Maud would treat her, if she took her in at all; better anything at that moment of volcanic passion than the cold and cutting repose, the icy calmness of the British matron's unemotional demeanour.

As Linnet was sitting there with her face in her hands, longing for Will's return, and half-doubting in her own heart whether she had done quite right, even from her own heart's standpoint, in coming straight away to him, Florian Wood, in a faultless frock-coat, with a moss-rose in his buttonhole, strolled by himself in a lazy mood down Piccadilly. It was Florian's way to lounge through life, and he was lounging as usual. He pulled out his watch. Hullo! time for dinner! Now, Florian was always a creature of impulse. He hesitated for a moment, with cane poised in his dainty hand, which of three courses to pursue that lay open before him. Should he drop into the Savile for his evening meal; should he go home by himself to Grosvenor Gardens; or should he take pot-luck with Will Deverill in Duke Street? Bah! the dinner at the Savile's a mere bad table d'hôte. At home, he would be lonely with a solitary chop. The social instinct within him impelled him at once to seek for society with his old friend in St James's.

He opened the door for himself, for he had a latch-key that fitted it. In the hall, Ellen was seated, and the man-servant of the house was standing by and flirting with her. "Mr Deverill's not at home, sir," he said, with a hurried start, as Florian entered.

"Never mind," the Epicurean philosopher replied, with his bland, small smile. "Pretty girl on the chair there. He's coming back to dinner, I suppose, at the usual hour. Very well, that's right; I'll go up and wait for him. You can tell Mrs Watts to lay covers for two. I purpose to dine here."

"Beg your pardon, sir," the man said, placing himself full in front of Florian's delicate form, so as to half-block the passage; "there's a lady upstairs." He hesitated, and simpered. "I rather think," he continued, very doubtful how to proceed, "Mr Deverill wished nobody to go up till he came back again. Leastways, I had orders."

"Why, it's Signora Casalmonte!" Florian broke in, interrupting him; for he recognised the pretty girl on a second glance as the housemaid at Linnet's. An expansive smile diffused itself over his close-shaven face. This was indeed a discovery! Linnet come to Will Deverill's! And with a portmanteau, too!—Will, whose stern morality had read him so many pretty lectures on conduct in the Tyrol. And Linnet—that devout Catholic, so demure, so immaculate, the very pink of public singers, the pure flower of the stage! Who on earth would have believed it? But there, it's these quiet souls who are always the deepest! While Florian himself, for all his talk, how innocent he was, how harmless, how free from every taint of guile, wile, or deception! What reconciled him to life, as he grew older every day, was the thought that, after all, 'twas so very amusing.

The man hesitated still more. "I don't think you must go up, sir," he said, still barring the way, "Mr Deverill told me if Hare Houseberger called, to say he wasn't at home to him."

Florian's face was a study. It rippled over with successive waves of stifled laughter. But Ellen, with feminine quickness, saw the error of the man's clumsy male intelligence. It would never do for Mr Wood, that silver-tongued man-about-town to go away and explain at every club in London how he'd caught the Casalmonte, with her maid and her portmanteau, on a surreptitious visit to Will Deverill's chambers. Better far he should go up and see the Signora herself. Principals, in such cases, should invent their own lies, untrammelled by their subordinates. The Signora might devise what excuse she thought best to keep Florian's mouth shut; and Will himself might come back before long to corroborate it.

"No, no," she said hastily, with much evident artlessness. "You can go up, sir, of course. The Signora's just waiting to see Mr Deverill."

Florian brushed past the man with a spring, and ran lightly up the stairs, with quite as much agility as so small a body can be expected to compass. He burst into the room unannounced. Linnet rose, in very obvious dismay, to greet him. She was taken aback, Florian could see—and glad indeed he was to notice it. This little contretemps was clearly the wise man's opportunity. Providential, providential! He grasped her hand with warmth, printing a delicate little squeeze on the soft bit of muscle between thumb and fingers. "What, Linnet!" he cried, "alone, and in Will Deverill's rooms! How lucky I am to catch you! This is really delightful!"

Linnet sank back in her chair. She hardly knew what to say, how to cover her confusion. But excuse herself she must; some portion at least of what had passed she must explain to him. In a faltering voice, with many pauses and hesitations, she told him a faint outline of what had happened that day—her quarrel with Andreas, his cruel treatment, how he had struck her and hurt her, how she had fled from him precipitately. She hinted to him even in her most delicate way some dim suggestion of her husband's letter to Philippina. Florian stroked himself and smiled; he nodded wisely. "We knew all that before," he put in at last, with a knowing little air of sagacious innuendo. "We knew Friend Hausberger's little ways. Though, how quiet he kept over them! A taciturn Don Juan! a most prudent Lothario!" It was the wise man's cue now to set Linnet still further against her husband.

"So I left him," Linnet went on simply, with transparent naïveté; "I left him, and came away, just packing a few clothes into my portmanteau, hurriedly. I didn't know where to go, so I came straight to Mr Deverill's. He was always a good friend of mine, you know, was Mr Deverill." She paused, and blushed. "I've sent him out," she continued, with a little pardonable deviation from the strictest veracity, "to see if he can find me some house among his friends, some English lady's, where I can stop for the present, till I know what I mean to do, now I've come away from Andreas. He's going to his sister's first, to see if she can take me in; after that, if she can't, he's going to look about elsewhere."

She gazed up at him timidly. She felt, as she spoke, Will was right after all. How could she brave the whole world's censure, openly and frankly expressed, if she shrank so instinctively from the prying gaze of that one man, Florian? God, who reads all hearts, would know, if she sinned, she sinned for true love; but the world, that hateful world, Linnet leant back in her seat and shut her eyes with horror.

As for Florian, however, he seized the occasion with avidity. He saw his chance now. He was all respectful sympathy. The man Hausberger was a wretch who had never been fit for her; he had entrapped her by fraud; she did right to leave him. What horrid marks on her arm, and on that soft brown neck of hers! Did the cur do that? What a creature, to lay hands on so divine a woman! Though, of course, it was unwise of her to come round to Will's; the world, and here Florian assumed his most virtuously sympathetic expression of face, the world is so cruel, so suspicious, so censorious. For themselves, they two moved on a higher plane; they saw through the conventions and restrictions of society. Still, it was always well to respect the convenances. Mrs Sartoris! Oh, dear, no! unsympathetic, out of touch with her! And yet, oh, how dangerous to stop here in these rooms one moment longer. With dexterous little side hints the wise man worked upon Linnet's fears insensibly. That fellow in the passage, now, the people of the house, so unwise, so uncertain; who could tell friend from enemy?

As he spoke, Linnet grew every moment more and more uneasy. "I wish Will would come back!" she cried. "I wish I had somewhere to go! It makes me so afraid, you see—this delay, this uncertainty."

Florian played a trump card boldly. "Why not come off with me at once, then," he suggested, "to my sister's?"

"Your sister's?" Linnet asked. "But I didn't know you had one!"

Florian waved his hand airily, with a compulsive gesture, as if he could call sisters to command from the vasty deep, in any required quantity—as indeed was the case. "Oh dear, yes," he answered. "She hasn't been long in town. She—er—she lives mostly in Brittany." He paused for a second to give his fancy free play. Ah, happy thought! just so!—a clergyman's wife would be the very thing for the purpose. "Her husband's chaplain at Dinan," he went on, with his bland smile, romancing readily. "She doesn't often come over. She's not well off, poor dear; but this year she's taken a house for the season . . . in Pimlico. You might go round there, at least, while you're waiting for Will. It's less compromising than this; and we could leave a note behind to tell him where he could find you."

Linnet debated internally. Florian paused, and looked judicial. "What sort of person is she?" Linnet asked at last, hesitating. "Kind, nice, sympathetic?"

"You've summed her up in one word!" Florian answered with a flourish. "Sympathetic, that's just it; she's bubbling over with sympathy. She goes out to all troubled souls. Though I'm her own brother, and therefore naturally prejudiced against her, I never knew anyone so intensely capable of throwing herself forth towards other people as my sister Marian. She's the exact antipodes of that unspeakable Sartoris woman; human, human, human, above all things human; she brims and overflows with the milk of human kindness! And she took such a fancy to you, too, when she saw you one night, in Cophetua's Adventure. She said to me, 'O Florian, do you think she'd come and stay with us? I'd give anything to know that sweet creature personally.' I told her, of course, you never stayed with anybody under the rank of a crowned head or a millionaire soap-boiler. She was quite disappointed, and she'd be only too delighted now, I'm sure, if she could be of any service to you."

He looked at her hard. He had provided a sister, mentally. As a matter of fact, he knew a lady, a most obliging lady, tolerably reputable, too, in a side street in Pimlico, who would be willing (for a slight consideration) to take Linnet in, and adopt any relation she was told to Florian. Once get a married woman (and a singer-body at that) away from her husband, into a house of your own choosing, and—given agreeable manners and a persuasive tongue—you can do before long pretty much what you like with her. So, at least, Florian's philosophy had always instructed him. He chuckled to himself to think pure chance should have enabled him thus to anticipate Will Deverill. And if Will was playing this game, this simple little game, why on earth shouldn't he play it too, and outwit his rival?

He went on to expatiate very enthusiastically to Linnet on the imaginary sister's sympathetic virtues. In a few minutes he had made her so absolutely charming, for he was a fluent talker, that at last Linnet, who, like all Tyrolese, was impulsive at heart, jumped up from her seat and exclaimed with a sudden burst, "Very well, then; I'll go there. It's safer there than here. We can leave a line for Will to let him have the address. I'll sit down and write it."

"No, no," Florian cried, eagerly, seizing a pen in haste. "I'll write it myself. Then we'll take a cab outside, and go round there together."

For if once Linnet was seen with him in a hansom in the street, after leaving her husband, her fate was sealed. She might as well do what all the world would immediately say she was bent on doing.

CHAPTER XLV

BY AUTHORITY

As Florian sat there, scribbling off a few lines of apology for their hasty departure, the door opened of a sudden, and Will Deverill entered.

Florian rose, a little abashed, though, to be sure, it took a good deal to abash Florian. He stood by the desk, hesitating, with his unfinished letter dangling idly in his hand, while he debated inwardly what plausible lie he could invent on the spur of the moment and palm off to excuse himself. But before he could make up his mind to a suitable story, Linnet, that impulsive southern Linnet, had rushed forward, all eager, with her own version of the episode. "O Will," she cried, spoiling all by her frank avowal, "I'm so glad you've come at last! I couldn't bear to wait here in doubt any longer; and Florian's so kind: he was just going to take me off for the night to his sister's!"

Will turned from her and gazed at Florian for a brief space in blank surprise. Then, as by degrees it dawned upon him what this treachery really meant, his face changed little by little to one of shocked and horrified incredulity. "Florian," he said, in a very serious voice, "come out here into the passage. This thing must be explained. I want to speak with you."

Florian followed him on to the landing, hardly knowing what he did. Will's eye was cold and stern. "Now, look here," he said, frigidly, fixing his man with his icy gaze, "it's no use lying to me. I know as well as you do, you've got no sister."

Florian smiled imperturbable. "Well, no," he said, blandly; "but—I thought I might improvise one."

Will took him in at a glance. He pointed with one hand to the stairs, impressively, "Go! without another word," he said. "You've behaved like a cad. Instead of trying to save and help this poor girl, you've concocted a vile plan in my absence to ruin her."

Florian turned to him, cynically. "You were looking out for a house to take her to yourself," he answered. "I don't suppose you meant to return her to her husband. If you may do it, why not I as well? Two can play at that game, you know. It's quits between us. You needn't pretend to such high morality at the very moment when you're engaged in enticing another man's wife away from her husband."

Will didn't deign any further to bandy words with the fellow. "Go!" he said, once more, pointing sternly to the doorway. Florian turned on his heel, and slunk down the stairs, as jauntily as he could, but looking for all that just a trifle disconcerted. Will leant over the banisters, as he went, with a sudden afterthought. "And if ever you dare to say anything to anyone on earth about having seen Linnet here, at my rooms, to-night," he called out, very pointedly, "I shall think you, if possible, even a greater cad than I think you now, and not hesitate to say so."

He returned to Linnet in his sitting-room. He wouldn't speak before her to Florian because he couldn't bear she should even suspect how bad an opinion the man had had of her, and what plot he had laid for her.

"You shall go round to Mrs Palmer's, Linnet," he said, taking her hand in his. "The place Florian spoke of isn't at all the right place for a girl like you. But Rue will receive you like a sister till we can arrange some other plan for you. At her house, you'll be safe from every whisper of scandal."

"You'll take me there, won't you?" Linnet inquired, gazing wistfully at him.

On that point, however, Will was firm as a rock. "No, dearest," he answered, laying one hand on her full round arm, persuasively. "You must go there alone, with only your maid. It's better so. Rue has a friend or two coming in to dine with her to-night. They'll see you arrive at her door by yourself; and if any talk comes of it, they'll know how to answer it."

Linnet flung herself upon him once more, in a last clinging embrace. She was wildly in love with him. Will pressed her hard to his heart; then he gently disengaged himself, and led her to the door. A cab was in waiting, the cab that brought him there. Linnet got into it at once, and drove off with Ellen. In twenty minutes more, she was in Rue's pretty drawing-room.

That night, when all the rest were gone, she and Rue sat up long and late, talking together earnestly. Their talk was of Will. Linnet didn't try to conceal from her new friend how much she loved him. Rue listened sympathetically, suppressing her own heart, so that Linnet ceased even to remember to herself how she had thought once of the grand lady as her most dangerous rival.

But all the time, Rue preached to her one line of action alone: "You must get a divorce, of course, dear, and marry Will Deverill." And all the time, Linnet shook her head, and answered through her tears, "A divorce to me is a mockery and a delusion. I'd rather stop with him openly, and defy the world and the Church together, than affront my God by pretending to marry him, when I know in my heart Andreas Hausberger is and must always be my one real husband."

At last they went to bed. Neither slept much that evening. Linnet thought about Will; Rue thought about Linnet. As things now stood, Rue would give much to help them. Since Will loved this woman far more than he loved her, she wished indeed Linnet might be freed at last from that hateful man, and they two might somehow be happy together. Only the Church stood in the way, that implacable Church, with its horrible dogma of indissoluble marriage.

Next day, Linnet spent very quietly at Rue's. Will never came near the house; but he wrote round a long and earnest letter to Linnet, urging her with all the force and persuasiveness he knew to go down that night as usual to the theatre. It was best, he said, in order to avoid a scandal, that she should appear to have left her unworthy husband on grounds of his own misconduct alone, and be anxious to fulfil in every other way all her ordinary engagements.

Linnet went, sick at heart. She hardly knew how she was to get through Carmen. But when she saw Will's face in a box at the side, watching her with eager anxiety, she plucked up heart, and, fired by her own excitement, sang her part in that stirring romance as she had never before sung it. She rushed at her Toreador as she would have rushed at Will Deverill. At times, too, as in the cigar factory scene, she was defiant with a wonderful and life-like defiance; for she marked another face in the stalls before her—Andreas Hausberger's hard face, gazing up at his flown bird with intense determination. Rue had come to see her through. At the end of the performance, Rue waited at the door for her. Will passed by, and spoke casually just a few simple words of friendly congratulation on her splendid performance; then she drove away, flushed, to Hans Place, in Rue's carriage.

It didn't escape her notice, however, that, as she stepped in, Andreas Hausberger stood behind, with his hand on the door of their own hired brougham. As Linnet drove off, he leaned forward to the coachman. "Follow the green livery," he called out in so loud a voice that Linnet overheard it. When they drew up at Rue's door, he was close behind them. But he noted the number, that was all; he had been there before, indeed, to Rue's Sunday afternoons, and only wished to make sure of the house, and that Linnet was stopping there. "Drive on home," he called to the man; and disappeared in the distance. Linnet looked after him and shuddered. She knew what that meant; and she trembled at the thought. He would come back to fetch her.

She was a Catholic still. If he came and bid her follow him, her lawful husband, how could she dare refuse him?

All that night long, she lay awake and prayed, torturing her pure soul with many doubts and terrors. In the lone hours of early morning, ghastly fears beset her. The anger of Heaven seemed to thunder in her ears; the flames of Hell rose up to take hold of her. She would give her very life to go back again to Will; and the nether abyss yawned wide its fiery mouth to receive her as she thought it. She would go back to Will, let what would, come;—but she knew it was wrong; she knew it was wicked; she knew it was the deadly, unspeakable sin; she knew she must answer before the throne of God for it.

Oh, how could she confess it, even to her own parish priest! How ask for penance, absolution, blessing, when she meant in her heart to live, if she could, every day of her life in unholy desire or unholy union! O God, God, God, how could she face his anger!

She rose next morning, very pale and haggard. Rue tried to console her. But no Protestant consolation could touch those inner chords of her ingrained nature. Strange to say, all those she loved and trusted most were of the alien creed; and in these her deepest doubts and fears and troubles they could give her no comfort. About eleven o'clock came a knock at the door. Linnet sat in the breakfast-room; she heard a sound of feet on the staircase hard by—two men being shown up, as she guessed, into the drawing-room.

The servant brought down two cards. Linnet looked at them with a sinking heart. One was Andreas Hausberger's; the other bore the name of her London confessor, a German-speaking priest of the pro-Cathedral at Kensington.

She passed them to Rue with a sigh. "I may go up with you?" Rue cried, for she longed to protect her.

But Linnet shrank back. "Oh no, dear," she answered, shaking her head very solemnly. "How I wish you could come! You could sit and hold my hand. It would do me so much good. But this is a visit of religion. My priest wouldn't like it."

She went upstairs with a bold step, but with a throbbing heart. Rue followed her anxiously, and took a chair on the landing. What happened next inside, she couldn't hear in full, but undertones of it came wafted to her through the door indistinctly. There was a blur of sounds, among which Rue could distinguish Andreas Hausberger's cold tone, not angry, indeed, but rather low and conciliatory; the priest's sharp German voice, now inquiring, now chiding, now hortative, now minatory; and Linnet's trembling speech, at first defiant, then penitently apologetic, at last awestruck and terrified. Rue leant forward to listen. She could just distinguish the note, but not the words. Linnet was speaking now very earnestly and solemnly. Then came a pause, and the priest spoke next— exhorting, threatening, denouncing, in fierce German gutturals. His voice was like the voice of the angry Church, reproving the sins of the flesh, the pride of the eyes, the lusts of the body. Linnet bowed her head, Rue felt sure, before that fierce denunciation. There was a noise of deep sobs, the low wail of a broken heart. Rue drew back, aghast. The Church was having its way. They had terrified Linnet.

For the first time in her life, the gentle-hearted American felt herself on the side of the sinners. She would have given anything just that moment to get Linnet away from those two dreadful men, and set her down unawares in Will's chambers in Duke Street. She tried hard to open the door, but the key was turned. "Linnet, Linnet!" she cried, knocking loud, and calling the poor girl by her accustomed pet name, "let me in! I want to speak to you!"

"No, dear; I can't!" Linnet answered through the door, gulping down a great sob. "I must fight it out by myself. My sin; my punishment."

The voices went on again, a little lower for a while. Then sobs came thick and fast. Linnet was crying bitterly. Rue strained her ear to hear; she couldn't catch a single syllable. The priest seemed to be praying, as she thought, praying in Latin. Then Linnet appeared to answer. For more than an hour together they wrestled with one another. At the end of that time, the tone of the priest's voice changed. It was mild; it was gracious. In an agony of horror, Rue realised what that meant. She felt sure he must be pronouncing or promising absolution.

So Linnet must have confessed!—must have renounced her sin!—must have engaged to go back and live with that man Andreas!

Right or wrong, crime or shame, Rue would have given ten thousand pounds that moment—to take her back to Will Deverill's.

As Rue thought that thought, the door opened at last, and the three came forth right before her on the landing.

Andreas and the priest wore an air of triumph. Linnet walked out in front of them, red-eyed, dejected, miserable. The Church had won; but, O God, what a victory!

Rue sprang at her and seized her hand. "Linnet, Linnet!" she cried agonised, "don't tell me you've let these two men talk you over! Don't tell me you're going back to that dreadful man! Don't tell me you're going to give up Will Deverill for such a creature!"

Linnet fell upon her neck, weeping. "Rue, Rue, dear Rue," she sobbed out, heart-broken, and half beside herself with love and religious terror, "it is not to him that I yield, O lieber Gott, not to him, but to the Church's orders."

"But you mustn't!" Rue cried, aghast, and undeterred by the frowning priest. "You must stop here with me, and get a divorce, and marry him!" And she flung herself upon her.

"There! what did I say?" Andreas interposed, with a demonstrative air, turning round to the man of God. "I told you I must take her away from London at once, at all costs, at all hazards—if you didn't want her to fall into deadly sin, and the Church to lose its hold over her soul altogether."

The priest looked at Rue with a most disapproving eye. "Madam," he said, curtly, in somewhat German English, "with exceeding great difficulty have I rescued this erring daughter from the very brink of mortal sin—happily, as yet unconsummated; and now, will you, a married woman yourself, who know what all this means, drive her back from her husband into the arms of her lover?"

"Yes, yes; I will!" Rue cried boldly—and, oh, how Linnet admired her for it! "I will! I will! I'll drive her back to Will Deverill! Anything to get her away from that man whom she hates! Anything to get her back to the other whom she loves! Linnet, Linnet, come away from them! Come up with me to my bedroom!"

But Linnet drew back, trembling. "Yes, yes; I hate him!" she wailed out passionately, looking across at her husband. "I hate him! Oh, I hate him! And yet, I will go with him. Not for him, but for the Church! Oh, I hate him! I hate him!"

The priest turned to Andreas. "I absolved her too soon, perhaps," he said, in German. "Her penitence is skin-deep. She is still rebellious. Quick, quick, hurry her off from this sinful adviser. You'll do well, as you say, to get her away as soon as you can—clear away from London. It's no place for her, I'm sure, so long as this man . . . and his friends and allies . . . are here to tempt her."

Rue clung hard to her still. "Linnet, dear," she cried, coaxingly, "come up to my room! You're not going with them, are you?"

"Yes; I am, dear," Linnet sobbed out, in a heart-broken tone. "Oh, how good you are!—how sweet to me! But I must go. They have conquered me."

"Then I'll go round this very minute," Rue burst forth through her tears, "and tell Will what they're doing to you. If it was me, I'd defy them and their Church to their faces. I'll go round and tell Will—and Will'll come and rescue you!"

The priest motioned Linnet hastily with one hand down the stairs. "Sie haben recht, Herr Hausberger," he murmured low. "Apage retro, Satanas! With temptations like these besetting her path, we shall be justified in hurrying away this poor weak lamb of our flock from the very brink of a precipice that so threatens to fall with her."

CHAPTER XLVI

HOME AGAIN!

Andreas Hausberger was always a wise man in his generation. The moment he knew Linnet had left his house, he realised forthwith that the one great danger to his interests lay in the chance of her obtaining a divorce, and marrying Will Deverill. To prevent such a catastrophe to his best investment was now the chief object in life of the prudent impresario. He had hurried away from home that first afternoon, it is true, to make sure how things stood with Philippina and her husband; but as soon as he found out no serious danger menaced him there, he rushed back to Avenue Road—to find Linnet flown, without a word to say whither. Now, Andreas, being a very wise man, and knowing his countrywomen well, felt tolerably sure Linnet was by far too good a Catholic to agree to a divorce, even if Will suggested it. She might run away to her lover in a moment of pique—and so shut herself out from the benefit of the English law on the subject by misconducting herself in return; but fly in the face of the Church, insult her creed, defy its authority, annul its sacraments, oh, never! never! Andreas was certain Linnet would do, just what Linnet really did; fling herself frankly upon Will Deverill's mercy, but refuse to marry him.

Moreover, with his usual worldly wisdom, the wirth of St Valentin saw at a glance that the Church was the only lever which could ever bring his revolted wife back to him. She had always disliked him; she now hated and despised him. But he was still, and must always be, in the sight of God, her lawful husband. Linnet feared and obeyed the Church, with the unquestioning faith of the genuine Tyrolese; it was to her a pure fetish, authoritative, absolute, final. Andreas recognised clearly that his proper course now was to enlist this mighty engine, if possible, in his own favour. To guard against all adverse chances, he must get Linnet back into his power at once, must carry her away from the sphere of Will's influence, and, if luck permitted, must hurry her off to some land where divorce was impossible.

Quick as lightning, he made up his mind. To throw up all her engagements in London forthwith would, of course, cost money, for she was engaged under forfeit, and to lose money was indeed a serious consideration. Still, in the present crisis, the temporary loss of a few stray hundreds was as nothing in Andreas's eyes compared with the possible prospective loss of Linnet's future earnings. He must risk that and more in order to snatch her from Will Deverill's clutches. He had meant to take his wife to America, on tour, a little later in the year; and he adhered to that programme: but not till she had quite got over her present fit of rebellion. For the moment, he judged it best on many grounds to venture on a bold step, no less a step than to go back with her to St Valentin. For this sudden resolve, he had ample reasons. In the first place, he would have her there under the thumb of Austrian law; divorce would be impossible, nay, even unthinkable. But, in the second place, and on this point Andreas counted far more, he would have her there in an atmosphere of unquestioning Catholicism, where all the world would take it for granted that to marry Will Deverill by judgment of an English court was an insult to Providence ten thousand times worse than to sin and repent, nay, even than to sin without pretence of repentance, but without the vain mockery of a heretical marriage. A few weeks in the Tyrol, Andreas thought in his wise way, surrounded by all the simple ideas of her childhood, and exposed to the exhortations of her old friend, the Herr Vicar, would soon bring Linnet back from this flight of unbridled fancy to a proper frame of mind again. Besides, the mountain air would be good for her health after so stormy an episode, ozone, ozone, ozone!—and he wanted her to be in first-rate singing voice, before he launched her on the fresh world of New York and Chicago. Lots of money to be made in New York and Chicago! Once get her well across the Atlantic in a White Star Liner, and all would be changed; she'd soon forget Will in the new free life of that Western Golconda.

To enlist the Church on his side was therefore Andreas Hausberger's first and chief endeavour. With this object in view, he took the unwonted step of confessing himself in due form to the priest of the pro-Cathedral the very day after Linnet left him. 'Twas a well-timed confession. Andreas admitted to the full his own misconduct, admitted it with a most exemplary and edifying show of masculine contrition. But then he went on to point out to the priest that between his wife's case and his there was a great gulf fixed, from the point of view of the ecclesiastical vision. He had sinned, it was true, and deserved reprehension; but he was anxious, all the same, to remain in close union as ever with his wife, to admit the obligation and sanctity of the sacrament. Frau Hausberger, on the other hand, had left his hearth and home, and seemed now on the very point of falling into the hands of heretics, who might persuade her to accept the dissolving verdict of a mere earthly court, and to marry again during her husband's lifetime, in open defiance of the Church's authority. Her soul was thus placed in very serious jeopardy. If she continued to remain with Will or with Will's friends, and if they over-persuaded her to obtain a divorce, she would become a Protestant, or at any rate would enter into an irregular union which no Catholic could regard as anything other than legalised adultery.

The justness and soundness of Herr Hausberger's views deeply impressed the candid mind of his confessor. It is pleasant indeed, in these degenerate days, to find a layman who so thoroughly enters into the Church's idea as to the obligation of the sacraments. Moreover, to let a well-known lamb of the flock thus stray from the fold before the eyes of all Europe, and on such a question, the confessor saw well would be a serious calamity. Indeed, the Church had somewhat prided itself in its way on Signora Casalmonte. It had pointed to her more than once as a conspicuous example of pure Catholic life under trying circumstances. A Tyrolese peasant-girl, brought up in a country where Catholic influences still bear undisputed sway, and transplanted to the most dangerous and least approved of professions, she had comported herself on the stage, in spite of every temptation, with conspicuous modesty and religious feeling. Beautiful, graceful, much admired, much sought after in all the capitals of Europe, she had resisted the many snares that beset a singer's career, and had shown a singular instance of pure domestic life in a sphere where such life is, alas, too uncommon. So much could the lessons of the Church effect; so great was the lasting power of early Catholic influences.

And now, if they must eat their own words publicly, and go back on their own encomiums, if Linnet, on whom they had prided themselves as a shining example of the success of their method, was to go off before the eyes of all the world with a non-Catholic poet, worse still, if she was to fly in the face of their most cherished principles, and request a divorce at the hands of purely secular judges, Catholicism itself would receive a serious blow in the eyes of many doubtful or wavering adherents. A person like the Casalmonte commands public attention. Of course, if the worst came to the worst, it would be easy enough for the Church to disown her; easy enough to remark, with a casual little sneer, that Rome had never approved of the theatrical profession, above all, for women. Still, it is a good pastor's duty, if possible, to save, above all things, the souls of his flock; and the first thing to do, it was clear, the confessor thought, was to bring the Casalmonte back again into subjection to her own husband. They must strain every nerve to prevent her obtaining or even demanding a divorce; they must strive, if they could, to obviate a gross and open scandal.

Actuated by such motives, and by many others of a more technical character, the confessor, after some demur, consented at last to the somewhat unusual course of calling upon the lost lamb, if her whereabouts could be found, and endeavouring to save her either from open sin or still more open rebellion. As soon as he learned she hadn't gone off with Will Deverill, but was quietly staying with a wealthy American lady, an intimate friend of her suspected lover's, the priest made up his sapient mind at once this meant a determination to seek a divorce, which must instantly be combated by every means in his power. So he worked upon Linnet's susceptible Southern nature by striking successively all the profoundest chords of religion, shame, penitence, remorse, and terror. He appalled her with the authoritative voice of the Church; he convicted her of sin; he overawed her with the mysterious sanctity of a divine sacrament. Before he had finished his harangue, Linnet crouched and cowered in abject fear before him. She loved Will with all her heart: she would always love him; she hated Andreas with all her soul: she couldn't help but hate him. Still, if God and the Church so ordained, she would follow that man she hated, till death them did part; she would forsake that man she loved, though her heart broke with love for him.

Andreas seized his opportunity; he struck while the iron was hot. His brougham was at the door; he had sent their luggage on to Charing Cross before him. In haste and trembling, he hurried Linnet away, hardly even waiting for Ellen to bring down the portmanteau with her jewellery and necessaries. They drove straight to Charing Cross, and took the Club train southwards. That night they spent in Paris. Linnet, heart-broken but calm, insisted on separate rooms; for that, at least, she must stipulate; she would follow him, she said, as the Church directed, to the bitter end, but never again while he lived should he dare to lay those heavy hands of his upon her. Next morning, they took the early express to Innsbruck, via Zurich and the Vorarlberg. Two evenings later, they sat together at St Valentin.

How strange it all seemed to her now, that familiar old world of her own native Tyrol! Everything was there, just as of yore, to be sure, land, people, villages, but oh, how small, how petty, how mean, how shrunken! St Valentin had dwindled down to a mere collection of farm-houses; the church, whose green steeple once looked so tall and great, had grown short and stumpy and odd and squalid-looking; the Wirthshaus, that once prosperous and commodious inn, seemed in her eyes to-day a mere fourth-rate little simple country tavern. To all of us, when we revisit well-known scenes of our childhood, space seems to have shrunk, the world to have grown smaller and meaner and uglier. But to Linnet, the change seemed even greater than to most of us. She had been taken straight away from that petty hamlet, and elevated with surprising rapidity into European fame, a popular favourite of Milan and Naples, Rome and Paris, Munich and Brussels, London and Vienna. The break in her life had been sudden and enormous; she had passed at once, as it were, from the village inn to the courts of kings and the adulation of great cities. And now, when she came back again, all was blank and dreary. The dear mother was dead; Will Deverill was away, and she might not see him; the Herr Vicar turned out a greasy, frowsy Austrian parish priest; Cousin Fridolin had a fat wife and two dirty-faced babies. The poetry seemed to have faded out of the Tyrol she once knew; the very cow-bells rang harsh, and Will Deverill, who could make music of them, was away over in London.

Only Nature itself remained to console her. And Andreas in his wisdom allowed her to commune much with Nature. The eternal hills had still some slight balm for her wounded spirit. Linnet and her husband stopped as guests at the Wirthshaus; it was Andreas's still, but he had let it to Cousin Fridolin. In the morning, after Linnet had gulped down the coffee and roll that seemed to half choke her, she would stroll up the hill behind the village inn, and sit on the boulders, just above the belt of pine wood, where she had sat long ago hand in hand with Will Deverill. The village children sometimes came and gazed at her, and whispered to one another in an awestruck undertone how this was Lina Telser, who once minded cows in a châlet on the Alps, and who was now the Casalmonte, a great, rich singer in England, with diamonds in her box, and grand rings on her fingers. Linnet dressed very simply for this mountain life, and tried to seem the same as of yore to Cousin Fridolin, and the priest, and the good old neighbours: but, ah me, how changed was the world of the Tyrol! And how curious it seemed to hear the same familiar chatter still running on about the same old gossips, the same petty jealousies, the same narrow hopes, and fears, and ideals, when she herself had passed through so much, meanwhile—had known other men, new ideas, strange cities!

So for a fortnight, Linnet lived on, scarcely speaking to Andreas, but sitting by herself on those springtide hills, where the globe-flowers scattered gold with a stintless hand and the orchids empurpled whole wide tracts of the meadows. She sat there, and thought of Will, and obeyed the Church, and followed Andreas. Yet, oh, how strange that God and our hearts should be thus at open war! that Nature should tell us one thing and the Church another! 'Twas a consequence of the Fall of Man, the Herr Vicar assured her; for the heart, the heart is deceitful above all things, and desperately wicked. And it was desperately wicked of her, no doubt, to think so much about Will; but there, Church or no Church, Linnet couldn't help thinking of him.

She was resigned, in a way; very much resigned; her heart had been crushed once for all when she married Andreas. It had flared up in a fitful flicker of open rebellion when she left his house and flung herself fiercely on Will Deverill's bosom; and then—Will himself had bruised the broken reed, had quenched the smoking flax, and sent her away hurt, bleeding, and humiliated. He did it for her own sake, she knew, but, oh, she would have loved him better if he'd been a little less thoughtful for her, less noble, less generous! Loved him better? Oh no; to love him better would be impossible! But they would both have been happier, with the world well lost, and present love for the reward of Paradise closed to them hereafter.

Purgatory? Ah, what did she care for their purgatory now! To count one year of love fulfilled with Will, she would gladly give her poor body to be burnt in burning hell for ever and ever. It was the Church that intervened to prevent it, not she; for herself, she was Will's; she could live for him, she could die for him, she could lose her own soul for him.

She never said a word to Cousin Fridolin and his wife, or to the people of St Valentin, of her relations with Andreas. Still, the villagers guessed them all. Simple villagers know more of the world than we reckon. She was rich, she was grand, they said, since she'd married the Wirth, and become a great lady: but she wasn't happy with Herr Andreas; he was cold and unkind to her. Those marks on her little wrists—they were surely the impress of Herr Andreas's big fingers; those red eyes, that pale face—they were surely the result of Herr Andreas's infidelities. Money, after all, isn't everything in this world: Lina Telser had diamonds and pearls at command, and she drank fine red wine, specially brought from Innsbruck; but she would have been happier, people thought at St Valentin in the Zillerthal, if she'd married Cousin Fridolin, or even Franz Lindner!

CHAPTER XLVII

SEEMINGLY UNCONNECTED

Franz Lindner! And how was Franz Lindner engaged during these stormy days? He was working out by degrees his own scheme in life for making himself rich, and so, as he thought, acceptable to Linnet.

With great difficulty, partly by saving and hoarding with Tyrolese frugality, partly by rare good luck in following a fortunate tip for last autumn's Cesarewitch, Franz had scraped together at last the five hundred pounds which he required for working his "system" at Monte Carlo. The royal road to wealth now lay open before him. So he started blithely from Victoria one bright spring morning, bound southward straight through by the rapide to Nice, with his heart on fire, and his capital in good Bank of England notes in his pocket. He meant to stop at Nice, not at Monte Carlo itself, because he was advised that living was cheaper in the larger town; and Franz, being a Tyroler, reflected with prudence that even when one's going to win twenty thousand pounds, it's best to be careful in the matter of expenditure till one's sure one's got them.

At Calais, he found a place in the through carriage for the Riviera. With great presence of mind, indeed, he secured a corner seat by pushing in hastily past a fumbling old lady with an invalid daughter. The opposite corner was already occupied by a handsome man—tall, big-built, rather dark, with brilliant black eyes, and abundant curly hair, of somewhat southern aspect. As Franz entered the carriage, the stranger scanned him, casually, with an observant glance. He had the air of a gentleman this stranger, but he was affable for all that; he entered into conversation very readily with Franz, first in English, then more fully in German, which latter tongue he spoke quite fluently. Part of his education had been acquired at Heidelberg, he said in explanation, before he went to Oxford; 'twas there he had picked up his perfect mastery of German idiom. As a matter of fact, he had picked it up rather by mixing with Jewish shop-boys from Frankfort in Denver City, Colorado; for the stranger was no other than Mr Joaquin Holmes, the Psycho-physical Entertainer, flying southward to restore his fallen fortunes at Monte Carlo.

Fate had used her Seer rather badly of late. His failure to sell Andreas's letter to Linnet was the last straw that broke the camel's back of Mr Holmes's probity. Thought-reading had by this time gone quite out of fashion; Theosophy and occult science were now all in the ascendant. There were no more dollars to be made any longer out of odic force; so Mr Holmes was compelled by adverse circumstances, very much against his will, to take refuge at last in his alternative and less reputable profession of card-sharper. With that end in view, he was now on his way to the Capital of Chance in the Principality of Monaco. Where gamblers most do congregate is naturally the place for a dexterous manipulator of the pack to make his fortune. Mr Holmes was somewhat changed in minor detail as to his outer man, in order to avoid too general recognition. His hair was cut shorter; his beard was cut sharper; his moustache, a hard wrench, was altogether shaved off; and sundry alterations in his mode of dress, especially the addition of a most unnecessary pince-nez, had transformed him, in part, from the aspect of a keen and piercing Transatlantic thought-reader to that of a guileless English mercantile gentleman. But his vivid black eyes were still sharp and eager and shifty as ever; his denuded mouth, now uncovered at the corners, showed still more of a cynical smile than before; and his complete expression was one of mingled astuteness and deferential benevolence, the former, native to his face, the latter, by long use, diligently trained and cultivated.

Before they reached Paris, Seer and singer had put themselves on excellent terms with one another. They had even exchanged names in a friendly way, the Seer giving his, for obvious reasons, as plain Mr Holmes, without the distinguishing Joaquin; it was safer so: there are plenty of Holmeses scattered about through the world, and the name's not compromising; while, on the other hand, if any London acquaintance chanced to come up and call him by it, such initial frankness avoided complications. Franz Lindner, more cautious and less wise in his way, gave his name unblushingly as Karl von Forstemann, a Vienna proprietor, out of pure foolish secretiveness. He had no reason for changing his ordinary style and title, except that he wished to be taken at Monte Carlo for an Austrian gentleman, not a music-hall minstrel. The Seer smiled blandly at the transparent lie; Franz's accent and manner no more resembled those of a Viennese Junker than his staring tweed suit and sky-blue tie resembled the costume of an English gentleman.

However, the prudent Seer reflected immediately to himself that this sort was created for his especial benefit. Behold, a pigeon! He was even more affable than usual on that very account to Herr Karl von Forstemann. He offered him brandy out of his Russia-leather covered flask; he invited him to share his anchovy sandwiches; he regretted there was no smoking compartment on the through carriage for Mentone, or he might have introduced his new friend to a very choice brand of fragrant Havana. Going to Cannes? or San Remo? Ah, Nice! that was capital. They'd travel together all night then, without change of companions, for he himself was going on straight through to Monte Carlo.

At that charmed name, which the Seer pronounced with a keenly cautious side-glance, Franz pricked up his ears. Monte Carlo! ach, so? really? Did he play, then? The cautious Seer smiled a deep and wary smile of consummate self-restraint. Play? no, not he; the Casino was rubbish: he went there for the scenery, the music, the attractions. Occasionally of an evening, to be sure, he might just drop into the Rooms to observe what was happening. If a run of luck came on any particular colour, or number, or series, as the case might be, now and again he would back it, once in a week or a blue moon, for pure amusement. But as to making money at it, bah, bah, what puerile nonsense! With odds on the bank, one chance in thirty-six, no scientific player could regard it in that light for one moment. As excitement—"I grant you," yes, all very well; one got one's fun for one's louis: but as speculation, investment, trial for luck, if it came to that, why, everybody knew it was all pure moonshine.

Franz listened with a smile, and looked preternaturally cunning. That was all very well in its way, he said, with a sphinx-like face, for the general public; but he had a System.

The Seer's eye was grave; the Seer's face was solemn; only about the corners of his imperturbable mouth could a faint curl have betrayed his inner feelings to the keenest observer. A System! oh, well, of course, that was altogether different. No one knew what a clever and competent mathematician might do with a System. Though, mark you, mathematicians had devised the tables, too; they had carefully arranged so that no possible combination could avoid the extra chances which the bank reserved to itself. However, experience, experience is the only solid guide in these matters. Let him try his System, by all means; and if it worked—with stress on that if—Mr Holmes would be glad for his own part to adopt. If it didn't, he could show him a trick worth two of that—a game where the players stood at even chances, with no rapacious bank to earn a splendid dividend and pay royally for the maintenance of a palatial establishment. And with that, he tucked himself up and subsided into his corner.

All night through, on their way to Marseilles, they slept or dozed at intervals—and then woke up once more to discuss by fits and starts that enthralling subject of winning at Monte Carlo. The fumbling old lady and her invalid daughter, propped upright in the middle seats, got no sleep to speak of, with their perpetual chatter. Before morning, the two men were excellent friends with one another. Franz liked Mr Holmes. He was a jolly, outspoken, good-natured gentleman, very kindly and well-disposed, and he recommended him to a good cheap hotel at Nice, lying handy to the station, for a man who wanted to run over pretty often to Monte Carlo. Franz went there as he was bid, and found it not amiss; 'twas pleasant, after so long a stay in England, to discover himself once more amongst compatriots, or next door—to talk in his native tongue with Swiss porters, Swiss waiters, Swiss boots, and Swiss chambermaids. With the great bare mountains rising abruptly in the rear, Nice almost seemed to him like his beloved Fatherland. The strange longing for home which is peculiar to mountaineers came over him with a rush at sight of their lonely summits. Ach, Gott, if it weren't that he had his fortune to make at Monte Carlo, he'd have gone on, then and there, straight through to St Valentin!

That first evening, he rested after the fatigues of the journey. He merely strolled about on the Promenade des Anglais, in the cool of the evening, and lounged along the Quays or through the Public Garden. It was a fine town, Nice, and Franz was very much pleased with it. He had given his name at the hotel as Herr Karl von Forstemann, a gentleman from Vienna; and as he sauntered along now through that gay little city, with five hundred pounds sterling in his trousers pocket, and twenty thousand awaiting him in the bank at Monte Carlo, he felt for the moment like the person he called himself. His strut was still prouder and more jaunty than ever; he stared at the pretty girls under the palm-trees of the parade as if they all belonged to him; he twirled his short cane by the arcades of the Place Masséna with a millionaire swagger. After all, it's easy as dirt to win thousands at roulette, if only you have a System. Strange how people will toil, and moil, and slave, and save, at a desk in London, when, here by this basking tideless Southern sea, this Tom Tiddler's ground of fortune, they might pick up coin at will just as one picks up pebbles!

Franz broke a bottle of champagne at ten o'clock, discounting his success, with two awfully jolly fellows he'd come across in the smoking-room. Nice seemed to be just cram-full of awfully jolly fellows! Then he went to bed early, and slept the sleep of the just till morning. After a cup of fragrant coffee and a fresh French roll, so unlike that bad bread man gets in London, he lounged over to the station, and took a first-class return to Monte Carlo. Oh, that exquisite journey! How bright it was, how sweet, how fairy-fair, how beautiful! Like all Tyrolese, Franz Lindner was by no means insensible to the charms of Nature; and that man must be blind and seared and dull indeed who wouldn't gaze with hushed delight, the first time he saw them, on those endless blue bays, those craggy cliffs, those towering heights, those jagged precipices. Villefranche, with its two promontories and its quaint white town; the Cap Ferrat and its twin lighthouses; the peninsula of St Jean, with its indented outline; the great bluffs of Beaulieu; the tunnelled headlands of the coast; green water breaking white on tumbled masses in the sea; Eza, perched high on its pinnacle of rearing rock; the bastions of Monaco, rising sheer like some basking whale from the purple waves beneath; the hanging gardens of La Condamine, the bare mountains in the background: Franz drank them all in with delight and enthusiasm. But all only sharpened his zest for the game he had in view; what an enchanted tract of coast it was, to be sure, this land that led him up to the Palace of Luck, where he was to woo and win his twenty thousand pounds sterling!

He wouldn't leave off till he had won it, every penny; on that he was determined. None of your beggarly ten or fifteen thousands for him! Twenty thousand pounds down was the goal he set before him. After that, well, who knows? He might perhaps stop . . . or, why this moderation?—he might perhaps go on, if he chose, and double it.

In such heroic mood, like a winner already, Franz mounted the broad steps of the great white Casino. Its magnificence for a moment abashed and daunted him. He had never yet entered so splendid a building; never trod so fine a room as that gorgeous atrium. However, he reflected next instant that he came there that day armed with the passport which makes a man welcome wherever he may go the wide world over—the talismanic passport of money in his pocket. Regaining his usual swagger as he mounted the steps, he followed the crowd into the office where cards of admission were issued, and gave his name boldly once more, in a very firm voice, as Herr von Forstemann of Vienna. Then, provided with the necessary pasteboard which ensures admission to the rooms, he still followed the stream into the vast, garish hall which contains the gaming tables. Its size and its gorgeousness fairly took the man's breath away. Though the hour was still early, as Franz now reckoned time in his cosmopolitanised avatar, he was surprised to find so immense a crowd of players gathered in deep rows round table after table, opening into long perspective of saloon after saloon in the farther distance. He drew up to the first roulette-board, and watched the play carefully for several minutes. Though he had studied the subject beforehand with books and diagrams, and had made sure, as he thought, of the truth of his System by frequent imaginary trials, it interested him immensely to see at last in real life, and with tangible actors, the scene he had so long contemplated in his feverish day-dreams.

The result was in some ways distinctly disappointing. He hadn't allowed to himself for so much bustle, so much noise, so many other players. In his mental picture, he had seen his own money only; he had staked and won, staked and lost, staked and won again incessantly, while croupiers and bank existed, as it were, for his sole use and benefit. But here in concrete reality, many complicating circumstances arose to distract him. Other people crowded round, row after row in serried order, to put on their own money without regard to his presence; and they put it all on in so many incomprehensible and ridiculous ways—backing dozens, or fours, or pairs, or columns, according to their Systems, which he had never thought of—that Franz for a stray minute or two felt thoroughly bewildered. He almost lost his head. The sweet simplicity of the little game he had played by himself on paper, against a bank which took no heed of any stake but his, now vanished utterly; in its place came chaos—a complex and distracting phantasmagoria of men and women flinging down gold pieces at cross-purposes on numbers and colours; sticking about their louis hap-hazard in reckless confusion on first or last dozens; raking in and grabbing up, with eager hands, in hot haste; till Franz's brain began to reel, and he wondered to himself, amid so many rolling coins, how each could tell at each turn what had happened to his own money. In idea, he had confined himself to the System alone; in practice, he found all the rest of the world engaged in playing ten different games at once—rouge-et-noir, passe-et-manque, pair-et-impair, and the rest of it—with distracting rapidity, at a single table.

For a minute or two, he watched, with cat-like eyes, before venturing to risk one of his hard-saved louis. But presently the sequence of numbers and colours on the board reached a point which appeared to him specially favourable for his System. Trembling greatly within, but swaggering outwardly still, Franz leaned over between two stout players who sat close by in front of him, and, edging himself sideways, passed through the jostling crowd, till he had deposited twenty francs on rouge, with a beating heart. For a minute he waited. Other people put their stakes unpleasantly close to his; coins rolled in casually, here and there, and were fixed by the croupier with his stick as voices behind directed. But Franz kept his eyes fixed fast on his own good louis. Whr'r'r, rang the roulette; "Rien ne va plus!" cried the croupier. For a second or two, as the thing spun, Franz felt his heart come up in his mouth with anxiety. The ball jumped out; his quick eyes couldn't follow it. Instinctively, he kept them fixed on his louis still. "Dix-sept gagne; impair, rouge, manque," cried the croupier. A flush of triumph rose up all unbidden on Franz's face. The System was justified then! he had won a louis!

By his side, the croupier raked in whole heaps of gold and silver. Then he began to pay out; here a beggarly five francs; there, ten broad yellow pieces. At last he came to Franz, and flung a louis carelessly by the side of the Tyroler's stake. Franz picked it up with a sense of ineffable triumph. A louis all at once! If he went on like this, he would soon grow rich! Twenty francs for a turn of the wheel! it was splendid, splendid!

He played again, and played on. Fortune favoured the beginner. They say 'tis a trick of hers. The siren lures you. Time and again, he staked and won; lost a little; won it back again. He was five louis to the good now—eight—six—four—eleven again. Then, for awhile, he went up steadily—twelve, thirteen, fourteen, fifteen, and so on to twenty. By that time, he grew elated. Why, the System was sure a royal road to riches. Lieber Gott, what fortune! He'd begun by thinking of twenty-franc stakes alone; he doubled them now, putting down at each time two napoleons together. Whr'r'r went the roulette afresh; black won; the inexorable valet raked in his two louis. Eighteen to the good now! never mind; try your luck again! Bravely he adventured another forty francs, this time on passe—so the System would have it. Twenty-two came out as the winning number! With joy and delight he saw his stake doubled; twenty to the good once more! Hurrah! this was splendid!

Stop now! The next coup demanded (by the System) that he should back a number—either twelve or twenty-four, as fancy dictated. With trembling fingers he laid down two louis on twelve. Once more, fortune favoured him. When he saw the croupier pay out seventy-two good gold coins on top of his own piece, Franz was almost beside himself. He clutched them up hurriedly, lest some grabber should snatch them, as often happens at the tables. While he did so, he felt a friendly tap on his shoulder from behind. He looked round suddenly. "So your System works well!" a cheery voice exclaimed, congratulatory. Franz nodded and smiled; 'twas his friend, Mr Holmes, that despiser of all Systems.

For the rest of that day, Mr Holmes hovered near, and kept an eye on Franz quietly. From time to time, to be sure, he followed some loser outside, and disappeared for half-an-hour in a mysterious way, after which little interval he somehow always turned up smiling. But whenever he came back it was to Franz's side; and he reappeared each time with the self-same question, "How much to the good now? been winning or losing?" And each time Franz was able, on the whole, in spite of fluctuations, to report progress;—seventy louis, ninety three, a hundred and one, a hundred and twenty! People about began to mark Franz's play by now. 'Twas another Mr Wells, they said; one would do wisely to follow him.

He played till evening. About seven o'clock, Holmes invited him to dinner at the Hotel de Paris. Franz strolled off, well content; why shouldn't he dine in peace? A hundred and thirty-four louis to the good was now the reckoning.

The affable stranger wished to stand champagne. But no Viennese gentleman with a Von to his name could permit such a reversal of the rules of politeness, when he was winning heavily. Franz ordered it himself, Dry Monopole of the best brand, and drank the larger half of it. After dinner, they hurried back to the tables once more. Franz soon got a seat; he was playing high enough now for Monte Carlo to respect him. For in the salles de jeu you are respected in precise proportion to your stakes. Mr Holmes, too, put down a quiet five-franc piece now and again on colour. "Just like my luck!" he exclaimed, as black turned up each time. "I'm the unluckiest dog at games of chance, I declare, that ever was born. I never touch them, somehow, but I burn my fingers. There's a fate in it, I think!" And so indeed it seemed. He lost every single silver piece he adventured.

But as for Franz, he won steadily. He had advanced his stake, now, with his advancing fortunes, to five louis a turn! When he saw five louis go, he hardly even noticed it. They came back again so soon, five, ten, fifteen, twenty. Oh, oh, but this was royal sport indeed! Three hundred louis one minute, then down again the next to two hundred and seventy, and up once more with a bound to two-eighty-five, two-ninety, three hundred. Coins became as counters to him: gold seemed to flow in and flow out like water. It was five louis lost, five won, five lost again. But as the rising tide first advances, then recedes, then once more advances, so, in spite of occasional temporary reverses, the tide of Franz's fortune rose steadily, steadily. He played on till the croupiers were clearing the tables for the night. When he left off at last, perforce, at the final spin, he reckoned to the good three hundred and twenty-seven bright French gold pieces.

CHAPTER XLVIII

THE BUBBLE BURSTS

Complacent Mr Holmes saw him safely off by the last train to Nice, before retiring for the night to his own snug quarters. 'Tis thus one prepares one's pigeons for the plucking. When Franz arrived at the hotel, he called for more champagne, to celebrate his victory; and, failing other friends, shared drinks with the waiter.

Next morning, he was over again at Monte Carlo betimes, though with a chastening headache. He got a seat at once, and sat down to it like a man who means to win a fortune. His experience of yesterday had only strengthened his preconceived belief in the infallibility of his System. Encouraged by luck, he began playing from the outset now on the basis of staking five louis a time on each turn of the roulette wheel. For the first two or three twirls, fortune still went with him. He won as easily as he had won the preceding evening. But, after a few hazards, the chance began to change; he lost once, twice, thrice, as quickly as he had won at the outset of his playing. Presently, he was aware of Mr Holmes at his side, watching his play with a self-restrained smile of cynical indifference. That smile put Franz Lindner at once upon his mettle. He began to plunge desperately. Five louis on black;—they went like water. Five louis on manque were equally unsuccessful. Time after time Franz played; and time after time he lost again. His winnings had gone down now to two hundred louis. He began to reflect whether it mightn't be wise to reduce his stake again for a while, during this run of ill-luck, from five louis to two. He even tried it once; but a disapproving murmur from a lady behind decided him to stick to the game he had so far been playing. "You should never change your stakes," she said, "when you're losing, you know; it's an insult to chance, and it brings bad luck with it." Franz was too good a Tyroler not to be thoroughly superstitious; so he accepted the bystander's disinterested advice, and continued to put down his five gold pieces.

But still, luck was hard. If it's easy to win three hundred pounds at a go, it's easier still to lose them. And yet, Franz felt sure that, sooner or later, the System must win; the System was infallible; his friend the betting man had made all that so clear to him. Recklessly and desperately he hurried on with his game—five louis, five louis, five louis once more—lost, lost, lost, lost—till he was sick and tired of it. Now and again, luck varied, to be sure, for a time, as it had varied yesterday; but while yesterday with minor fluctuations it steadily rose, to-day with minor fluctuations it as steadily fell again. By two o'clock that afternoon, he had lost the whole of his last night's winnings, and was reduced once more to his original capital.

He was going to stake yet again, somewhat haggard and feverish, when Joaquin Holmes, who had been watching him with the profoundest interest, tapped him lightly on the arm and invited him to luncheon. "You want food," he said "—and wine. After a good glass of Mumm, you'll play better and stronger again!" In the altered state of the money-market, Franz felt himself less punctilious on the score of treats than the day before; he accepted the lunch, and the offer of champagne, with despondent alacrity. The Seer, ever prudent, stood a bottle of the best wine the cellar of the Hotel de Paris could produce. It was excellent and invigorating. As lunch proceeded, Franz's spirits returned; the champagne supplied him with fresh sinews of war—Dutch courage for the onset. "If I were you, Von Forstemann," the Seer said in his friendliest and most insinuating tone, "I wouldn't play any more. You're sure to lose in the end by it." But Franz stood by his colours. "Ah, no," he answered, smiling, "I can't lose. I've got a System. It's been tried before. A friend of mine, do you know, made twenty thousand pounds in these very rooms by it."

Flushed and fired by his wine, he went back to the tables. The Seer paid the bill for their lunch, and followed him. Franz had found another seat, and was deep in his play. But he lost, lost, lost—won a little—then lost again. All the afternoon long, he kept on losing. The Seer walked about, exchanging a word or two at times with friends and with ladies of his acquaintance (some of whose faces Franz fancied he had seen before at the London Pavilion), but came back again to his side after each such excursion, with friendly persistence.

"How much have you lost now?" he asked each time.

And Franz, very shamefaced, yet proud in a way that he could own to such losses, made answer again and again, as the case might be, "A hundred and twenty," "Two hundred and thirty," "Three hundred and twenty-seven." Ach Gott, it was pitiful!

At last, about six o'clock, the Tyroler found himself reduced to a hundred and fifty pounds of his original capital. He couldn't understand it; this was strange, very strange; the System somehow didn't seem to work as it ought to do. In his despair, he almost began to disbelieve in its virtues. Just then, the Seer strolled casually by once more, chatting gaily to a lady. He paused, and looked at Franz. In the thirst for human sympathy we all feel at such times, Franz beckoned him up with one hand, and confided to him in a hoarse whisper the painful state of his exchequer. "Come out and have a drink," the Seer said, bending low, with his most courteous manner. "Let's work this thing out. Just you show me your System?"

Franz followed him blindly across to the café opposite. The Seer ordered two cognacs and a syphon of soda-water. "Now, tell me how you do it," he said, in a very grave voice. And, with some little reluctance, looking down at the table, Franz proceeded to disclose to his attentive listener the main points of his System.

It was a transparent fallacy, of course. Such systems always are; and the Seer, who was no fool at the doctrine of chances, saw through it at a glance. His lip curled lightly. "You're a good mathematician?" he asked, with a well-suppressed sneer.

And Franz was obliged perforce to admit, in this critical moment, that he had got no further in that abstruse science than the first four rules of arithmetic.

The Seer assumed his kindliest and most didactic manner. "Now, you look here, Herr von Forstemann," he said, leaning over towards his new friend confidentially; "you've allowed yourself to be duped; you've been grossly imposed upon. I can show you in a minute your System's all bosh. The bank stands always its regular chance to win, no matter what you do, and it dodges you exactly where you think you've dodged it."

He took out a pencil and paper, and began with great show of care and patience to make the fallacy as clear as day to his unwilling pupil. Franz leant over him and looked. Step by step the clever American unravelled before his eyes all the tangled mass of false assumptions and baseless conclusions Franz called his System. Poor Franz stood aghast; the demolition was patent, irresistible, crushing. Joaquin Holmes was in his element; he was a specialist on games of chance; he demonstrated with loving care that in this case, as in all others, the bank had exactly thirty-seven chances for itself, against thirty-six for the players. Franz saw it with his own eyes: sorely against his will he was forced to see it. He couldn't gainsay it: it was clear as mud; he could only murmur in a feebly illogical way, "But my friend made twenty thousand pounds in these rooms right off with it."

The Seer was remorseless. "Accident!" he answered, calmly, with a bland wave of the hand. "Pure luck! Coincidence! And if it happened once, by a mere fluke, to pull itself off so well, all the less reason to believe such a wonderful sequence of happy shots would ever manage to repeat itself. The bank stands always its fixed chance to win in a certain proportion; by good fortune you may circumvent it, by calculation, never!"

Franz was convinced against his will. But the blow was an appalling one. He had lost three hundred and fifty pounds already; he saw no hope of recovering it. And, what was far worse, he had practically lost twenty thousand into the bargain. During all those years while he had been saving and scraping, he had considered his fortune as good as made, if he could but once go to Monte Carlo with five hundred pounds of ready money in his pocket. In five short minutes the affable stranger had knocked the bottom out of his drum—demolished the whole vast superstructure of false facts and bad reasoning Franz had reared so carefully; and now, like a house of cards, it had tumbled about his ears, leaving the poor duped Tyroler blankly hopeless and miserable.

The reaction was painful and piteous to behold. From a potential millionaire, Franz descended at once to be the owner of a paltry hundred and fifty pounds in English money. The Seer did his best in these straits to console and comfort him. He pointed out that while no man can ensure a fortune at games of chance by trying to play on a system, any man may have the good luck to win large sums if he treats it frankly as a question of fortune, not of deliberate planning. "Only," he added, with a significant glance towards the Casino, "it's foolish to play where one backs one's luck against a public bank which stands to win, by its very constitution, a certain regular proportion of all money staked against it."

His words fell on stony ground. Franz was simply inconsolable. The longer he looked at those irrefragable calculations, the more clearly did he recognise now that the Seer was right, and the System on which he had staked his all was a pure delusion. But Mr Joaquin Holmes extended him still the most obtrusive sympathy. "I'm awfully sorry for you, Herr von Forstemann," he said, over and over again, regarding his figures sideways. "This has been a hard trial to you. But you mustn't give up because you've been bitten once. Sooner or later, luck must turn. You've lost a great deal; all the sooner, then, must it change for you. Give me the pleasure of dining with you at the restaurant round the corner. You'll see things in a truer light, you know, when you've digested your dinner."

Franz followed him mechanically. He had no heart for anything. The Seer ordered a choice repast, and plied his pigeon well with the best wines in the cellar. All the while, as they dined, he harped still on three chords—his own persistent ill-luck at all games of chance; the folly of playing where the odds are against you, no matter how little, at a public table; and the certainty of winning back, on the average, what you've lost, if only you play long enough at even betting.

Emotions, once well roused, tend to flow on unchecked, in spite of temporary obstacles, in an accustomed channel. As the dinner digested itself, and the Dry Monopole fired Franz's brain once more, the thrasonic mood of the gambler came over him yet again as strong as ever. Like a born braggart that he was, a true Tyrolese Robbler, he began to boast in thick tones of how he would get the better still of those swindling tables. The Seer encouraged him to the echo in this gallant resolution, but thought ill of his chances at the unfair roulette-board, against the certain dead-weight of a mathematical calculation. "Come up with me to my room after dinner," he put in, carelessly, "and I'll show you a little game I learnt when I went buck-shooting in the Rockies some years ago. It's perfectly fair and square, with no sort of advantage to one side over the other. None of your beastly zeros: all even chances. I won't play it with you myself—or at least, only for a turn or two, just to show you how it's done—I'm so deuced unlucky. But there are lots of fellows around who'll be glad enough to give you a chance of your revenge; and, in my opinion, it's just about the very evenest game a sensible man ever put his money down upon."

Franz submitted to be taught with a very good grace. He was ready enough now for anything on earth that would help him to win back his solid lost sovereigns. They went round to a large hotel in the direction of La Condamine. People were moving in and out of the doorway by degrees, for it was just after dinner, and the town was crowded. Franz followed the Seer upstairs to a nicely furnished bedroom on the second floor, arranged as a salon, with an alcove for the bed, after the continental fashion. Nobody took much notice of them; come and go is the rule at Monte Carlo everywhere; and, besides, Mr Joaquin Holmes, that affable new-comer, was very much in the habit of taking strangers to play in his bedroom.

They sat down at the table, and the Seer, after much show of fumbling in his box, produces at last a pack of English cards, the cover still unbroken. With an innocent air of very slight acquaintance with the game he had proposed, he shuffled and cut them. "Let me see," he said, knitting his brows, and pretending to recollect. "It's like this, I think. Ah, yes, I remember." And he dealt out a card to himself, and another to Franz, with most ingenious carelessness.

Then he went on to explain in very glowing terms the simplicity of this game, and its peculiar guilelessness. "You back your card for what you like, and if I choose, I double you. You see, it's even chances. We each stand to win equally. It's easy as A.B.C. But my luck's so bad, I won't play you for money. Let's stake an imaginary five pounds on the turn-up."

They tried a deal or two, for love, on this imaginary basis, and Franz won twice out of three times. He wished it had been for sovereigns. He tried again and again, the Seer manipulating his pack all the time with conspicuous awkwardness, and managing to lose with surprising regularity. What a pity the man was so shy of tempting fate, Franz thought; though, to be sure, it was no wonder. For he lost, lost, lost, with almost incredible persistence. Still, Franz was annoyed to think that so many lucky shots, at so even a game, should all go for nothing. And he himself—why, he could win at this play like wildfire. If only he could find such a pigeon to pluck! He'd drain his man dry of all he had at a sitting!

"Come, put a louis on it!" he exclaimed at last, with a "Who's afraid" sort of air, to the reluctant stranger.

The Coloradan hesitated. He pulled out a purse full of notes and gold. "No; I can't go to a louis," he answered, gingerly, after a pause. "I've such beastly bad luck. But I'll tell you what I'll do; I'll lay you ten francs on it!"

His air was candid enough to disarm the most suspicious mind. He played, and lost. Franz picked the coins up nimbly. "Try it again," he said, with a broad smile; and Joaquin Holmes tried it. Four times running Franz won; then the American lost patience. "I'll go you a louis," he cried, warming up, and drawing a coin from his purse. Franz took him, and won it. At that, Holmes, as the Robbler thought, lost his head and grew frantic. He plunged; he doubled; he lost; he cursed his luck; and once more he boldly plunged again. Now and then, to be sure, he won; but 'twas always on the times when he omitted to double. This was a first-rate game, Franz thought; he was winning back his own again.

After a while, the Seer pulled up his chair, and settled down to it seriously. "I'm a devil of a gambler," he said, with a smile, "when once I get well into it. I won't leave off now till you've broken my bank, and got my bottom dollar. I've eight hundred pounds here"—which was a simple trade lie—"and I won't stop now till I've lost every penny of it."

Ha, ha; that was game! They buckled to in earnest. Franz played with a will. He won, won, won; he laughed loud; he picked up gaily; then, suddenly, strange to say, he lost, lost, lost again. All at once, the Seer's fingers seemed to go like lightning. He dealt fast and furious; he doubled every time; luck had somehow changed; he was winning now heavily. Franz didn't think quite so well of the game as it proceeded; he began to regard it, in fact, as little short of a swindle. But, as his pile diminished, the Seer gave him scant time to reflect between deals. "Stake! I double you!" Flash went the card; the Seer raked in the money. That was very strong champagne, and Franz's head was reeling. Still he played, played, played, lost, lost, lost, yet played again. His pile was dwindling now with appalling rapidity. He took a pull at the brandy and soda the Seer had obligingly placed by his side. What was this? The affable stranger was clearing him out every time. Franz began to suspect a plant. Could the man be a swindler?

He glanced at his little heap. A cold thrill coursed through him. Only seven louis left! When those seven were gone, why, then he would be penniless!

The Seer dealt again. With a loud German oath, Franz seized his hand and stopped it. "I saw you do it," he cried. "You rogue, I've found you out! You felt one card, changed it, and then pushed out another."

The Seer sprang up angrily. "That's an imputation on my honour," he cried, standing up and facing him with an air of indignant virtue. "I'm an English gentleman. If you insult me like that—"

But before he could say another word, quick as thought, a knife flashed in the air with unspeakable swiftness. The Seer's hand darted into his pocket for the trusty six-shooter. It was dagger against pistol, Tyroler against Westerner. But Franz was too sharp for him. Before the Coloradan's deft fingers could reach the trigger of the revolver, that keen blade was buried deep in his exposed left breast—buried deep and gurgling. Without a word, without a groan, the American dropped back short into the easy-chair he had that moment quitted. Blood spurted from the wound—spurted fast in little jets. It had penetrated his heart. He was dead in a second.

In less time than it takes to say it, Franz realised what he had done, and pulled himself together from his paroxysm of passion. Leaving the notes where they lay, he crammed his own gold hastily into his waistcoat pocket. He let the knife stop in the wound; it was in no way compromising. Then he opened the door, and walked calmly out, and down the broad stone steps, and into the streets of Monte Carlo.

CHAPTER XLIX

THE PIGEON FLIES HOME

A Robbler's not a man to be lightly discomposed by the mere accident that he happens to have committed a murder. Franz's first impulse, indeed, as he left that blood-stained room, was to run away helter-skelter from the scene of his hasty crime, to disappear into space, London, the Tyrol, anywhere, without even going back to his hotel at Nice to reclaim his portmanteau. But second thoughts showed him how foolish so precipitate a retreat would be. By adopting it, he would be throwing away many valuable chances which now told in his favour. It was wholly to the good, for example, that he'd happened to give his name all along the line as Karl von Forstemann from Vienna. Even if the authorities found reason to suspect him of having killed this man Holmes, they'd lost much useful time in trying to track down the imaginary Von Forstemann; while he himself might be making his way quietly across the length and breadth of the continent, meanwhile, under his own true name as Franz Lindner of the London Pavilion. Though, to be sure, there was no reason why they should ever suspect him. Hundreds of people flock in and out of Monte Carlo every day; hundreds of people come and go at every hotel, unnoticed. Besides, it wasn't likely the body'd be discovered till to-morrow morning; and by that time, Gott sei dank, he'd be safe and away across the Italian frontier.

It was early still, only a little past ten. Tremulous and startled by the magnitude of his crime, he strolled about for awhile to cool himself in the Casino gardens. Then a happy thought struck him, he'd go in and play for a bit to avoid suspicion. Hot at heart as he was, but trying his best to look unconcerned, he passed into those huge over-heated rooms once more, and played for half-an-hour with very languid attention. The greater stake now in jeopardy made it difficult for him when he won to remember even to take up his money; he let it lie once or twice on the board till it doubled and trebled itself. But that was all to the good; it suited his book well: people noticed only the more how coolly he was playing. Strange to say, he was winning, too, when he cared so little whether he won or lost—winning pounds at a time on every turn of the tables. It was a master-stroke of policy, and Franz plumed himself not a little on being clever enough to think of it. How could people ever say it was he who killed the man, when he'd spent half the night at play in the gambling rooms of the Casino?

At eleven, he left off, several pounds to the good, and strolled down to the station with well-assumed carelessness. He returned in a carriage with the two jolly young Englishmen. Casually, on the way, he mentioned to them that he was going to leave Nice next morning. At the hotel they broke another bottle of champagne together. Franz sat up, and talked excitedly, and even sang comic songs; he was afraid to go to bed; though still self-possessed, and by no means panic-stricken, he was nervous and agitated.

That night, he never undressed. He lay in his clothes on the bed, and slept by snatches fitfully. In the morning, he rose early, and looked hard for spots of blood as he washed and dressed himself. But he had done his work far too neatly to spatter his clothes. "Coffee, quick, and my bill!" he said to the waiter who answered the bell; "I want to catch an early train at the station for England." He said England on purpose, though he meant it to be Italy. With a true Tyroler's instinct, he would strike straight home—by Milan, Verona, and the Brenner, to St Valentin.

At the station, he took a through ticket, first-class, for Genoa. He had to pass Monte Carlo, and he did so with repugnance. Yet he wasn't much afraid; the Robbler instinct was still strong within him. A couple of fat Frenchmen got into the carriage at Monaco; they were talking of some tragedy that had happened last night at an hotel at La Condamine. Franz pricked up his ears but tried to look unconcerned. "Somebody dead?" he inquired in his Teutonic French, with a show of languid interest.

"Yes; another suicide," one of the Frenchmen answered, shrugging his shoulders, with a smile. "Que voulez-vous? An Englishman, a fellow called Holmes, or, some say, an American. He stabbed himself last night, after losing heavily. He was stopping at my hotel: he went to bed all well; the servants knocked this morning, got no answer, went in and found the body in a fauteuil, where the malheureux had stabbed himself."

Franz's eye gleamed bright. So at first they had put the best interpretation upon it! The mere suspicion of a suicide might give him a start that would enable him to escape. He shrugged his shoulders in return. "A common episode of life as things go at Monte Carlo!" he murmured, philosophically.

The Frenchmen got out and left the train at Mentone. At Ventimiglia, Franz crossed the frontier with a beating heart; so far, at least, no telegram to arrest or detain him. All morning, the train crawled on at a snail's pace towards Genoa. Franz chafed and grumbled, eating his heart out with impatience. At San Pier d'Arena, the junction-station, he took his portmanteau in his hand, and re-booked for Milan. There he spent that second night in fear and trembling. On his way up to an hotel, he bought a copy of an evening paper, the Corriere della Sera. The same story still—Suicidio a Monte Carlo.

He didn't sleep much; but he slept—that was ever something. At seven o'clock, he was up, and walked out towards the Cathedral. But that mount of marble, with its thousand spires and its statued pinnacles in the myriad niches, had no power on such a day to arrest his attention; beside the great west door, he was looking for a boy with a morning newspaper. Soon he found one, and tore it open under the arcades of the Piazza. He knew no Italian, but by the aid of his scanty French he could make out the meaning of one sinister paragraph. "It is now believed that the man Holme or Holmes, who was found stabbed in his room at the Hotel des Étrangers, at Monte Carlo, yesterday morning, met his death by foul means, and not, as was at first suspected, by suicide. The doctors who have examined the wound concur in the opinion that it could hardly by any possibility be self-inflicted. Holmes is now known to have been a notorious card-sharper, and it is surmised that he may have been murdered in a fit of revengeful passion by one of his victims, several of whom he is said to have duped during the last few days in the neighbourhood of the Casino. No clue, however, has as yet been obtained to the name or personality of his supposed assailant."

Murder! they called it murder to stab that cheating rogue! and they took him for a murderer just because he'd revenged himself! When they'd got as far as that, it was probable before long they'd track the deed home to Herr Karl von Forstemann. Franz saw clearly enough now what his next move must be. Herr Karl von Forstemann must disappear as if by magic from this earthly scene, and

Franz Lindner of St Valentin, and of the London Pavilion, that honest and simple-minded Tyrolese musician, must at once replace him.

He paid his bill at the hotel, took a cab to the station instead of the omnibus, and caught the through train to Venice direct—throwing the police off his track, if it came to police, by getting out short, portmanteau in hand, at Verona, for the Brenner. All day long, he travelled on by that beautiful mountain line, up the Adige towards Botzen; and, though he was flying for his life, it gave him none the less a genuine thrill of joy when he beheld once more those beloved Tyrolese peaks, and heard the German tongue spoken with a Tyrolese accent. He slept that night at Botzen. There, he felt his foot once more upon his native heath. In the morning, he rose early, and went into a hatter's, where he bought a Tyrolese hat of the old conical pattern; all fugitive that he was, the ingrained instincts of his youth yet made him turn the blackcock's feather in it the wrong way forward, Robbler-wise. Vain-glorious still and defiant, nobody would ever have taken him for a runaway criminal. He bought also a pair of stout Tyrolese boots, and introduced a few other little changes in his costume, sufficient to transform him at once from the cosmopolitan snob into the simple Franz Lindner of the old days at St Valentin. Then he took the train north again, right through to Innsbruck, where he slept his third night, more confident than before, and had a chance of reading all in a Vienna paper.

That all was bad enough. No doubt now remained on the minds of the French police that Joaquin Holmes had been really murdered. The hypothesis of suicide broke down at every step. Suspicion pointed most to one or other of three persons whom he was believed to have duped just before the murder. One of these three was being traced by detectives to Marseilles and Paris; the other two, it was believed, had gone on to Italy. In the interests of justice, the police would mention no names at present, but one of these three, they held, must almost certainly be the murderer.

Still, the instinct of his race urged Franz on to St Valentin. He took the afternoon train north as far as Jenbach; then he tramped all the way on foot to his native village. It was late when he arrived, and, tired and hunted down, he went straight to the Wirthshaus. Cousin Fridolin held up his hands in astonishment to see the wanderer. It wasn't merely surprise that Franz should come back at all, but that he should come back as he went, a genuine Tyroler. All were well in the place: the Herr Vicar and everyone. And Andreas Hausberger and Linnet were here as well, returned home for a holiday.

It was Franz's turn now to start back in surprise. What, Andreas and Linnet come back to St Valentin! Impossible! You don't mean it!

But Cousin Fridolin did mean it, with his thumbs in the armholes of his red Tyrolese waistcoat. They'd retired for the night, they were here at the inn; but he'd knock at their door (full of country hospitality as he was, the simple soul!) and tell them to come out and welcome a friend home again.

Franz seized his arm to prevent him. "Oh no," he cried; "not that. . . . There are reasons why you mustn't. . . . Andreas and I had a difference some years ago at Meran; and though we patched it all up again in a way in London, I don't want to see him now, at least, not till to-morrow."

As for Cousin Fridolin, standing back and regarding him in surprise, he could hardly understand these fine town-bred manners. If Franz had come back a true Tyroler in dress, he brought with him none the less all the airs and graces of Western civilisation, as understood by the frequenters of the London Pavilion. They sat awhile and talked, while Franz ate the rough supper and drank as much as was good for him of the thin country beer; but Cousin Fridolin noticed that his old rival and companion seemed unaccountably stiff and reserved in his demeanour. Especially did he shirk any obtrusive questions as to whence he had come, and by what route he had got there. As they parted for the night, Franz turned to Cousin Fridolin, who alone in the village had yet seen or spoken with him. "Don't tell Andreas and Linnet I came here to-night," he said. "I want them not to know till they meet me as a surprise to-morrow morning."

Cousin Fridolin, much wondering, promised compliance with his wish. He lighted Franz to his room, and bade him good-night in a very audible whisper. Herr Andreas and his wife had the next rooms to him, he said. Franz nodded a distant assent, and shook his hand somewhat coldly. The terror that had stood over him since he left Monte Carlo grew somehow much deeper, much nearer, much more real, as he found himself once more in these familiar surroundings. He bolted the door with its little wooden button, and sat alone on the bed for some minutes in silence. The solitude appalled him more than ever before; he felt conscious, in some dim way, the hue-and-cry of the police was now well after him.

As he sat there and listened to his own heart beating, while the tallow candle guttered on the table by his side, a low sound from the next room began to attract his attention. It was a stifled sound, with a choking sort of sob in it. Just at first, too preoccupied with his own emotions, Franz hardly noticed it; but at last it obtruded itself upon him by its very unobtrusiveness. Of a sudden, he realised to himself what manner of noise this was. It was the deep suppressed sound of a woman weeping. With her head under the bed-clothes, she was crying, crying, crying silently.

Rising up from his bed, Franz crept over to the door of communication between the two rooms, his mind for the moment distracted by the sound even from his own immediate and pressing danger. For it was borne in upon him at once by what Fridolin Telser had said, that the woman in the next room was none other than Linnet!

Sob, sob, sob, the voice continued, chokingly. Franz could feel rather than hear that the noise was muffled by the intervention of the bed-clothes, and that Linnet, if it was she, was doing the very best she knew to check it. But, in spite of her efforts, the sobs broke out afresh every now and again, spasmodically; she was sobbing, sobbing, sobbing, as if her heart would break, sobbing by herself in the solitude of her bedroom.

All terrified as he was, Franz's heart stood still at it.

Presently, another door on the far side seemed to open, and a voice was heard saying in low, angry tones, "Won't you stop that noise? I can't sleep for hearing you."

It was Andreas Hausberger's voice; Franz clenched his hands to hear it. But Linnet seemed to raise her head from the bed-clothes at those words, and speak at last with a great effort to calm herself. "Andreas," she said, through her sobs, "as the Church bids, I follow you; but I can't help crying when I think how you treat me. I cry as silently and quietly as I can to myself. If I keep you awake, you must take another room a little farther off from me."

That was all. She said no more; and Andreas closed the door, as Franz judged, and went back again. But even in his own hour of peril and terror, perhaps all the more keenly because of all that had happened to him, Franz read in those few words the whole story of Linnet's unhappy marriage. He had suspected it before, of course, but now he knew it. Andreas's gruff tone of reproof, poor Linnet's shrinking accent of despairing misery, were more eloquent in his ears than whole hours of deliberate and demonstrative talking. This episode meant much to him. It was for Linnet he had hazarded and encountered everything, it was for Linnet, indirectly, he had risked his own life by stabbing that wretched man away over at Monte Carlo!

His anger burned bright against Andreas Hausberger; Hausberger who had cheated him of his Linnet long ago; Hausberger who was making his Linnet's life a burden to her! The cold-blooded wretch! How Franz wished it was into him he had plunged that good knife that did swift execution on the dead cheat at Monte Carlo! Ah well, ah well, it was not too late even now! If he couldn't marry Linnet, he could at least avenge her! He could have wiped out old scores and redressed new wrongs, if it had only been Andreas in place of that other man!

CHAPTER L

ANDREAS HAUSBERGER PAYS

That night again Franz didn't trouble to undress. He lay on the bed in his clothes, and let the candle burn out as it would in its socket. Early next morning, with the restlessness of a hunted man, he rose betimes, and went down to the wonted breakfast of the inn with Cousin Fridolin. Their talk over their coffee was of Linnet and Andreas. Fridolin retailed to him, bit by bit, all the sinister surmises of the village gossips; people thought at St Valentin Andreas was jealous at last of his beautiful Frau, Fridolin let his voice drop to a confidential key, and had brought her away hither from some lover in London. Franz smiled bitterly at that thought; why, the man hadn't heart enough in him to be even jealous, for one may be beneath jealousy as one may be above it. Was he unkind to her? Franz asked, curiously, as Cousin Fridolin broke off in the midst of a sentence.

Well, he didn't exactly strike her, Cousin Fridolin believed; though, to be sure, when she first came to the inn, she bore marks of violence. But she cried all day, and she cried all night; and folks fancied in the village it might perhaps be for Will Deverill. At any rate, she and Andreas lost no love between them; man said it was only as a good Catholic she stopped with him.

After breakfast, Franz rose up and walked out on the road aimlessly. Restless still, with the ever-present fear of detection upon him, and with the fiery Tyrolese heart eating itself out within, he walked on and on, hardly knowing why he did so. At last he reached Zell, the little capital of the valley. It was early still, for he had started at daybreak; but already a strange group of whispering villagers crowded agog round the door of the post-office and telegraph, where the post-master was affixing an official notice. Franz joined them, and read. His blood ran cold within him. It was a Kaiserlich-Königlich police announcement of a public reward of ten thousand florins for information leading to the capture of one Karl von Forstemann of Vienna, age, height, and description as below annexed, accused of the murder of Joaquin Holmes, an American citizen, at Monte Carlo, and known to have returned to Austrian territory by Verona and Botzen, where he had altered his clothing, and gone on to Innsbruck.

As Franz read those damning words, he knew in a second all was really up with him. Once they had tracked him so far, they must track him to St Valentin. Again the instinct of his race drove him back towards his native village, after a word or two interchanged with his friends at the post-office. Those simple country souls never dreamt in their hearts of suspecting their old comrade, Franz Lindner the jäger, who had come back unexpectedly, like Andreas and Linnet, of being the Karl von Forstemann of Vienna referred to in the announcement. But Franz knew it couldn't be long before the police were on his track; and he turned and fled upwards to his old home at St Valentin, like a fox to its lair, or a rabbit to its burrow.

All the way up the hill his soul seethed within him. He would sell his life dear, if the worst came to the worst; they should fight for it now before ever they took him. He had stopped at a shop at Zell to buy a jäger's knife, in place of the one he had left behind him at Monte Carlo, in the card-sharper's body. He stuck it ostentatiously in the leather belt he had bought at Botzen to complete his costume; as he went on his way, he fingered it ever and anon with affectionate familiarity. Old moods came back to him; with his feather in his hat and his blade by his side, he felt himself once more a true Tyrolese Robbler. The thin veneer of Regent Street had dropped off as if by magic; when they wanted to arrest him, they should fight for it first; who would take him, must follow him like a fleet-footed chamois up the rocks behind St Valentin. And whoever came first should receive that good knife, plump, so, in his bosom, or plunge his own, if he could, into Franz's. He would die like a man with his dagger in his hand. No rope or axe should ever finish the life of a free mountain jäger!

Thus thinking to himself, at last he reached the inn. On the threshold, Cousin Fridolin met him, distinctly penitent. "Andreas knows you're here, friend Franz," he said, with a reluctant air. "I didn't quite tell him, but he guessed it, and wormed it out of me. He's gone for a walk just now with Linnet, she's grown such a fine lady. But there, I forgot; you've seen her in London."

"Yes; I've seen her in London," Franz answered, half-dreamily, in a musing undertone. His voice was as the voice of a condemned criminal. He knew he was doomed. He knew he must die. It might be to-day, or it might be to-morrow; but, sooner or later, he felt sure, the police would be after him.

He stalked moodily into the inn, and dropped, tired, into a chair in the parlour bar, with his legs extended straight in front of him in a despondent attitude. There he sat and reflected. Cousin Fridolin's voice ran on, but Franz never heeded it. How little it meant to him now, Cousin Fridolin's chatter about Linnet and Andreas! What did he care whether they were rich enough to buy up the whole parish, as Fridolin asserted, and have money left over? In a few short weeks, nothing on earth would make any difference. He gazed at his feet, and knit his brows, and breathed hard. Cousin Fridolin by his side ran on unchecked. Franz answered him nothing.

By-and-by the latch lifted, and Andreas Hausberger entered, followed close by Linnet.

Andreas gazed at his man angrily. Then he turned round to his wife. "Go to your room, Linnet," he said, in his stern tone of command. "I must speak with this fellow."

Linnet, cowed and trembling, slank off without a word. Franz could see she was pale, and had suffered greatly. Her cheeks had fallen in, her colour had flown, her lips were bloodless, her eye had lost its lustre. Andreas spoke to her in an ugly, domineering voice. Franz glared at him in his wrath. Surely, surely it was high time old scores were wiped out, and this question at least of Linnet's happiness settled.

He must die himself soon; of that he felt quite sure; 'tis a chance which a Robbler has long been accustomed to keep vividly before him. But it would be something at least to feel he didn't lose his own life in vain; that he was avenging himself on Andreas, and freeing Linnet. If guillotined he must be, it was better he should be guillotined for killing Andreas Hausberger on a woman's behalf, than for stabbing a base card-sharper in a drunken brawl at Monte Carlo.

In such temper, at last, did Franz Lindner stand up and confront with mortal hate his old unforgiven enemy. Andreas turned to him with a little sneer. He spoke in English, lest Cousin Fridolin, bustling about behind the bar at his business, should overhear him and know what they were saying. "Well, what are you doing here?" he asked, with a contemptuous curl of those cynical lips. "Deverill sent you, I suppose. You've come all this way to spy upon me and my wife as his flunkey."

Franz took a step forward, and glared at him fiercely from under his eyebrows. "I have not, liar," he answered, his fingers twitching. "I didn't know you were here, and I am no man's flunkey."

The return to his native air and his native costume, coupled with the gravity and danger of the situation, seemed to have raised him all at once from the music-hall level to the higher and nobler plane of the Tyrolese mountaineer. He looked and moved every inch a freeman, nay, more, he confronted Andreas with such haughty self-confidence that his enemy, surprised, drew back half-a-step and surveyed him critically. "That's a very strange coincidence," Andreas murmured, after a short pause. "It's curious you should choose the exact moment to come when I happened to be at St Valentin."

Franz scowled at him yet again. "You can take it how you like," he retorted, in German, with a toss of the head in his old defiant fashion. "If you choose to think I came here to follow you and fight you, you're at liberty to think so. I'm ready, if you are. I've an old cause of quarrel against you, recollect, Andreas Hausberger. You robbed me by fraud long ago of the woman I loved; you married her by force; and you've made her life unhappy. If I dogged you, which I haven't done, I'd have cause enough and to spare. You remember that first night when I saw you in London, in Mrs Palmer's box at the Harmony Theatre? Well, if it hadn't been for the presence of the woman I loved, the woman you stole from me, that very first night, you false cur, I'd have buried my knife in you."

Andreas drew back yet another pace. He was taller than Franz, very big and powerful. With a contemptuous look, he measured his enemy from head to foot. "Why, you couldn't, you fool," he answered, drawing himself up to his full height. "I never yet was afraid of you or of any man. Many's the time I've turned you, drunk, out of this very room. I'll turn you out again if you dare to speak so to me!"

He was wearing a Tyrolese hat, just like Franz's own; he had bought it at Jenbach on his eastward route, to return, as was his wont, at each fresh visit home, to the simplicity and freedom of his native mountains. Before Franz's very eyes he removed it from his head, and, with a sneer on his face, turned the blackcock's feather Robbler-wise as a challenge of defiance.

No Robbler on earth could overlook such a wager of battle. Trembling with rage, Franz Lindner sprang forth, and leaped angrily towards him. His face was black as night; his brow was like thunder. He snatched the hat from Andreas's head with a deft flank movement, and tore hastily from its band the offending emblem.

"Was kost die Feder?" he cried, in a tone of angry contempt, holding it up triumphantly before its owner's eyes. All the west was blotted out; Franz Lindner was himself again. He was a Robbler once more, with the hot blood of his Robblerhood boiling fierce within him.

Quick as lightning, the familiar answer rang out in clear tones, "Fünf Finger und ein Griff!" Andreas brooked no such insult. "Five fingers and a grip"—he should have if he wanted them.

Before Cousin Fridolin had time to understand what was passing before his eyes, or to intervene to prevent it—in the twinkle of an eye, with extraordinary rapidity, the two men had closed, hands and arms fast locked, and were grappling with one another in a deadly struggle. Franz flung himself upon his foe like a tiger in its fury. One moment, his knife flashed high in air. Cousin Fridolin rushed forward, and strove to tear them asunder. But, before he could reach them, that gleaming blade had risen above Franz's head and flashed down again, with unerring aim, on Andreas Hausberger's bosom. The big man fell back heavily, both hands pressed to his heart, where black blood was oozing out in long, deep, thick gurgles.

With a sudden jerk, Franz flung down the knife he had wrenched from the wound. It stuck quivering by its point in the wooden flooring. Then he thrust his hands into his pockets, with one foot pushed forward. He clenched his teeth, and bent his head towards the dying man's body. "I always meant to kill you," he cried, in his gratified rage, "and, thank God and all blessed saints, to-day I've done it."

Cousin Fridolin jumped forward, and bent aghast over the body. But Franz stood still, gazing on it calmly. At that moment, the door opened, and Linnet entered.

CHAPTER LI

EXIT FRANZ LINDNER

The first thing Linnet felt, as she sprang forward to her husband, who lay dying or dead on the floor in front of her, was a pervading sense, not of sorrow or of affection, but of horror at a great crime successfully accomplished. "You've killed him, you've killed him!" she cried aloud to Franz. "O Fridolin, quick, quick, run and fetch the Herr Vicar! He's breathing still; I can hear him ever breathing! Perhaps there's time yet for him to receive extreme unction."

To all of them, the sacraments were the chief things to be thought of. Fridolin hurried off as he was bid, rousing the house as he went with a loud cry of alarm to come and look after Linnet. But Linnet herself sat on the ground all aghast, with her husband's head laid heavy in her lap, trying to staunch his wound helplessly, and wringing her hands now and again in a blind agony of terror. Meanwhile, Franz stood by as if wholly unmoved, regarding the entire scene with a certain sardonic and triumphant self-satisfaction. He wouldn't die for nothing, as things had turned out now; he had avenged himself at least on his lifelong enemy!

He stood there many minutes, with his hands in his pockets, growing cooler and cooler as he reflected on his deed, and more and more glad in his heart to think he had done it. So Linnet at least would be free! it was ever something to have rid her of Andreas Hausberger! Men and women came in, and lifted Andreas where he lay, and stretched him on the bed in the adjoining room, and stripped off part of his clothes, and washed the wound, and examined it. But nobody as yet thought of arresting Franz or molesting him in any way. He stood there still, the one wholly unconcerned and careless person in that excited assembly. His rage had cooled down by this time, and he was perfectly collected. He was waiting for the village authorities to come and take him into custody.

The priest arrived in due time, with the holy oil and the viaticum; but, pronouncing Andreas dead, refused to administer the sacraments. The doctor came, too, a little later than the priest, and confirmed the Herr Vicar's unfavourable verdict. Linnet sat and wrung her hands by the bedside where he lay, more at the suddenness of the event, and the unexpected horror of it, than from any real sense of affection or bereavement. The little crowd in the room gathered in small knots and whispered low around Franz. But Franz stood coolly looking on, without making an attempt to escape, less interested in what had occurred than anyone else in the village. What was one murder more to the man who was wanted from Monte Carlo to St Valentin?

By-and-by, a fresh commotion arose outside the inn. The crowd in the room divided, and buzzed eagerly. The Herr Landrath, they said, had come to arrest the murderer. Franz looked around him defiantly, as they whispered and stared at him. But no man laid a hand on him. No man dared to touch him. The Landrath himself hesitated to enter the place where the dead man lay, and arrest the murderer, red-handed, in presence of the priest, the corpse, the widow. "Is Franz Lindner in there?" he asked solemnly from the doorway.

And Franz answered in a firm and unshaken voice, "He is so, Herr Kaiserlich-Königlich Commissary."

"Come out," the official said. And with a bold and haughty tread Franz Lindner came out to him.

"In the name of the Emperor-King, I arrest you, Franz Lindner, for the wilful murder of Andreas Hausberger in this village," the Commissary said sternly, laying his hand on his prisoner's shoulder.

Franz laughed a discordant laugh. "And, in the name of the Emperor-King, you shall run for it, by Our Blessed Frau," he answered, contemptuously. He shook the hand from his shoulder with an easy jerk, and pushed back the Landrath, who was a heavy man of more than middle-age, with those two stout arms of his. "Follow and catch me, who can," he cried, laughing loud once more, "Kaiserlich-Königlich Commissary!" And before they all knew what was happening under their eyes, with a bound like a wild beast Franz had darted to the door, pushed his way through the little group that obstructed the threshold, hit out right and left with elbows and fists against all who strove to stop him, tripped up the first man who tried to seize him by the coat, and sprung by the well-known path up the free mountains behind them.

"Follow him!" the Commissary gasped out, collecting his breath, and pulling himself together again after the unexpected shaking. "In the law's name and the Emperor-King's, all good subjects, follow him!"

Three or four of the younger men, thus adjured and called on personally to arrest the criminal, darted after him at full speed up the slope of the mountain. But they followed just at first with somewhat half-hearted zeal; for why should they wish thus to seal the fate of an old friend and comrade? As they advanced, Franz waved his hat derisively a hundred yards in front of them. In his old jäger days, not Fridolin Telser himself was so swift to follow the clambering chamois among the peaks and pinnacles above the pine-clad forest. All those years of indulgence in crowded cities had weakened his bodily vigour and relaxed his muscles; but in soul he felt himself still once more as of old the free mountain hunter. "Come on!" he shouted aloud, with a wild jodel of challenge. "Come, and catch me if you can. Who comes first, gets my fist in his face and knife in his heart. Arrest me if you dare. If you try it, you may sup to-night in purgatory, at a table side by side with Andreas Hausberger!"

He fled up the mountain with incredible speed for a person so out of training; but his native air braced him, and the double excitement of the last few days seemed to stimulate his nerves and limbs to extraordinary energy. A man runs his best when he runs for his life. On and on Franz mounted, past the pinewood and the boulder where Linnet sat long ago with Will Deverill, and up to the crags beyond, where blank patches of snow still lurked here and there in the sunless crevices. Every now and again he looked back to see how far he had distanced his pursuers. He gained at each step. He had one great advantage. He was flying for dear life, whither or why he knew not; they were following unwillingly, in the name of the law, the footsteps of an old friend and boon companion.

Above, all was snow. In those northward valleys winter loiters late, and spring comes but tardily. Once among the firn, Franz could give them the slip, he felt sure; he could lurk behind rocks, or hide among the klamms, and let the baffled pursuers pass by unnoticing. But no, but no, ach, Gott! the footprints! With a sudden revulsion he realised his error. Those years in milder climates had made him forget for a moment the hopelessness of escaping if once he reached the snow-line. Appalled and dismayed, he turned and hesitated. Then he dashed off at an angle, horizontally along the hill, at the same general level, so as to avoid the snow-covered glaciers. That one false move lost him. His pursuers, seeing him double, headed forward diagonally across the third side of the triangle, and gained on him visibly. Franz was blown and panting. His heart throbbed hard; he had overtaxed it sadly in that first wild burst up the ramping hillside. Again he paused, and looked back. The hopelessness and futility of the whole thing broke in upon him. If he ran all day and all night as well, if he distanced that little body of amateur pursuers for the moment, what would it profit him in the end? Could he evade arrest at last? could he escape the clutches of the Austrian law, shake off the strong hand of the Kaiserlich-Königlich government?

All at once, seized with a sudden little access of despair, he sat down on the hillside, and laughed aloud audibly. "Ha, ha, ha," he cried, hoarsely, at the very top of his voice, as his antagonists drew nearer, "So you think you'll catch me! You think you'll get well paid! You want to earn a reward on me! Well, look here, Ludwig Dangl," and he shouted through his bent hand to the foremost of his pursuers, "there's ten thousand florins set on my head already for stabbing a man dead in an hotel at Monte Carlo, and it's yours . . . if you catch me! Come on, friend, and earn it!"

He had grown reckless now. The dare-devil spirit of the man who knows well he has forfeited his life and has no chance of escape left, had wholly taken hold of him. He sat there, by the Kamin, waiting till the pursuers were almost upon him. "Ten thousand florins!" he shouted aloud once more, waving his hat above his head, as he jumped up when they neared him. "Ten thousand florins is a nice round sum! Will you have it, Ludwig Dangl? will you have it, Karl Furst? will you have it, Fritz Mairhofer?"

His very recklessness appalled them. The men thought he must be mad. They paused, and stared hard at him. There were only three now. Neither liked to advance first. Franz waved his hat frantically, and beckoned them on towards the weathered crags that overlook St Valentin. Great rocks there rose sheer over fissured gullies. The men hardly ventured to follow him up to those frowning heights. Heaven knows what a madman, in such a mood as that, may do or dare among the cleft troughs and gorges! They halted, debated, then came on towards him, abreast, more slowly, step by step, in a little formed body. But Franz, now restored by a momentary pause, leaped upward like a chamois over the steep path in front of him. The fresh mountain air seemed to nerve and invigorate him. On, on, he bounded swift over the jagged steps in the rock, till he poised himself at last like a mountain goat on the very edge of the precipice. It was a sheer cliff that looked down on a great snowdrift in a ravine two hundred feet beneath him. The Robbler instinct in Franz's blood had now gained complete mastery. He waved his hat again, with its feather turned insultingly. "Ten thousand florins!" he cried once more, in his loudest voice. "Ten thousand florins! Who wants them? Who'll earn them?"

He laughed aloud in their faces. The three men drew on cautiously. Franz waited till they came up. Then Ludwig Dangl, mustering up courage to take the first step, stood forward and laid hands on him. Straightway Franz seized his assailant round the body with a wrestler's grip. Ludwig tried to disengage himself; but 'twas a narrow and dangerous spot for wrestling. With a sudden wrench, Franz lifted him from the ground. Holding him grasped in his arms, he looked over the edge of the precipice. Next instant, he had leaped, with Ludwig Dangl in his embrace. One loud cry burst at once from both their straining throats. A cry of wild triumph; a cry of fierce despair. Then all was silence.

The other two men, looking awestruck and horrified over the edge of the crag, saw them fall two hundred feet sheer into the soft snow beneath. It received them gently. Not a sign marked the spot where the two bodies sank in. The soft snow closed over them. But they must have been dead many seconds before they reached the bottom.

CHAPTER LII

A CONFESSION OF FAITH

It was a terrible time for Linnet, those few days at the inn, while she waited to bury her murdered husband. She felt so lonely, here among her own people; her isolation came out even more vividly than she could have expected: she had outgrown them, that was the fact, and they could no longer sympathise with her. Their very deference and respect chilled her heart to the core in that appalling season of solitary wretchedness: they regarded her just in the light of the great lady from London, too grand and too fine for them to venture upon comforting her. So Linnet was forced to have out her dark hour by herself, and be content for the rest with the respectful silence of her poor fellow-country-people.

The first night, in particular, was a very painful trial to her. By evening, they had brought back Franz's body from the snowdrift; and now it lay with Ludwig Dangl beside her dead husband's in the dancing-hall that stood just below the very room where Linnet had to spend the first night of her widowhood. Though she kept the candle burning, and the crucifix by her side, the awful sense of solitude through the long slow hours, with those three hostile corpses lying side by side in the hall beneath her, made her shudder with affright each time she woke with a start from a snatch of hurried sleep, much disturbed by hateful dreams, to the reality of her still more hateful position.

Early next morning, however, a messenger arrived post haste from Zell, with a telegram directed to Frau Hausberger, St Valentin. Linnet tore it open mechanically, half dreading some fresh surprise. As she read it, she drew a deep breath. Oh, that dear, dear Rue! This was quite too good of her. "Have heard of your trouble, and sympathise with you deeply. Am on my way to join you. Shall reach St Valentin to-morrow evening."

It was a measure to Linnet of how English she had become, that, as she stood on the platform at Jenbach next day, awaiting the arrival of Rue's train from Innsbruck, she felt as though she were expecting the advent of some familiar home-friend, coming to cheer her solitude in a land of strangers. When at last the train drew up, Rue leapt from the carriage into her rival's arms, and caressed her tenderly. Linnet looked sweet in her simple dark dress, the plainest she possessed, for she hadn't yet had time to get her mourning ready. "How did you hear of it all, you dear kind Rue?" she inquired, half-hysterically, clasping her new friend to her bosom in a sudden outburst of sated sympathy. "It couldn't surely have got so soon into the English papers."

"No, dear," Rue answered, in her tenderest tone, laying one soft hand soothingly on the pale cheek as she answered. "I'd written to St Valentin beforehand, to some one whose address Will Deverill gave me, asking for news of you every day, and enclosing money; and he telegraphed to me at once as soon as all this happened. His name's Fridolin Telser, and Will says he is a cousin of yours. So, of course, as soon as I heard, I felt I must come out, post haste, to join you; for I knew, Linnet, how lonely you'd be, and how much in need of a woman's sympathy."

Linnet answered nothing. That "of course" was too much for her. She burst into tears instead, and sobbed her full heart out contentedly on Rue's friendly shoulder. They drove back to St Valentin hand-in-hand together. That night, Rue slept with her, in a little room in the village; and though they talked for hours with one another, and only dozed at intervals, Linnet rose next morning fresher and stronger by far than she had felt at any time since the day of the murder.

Rue stopped on with her all that week, till Andreas was buried, and she could leave St Valentin. Linnet shrank now from taking anything that had ever been his. The Wirthshaus was to be sold: Cousin Fridolin bought it at a low price with his hoarded savings, and the proceeds were to be devoted to a new school for the village. The Herr Vicar, too, was richer by many masses for the repose of the unworthy soul which Linnet felt sure had now much need of his orisons. Nor were even Franz Lindner and Ludwig Dangl forgotten: the shrine on the hill-top, by the Chamois Rocks, marking the spot whence they took their fatal leap, was erected, the guides will tell you, "by the famous singer, Casalmonte, who came originally from this village."

Rue went back with her friend to London, stopping a week or two by the way at quiet country spots in the Bavarian Highlands, on the Rhine, and in Belgium. 'Twas early June when they reached town. Rue wouldn't hear of Linnet's returning to her old house in St John's Wood, where everything would remind her of that hateful past: she insisted that her "new sister," as she called her, must share for the present her home in Hans Place, till other arrangements could be made for her. "Besides," she added, with a little smile, full of deeper import, "it'll save scandal, you know. You mustn't live alone. It's best you should stop in some other woman's house, till you've arrived at some fixed understanding as to your future."

It was in Rue's drawing-room, accordingly, a few weeks later, that Linnet for the first time saw Will Deverill once more after all that had happened. With the same generous self-restraint he had always shown wherever Linnet's reputation was concerned, Will had denied himself for many days the pleasure of calling upon her. When at last he came, Linnet made up her mind beforehand she should receive him with becoming calmness and dignity. But the moment Will entered the room, and took her two hands in his, and looked deep into her dark eyes, and stood there silent, thrilling through from head to foot at sight of her, yet rejoicing in heart at his one love recovered, why, as for Linnet, she just looked up at him, and drew short gasps of breath, and held his hands tight in her own, and then with a sweet half-unconscious self-surrender let herself fall slowly, slowly upon his bosom. There he allowed her to lie long without speaking one word to her. What need of words between those two who understood one another instinctively? what chance of concealing the hope and joy each felt, and knew, and communicated, unspoken, by mere contact to the other? For touch is to love the most eloquent of the senses.

At last they found words, and talked long and eagerly. There was no question between them now in what relation they must henceforth stand to one another. It was mere details of time, and place, and propriety, the when and how and where, that interested them at present. "But you can get a dispensation for me?" Linnet asked, nestling close to him.

Will smiled a gentle smile. "There's little need of dispensation, for you and me, my darling," he said, holding her hand tenderly. "You would have given me yourself once, in spite of the Church and the world: you can surely give me yourself now without a qualm of conscience, when the Church and the world will both smile approval. To me, Linnet, the whole sanctity of a union between us lies infinitely deeper than any man's sanction, be he priest or Pope or king or lawgiver. As I said to you, once before, you are mine, and I am yours, not by any artificial bond, but by the voice of our hearts, which is the voice of nature and of God within us: and whom God hath joined together, man cannot join firmer, nor yet put asunder. But if it pleases you to ask some priest's leave for the union no priest on earth can possibly make sacreder, yes; set your heart at rest about that, darling;—I've seen the Archbishop already, and he's promised to get you the regular papal dispensation."

Linnet leant back, and gazed up at him. Her gaze was half fear, half frank admiration. "Dearest Will," she said, pleadingly, in her pretty foreign English, "you're a man, I'm a woman, and therefore illogical: forgive me. I've been brought up to think one way, which I know is a dreadful way: my own heart tells me how foolish and cruel and wicked it is to think so; and yet, may the Blessed Madonna and all holy saints forgive me for saying it, I should be afraid of their anger and the eternal hell if I dared to disbelieve in what seems so cruel. You speak to me of another way, which my own heart tells me is just and pure and good and beautiful, which my head approves as common-sense and sound reasoning; and yet, may the Blessed Madonna forgive me again, though I try hard to believe it, the teachings of my childhood rise up at every step and prevent my accepting it. I can't understand this mystery of open war between God and our hearts, between God, who made them, on the one hand, and what is best, not what is worst, within them, on the other. I pray for light, but no light comes. Why should God's law fight so hard against God's instincts in our souls, against all that we feel to be purest, noblest, truest, best in our nature?"

"Not God's law," Will said gently, smoothing her hand with his own, "but the priests', Linnet, the priests', which is something quite different. God's law is never some precept beyond and outside us: it is the law of our own being, the law of our own hearts, the law of the native instincts and impulses that stir us. Your marriage with Andreas, were it twenty times blessed by priest or by Pope, was from the very first moment an unholy and unnatural one. It was a sin against purity and your own body; it was a legalised lie, a lifelong adultery. You felt its shame yourself, and shrank from the man physically. Your heart was not his, so how could your body be? Even the laws of men would have allowed you to leave him and come home to me, whose complement and mate you are by nature, after his treatment of you that day, and your discovery of his letter to Philippina. But the laws of your Church, which are not the laws of men but the laws of priests, and therefore worse and more unnatural than even the common laws of mankind, forbade you to take advantage of the loophole of escape which divorce would permit you from that wicked union your priests had imposed upon you. The Church or the law that bids you live with a man you loathe and despise, that Church or law dishonours your own nature; that Church and that law is not of God, nor even of man, but of priests and the devil. The Church or the law that forbids you to live with the man your own heart dictates and points out to you, is equally of the devil. And see how it proves itself so! It needed the intervention of Franz Lindner's knife to free you from your false union with Andreas Hausberger! Can that Church and that law be right or sound which make a murder the one loophole by which a soul can free itself from the unholy bond they would unwillingly impose upon it? Your own heart told you it was wrong and dishonouring to live with Andreas; your own heart shrank from his loveless embraces; your own heart showed you it was right to leave him, and fly away to the man you loved, the man that loved you. Will you believe that God's law is worse than your own heart? Will you think there's something divine in an institution of men which compels you to degrade and dishonour your own body, to sin so cruelly against your own pure instincts? Nothing can be wickeder, I say, than for a woman to sell herself or to yield herself in any way to a man she loathes. No Church and no law can make right of that wrong: it's degrading and debasing to her moral nature. The moment a woman feels she gives herself up against her own free will and the instincts of her own heart, she is living in sin, and you know it, Linnet, though all the priests and all the Popes on earth should stretch robed arms and hands to bless and absolve her."

He spoke with fierce conviction. Linnet nestled against his breast: his words overcame her. "I know it, Will, I know it," she exclaimed, half-hysterically. "My heart told me so always, but I couldn't believe it. I can't believe it now, though I know you're right when I hear you speak so. Perhaps, some day, when I've lived with you long enough, I shall come to think and feel as you do. . . . But for the present, my darling, I'm so glad, oh, so glad, don't laugh at me for saying it—that you've got a dispensation."

Charles Grant Blairfindie Allen was born on February 24th, 1848 at Alwington, near Kingston, Canada West (now part of Ontario). He was the second son of the Rev. Joseph Antisell Allen, a Protestant minister from Dublin, Ireland and Catharine Ann Grant, the daughter of the fifth Baron of Longueuil.

Grant was educated at home until he was thirteen at which time the family moved, initially to the United States, then France and finally settling in the United Kingdom.

Whilst growing up the family background was obviously religious but Grant developed his own views on life and the world and turned to agnosticism and socialism.

He was educated at King Edward's School in Birmingham and Merton College in Oxford. After graduating, Grant studied in France and also taught at Brighton College. By 1870, still only in his mid-twenties, he became a professor at Queen's College, a black college in Jamaica.

Whilst in Jamaica Grant met and married his first wife Ellen Jerrard in 1873 and they produced a son five years later; Jerrard Grant Allen, who grew up to become a theatrical agent/manager.

In 1876 Grant and his family left Jamaica to return to England with both the talent and ambition to become a writer.

He quickly turned to writing essays, gaining a reputation for his work on science and literary works. An early article, 'Note-Deafness' a description of what is now called amusia, was published in 1878 in the learned journal Mind and was cited approvingly by Oliver Sacks very recently.

From essays in magazines and journals he now turned to books, initially on scientific subjects. These include Physiological Æsthetics 1877 and Flowers and Their Pedigrees 1886.

His first major influence was associationist psychology, as then expounded by Alexander Bain and Herbert Spencer, the latter is often considered the most important individual in the transition from associationist psychology to Darwinian functionalism. In Grant's many articles on flowers and perception in insects, Darwinian arguments now replaced the old Spencerian terms.

On a personal level, a long friendship that started when Grant met Herbert Spencer on his return from Jamaica, turned eventually to one of unease over its long course. Grant was to write a critical and revealing biographical article on Spencer that was published after Spencer was dead.

In the early 1880's Grant began to assist Sir W. W. Hunter in his Gazeteer of India. It is at this time that Grant now turned his full attention away from the factual and towards the world of imagination and fiction.

Between this shift to fiction in 1884 and his death fifteen years later Grant was to write about 30 novels.

Many were adventure novels which were very common in the late Victorian period as writers turned their literary talents to the voracious appetites of the weekly or monthly serial magazines.

Some however were to cause quite a stir. For instance in 1895 Grant took the subject of children born out of wedlock as his subject matter. The result was The Woman Who Did, that suggested, indeed pushed, for its time, certain quite startling views on marriage and related areas. In keeping with his then glowing reputation it became a bestseller despite it being seemingly at odds with society's unease at its provocative subject matter.

Interestingly Grant wrote novels under female pseudonyms. One of these was the short novel The Type-writer Girl, which he wrote under the name Olive Pratt Rayner.

Another work, The Evolution of the Idea of God 1897, propounding a theory of religion on heterodox lines, has the disadvantage of endeavoring to explain everything by one theory. This "ghost theory" was often seen as a derivative of Herbert Spencer's theory. However, at the time, it was well known and brief references to it can be found in a review by Marcel Mauss, Durkheim's nephew, in the articles of William James and in the works of Sigmund Freud. The young G. K. Chesterton wrote on what he considered the flawed premise of the idea, arguing that the idea of God preceded human mythologies, rather than developing from them. Chesterton said of Grant Allen's book on the evolution of the idea of God "it would be much more interesting if God wrote a book on the evolution of the idea of Grant Allen".

From this and other instances, it can be seen that his work was in debate and whether agreed with or not could always ensure a lively discussion.

Grant also helped to pioneer science fiction, with the 1895 novel The British Barbarians. This book, was published at about the same time as H. G. Wells was to publish The Time Machine. The plots are quite different but both describe time travel. A few years later his short story The Thames Valley Catastrophe (published 1901 in The Strand magazine) describes the destruction of London by a massive volcanic eruption. Whilst the premise now may seem outlandish, at the time genuine panic and concern set in as, like his contemporary, Jules Verne, much of great science fiction writing is rooted in a plausibility that is set out very convincingly.

In detective fiction too his works include female detectives, very much an innovation in the young genre and his gentleman rogue, Colonel Clay, is seen as a forerunner to other, perhaps more famous characters, by other later writers.

In 1881 he had settled at Dorking, where he took great delight in botanical walks in the woods and sandy heaths. He never enjoyed particularly good health and so almost every winter he would depart for milder climes, to winter in the south of Europe, usually at Antibes, though occasionally as far as Algiers and Egypt.

In 1892 he bought land almost on the summit of Hind Head, and built himself a charming cottage which he called the Croft. Here he found that it was possible to endure the vagaries of the English winter and in landscape more beautiful and wilder than at Dorking and that his long scientific training could better appreciate.

His growing re-discovery and interest in art in the later part of his life allowed him to blend together literature, art and history in a series of guide books on Paris, Florence, Venice, and the cities of Belgium.

On October 25th 1899 Grant Allen died at his home in Hindhead, Haslemere, Surrey, England. He died just before finishing Hilda Wade. The novel's final episode, which he dictated to his friend, doctor and neighbour Sir Arthur Conan Doyle from his bed appeared under the appropriate title, The Episode of the Dead Man Who Spoke in the Strand Magazine in 1900.

Grant Allen is rarely heard of today, although an occasional short story can be heard on the radio or reprinted among magazine enthusiasts but in his time he did much to entertain the masses and push several genres along a richer journey they are still proceeding on today.

Grant Allen – A Concise Bibliography

Physiological Æsthetics. 1877
The Colour-Sense: Its Origin and Development. 1879
Evolutionist at Large. 1881
Vignettes from Nature. 1881
The Colours of Flowers. 1882
Colin Clout's Calendar. 1883
Flowers and Their Pedigrees. 1883
Philistia. 1884
Strange Stories. Short Stories. 1884
Babylon. A novel in 3 volumes. 1885
For Mamie's Sake. 1886
In All Shades. 1886
The Beckoning Hand & Other Stories. 1887
This Mortal Coil: A Novel. 1888
Force and Energy. 1888
The Devil's Die. 1888
The White Man's Foot. 1888
Falling in Love. 1889
The Tents of Shem. 1889
Wednesday the Tenth. 1890
The Great Taboo. 1890
Dumaresq's Daughter. 1891
What's Bred in the Bone. 1891
The Duchess of Powysland. 1892
The Scallywag. 1893
Michael's Crag. 1893
The Lower Slopes. 1894
Post-Prandial Philosophy. 1894
The British Barbarians. 1895
At Market Value. 1895
The Story of the Plants. 1895
The Desire of the Eyes. 1895
The Woman Who Did. 1895
The Jaws of Death. 1896
A Bride from the Desert. 1896
Under Sealed Orders. 1896
Moorland Idylls. 1896
An African Millionaire. Colonel Clay's novel. 1897
The Evolution of the Idea of God. 1897
Paris. 1897
The Type-writer Girl. (as Olive Pratt Rayner) 1897
Tom, Unlimited. (as Martin Leach Warborough) 1897
Flashlights on Nature. 1898

The Incidental Bishop. 1898
Venice. 1898
The European Tour. 1899
A Splendid Sin. 1899
Miss Cayley's Adventures. 1899
Twelve Tales: With a Headpiece, a Tailpiece, and an Intermezzo. 1899
Hilda Wade (finished by Arthur Conan Doyle). 1900
Linnet. 1900
The Backslider. 1901
Sir Theodore's Guest & Other Stories. 1902
Evolution in Italian Art. 1908
The Hand of God. 1909
The Plants. 1909

Short Stories
The Empress of Andorra. 1878
My New Year Among the Mummies. 1878
Lucretia. 1879
My Circular Tour. 1880
A Ballade of Evolution. 1880
Ram Das of Cawnpore. 1880
The Chinese Play at the Haymarket. 1880
The Senior Proctor's Wooing. 1881
Pausodyne. 1881
Caribbean Twelve Per Cents. 1882
An Episode in High Life. 1882
Mr Chung. 1882
Isadine and I. 1883
The Backsider. 1883
The Reverend John Creedy. 1883
The Foundering of the Fortuna. 1883
The Third Time
The Gold Wulfric
My Uncle's Will. 1884
Carvalho. 1884
The Mysterious Occurence in Piccadilly. 1884
Dr Greatex's Engagement. 1884
Hugh Portledown's Return from Normandy. 1884
The Child of Phalanstery. 1884
The Curate of Churnside. 1884
John Cann's Treasure. 1884
Olga Davidoff's Husband. 1884
The Search Party's Find. 1885
The Two Carnegie's. 1885
Professor Milliter's Dilemma. 1885
In Strict Confidence. 1885
The Beckoning Hand. 1885
The Third Time. 1886
Harry's Inheritance. 1886
The Gold Wulfric. 1886

Mr Pierpoint's Repentance. 1886
Claude Tyack's Ordeal. 1887
Leonard's Recovery. 1887
A Social Difficulty. 1887
Dr Palliser's Patient. 1888
My Christmas Eve at Marzin. 1888
The Sultan's Sister. 1888
His First Crime. 1889
The Mayfield Mystery. 1889
Andre Canivet's Curse. 1890
Old Margaret. 1890
My One Gorilla. 1890
Dick Prothero's Luck. 1890
A Deadly Dilemna. 1891
Jerry Stokes. 1891
Selwyn Utterton's Nemesis. 1891
General Passavant's Will. 1891
The Briefless Barrister. 1891
Melissa's Tour. 1891
Karen – A Canadian Romance. 1891
The Prisoner of Assiout. 1891
The Abbe's Repentance. 1891
Masie Bowman's Fate. 1891
Naomi's Christmas Eves. 1891
That Friend of Sylvia's. 1892
The Conscientious Burglar. 1892
The Minor Poet. 1892
The Governor's Story. 1892
The Pot Boiler. 1892
The Great Ruby. 1892
Ewen Murray's Swim. 1892
Ivan Greet's Masterpiece. 1892
Pallinghurst Barrow. 1892
Langalula. 1893
The Assasin's Knife. 1893
The Artist and the Penny-a-Liner. 1893
A Casual Conversation. 1893
How To Succeed in Literature. 1893
Torrigiano. 1893
A Modern Sibyl: A Florentine Sketch. 1893
Nemesis Wins. 1894
Cecca's Lover. 1894
A Self Respecting Servant. 1894
Passiflora Sanguinea. 1894
An Excellent Match. 1894
Major Kinfaun's Marriage. 1894
Grateful Joe. 1894
An Idyll of the Ice. 1894
Criss Cross Love. 1894
Poor Little Soul. 1894
Amour de Voyage. 1894

The Dynamiter's Sweetheart. 1894
A Triumph of Civilisation. 1894
Dr Wardroper's Lie. 1894
The Miraclous Explorer. 1894
Leon and Leonie. 1895
A Comic Emotion. 1895
Joe's Rascality. 1895
Evelyn Moore's Poet. 1895
Frasine's First Communion. 1895
TheDead Man Speaks. 1895
A Study From the Nude. 1895
Cecca's Choice. 1895
The Desire of the Eyes. 1895
The Making of a Poet. 1895
The Man From Cumbrae. 1895
Fogo Skerries. 1895
The Great Californian Heiress. 1895
Cap'n Tom Woolley. 1895
The Girl at the Fair. 1895
Love's Old Dream. 1895
A Modern Pygmalion. 1895
A Bride From the Desert. 1895
The Practical Test. 1896
A Confidential Communication. 1896
The Great Temperance Preacher. 1896
A Day on the River. 1896
The Episode of the Mexican Seer. 1896
A Midsummer Episode. 1896
The Episode of the Diamond Links. 1896
Omar at Marlow. 1896
A Mere Matter of Standpoint. 1896
Fair Exchange. 1896
The Cowardly Dynamiter. 1896
The Episode of the Old Master. 1896
The Episode of the Tyrolean Castle. 1896
Janet's Nemesis. 1896
Entirely Accidential. 1896
The Episode of the Drawn Game. 1896
Wolverden Tower. 1896
The Episode of the German Professor. 1896
The Episode of the Arrest of the Colonel. 1896
The Episode of the Seldom Gold Mine. 1897
The Camisard's Bride. 1897
The Episode of the Japanned Dispatch Box. 1897
Llanfihangel Skerries. 1897
The Episode of the Game of Poker. 1897
The Episode of the Bertillon Method. 1897
A Lady of Florence. 1897
The Episode of the Old Bailey. 1897
A British Verdict. 1897
A Domestic Tragedy. 1897

A College Charm. 1897
A Freak of Memory. 1897
The Judge's Cross. 1897
The Thames Valley Catastrophe. 1897
The Great Oriental Seer. 1897
The Adventures of the Cantankerous Old Lady. 1898
The Adventure of the Supercilious Attache. 1898
The Pirate of Cliveden Reach. 1898
The Adventure of the Amateur Commission. 1898.
The Adventure of the Impromptu Mountaineer. 1898
Joe's Wife. 1898
The Adventure of the Urbane Old Gentleman. 1898
The Adventure of the Unobtrusive Oasis. 1898
The Adventure of the Pea Green Patrician. 1898
Isenberg's Regiment. 1898
The Adventure of the Magnificent Maharajah. 1898
A Woman's Hand: A Story. 1898
The Adventure of the Cross Eyed QC. 1898
The Christmas Eve Concert. 1898
The Adventure of the Oriental Attendant. 1899
Joseph's Dream. 1899
The Adventure of the Unprofessional Detective. 1899
Hobbling Mary. 1899
The Episode of the Patient Who Disappointed Her Doctor. 1899
The Episode of the Gentleman Who Had Failed For Everything. 1899
The Episode of the Wife Who Did Her Duty. 1899
The Episode of the Man Who Would Not Commit Suicide. 1899
A Regrettable Error. 1899
Peace-At-Any-Price Bill. 1899
The Episode of the Letter with a Basingstoke Post-Mark. 1899
The Episode of the Stone That Looked About It. 1899
His Ways Inscrutable. 1899
The Episode of the European With A Kaffir Heart. 1899
The Episode of the Lady Who Was Very Exclusive. 1899
The Episode of the Guide Who Knew the Country. 1899
Luigi and the Salvationist. 1899.
A Christmas Adventure. 1899.
The Episode of the Officer Who Understood Perfectly. 1900
Meriel Stanley, Poacher. 1900
The Episode of the Dead Man Who Spoke. 1900
A Question of Colour. 1900
Fra Benedett's Medal: A Story. 1900
The Temple of Fate: A Fable. 1900
The Way to Keronan. 1902
Lucy Lockett. 1902
Spencerian. 1904

Articles
1878. Hellas and Civilization, Gentleman's Magazine, Vol. CCXLIII
1878. Nation-making: A Theory of National Characters, Gentleman's Magazine, Vol. CCXLIII

1878. The Origin of Fruits, in Popular Science Monthly Volume 13
1879. Why Do We Eat our Dinner? in Popular Science Monthly Volume 14
1879. A Problem in Human Evolution, in Popular Science Monthly Volume
1879. Pleased with a Feather, in Popular Science Monthly Volume 15
1880. Why Keep India? The Contemporary Review, Vol. XXXVIII
1880. The Growth of Sculpture, The Cornhill Magazine, Vol. XLII
1880. The English Chronicle, Gentleman's Magazine, Vol. CCXLV
1880. The Venerable Bede, Gentleman's Magazine, Vol. CCXLIX
1880. The Dog's Universe, Gentleman's Magazine, Vol. CCXLIX
1880. Evolution and Geological Time, Gentleman's Magazine, Vol. CCXLIX
1880. Geology and History, in Popular Science Monthly Volume 17
1880. Aesthetic Feeling in Birds, in Popular Science Monthly Volume 17
1880. Aesthetic Evolution in Man, in Popular Science Monthly Volume 18
1881. The Story of Wulfgeat, Gentleman's Magazine, Vol. CCLI
1882. An English Shire, Gentleman's Magazine, Vol. CCLII
1882. The Welsh in the West Country, Gentleman's Magazine, Vol. CCLIII
1882. The Colours of Flowers, The Cornhill Magazine, Vol. XLV
1882. An English Weed, The Cornhill Magazine, Vol. XLV
1882. Sir Charles Lyell, in Popular Science Monthly Volume 20
1882. Hyacinth-Bulbs, in Popular Science Monthly Volume 20
1882. Who was Primitive Man? in Popular Science Monthly Volume 22
1883. The Pedigree of Wheat, in Popular Science Monthly Volume 22
1883. From Buttercups to Monk's-Hood, in Popular Science Monthly Volume 23
1883. Honeysuckle, Gentleman's Magazine, Vol. CCLV
1884. The Garden Snail, Gentleman's Magazine, Vol. CCLVI
1884. Our Debt to Insects, Gentleman's Magazine, Vol. CCLVI
1884. Idiosyncrasy, in Popular Science Monthly Volume 24
1884. The Ancestry of Birds, in Popular Science Monthly Volume 24
1884. The Milk in the Cocoa-Nut, in Popular Science Monthly Volume 25
1884. Our Debt to Insects, in Popular Science Monthly Volume 25
1884. Hickory-Nuts and Butternuts, in Popular Science Monthly Volume 25
1884. Queer Flowers, in Popular Science Monthly Volume 26
1885. Food and Feeding, in Popular Science Monthly Volume 26
1885. Concerning Clover, in Popular Science Monthly Volume 28
1886. A Thinking Machine, Gentleman's Magazine, Vol. CCLX
1886. Fish Out of Water, in Popular Science Monthly Volume 28
1886. A Thinking Machine, in Popular Science Monthly Volume 28
1886. Thistles, in Popular Science Monthly Volume 30, November 1886
1887. A Mount Washington Sandwort, in Popular Science Monthly Volume 30
1887. Among the Thousand Islands, in Popular Science Monthly Volume 31
1887. The Progress of Science from 1836 to 1886, in Popular Science Monthly Volume 31
1887. American Cinque-Foils, in Popular Science Monthly Volume 32
1888. Gourds and Bottles, in Popular Science Monthly Volume 33
1888. A Living Mystery, in Popular Science Monthly Volume 33
1888. Evolving the Camel, in Popular Science Monthly Volume 34
1889. From Africa, Gentleman's Magazine, Vol. CCLXVII
1889. Genius and Talent, in Popular Science Monthly Volume 34
1889. Plain Words on the Woman Question, in Popular Science Monthly Volume 36
1890. The Girl of the Future, Universal Review, Vol. VII.
1891. Democracy and Diamonds, The Contemporary Review, Vol. LIX
1892. A Desert Fruit, in Popular Science Monthly Volume 41

1893. Ghost Worship and Tree Worship I, in Popular Science Monthly Volume 42
1893. Ghost Worship and Tree Worship II, in Popular Science Monthly Volume 42
1897. Spencer and Darwin, in Popular Science Monthly Volume 50
1898. The Romance of Race, in Popular Science Monthly Volume 53
1898. The Season of the Year, in Popular Science Monthly Volume 54

Poetry

Grant Allen wrote various poems published in many magazines etc. We have not listed them here
but hope to record some of them in the future.

www.ingramcontent.com/pod-product-compliance
Lightning Source LLC
Chambersburg PA
CBHW061147170626
46809CB00003B/1014